THE END

A Love Story

David R Mann

Publisher: David R Mann

Copyright © 2025 David R Mann

All rights reserved

The characters and events portrayed in this book are fictitious. Any similarity to real persons, living or dead, is coincidental and not intended by the author.

No part of this book may be reproduced, or stored in a retrieval system, or transmitted in any form or by any means, electronic, mechanical, photocopying, recording, or otherwise, without express written permission of the publisher.

Cover design by: David R Mann

CONTENTS

Title Page
Copyright
Chapter 1 Discovery   1
Chapter 2 Trajectory   13
Chapter 3 Celestial Crossroads   43
Chapter 4 Juno   77
Chapter 5 Kaʻepaokaʻāwela   95
Chapter 6 Arrival   123
Chapter 7 White   156
Chapter 8 Fiery Red and Flat Black   183
Chapter 9 Spring Green   207
Chapter 10 Abduction   244
Chapter 11 Invasion   261
Chapter 12 Occupation   292
Chapter 13 The Beggar at the Gate   339
Chapter 14 Reunion   375
Dedication   393
Acknowledgments   394
Author's Notes: 396

CHAPTER 1
DISCOVERY

Beneath the Hawaiian sun, Caleb glided across the turquoise waves at Diamond Head, his morning ritual of surfing a perfect blend of physical effort and mental clarity. The ocean's rhythm often mirrored the cosmic dance he studied by night, sparking moments of inspiration—though today, his thoughts kept wandering to Emma Kanoa.
He'd never kissed her, never dated her, never even mustered the courage to ask her out. Yet, Emma had a way of slipping into his mind uninvited. Her easy smile, the way she lit up when explaining a complex idea, even the lilting cadence of her voice—it all lingered like a sweet refrain. He often wondered if she'd noticed how his gaze lingered a second too long or how he always seemed to find excuses to talk to her at work.

Diamond Head, a peaceful escape near his apartment and work, usually centered him. The crescent-shaped beach, framed by swaying palms and lapped by crystalline waves shaped by an offshore reef, was his sanctuary. But today, even as fish darted beneath his board and a sea turtle surfaced briefly nearby, his focus wavered.

He found himself imagining what Emma might think of this place, its quiet beauty, so different from the bustling Waikiki scene. Would she appreciate the peaceful rhythm of the waves or find herself distracted, like he so often was? As Caleb floated on his board, staring at the endless blue above, a question tugged at him: could he ever find the courage to invite her into this part of his life, where the world felt wide open and full of possibilities?

Dr. Caleb Jacobson was a postdoc at the University of Hawaii's Institute for Astronomy (IfA). To put it plainly, he was an astronomer, an occupation he had dreamed of since he first gazed at the Milky Way in a moonless sky as a child growing up in Oklahoma. His parents loved camping with their two children, Caleb and his sister, Bethany. They tried to find campsites a few hours away by car from Oklahoma City where they lived. Camping on the shore of a lake was always their first choice but sometimes they just had to settle for a pool, usually an above ground pool and usually the pool was overcrowded and unheated.

Caleb's introduction to the Milky Way took place at Liberty Lake, just north of the city but far enough to avoid light pollution. It was time for bed, the campfire was doused. The kids had used the toilets. Walking back to the camp chairs around the fire ring, Caleb noticed his parents looking up.

"Whatcha looking at?" asked Caleb.

"The Milky Way," answered his Dad, Jake Jacobson. "Come here. Look at this. See where I'm pointing at. It goes from there to there. It's like a river of light in the sky."

Caleb was mesmerized.

"What is it?" he asked.

"It's the galaxy that we live in," said his mom. "I guess we are kind of on the edge of it looking back at it."

"What's our galaxy?"

"It's a hundred billion stars, thousands of trillions of miles away," she answered.

"How come I've never seen it before?" Caleb asked.

"It's easier to see on a clear, moonless night without any lights nearby. Now that you know what it looks like you might be able to find it in the sky at home," said his dad. "It won't be near as spectacular."

His dad continued, "While we are studying the stars, we should tell you a couple more things that might save your life."

His mom, Jean, gave Jake a puzzled look. *Save his life?* She mouthed at Jake.

"Look here," said his Dad, pointing to the north sky. "That's the Big Dipper. It's always in the north. The Big Dipper is made up of seven bright stars that form a distinct shape resembling a large ladle or a scoop. The bowl of the dipper is made up of four stars, while the handle extends out from one side, made up of three stars. Now a ladle is what your mother uses to fill your bowl with soup. The ladle that she uses has a round bowl, the Big Dipper has a squarish bowl and a bent handle. You see it?"

"Sure Dad," Caleb answered. "How will that save my life?"

"Because it tells you where North is.If you are ever lost at night and you know what direction you need to go but you don't know which way it is, you can figure it out if you can see the Big Dipper. If you just want to know roughly which way is North just look for the Big Dipper. It is Northish. If you need to know precisely which direction is North, look at the two stars on the edge of the Big Dipper's bowl. You know, the part that holds the water. These two stars are like a pointer," said Jake.

"Imagine a straight line going through these two stars and keep following that line in the sky. Remember that's in the direction up for the dipper itself, imagining that the bowl is holding water. Everything in the sky rotates so the Big Dipper may appear upside down. So the line could seem to be up, down or sidewise. "

"After you follow the line for a bit, you'll see a bright star. This star is Polaris, also known as the North Star. Polaris is special because it always points exactly north. If you're lost, you can find Polaris to figure out which way is north. If you know north then you can figure out south, east and west." said Jake, pointing out the other three directions.

-

Although their telescopes were located at the tops of dormant volcanoes, UH astronomers were based at the IfA headquarters building in the part of Honolulu known as Mānoa Valley, near the main campus of the University of Hawai'i on the island of Oahu. From there, it was quite a journey to get to Mauna Kea on the Big Island of Hawaii where you could find over a dozen multi-multi-million dollar high tech telescopes.

The Thirty Meter Telescope (TMT), envisioned as one of the world's most advanced astronomical observatories, never materialized. Planned for Mauna Kea, Hawaii's highest peak and an ideal site for stargazing due to its altitude, dry climate, and minimal light pollution, the project faced fierce opposition. Native Hawaiians, environmentalists, global activists, and some politicians united against it, citing cultural, spiritual, and ecological concerns.

To Native Hawaiians, Mauna Kea is sacred—a meeting place of heaven and Earth, home to gods, and an ancient burial ground. Many saw telescope construction as desecration, intensifying long-standing grievances tied to Hawaiian sovereignty and the legacy of U.S. annexation. Ecological concerns over the mountain's fragile environment further fueled protests. In the end, science gave way to cultural and environmental preservation, marking the TMT as a project that never found its place.

Caleb's telescope wasn't on Mauna Kea. Named Pan-STARRS, the Panoramic Survey Telescope and Rapid Response System, it was at the Haleakalā Observatory at the dormant volcano of the same name on the island of Maui.

"First thing" for Caleb as with the other observational astronomers started about 1 PM. After his surf session, Caleb would take care of chores and errands, often meeting up with other astronomer's for "lunch" at 6 PM at the University's Gateway Cafe and finally making his way to his office at the IfA.

Although Caleb visited the Haleakalā Observatory many times, he did his observing at the Institute for Astronomy (IfA) complex on the campus of the University of Hawaii in Honolulu on the Island of Oahu.

During his infrequent expeditions to Haleakalā, he was always struck by the serene solitude that enveloped the summit. The volcano's peak, crowned with telescopes reaching out to the cosmos, was devoid of the tension found elsewhere. Not once did he encounter a protester among the observatories perched on the ancient shield volcano. The only sounds were the whispering winds and the distant hum of scientific equipment, undisturbed by the human conflicts that often accompany progress.

However, the atmosphere shifted dramatically on his rare visits to Mauna Kea. Each time he ascended the sacred mountain, he was met with a poignant reminder of the deep-rooted struggle that gripped the land. At the base of the mountain, he passed by a semi-permanent encampment—a site that had become a symbol of both resistance and reverence. The "Protectors of Mauna Kea," a diverse group of individuals committed to defending the sacred summit, stood their ground. The camp was an amalgamation of environmental activists, native Hawaiians, and Kupuna—the revered elders of the Native Hawaiian community, whose presence lent the protest a profound sense of gravitas.

Each time he passed by, the camp served as a quiet yet powerful reminder of the complex interplay between science, culture, and the deep spiritual connections that bind people to the land.

-

Caleb's office at the IfA was just a worn plywood top folding table pushed up against the wall off of which four different sized monitor's hung. The table was cluttered with star charts, research papers, and an old beat up surfboard was tucked under the table to level it - a table leg had broken off.

This was where he transformed from surfer to astronomer.

Ironically, astronomer's called the large air-conditioned room full of tables and monitors, the warm room. A carry over from the recent past when telescopes lost their eyepieces and were first fitted with high resolution CCDs, astronomers would work in a room adjacent to the telescope and observe by looking at a monitor. Unlike the room the telescope was in, which had to be exposed to the elements, the astronomers' room could be kept warm. Hence the term, "warm room".

When she happened to be observing in the warm room, Caleb found his thoughts increasingly tangled in distraction, courtesy of Dr. Emma Kanoa. Emma, with her flowing black hair that seemed to capture the light, had a quiet magnetism that Caleb found impossible to ignore. Her deep brown eyes held a spark of intelligence and warmth, and her graceful presence could brighten even the dim, utilitarian space of the observatory.

Emma had joined the Institute for Astronomy about two years after Caleb. A native of Hawaii, she'd ventured to the mainland for her education, where she had been fiercely focused on her studies, brushing off any distractions—especially romantic advances—with a resolute determination. Now, with her academic achievements behind her and her career firmly established, Emma seemed to have relaxed that stance, her once-automatic rebuff setting now set to manual. The change only added to her allure, leaving Caleb both intrigued and more hesitant than ever to act on his growing feelings.

Caleb admired Emma's intelligence and dedication, often finding excuses to collaborate with her on projects or linger in conversations. He noticed how her eyes lit up when she talked about her research, and how her laughter had a musical quality that lingered long after she left the room.

One evening, on a coffee break, Caleb and Emma found themselves alone on the institute's grounds. The night was serene, the cool ocean breeze carrying the rhythmic crash of distant waves. Overhead, the stars sparkled like fragments of crystal scattered across a velvety black sky, the Milky Way arcing above them like a celestial river. The air was fragrant with the sweet blend of night-blooming jasmine and plumeria.

"Caleb," Emma said softly, breaking the silence, "I've been thinking a lot lately… about our work and… other things. Moments like this make me realize there's more to life than just research."

As the words left her mouth, she winced inwardly. *So cliché,* she thought, resisting the urge to cringe.

Caleb's pulse quickened, her words igniting something unfamiliar yet undeniable in him. "I know what you mean," he said, his voice carefully steady and his eyes fixed on hers. "The universe is full of mysteries, but sometimes the most meaningful discoveries are right in front of us."

Could I sound any more obvious? Caleb thought, feeling his stomach twist.

Emma turned toward him, her dark eyes glimmering with reflected starlight. *At least he's not laughing at me,* she thought, her lips curving into a tentative smile. "Do you ever wonder what's next? Beyond... all of this?"

So trite. Why am I so bad at this? But he's still here, he hasn't run away, yet, Emma realized, a small spark of courage flickering in her chest.

"All the time," Caleb admitted after a pause, his voice softer now. "I think it's time I started exploring those possibilities—not just professionally, but personally too."

Corny, Caleb thought. *Absolutely corny.* But as Emma's smile deepened, the faint blush on her cheeks catching the glow of the starlight, his self-consciousness ebbed.

Now that I have totally humiliated myself, I might as well just go for it, Emma thought. "Maybe," she said, her voice tinged with quiet hope, "we could explore some of those possibilities together."

A COSMIC SHIFT! A QUANTUM LEAP! Caleb's chest swelled with a mixture of exhilaration and disbelief. Under the vast Hawaiian sky, surrounded by the perfume of blossoms and the timeless expanse of the cosmos, *he knew it,* as though the universe itself had conspired to bring them to this moment. Whether navigating the stars or the uncertain currents of the heart, Caleb knew one thing: he was ready to move forward, and he hoped Emma would be by his side.

Magically, the air filled with the sound of a resonant chime followed by a rising crescendo of harmonic tones. Imagine a deep, clear bell-like tone that signifies the gravity of a moment, followed by a cascade of uplifting, shimmering notes that evoked a sense of wonder.

It was Caleb's phone at the most inconvenient moment imaginable, it had received an urgent notification. Frustrated, he tried to mute it but he couldn't miss the message on the screen. **ISO**. Three letters large and blinking on the screen. Emma, of course, also saw the alert.

"Go!" she exclaimed. "We will continue this later. Go!"

Caleb sprinted back to the warm room and his station. Apparently, their first kiss could wait.

Pan-STARRS thought it had found another Interstellar Object. Like Oumuamua or perhaps 2I/Boris and yet quite unlike either one.

Caleb called up the image on his monitor. A faint trail, a single pixel wide, traveling east to west. The longest trail he had ever seen from Pan-STARRS.

Has someone changed the magnification, he wondered.

He quickly confirmed that no one had messed with the settings. The trail corresponded to an object traveling 12 degrees per day. He projected the trail backwards 12 degrees and called up the corresponding image from the previous evening.

There it is! Far fainter and missing a few pixels but easy enough to see when you know where to look, he thinks. Just a little too faint for Pan-STARRS to catch. Enough evidence to report it to the Minor Planet Center, he decided.

He quickly summarized and submitted his findings to the Minor Planet Center, the organization responsible for the designation of minor bodies in the solar system. It was the middle of the working day in Cambridge, Massachusetts, where the MPC resides and so it was not a big surprise to receive a conditional interim designation: MPEC 2024-N108

Soon it will be time to give it a real name, he thinks. *I could ask Emma for suggestions.*

Instead of rushing to find Emma, Caleb did what protocol demanded —he reached out to his supervisor, Dr. Helen Wright. He was meticulous in reporting everything he had discovered, fully aware that transparency was key in situations like this. Dr. Wright, who had been with the IfA long before the discovery of Oumuamua by Dr. Robert Weryk on October 19, 2017, was a seasoned professional. A product of the GI Bill's "kicker" program, she had the expertise and discipline to lead efficiently. She quickly took charge, appointing herself head of the post-discovery team. Her first priority was securing telescope time to study MPEC 2024-N108 across as many observatories as possible.

Dr. Wright knew exactly whom to call. As she confidently reminded Caleb, she had longstanding relationships with the directors of nearly every major telescope, and they knew her well enough to accommodate her requests. With the groundwork laid, she deftly delegated responsibilities to various post-docs, including Emma, assigning tasks based on their specific qualifications and competencies. Recognizing the potential media storm, Dr. Wright suggested Caleb take on the role of team spokesperson. She knew he would be swamped with requests, and his calm, knowledgeable demeanor would represent the team well.

Caleb felt like Dr. Eleanor Arroway (Jodi Foster) in the movie Contact when Dr. David Drumlin (Tom Skerritt) took over her SETI project. No one was taking credit for his discovery but he was going to be so busy answering questions that he would have little time to study his own discovery.

Caleb stood at the edge of the warm room, gazing at the monitors displaying data from Pan-STARRS. The excitement of discovering another interstellar object, tentatively designated as MPEC 2024-N108, was dampened by the responsibilities now thrust upon him. Dr. Helen Wright had taken charge, efficiently organizing the post-discovery team's efforts to study the object. Emma was deep into her assigned tasks, and Caleb found himself juggling his newfound role as spokesperson.

Caleb would have preferred to stay and study the intriguing object, which was traveling at an astonishing 30 miles per second and measured at least 15 miles in diameter. It was entering the solar system from the north, from the direction of Vega. But his focus was soon pulled elsewhere when he received a formal summons to Washington, D.C., to testify before a joint congressional and senate committee about his discovery and the team's findings.

As Caleb boarded the plane to Washington, he couldn't help but think about the significance of their discovery. This new interstellar object was not only larger than 'Oumuamua or Borisov but also moving at an incredible speed, suggesting a journey of potentially millions of years. He knew the scientific community was buzzing with theories and speculations, but now he had to face the political arena—a place he was far less comfortable.

The hearing room was packed with reporters, scientists, and politicians. The room was grand, with high ceilings adorned with ornate moldings and large windows that let in streams of natural light. Dark wood paneling lined the walls, giving the space a formal and imposing atmosphere. The smell of polished wood and a hint of old paper filled the air, a mix of the room's history and the many documents that had been debated there over the years.

Caleb felt a wave of anxiety but reminded himself that this was his opportunity to share the importance of their discovery with the world.

"Dr. Jacobson," began Senator Reilly, a stern-looking man with graying hair, "can you explain to us the significance of your discovery?"

Caleb took a deep breath. "Thank you, Senator. I was just informed that the Minor Planet Center has confirmed our findings for MPEC 2024-N108 and has accepted the suggestion of a name by one of the team members, Dr. Emma Kanoa of Alohanui which in Hawaiian means "Great Love." The object is an interstellar visitor traveling at 30 miles per second. It's at least 18 miles in diameter and appears to be coming from the direction of Vega. This speed and size suggest it is unlike any comet or asteroid we've studied within our solar system. Its path and velocity indicate it has been traveling through interstellar space for a very long time, possibly millions of years."

"How do you know it's interstellar?" asked another committee member.

"We tracked its trajectory using the Pan-STARRS telescope. Its speed and direction don't align with any known solar system bodies. Its speed exceeds the escape velocity of the sun. That means it didn't originate in our solar system and it will leave our solar system. Additionally, its composition and behavior, observed through multiple telescopes, further support its interstellar origin," Caleb explained.

Another committee member, Congresswoman Nora Palmer, a woman with sharp eyes and a no-nonsense demeanor, leaned forward. "Dr. Jacobson, is there any chance that MPEC 2024-N108 or Alohanui, as it shall henceforth be known, could hit Earth?"

Caleb shook his head confidently. "No, Representative Palmer. The closest it will come to Earth is about 30 million miles. It poses no threat to our planet."

Senator Reilly wanted a little more face time and so he asked, "You testified it came from the direction of Vega. In the movie, *Contact*, the radio signal came from the direction of Vega and it was a fake. Any chance of this being a fake?"

"No, Senator, this is the real thing."

"Just one more question," said Reilly. "As I understand it, the main purpose of Pan-STARRS was to identify asteroids that might pose a hazard to Earth, to mankind. You testified that this Interstellar Object poses no threat to our planet. I suppose I'm just wondering who's watching the store? Here's my question: are we potentially missing a planet-killer while all the telescopes in the world are pointed at Alohanui."

"I can see why you might worry about that but Pan-STARRS1 was never taken off its regular duties. It's still looking for as yet unidentified asteroids. Almost all the telescopes now directed at Alohanui are using the telescope director's discretionary time. This is time available because these telescopes were not fully booked and because we have benefited from unusually good observing weather lately especially in Hawaii and South Africa. I expect that many many amateur astronomers are pointing their telescopes at Alohanui as they would any newly discovered comet. Amateurs like Gennady Borisov, discoverer of 2I/Borisov. So some amateurs are not looking for planet-killers right now but they will get back to it once the novelty of Alohanui wears off. I also expect that many people who up to now haven't been amateur astronomers will buy a telescope and start observing!"

After the hearing, Caleb was swarmed by reporters. He managed to answer a few questions before making his way back to his hotel. There, he finally had a moment to himself to reflect on the day's events. His thoughts drifted to Emma and their conversation under the stars. He pulled out his phone and sent her a quick message.

"I wish you were here. This is all so overwhelming."

A few minutes later, his phone buzzed. "I wish I was there too. You did great today. Can't wait to hear all about it when you get back."

Upon returning to Hawaii, Caleb was eager to dive back into the research. He and Emma met up at their favorite spot on the institute's grounds, where they could talk freely away from the hustle and bustle of the warm room.

"How was Washington?" Emma asked, genuinely curious.

"Intense," Caleb replied. "But it felt good to share our work with a wider audience. Now, I'm happy to get back to you and this interstellar visitor. There's so much more to uncover."

Back at the IfA, the team worked tirelessly. Dr. Helen Wright had secured observing time on multiple telescopes, including the James Clerk Maxwell Telescope and the Subaru Telescope. Emma's role involved analyzing the spectral data, while Caleb focused on the object's trajectory and potential origins.

As the weeks passed, the team uncovered more details about Alohanui. For example, it had little or no coma, the halo/tail that comets have. Its composition was unlike any comet or asteroid in our solar system, suggesting a completely different origin. Spectral analysis revealed it contained rare elements not typically found in known celestial bodies.

One night, while studying the data, Caleb and Emma found themselves alone again. The sky was clear, and the stars were shining brightly.

"Emma," Caleb said, breaking the silence, "I'm glad we're doing this together. There's no one else I'd rather be on this journey with."

Emma looked at him, her eyes reflecting the starlight. "Me too, Caleb. This is just the beginning of something incredible."

CHAPTER 2
TRAJECTORY

The whirlwind of attention that had engulfed Caleb following the groundbreaking discovery had finally begun to wane. Faded into the background were the relentless demands for testimony, the barrage of media requests, and the constant scrutiny. For the first time in what felt like ages, Caleb found himself with the luxury of time—time to return to his true passion for astronomy, and hopefully to spend more moments with Emma.

Emma, along with the rest of the team, was deeply absorbed in the monumental task at hand. They were working tirelessly, their days and nights consumed by the meticulous analysis of data pouring in from telescopes scattered across the globe. Each new piece of information brought them closer to unraveling the mysteries of Alohanui, the enigmatic interstellar visitor that had captivated the scientific community.

Alohanui, with its trajectory from the far reaches of the north, was on a path that would soon take it perilously close to the sun. As it approached, the object would slip behind the blinding brilliance of the sun, rendering it invisible to telescopes on Earth. This impending reality was a source of frustration for astronomers, who knew all too well the limitations of their instruments. Modern telescopes, with their delicate CCDs, couldn't risk being pointed too close to the sun, lest they be irreparably damaged. The same fate awaited the eyes of anyone foolish enough to peer through an old-fashioned telescope at the fiery orb—blindness.

As Alohanui edged closer to the sun, the scientific community braced itself for the inevitable: the interstellar object would soon be out of sight, hidden in the sun's overwhelming glare. The sense of anticipation and anxiety was palpable as they waited for the moment when Alohanui would disappear from view, knowing that they could only hope for its reappearance on the other side.

In the midst of this tension, Caleb was stunned to see the headline splashed across the front page of the Oahu Observer, the local newspaper: "ALOHANUI PLUNGES INTO SUN!" The words seemed to scream from the page, a stark contrast to the measured scientific reports he had been following. Caleb couldn't believe the paper had resorted to such sensationalism, crafting a headline that so grossly misrepresented the situation. The implication that Alohanui had crashed into the sun and been annihilated was not only misleading but a complete distortion of the facts.

The truth was far less dramatic but no less significant. Alohanui was simply moving out of view, its journey continuing behind the sun from Earth's perspective. The object was not doomed, nor was it destroyed. But the newspaper, in its quest for readers, had twisted reality into a headline that was as false as it was alarming.

Caleb felt a surge of frustration at the thought of how easily misinformation could spread, especially when dealing with something as important as an interstellar object. But even as he fumed over the misleading headline, he knew that the truth would eventually emerge. For now, all he could do was wait, just as the rest of the world would have to, for Alohanui to reappear from behind the sun, continuing its mysterious voyage through the cosmos.

The latest observations revealed that as Alohanui drew closer to the sun, it began to decelerate and subtly alter its trajectory. This behavior, while intriguing, wasn't entirely unexpected. After all, both 'Oumuamua and 2I/Borisov had exhibited similar course changes as they approached the sun.

Borisov, for instance, was a comet, albeit one of interstellar origin. Despite its exotic beginnings, it behaved much like a typical local comet, complete with a visible coma—a cloud of gas and dust released as the sun's heat caused it to off-gas. Its trajectory shift was consistent with the gentle push from these escaping gasses, a predictable behavior for a comet nearing the sun.

'Oumuamua, however, presented a more puzzling case. Unlike Borisov, it had no detectable coma—no visible halo of dust and gas that could explain its sudden acceleration and change in course. Astronomers were left scratching their heads, as there were no signs of the frozen gasses typically expected to vaporize and produce the kind of thrust needed to alter its trajectory. Yet, the object sped up, seemingly propelled by some unseen force.

The leading hypothesis suggested that 'Oumuamua might have acted like a solar sail, its surface subtly pushed by the pressure of the sun's radiation. This idea, though speculative, was supported by the object's unusual shape and the lack of any other apparent mechanisms for its acceleration. It was as if the sun's photons were gently nudging it along, steering it on a path that defied conventional expectations.

Now, as Alohanui approached the sun, its deceleration and trajectory change raised similar questions. Was it following the same mysterious principles that guided 'Oumuamua or was there another, yet-to-be-understood phenomenon at play? The observations were clear: Alohanui's behavior was a blend of the familiar and the enigmatic, a reminder that even with all the knowledge gleaned from previous interstellar visitors, the universe still held secrets that defied easy explanation.

With Alohanui now passing behind the sun, all they could do was wait. The Institute for Astronomy (IfA) team, along with hundreds of astronomers around the globe, had meticulously calculated its trajectory. They knew precisely where and when Alohanui would reemerge, and anticipation filled the air as they prepared for the moment it would once again grace the night sky.

With an unexpected lull in their hectic schedules, Caleb decided to seize the moment and invited Emma to join him for a late morning surf at Diamond Head. The sun was already climbing in the sky, casting a golden glow over the shimmering waves and the lush green foliage that bordered the beach. The scent of saltwater mingled with the sweet fragrance of plumeria carried on the gentle breeze, while the rhythmic sound of the surf crashing against the shore created a serene soundtrack to the day.

Caleb arrived at the beach with a sense of excitement and anticipation. He had brought along an extra surfboard, well-worn and seasoned by countless rides on the waves, fully intending to teach Emma the art of surfing. The idea of sharing one of his favorite pastimes with her filled him with a boyish enthusiasm. As they made their way down to the water, the sand warm and soft beneath their feet, Caleb was eager to play the role of the instructor.

The beach was stunning in its simplicity, framed by the iconic silhouette of Diamond Head crater in the distance. Palm trees swayed gently along the shoreline, their fronds rustling in the wind, casting dappled shadows on the sand. The water was a mesmerizing shade of turquoise, clear and inviting, with the waves rolling in with a perfect rhythm—just right for a day of surfing. A few seabirds glided effortlessly over the ocean, their cries punctuating the calmness of the scene.

Emma stood at the edge of the surf, the sunlight casting a warm, golden hue over her as she gazed out at the ocean. She wore a simple, elegant tankini version of a bikini, a perfect fit for someone who moved through the water with such grace and ease. The color of the tankini, a deep ocean blue, contrasted beautifully with her sun-kissed skin, giving her an air of effortless style.

Her hair, slightly tousled by the sea breeze, fell in loose waves around her shoulders, the strands catching the sunlight and glinting like strands of gold. She adjusted her sunglasses, a playful smile tugging at the corners of her lips as she turned to Caleb, the joy of the day reflected in her eyes.

As she moved, there was a natural, unassuming confidence in her posture, the kind that came from someone completely at ease in her own skin. Every step she took left delicate imprints in the wet sand, the ocean lapping at her feet, drawing her closer to the water's edge where she felt most at home. The breeze played with the ends of her hair, and she tilted her head back slightly, enjoying the warmth of the sun on her face.

The tankini showcased her athleticism, a testament to her years spent surfing and swimming in these waters. It was clear that she belonged here, among the waves and the salt air. Emma carried herself with a blend of strength and grace, her movements fluid and purposeful, embodying the spirit of the ocean that she loved so much.

Even in this casual setting, there was something undeniably captivating about Emma—a blend of beauty, strength, and a deep connection to the natural world around her. It was this mix that drew Caleb's admiration, making him feel a profound sense of connection to the woman beside him, a connection that deepened with every shared wave and moment in the sun.

As they reached the edge of the water, Caleb turned to Emma, his expression a mix of awe at her beauty and a bit of playful condescension. "Okay, so the first thing you need to know about surfing is—"

Emma cut him off with a knowing smile, her eyes sparkling with mischief. "I've got it, Caleb," she said, her voice light and teasing.

He blinked in surprise, taken aback by her confidence. Before he could respond, Emma had already grabbed the surfboard from him with a practiced ease and waded into the water. Caleb stood there for a moment, processing what was happening, his plans for the day suddenly upended.

Emma paddled out with a fluid grace that came only from years of experience. Caleb watched, his mouth slightly agape, as she effortlessly caught the first wave, popping up onto the board with the skill of someone who had spent her life on the water. She rode the wave with the kind of finesse that made it clear she was no novice.

Caleb couldn't help but feel stupid for assuming he would be the one doing the teaching. After all, she was born in Hawaii. He shook his head with a sheepish grin, laughing at himself as he waded out to join her. As Emma paddled back out, she caught his eye and winked, the sun catching in her hair, turning it into a halo of gold.

"You were going to teach me, huh?" she teased, her tone light but affectionate.

Caleb chuckled, a warm feeling spreading through him that had nothing to do with the sun. "I guess I'll learn a thing or two from you instead," he replied, his voice carrying a note of admiration.

They spent the rest of the morning together, riding the waves, sharing laughter, and enjoying the easy companionship that had grown between them. The beach, with its vibrant foliage and sparkling waves, became their private playground. As they took breaks, lounging on their boards and letting the sun dry their skin, Caleb found himself captivated not just by Emma's skill but by the way she seemed so at home here, in her element.

It wasn't just about the surfing—it was about the connection they were building, the unspoken understanding that grew with each passing moment. Caleb felt a growing affection for Emma, one that went well beyond friendship and into something deeper, something he hadn't quite expected but welcomed all the same.

As the sun climbed higher and the waves began to lose some of their morning perfection, they eventually paddled back to shore. The beach, now busier with the midday crowd, felt like a different place from the quiet retreat they had enjoyed earlier.

Caleb glanced over at Emma as they walked back up the beach, their surfboards tucked under their arms, and couldn't resist a smile. "Next time, I'll let you choose the activity," he said, his voice warm with affection.

Emma laughed, her eyes sparkling as she looked at him. "Deal," she replied, her smile holding a promise of more shared adventures to come.

Finally, as the sun dipped low on the horizon, casting a warm amber glow over the city, Caleb and Emma made their way to the Gateway Café. It was just after 6 PM, and the air was filled with the subtle promise of evening—a perfect time to unwind after a long day. The café, nestled on a quiet street corner not too far from the "warm room", was a favorite among the astronomers and researchers who frequented the area. Its unassuming exterior, adorned with ivy and soft, glowing lanterns, gave way to a cozy interior that felt like a home away from home.

Inside, the café was a blend of rustic charm and modern touches. Wooden beams crisscrossed the ceiling, and the walls were lined with bookshelves filled with everything from well-worn scientific journals to classic novels. The soft hum of conversation mixed with the clinking of cutlery and the occasional burst of laughter, creating an atmosphere that was both lively and intimate. The scent of freshly brewed coffee and baked goods lingered in the air, mingling with the savory aroma of the evening's specials.

Caleb and Emma spotted the rest of the team already gathered around a large, sturdy wooden table near the back of the café. The table was littered with menus, notebooks, and half-finished drinks —evidence of a group that was equally passionate about their work and their camaraderie. The group included Dr. Helen Wright, the seasoned astrophysicist with silver-streaked hair pulled back into a no-nonsense bun, who was in the middle of an animated discussion with a younger colleague about the latest data regarding Alohanui. Her voice, calm yet authoritative, carried just enough to draw the attention of those nearby, adding to the intellectual buzz of the café.

Next to her sat Mark, a lanky, bespectacled postdoc who always seemed to be halfway between a brilliant idea and a sip of his ever-present cappuccino. He was flipping through a well-annotated notebook, occasionally glancing up to interject with a thought or two, his fingers absently drumming on the table in time with the music softly playing in the background. Across from Mark was Lisa, a vibrant astronomer with a contagious laugh, who was currently regaling the group with a humorous story from her last observing trip. Her expressive gestures and wide smile lit up the corner of the room, drawing chuckles and smiles from the team.

As Caleb and Emma approached, they were greeted with a chorus of welcomes and the scraping of chairs as space was made for them at the table. Caleb couldn't help but feel a warm sense of belonging as he took his seat next to Emma, their shoulders brushing in the close quarters. The café's dim lighting and the flicker of candles on the tables created a relaxed, almost intimate ambiance, a sharp contrast to the intensity of their work but a much-needed reprieve.

The conversation ebbed and flowed, touching on everything from the latest astronomical findings to more mundane topics like where the best food trucks were outside the city. Plates of food began to arrive—hearty sandwiches, fresh salads, and steaming bowls of soup—all served with the kind of care and attention that made the Gateway Café a favorite among the local academic community.

Caleb found himself caught up in the easy banter, the stress of the day melting away with each passing moment. He exchanged knowing glances with Emma as they shared a plate of sweet potato fries, the simple act of passing food between them deepening the unspoken connection that had been growing since their first meeting. The laughter of their colleagues, the clatter of dishes, and the background hum of the café all blended into a soothing symphony, creating a moment that felt both timeless and fleeting.

As the evening wore on, the conversation shifted to more personal topics, and the camaraderie around the table grew even stronger. It was clear that this was more than just a team of colleagues—they were friends, bonded by shared experiences and a mutual passion for the stars. And in this cozy corner of the Gateway Café, surrounded by good food and even better company, Caleb realized that this was exactly where he wanted to be.

However, the mood shifted when the shrill ring of a phone cut through the chatter. All heads turned as Dr. Helen Wright reached into her bag, her expression instantly serious as she answered the call.

She listened intently, her brow furrowing as the voice on the other end relayed what was clearly urgent news. The minutes ticked by, and the group gradually noticed the change in her demeanor, but the buzz of conversation continued unabated. When the call finally ended, Dr. Wright stood up, her eyes scanning the table as she tried to get everyone's attention. Her first attempts to speak were drowned out by the ongoing discussions, so without hesitation, she took a bold step.

In one fluid motion, Dr. Wright climbed onto her chair and then onto the sturdy wooden table, her presence commanding the room. This unexpected move had the desired effect; the animated conversations quickly died down, and a hush fell over the group. All eyes were now on her, their expressions ranging from curiosity to concern.

Holding up her phone like a conductor readying her orchestra, Dr. Wright addressed the team with a voice that, though calm, carried the weight of urgency. "That was SALT—the South African Large Telescope," she began, her gaze sweeping over the faces around the table. "They've been scanning the skies for Alohanui for the past two hours, but they've come up empty. It's not where we predicted it would be."

A ripple of surprise and anxiety passed through the group. Alohanui had been the focus of their work for weeks, and the idea that it could slip through their grasp was unsettling.

Dr. Wright continued, her tone now brisk and decisive. "Our observation window opens in fifteen minutes, which means we need to be ready and in position when our telescopes come online. We can't afford to miss this opportunity."

She turned her attention directly to Caleb, her expression serious. "Caleb, I need you to head over to the control room right now and take a look at the data SALT has gathered. We need to figure out what's going on and fast."

The weight of the moment pressed on Caleb as he nodded, already mentally preparing for the task ahead. The relaxed atmosphere of the café was quickly replaced by the gravity of their work.

Dr. Wright then looked around at the group, her voice softening just a bit. "I know this was a great time, and we all needed the break, but it's time to get back to work. Alohanui isn't going to wait for us."

With that, the group began to stir, the camaraderie of moments before giving way to the focused determination that had driven them all to this point. Dr. Wright stepped down from the table, her leadership unchallenged, and the team quickly gathered their belongings, the urgency of the situation clear in their movements.

Caleb exchanged a brief, reassuring glance with Emma before making his way toward the door. The evening, which had started so leisurely, was now charged with a sense of purpose. As he left the warmth of the café behind and stepped into the cool night air, Caleb's mind was already racing, filled with calculations and questions about where Alohanui could be.

Back in the warm room, Caleb's phone buzzed sharply on the desk, slicing through the din. His heart skipped a beat as he saw Dr. Wright's local flash on the screen. Bracing himself, he answered, but before he could even speak, her voice cut in, sharp and tense.

"It's leaked," she said, her tone tight with frustration. "It's everywhere now. Alohanui Lost! That's one of the kinder headlines. Others are worse—Alohanui Misplaced!—as if we dropped it like a set of car keys."

Caleb felt a knot tighten in his stomach as she continued. "The media's having a field day. I've been fielding calls from reporters non-stop since the story broke. It's out of control. Everyone's looking to us for answers, and they're expecting them now. I'm doing what I can to hold them off, trying to call in every favor for telescope time that I've already burned through."

She paused for a breath, and Caleb could practically hear the exhaustion in her voice. "This is more than a PR nightmare, Caleb. We're on the edge here, and if we don't find Alohanui soon, the whole team, the Institute, our reputation—it could all take a massive hit. People are already starting to whisper about incompetence, and if they start thinking we can't track a major interstellar object, what's next? Little green men jokes? Conspiracy theories? That we can take but the idea that we could lose an asteroid makes us completely useless. We can't do the job we were hired to do. It will be hard at budget time when we are trying to justify our salaries."

Caleb's mind raced. He knew she was right. The stakes had been high before, but now they were skyrocketing. The entire world was watching them, waiting for answers—answers they didn't have yet. The pressure to locate Alohanui had shifted from scientific curiosity to a desperate need for damage control.

Dr. Wright's voice softened, but the urgency was still there. "Caleb, please, for all our sakes, find it. I'll try to keep the press off your back. Just shut off your cell and don't answer your local. We can't afford any more setbacks. Get creative. Use whatever resources you need. Just… find it."

As she hung up, Caleb sat there, phone still in hand, staring blankly at its screen. His mind was already racing ahead, calculating the next steps, running through the possibilities. There was no room for error now.

He turned to continue his walk to the warm room, the cool night air carrying the scent of tropical blooms that filled the university grounds. The path was lined with towering palm trees swaying gently in the breeze, their leaves rustling softly against the backdrop of the star-studded sky. The soft glow of the campus lights cast long shadows across the neatly manicured lawns, where clusters of vibrant hibiscus and plumeria added bursts of color to the night.

As he walked, preoccupied with the missing interstellar object, Emma suddenly appeared, seemingly out of nowhere. Without a word, she grabbed his hand, her touch warm and urgent, and pulled him behind one of the palm tree groves that dotted the pathway. The world seemed to fall away, the sounds of the night fading into the background as she turned to face him.

Before he could react, she reached up, cupping his face with both hands, her eyes locking onto his with an intensity that took his breath away. Then, without hesitation, she kissed him. It was a kiss filled with a mix of emotion—hope, desperation, and something deeper that had been simmering between them for a while.

When she finally pulled back, her eyes still searching his, she gave him a small, almost shy smile. "For luck," she whispered, her voice soft but filled with sincerity.

For a moment that Caleb couldn't afford, they stood there, the cool bark of a palm tree against Caleb's back and the warmth of Emma's hand still in his. The kiss lingered in the air between them, a silent promise that whatever came next, they would face it together.

The stars overhead twinkled brightly, oblivious to the drama unfolding below. But for Caleb, Emma, and the rest of the team, the night was just beginning. The universe had thrown them a curveball, and now it was up to them to catch it. They walked back to the warm room hand in hand.

"We've got to find it again," Dr. Caleb Jacobson muttered, more to himself than to anyone else in the room. "We'll need long exposures to track it, especially with the target so close to the sun. It's tricky, but we have no choice. Whatever it is, it's changed its trajectory—far more dramatically than any comet we've ever seen."

Talking to himself was a habit Caleb found oddly helpful, so he continued, his thoughts racing. "Alright, let's push the boundaries. Think outside the box. It changed it's trajectory more than off gassing could account for. What if we assume something wild—assume it's a spacecraft piloted by something intelligent? If that were the case, wouldn't it aim for Earth? What would its path look like if Alohanui, with its apparent 18-mile-wide solar sail, was trying to come here? To do that, it would need to enter the ecliptic plane. How much thrust would that require? Could a solar sail provide enough?"

"Did you just say ecliptic?" Emma asked, suddenly alert. "If we can narrow our search to the ecliptic plane, we might be able to wrap this up tonight."

"What's 'ecliptic' mean?" came a voice from beneath the table.

Caleb blinked, looking around. "Who's asking?" he inquired, couldn't be an astronomer. After all, the ecliptic plane was taught in Astronomy 101—day one, lesson one, the ecliptic plane.

"Eric from IT," the voice responded.

"Oh, that explains it," Emma said with a chuckle. "What are you up to down there, Eric?"

"Professor Wright asked me to swap out the 1 gigabit switches for new 10 gigabit ones. These were originally intended for the Computer Science Lab but somehow you guys moved up the ladder. And they really are 10 times faster," Eric replied from his spot under the table adding in a whisper, "Well 9 times really but who would notice?".

"Tonight?" Caleb asked, surprised.

"Yes, she thought you might appreciate a bit more bandwidth," Eric explained.

"Absolutely," Caleb agreed. "So, about your question—the ecliptic plane is essentially the flat, imaginary surface formed by Earth's orbit around the Sun. Think of it as a giant tabletop. The planets in our solar system mostly stay within this plane as they move around the Sun, which makes it crucial for tracking their movements in the sky."

Emma jumped in to help, "Eric, imagine you're tiny and standing on this table. You can see all the planets by just turning around; you don't need to look up or down, just left and right."

"So," Eric said thoughtfully, "if Alohanui is intelligent and aiming for Earth, you'd only need to search a small part of the sky."

"Exactly," Caleb nodded. "By the way, did Dr. Wright mention anything else when she gave you this task?"

Eric hesitated before answering, "Well, she did say if I shared anything I overheard, I'd be fired."

Emma and Caleb exchanged amused glances. "That's exactly right, Eric," Caleb said with a grin.

"Any other questions, Eric?" asked Caleb.

"Yes, why is this surfboard under here? It makes it hard to run wires."

Professor Wright sat in her office, surrounded by the controlled chaos that came with managing a groundbreaking project. Her office, tucked away in a quiet corner of the Institute for Astronomy, was a blend of meticulous organization and the inevitable clutter that accompanied her many years of research. Shelves lined with thick volumes on celestial mechanics, star charts pinned to the walls, and a large, wooden desk covered in stacks of papers and open notebooks reflected her lifelong dedication to the mysteries of the cosmos. The soft hum of her computer, the muted rustle of papers, and the occasional beep from her phone were the only sounds in the room, a stark contrast to the storm of activity she was coordinating.

She was in the midst of fielding a barrage of telescope requests from her astronomers and pushback from the telescope directors across the globe. Out of years of habit, she kept the ceiling lights off even when she wasn't observing. The room had an air of quiet urgency, with the large windows letting in a little light from a crescent moon very low in the sky, casting long shadows over the star charts scattered across her desk. This was the nerve center of their operation, where decisions were made that could change the course of their research.

Caleb, sat in his office, the warm room, shared with dozens of other astronomers. He hesitated before dialing her number. He knew the gravity of what he was about to suggest. The entire team—and indeed the broader astronomical community—had so far treated Alohanui as a natural phenomenon. But the latest data, or lack thereof, had thrown them a curveball. The idea that this object might be something more, something intelligent, was an uncharted territory that brought with it a risk of professional ridicule. The very thought of the Institute for Astronomy (IfA) being associated with a belief in "little green men" was almost laughable. It could easily become fodder for jokes and undermine the credibility of their work. If word got out that they were diverting resources based on such a wild theory, the potential embarrassment could ripple through the team, the university, and even the international scientific community.

But the situation demanded action. Alohanui had gone missing, its trajectory no longer aligning with their predictions. The idea that it might have changed course deliberately was growing harder to ignore. Caleb knew they needed to explore every possibility, even the most unconventional ones.

With a sense of trepidation, he picked up the phone and dialed

Professor Wright's number. He expected her to be too busy, or worse, skeptical of his suggestion. But to his surprise, she answered almost immediately, cutting through the anticipated wait with her signature efficiency.

"Professor Wright here," her voice came through, calm and direct, yet carrying the weight of someone juggling a hundred responsibilities at once.

Caleb quickly laid out his thoughts, bracing for the pushback he was certain would follow. But instead of the resistance he feared, there was a moment of silence as she considered his words, followed by a response that caught him completely off guard.

"We'll redirect the telescopes," she said with a calm decisiveness that set Caleb at ease. "Alohanui is lost. We've got to start looking somewhere, and the ecliptic is as good a place as any."

Her swift agreement was a relief, but also a testament to the gravity of the situation. Professor Wright was not one to entertain fanciful ideas, yet she recognized the importance of exhausting every possibility. Caleb could almost picture her in her office, standing amidst her organized chaos, making decisions with the kind of clear-headed pragmatism that had earned her respect throughout the scientific community.

The decision was made, and with it came the weight of knowing they were venturing into uncharted territory. They were about to test a theory that could either lead to a monumental discovery or an embarrassing dead end. But for now, all that mattered was finding Alohanui again, wherever it might be, and whatever it might turn out to be. As Caleb hung up the phone, he felt a renewed sense of purpose. The night was far from over, and their search had just taken a turn that no one could have predicted.

Caleb quickly composed a request to the Catalina Sky Survey, urgently seeking immediate observation time on their 1.5m Cassegrain Reflector, perched atop Mt. Lemmon, just north of Tucson, Arizona. The sun would soon be rising over Tucson, marking the end of the observatory's observing period, but there was still a slim window of opportunity. The last hour of their schedule was often set aside for follow-up requests, and Caleb was hoping that no one else had claimed it.

He meticulously input the coordinates where Alohanui might be if it had used a solar sail to shift into an ecliptic trajectory without altering its velocity. It was a long shot, but Caleb couldn't shake the feeling that maybe, just maybe, this mysterious object wanted to be found. "I guess I'm hoping they want to be seen," he murmured to himself as he pressed the enter key, committing his request to the ether.

The next step was a waiting game—a test of patience. The process was anything but instantaneous. There was the inevitable latency as his request made its way across the internet, followed by the time required for the telescope to align with the target coordinates. Once locked in, the telescope would begin its exposure—a 30-second window capturing whatever lay in the vastness of space. But that was just the start. After the exposure, there was another bout of latency as the data made its way back to Caleb, a 111-megapixel image slowly transmitting to his monitor. He had requested a series of images, each one tracking along the ecliptic trajectory, expecting a new frame every 37 seconds.

As Caleb watched the progress bar inch forward, he couldn't help but feel the weight of the moment. This was no ordinary observation; it was a leap into the unknown. The coordinates he had sent could be completely off, or they could be the key to unlocking the mystery of Alohanui. For now, all he could do was wait, the seconds stretching into what felt like hours, each tick of the clock heightening the tension as he awaited the first image.

Was it pure hubris that led Dr. Jacobson to configure his monitor to display a magnified view of the exact spot in the cosmos where he calculated Alohanui should be? Maybe. But as the first image loaded, his anticipation quickly turned to dismay—there was nothing there. A blank patch of space, empty and unremarkable.

"What did you expect?" he muttered to himself, the reality sinking in. This was a long shot—a long shot in the dark, really—and it hadn't paid off. Doubts began to creep in. What have I gotten myself into? His thoughts drifted to a simpler moment, one where he was strolling through the university gardens with Emma, the sun warm on his back and the scent of blooming flowers in the air. That seemed a world away from the cold, indifferent expanse of space he was staring at now.

But instead of giving in to frustration, he did his job. He methodically began zooming out from the pinpoint he'd so confidently chosen. As he widened the field of view, the screen filled with a familiar tapestry of stars, but still no sign of Alohanui. The void where the object should be felt almost mocking, a silent reminder of the enormity of space and the fragility of human calculations.

With a sigh, Caleb decided to zoom all the way out, expanding the view to show the full extent of the image. It felt like a concession, an acknowledgment that he might have missed the mark entirely. But then, just as he was about to resign himself to defeat, something caught his eye—a streak, faint but unmistakable, running along the top edge of the screen.

His heart leapt in his chest. Excitement, relief, and a tinge of disappointment flooded through him all at once. The streak was long, clearly a moving object, and almost certainly Alohanui. The excitement surged first—he hadn't lost it, after all. There it was, the elusive interstellar visitor, still out there, still moving. Relief followed quickly; he wouldn't go down in history as the astronomer who lost track of the most significant object to ever enter our solar system.

But then came the shadow of disappointment, creeping in to douse the initial spark of excitement. The streak on the image was all wrong. Alohanui's trajectory wasn't heading toward Earth, and its path deviated just enough from the ecliptic plane to deflate his bold theory. Caleb had to admit it: his idea, as audacious as it had been, was incorrect. This wasn't skill; it was sheer luck. Alohanui lingered on the very edge of the frame, precariously close to slipping into oblivion. Had the image been captured a minute later, Alohanui would still be lost.

The realization weighed heavily on him: *I wasn't good, just lucky.* The words looped in his mind, a mantra equal parts frustration and humility. It wasn't his sharp insight that uncovered Alohanui but the cold, unerring precision of Pan-STARRS—the software, the hardware—working without bias or ego. It wasn't his brilliance that led to the discovery but the random chance of being on duty at the exact right moment. If anything, he owed his success to the fortunate timing of the universe rather than his own merit. Awards for astronomers were a curious thing, he thought; if they gave them to telescopes instead, Pan-STARRS would have had this one in the bag.

Still, his flawed theory—though riddled with mistakes—had nudged the telescope just close enough to the truth to salvage the moment. A cosmic near-miss. Caleb couldn't help but smirk ruefully. *Lucky to have made it this far, lucky to have dodged disaster.*

And then his thoughts shifted. *Now, Emma—she's the real deal. She's actually good. And, if I'm being honest, she's the luckiest thing that's ever happened to me.*

The corners of his lips turned up as a wry saying floated to the surface of his thoughts: *Better to be lucky than good.* It rang truer now than ever. He let the idea settle in, not as a burden but as a truth he could live with. *I'm lucky,* he thought, leaning back with a quiet grin. *And I can work with that.*

Caleb leaned back in his chair, his eyes fixed on the streak that stretched across his screen—a streak that embodied both immense potential and profound mystery.

Without wasting another moment, Caleb picked up the phone and made a short call to Dr. Wright. As the call connected, he also sent her a link to the latest image from the Cassegrain Reflector, the one with the streak that had reignited his hope. The image contained all the necessary metadata to help determine if this was indeed Alohanui, or if it was something else—perhaps an uncataloged asteroid, a long-forgotten piece of space debris, or maybe even an old Soviet booster drifting aimlessly through the void.

"Someone needs to check my work," he said, his voice tinged with both excitement and caution. "The streak is so long, if this isn't Alohanui, then we might be dealing with another interstellar visitor altogether."

Dr. Wright didn't miss a beat. "I'll get Mark on it right away," she replied, her tone decisive. "I'll give him a couple of hours to analyze it before we bring in the rest of the team. In the meantime, I want you to retask the Cassegrain to capture a few more images of whatever this is. We need to nail down its trajectory."

Caleb nodded, already pivoting back to his console with renewed focus. He quickly drafted a new request to the Catalina Sky Survey, canceling the previous one and urgently calling for the retasking of the 1.5m Cassegrain Reflector. Time was slipping away—there were only minutes left in Catalina's observation window. Yet, to his relief, the request was instantly granted. It felt almost surreal—astronomy on demand, with the universe just waiting for their next move.

Still, Caleb couldn't help but wonder: *Was this luck, or had Professor Wright leaned on her considerable influence to push my requests to the front of the line?* He smirked at the thought, deciding it was a blend of both—luck that his boss had that kind of pull and luckier still that she chose to use it now.

The chase was back on, and with every new image, they were one step closer to uncovering the truth about this enigmatic object. Whether it was Alohanui or something entirely different, Caleb knew one thing for certain: they were on the brink of something big, and they couldn't afford to miss a single detail.

While the team at the Institute for Astronomy (IfA) was neck-deep in their search for Alohanui, the media was having a field day. Headlines blared sensational claims, none more outrageous than the one splashed across the front page of the *Oahu Observer*: "ALOHANUI PLUNGES INTO SUN! LOST FOR GOOD." Caleb could hardly believe his eyes. How could they write that? It was a blatant lie, a headline designed to grab attention rather than report the truth.

The article's body, however, was more measured. It accurately stated that Alohanui hadn't been found where and when they had expected it to appear. But of course, the journalists were in the dark about the latest developments—especially the promising image from the

Cassegrain Reflector.

Meanwhile, Dr. Mark Hourigan's time was up. He had spent two intense hours poring over the faint trail captured in the Cassegrain image, trying to determine what exactly they were looking at. Neither Dr. Jacobson nor Dr. Wright wanted to disrupt his focus, but they couldn't ignore the need for more data. As new images became available, they sent them his way—Caleb forwarding the latest from the Catalina Sky Survey, and Professor Wright securing additional frames from Pan-STARRS1.

Now, they finally had something solid to work with. The new images provided them with parallax—or in more familiar terms, triangulation. With Hawaii and Arizona separated by 2,500 miles, and Alohanui roughly 93 million miles away, they were in a perfect position to measure the tiny shift in the object's position against the background stars. For astronomical purposes, the stars themselves were essentially fixed points, infinitely far away, making any discrepancy between the images highly valuable.

When they superimposed the two pictures taken at the exact same time from these distant observatories, they noticed a slight but crucial difference in the background star positions. This allowed them to calculate, albeit roughly, the distance of the object they were tracking. The result would reveal whether the mysterious streak they were observing was something in Earth's orbit, a stray piece of space debris, or the elusive Alohanui near the sun.

The calculation took only seconds. The object in the frames was definitely near the sun, almost certainly Alohanui.

Finally, with this critical data in hand, the team could begin to unravel the mystery of what they were really looking at. The pieces were starting to come together, and the truth about Alohanui was within their grasp.

It was time for a press conference. The IfA needed a chance to set the record straight and dampen the hype. Of course, Dr. Wright wanted Caleb to do it. Caleb had come to admire her more and more as they worked together and so he felt he owed it to her to carry on as spokesman for the team.

"Looks like you're going to be thrown back into the spotlight as the spokesperson," Emma said, her tone light but with an underlying note of concern. She knew all too well how the media would latch onto the latest developments, probably spinning wild theories that Alohanui was some colossal spacecraft piloted by super-intelligent extraterrestrials. "I have a feeling the headlines will be full of alien invasion theories by tomorrow morning," she added with a half-smile. "I'm going to miss having you around."

Caleb glanced at her, catching the mix of teasing and genuine concern in her eyes. He tried to play it off, but even he knew his words lacked conviction. "Come on, it won't be as crazy as before. I'll still be around," he said, attempting to sound reassuring, but the uncertainty in his voice was unmistakable.

Emma raised an eyebrow, clearly not buying it. "Really? Because last time, you were barely able to squeeze in a lunch break, let alone any actual research time. And now, with all this new attention, they're going to have you on every news channel, answering every outlandish question they can come up with."

Caleb sighed, rubbing the back of his neck. "I know... It's just... I didn't sign up for this to become some kind of media figure. I just want to study the stars, to understand what Alohanui really is, without all the noise."

Emma's expression softened, and she reached out, placing a hand on his arm. "I know you did. And that's exactly why they want you out there—you're the one who made the discovery, the one who understands it better than anyone else. But just don't forget why you're here, Caleb. Don't let them pull you so far away from the work that you lose sight of what really matters."

He looked down at her hand on his arm, then back into her eyes, feeling a rush of gratitude for her understanding. "I'll try not to," he said more sincerely this time. "But I'm going to need you to remind me of that when things get hectic."

Emma smiled, a mix of warmth and resolve in her expression. "You can count on it. Just remember, while you're out there answering questions, I'll be here, making sure we don't miss anything. We're in this together, right?"

Caleb nodded, feeling a renewed sense of determination. "Right. Together."

But as they stood there, Caleb couldn't shake the nagging feeling that the demands of the media circus were about to pull him further away from the work that truly mattered to him—and from the person who mattered even more. He knew Emma was right; the next few weeks could easily spiral out of control if he wasn't careful. And as much as he tried to reassure her—and himself—he knew that staying grounded in their research, and in their connection, would be his biggest challenge yet.

Dr. Wright managed to reserve the largest hall at the University and scheduled it for 4PM.

By 3:30 pm the hall was packed. Reporters filled the room, their cameras and recorders ready.

Caleb took the podium.

"Before we take questions, I'd like to report on what we know to date," he said.

The first Cassegrain image appeared on a huge screen.

"This was taken yesterday by the 1.5m Cassegrain Reflector, part of the Catalina Sky Survey in Arizona. We believe that this is Alohanui. It is not where we expected it to be when it reappeared from the far side of the sun, in fact it is almost a quarter million miles from where we expected it to be."

The screen then showed successive images from the Cassegrain and then showed a montage of those images showing the long trail of Alohanui's trajectory.

"This is a composite of all the Cassegrain images showing Alohanui's trajectory. We haven't done enough observing over a long enough period of time to get an accurate trajectory but we think that it will travel through the solar system and then back to interstellar space."

"I'll take questions now."

They had set up a microphone on the auditorium floor and reporters scrummed to be first in line.

"Adison James, Oahu Observer. Dr. Jacobson, how did you lose an object 20 miles wide?"

"Every comet and every interstellar object that we know about so far, undergoes small course changes when it gets close to the sun. Comets off-gas and that produces thrust that pushes the comet in a direction away from the sun. 'Oumuamua, even though it didn't seem to have any frozen gasses on its surface, experienced accelerations that were unexpected. With Alohanui, like 'Oumuamua doesn't seem to have any frozen gasses on its surface so we didn't expect outgassing and thrust. But Alohanui does have a large surface. Now we did calculate the force of sunlight pushing on this interstellar object and we did expect some changes in trajectory but what we did not anticipate was that Alohanui might not be spherical. We now believe that Alohanui presented a flat surface to the sun as it went around the back of the sun and that like a sailboat, it tacked changing its trajectory in a way we didn't anticipate and in fact couldn't have anticipated. But we reaquired it really fast, however not fast enough for the media."

"So Alohanui has a solar sail?" asks Adison.

"Probably not, but it probably does have a large flat surface. It's certainly not a spheroid."

"Any chance that Alohanui will hit earth?"

"None at all, as I said, it will travel through the solar system and back into interstellar space. Won't come within 10 million miles, I assure you, I guarantee it." As the words come out of his mouth Caleb instantly regrets them. After all Alohanui has surprised him before, who knows what surprises Alohanui might have left.

"How do you think that Alohanui came to have a flat surface aren't most asteroids and comets roundish?"

"Possibly a collision, splitting a spheroid apart. It would be wonderful to get a close up look at it but we will probably never know."

As Alohanui journeyed farther from the sun and drew nearer to Earth, its unique characteristics became increasingly apparent. Unlike 'Oumuamua, which remained elusive—only visible as a faint streak in time-lapse photographs due to its small size and great distance—Alohanui was large enough to offer a clearer glimpse into its mysteries.

Once Alohanui had passed behind the sun and moved far enough away for telescopes to safely capture detailed images without risking damage to their sensitive CCDs, astronomers worldwide seized the opportunity. Observatories across the globe pivoted their instruments toward the enigmatic visitor, eager to unlock the secrets it held. Even the James Webb Space Telescope (JWST) dedicated an hour to study Alohanui at its closest approach to Earth, capturing data that promised to shed light on its origins and composition.

The global astronomical community, fueled by both curiosity and a sense of urgency, focused intently on Alohanui, knowing that every new image brought them closer to understanding this rare interstellar traveler.

Even with the most advanced, high-resolution telescopes in existence trained on Alohanui, the images produced were nothing more than a single pixel. This fact, however, didn't make it into the headlines of newspapers or online articles. What the public wanted—what they demanded—was a picture. Something tangible, something they could see and interpret, even if it was just a representation. And so, the concept of an "artist's impression" was born. Each pixel captured by the telescopes, though seemingly insignificant, was a treasure trove of data. That pixel fluctuated subtly from moment to moment, changing its signature across the entire electromagnetic spectrum—from radio waves to microwaves, infrared, gamma rays, and beyond. The astronomers were drowning in information, extracting as much as they could from that tiny dot of light. But the public wasn't interested in the complexities of data analysis—they wanted an image, something to visualize the mysterious object hurtling through space.

They would get their picture—a magnificent image painstakingly crafted to combine all the best educated guesses from the scientists studying Alohanui. And somewhere, in very fine print beneath the illustration, would be the words "Artist's Impression," a disclaimer that most would overlook but that would safeguard the scientists from accusations of misleading the public.

It was Emma who first noticed something extraordinary. Her eyes widened with a mixture of excitement and disbelief as she studied the waveform on her monitor. "Caleb, you need to see this," she called out, her voice tinged with both awe and trepidation.

The data she was looking at wasn't an image in the traditional sense—not a photograph—but the radar signature of Alohanui. This signature wasn't static; it changed as Alohanui rotated, presenting different sides to the telescopes from millions of miles away. Neither Caleb nor Emma were experts in radar astronomy, but Emma had a chart that compared radar signatures of various objects: a sphere, naturally the most common shape in space; a cigar shape; a cube; a square prism; a rectangular prism; a triangular prism; a pyramid; and more.

"What do you think?" Emma asked, pointing to the long, wavy line scrolling across her monitor. It resembled an electrocardiogram, and as Caleb and Emma discussed the different segments of the line, they might have been mistaken for two cardiologists consulting over a heart patient.

"That section here is clearly a square," Caleb said, tracing a portion of the waveform with his finger. "But then it shifts—here, it looks more like a four-sided pyramid, and over here, it resembles a triangular prism. A cube would appear as a three-sided pyramid if viewed from a corner, and we do see that signature here, but the four-sided pyramid shows up even more strongly over here."

"This is definitely outside my wheelhouse," Caleb admitted, shaking his head slightly.

Emma nodded, her gaze still fixed on the monitor. "I think we can safely rule out an oblate spheroid," she said. That term applied to almost every large object in the solar system—planets, moons, and even many asteroids—but it clearly didn't apply to Alohanui.

Whatever this object was, it defied the norms of celestial shapes.

They both stared at the waveform in silence for a moment, the weight of their discovery settling in. Alohanui wasn't just another rock in space—it was something different, something that didn't fit neatly into the categories they were familiar with. The object's changing radar signature hinted at an incredibly complex geometry, far beyond the simple, rounded shapes that dominated the cosmos.

As they continued to analyze the data, Caleb and Emma knew they were on the verge of understanding something extraordinary, something that could reshape their understanding of the universe. The more they studied the waveform, the more certain they became that Alohanui was unlike anything humanity had ever encountered —a mysterious visitor from the depths of space, with secrets still waiting to be revealed.

"It's... a square prism, maybe a cube, final answer!" Caleb murmured, his mind racing with the implications. The sheer size and geometric precision of the object were beyond anything they could have anticipated.

News of Alohanui's shape spread like wildfire. Headlines blared sensational stories, speculating wildly about the nature of this massive cube hurtling through space. "Giant Solar Sail or Alien Craft?" some questioned. Others drew parallels to the Borg from *Star Trek*, fanning fears and fascination alike. The idea of Earth being "assimilated" by an alien civilization became a hot topic on social media and news networks.

In response to the growing media frenzy, Caleb found himself at the center of a whirlwind he had never expected. The university's grand auditorium, normally a sanctuary for academic discussions and lectures, was now a battleground of flashing cameras and shouted questions. The room, with its high ceilings and imposing portraits of long-deceased scholars, seemed to preside over the affair, adding to the gravity of the situation.

A large screen behind the podium showcased the now-famous artist's impression, an image of Alohanui—a cube of staggering dimensions, hanging ominously against the backdrop of the stars.

The stark, unnatural geometry of the object seemed almost surreal in the vastness of space, a sight that no one in the room would soon forget.

Dr. Helen Wright stood off to the side, her presence exuding a calm authority that was both reassuring and commanding. Dressed in a sharp navy suit, her silver-streaked hair pulled into a sleek bun, she radiated professionalism, a stabilizing force amid the chaos. Nearby, Emma stood with a tablet in hand, her focused expression revealing her readiness to assist Caleb at a moment's notice. Her calm demeanor, coupled with her innate intelligence, added a sense of order to the otherwise frantic environment.

The press conference began with a barrage of questions, the noise overwhelming as reporters pushed forward, eager to get their microphones closer to Caleb. The cacophony was almost dizzying, but Caleb took a deep breath, grounding himself before addressing the throng.

"Dr. Jacobson, is this the Borg? Is Earth in danger of being assimilated?" one reporter shouted, his voice rising above the clamor and eliciting nervous laughter from the crowd.

Caleb offered a reassuring smile and shook his head lightly. "Let me ease your concerns—Star Trek and the Borg are purely fictional, even if they're still captivating in reruns and grainy low definition. What we're dealing with here, with Alohanui, is undeniably extraordinary, but it remains firmly grounded in the natural world. Its cubic shape and unusual behavior are unlike anything we've observed before, but as of now, we have no concrete evidence to suggest it's anything other than a natural celestial phenomenon."

He paused, reading the anticipation in the room before continuing. "Now, I understand the big question on everyone's mind—could this be piloted or created by an intelligence? I can't definitively say one way or the other, but I can tell you this: we've been actively trying to communicate with Alohanui. We've sent messages using radio waves, lasers, microwaves—every form of signal we can think of. So far, we've received nothing back. No response, not even a hint."

Caleb's expression grew more thoughtful as he elaborated. "Even without us trying to get its attention, any intelligent entity would likely have noticed Earth. Our planet is practically a beacon, emitting every type of electromagnetic signal possible, not to mention neutrinos from our nuclear power plants—signals that have a very distinct signature. So, if there's intelligence behind Alohanui, why hasn't it acknowledged us? And why is it seemingly headed for Jupiter instead of Earth?"

He leaned in slightly, as if to emphasize the point. "Yes, it changed course, but let's not forget that both 2I/Borisov and 'Oumuamua—other interstellar objects—also altered their trajectories. There are those who believe 'Oumuamua was an alien spacecraft, and I have no doubt those same voices will say the same about Alohanui. But until we have more evidence, we have to consider all possibilities—natural and otherwise."

The room was silent for a moment as the reporters processed his words, the atmosphere thick with both skepticism and intrigue. Caleb could sense the weight of what he had just said, knowing that the questions would only grow more intense as the mystery deepened. But he was ready for them, grounded in the pursuit of knowledge, whether the answers lay in the natural world or somewhere far beyond.

As the initial frenzy subsided, a reporter raised their hand and asked, "What is albedo, and why is the albedo of Alohanui so high?"

Grateful for the shift to a more technical question, Caleb explained, "Albedo refers to the percentage of light that an object reflects. For instance, fresh snow has a high albedo because it reflects most of the sunlight that hits it. Alohanui's albedo is nearly 1—meaning it reflects almost all the light that encounters it, similar to freshly fallen snow. This level of reflectivity, especially in an object so large and geometrically perfect, is highly unusual and is something we're actively studying."

Another reporter, trying to keep the momentum, yelled out, "Have you got a better sense of the trajectory?"

"Yes, yes we do," Caleb answered confidently. "With every additional observation, we gather more data on Alohanui's trajectory. While it will ultimately leave the solar system and continue into interstellar space, what's particularly interesting is that it's going to pass very close to Jupiter. The Juno spacecraft, which has been orbiting Jupiter since 2016, is still operational. When we refine our calculations of Alohanui's path sufficiently, NASA may be able to adjust Juno's orbit to capture some incredible close-ups. That possibility is very exciting."

As Caleb continued to field questions, the atmosphere in the auditorium began to shift. The initial shock and sensationalism were giving way to genuine curiosity and a deepening interest in the scientific implications of this discovery. The cube-shaped Alohanui had captured everyone's imagination, from seasoned scientists to casual observers.

"It's a cube!" one reporter exclaimed. "How can that possibly be a natural phenomenon? Can you give us an example of anything cubic in nature?"

Caleb smiled, welcoming the challenge. "Sure. Crystals, for example. In fact, Alohanui has had more spectrometers directed at it than any other celestial object in history. The square face of Alohanui that is presently presenting itself to our telescopes appears to be made of quartz. Imagine that—an enormous, 18-mile-wide quartz crystal! While a crystal of this size is extraordinary, it's not entirely outside the realm of possibility in a universe as vast and varied as ours. There might be processes at work in interstellar space that can form such massive structures. While I'm not saying Alohanui is just a single quartz crystal, at this point, it's a possibility we can't rule out."

The room buzzed with a renewed sense of wonder and excitement. Alohanui was no longer just an anomaly—it was a window into the boundless possibilities of the cosmos, sparking imaginations and pushing the boundaries of human understanding.

The next day at "lunch," which for astronomers came at 6 PM, Dr. Helen Wright once again commandeered the Alohanui team's attention by climbing onto the table. She addressed the room with her usual mix of authority and candor. "Alohanui won't be near Jupiter for another 18 months. Can you believe how fast it's moving? Juno took five years to get from Earth to Jupiter, and Alohanui is making that journey from the Sun in just 18 months."

She paused, scanning the room and making deliberate eye contact with as many team members as she could, ensuring her words resonated. "But here's the thing. Every single one of you has poured hours—weeks—of unpaid overtime into this project. You've been relentless, and it shows in the work. But now, I'm saying you need to take a step back. Rest. Recharge. I don't know what's coming in the next 18 months, but when Juno starts sending back those pictures, we'll be busier than ever. So, starting tomorrow, I want everyone to take a month off."

The room erupted in a mixture of cheers, laughter, and audible sighs of relief. Faces etched with exhaustion suddenly glowed with smiles, the weight of long nights and unrelenting effort temporarily lifted. Caleb surveyed the scene, sensing the collective exhalation but also noting a subtle unease. For many, the idea of stepping away from work that had consumed their lives for months felt foreign—almost unnatural. He himself felt a flicker of doubt. What if slowing down made it harder to gear up again when the time came?

Still, he acknowledged the wisdom in her words. This pause wasn't just a respite; it was a necessary preparation for the chaos to come. In a year and a half, the data from Alohanui would demand more from them than ever before. For now, they had to rediscover how to rest and hope that, when the moment arrived, they'd be ready to rise to the challenge once more.

CHAPTER 3
CELESTIAL
CROSSROADS

A month off! Caleb thought, a wave of relief washing over him. I could definitely use that—like a mini sabbatical. Maybe even finally take Emma on a proper date.

The room was filled with the rich aroma of coffee and the comforting scents of a late-night meal. The team had gathered around a large wooden table, its surface scratched and worn from years of use, each mark telling a story of late-night brainstorming sessions and impromptu celebrations. Plates and mugs were scattered across the table, remnants of the team's hastily assembled dinner. Caleb had a half-eaten sandwich in front of him, its crusts pushed to the side, while Emma was finishing a fresh, colorful salad, the vibrant greens and reds contrasting with the simple white plate. Mark, ever the minimalist, was working through a bowl of tomato soup, the steam rising gently as he dipped a crusty piece of bread into it.

Professor Helen Wright, still standing on top of the table, looked like she had more to say. The overhead lights cast long shadows, making her presence even more commanding. Her tailored suit was a sharp contrast to the casual wear of the others, yet she managed to look both professional and approachable at the same time.

"While I have all of your attention," she began, her voice strong and clear, "I want to take a moment to acknowledge the incredible work each of you has put in over the past year since the discovery of Alohanui. This has been a journey unlike any other, and I'm proud of what we've accomplished together."

She paused, scanning the room, making eye contact with each team member. The room was quiet, save for the occasional clink of silverware against plates.

"But I want to especially recognize three individuals whose contributions have been nothing short of extraordinary," she continued. "Dr. Emma Kanoa, Dr. Mark Hourigan, and of course, Dr. Caleb Jacobson."

At the mention of his name, Caleb felt a mix of pride and humility. He glanced at Emma, who gave him a warm, encouraging smile, and then at Mark, who nodded subtly, his expression one of quiet satisfaction.

Professor Wright's gaze settled on Caleb as she delivered the news that left him momentarily speechless. "It's official, but it hasn't been announced yet—the U.S. Astronomy Group has selected Dr. Caleb Jacobson to be this year's recipient of the Edwin Powell Hubble Medal of Honor for the most important discovery of the year."

The room erupted in applause, the sound echoing off the walls, filling the space with a sense of shared accomplishment. Caleb's heart raced, the magnitude of the recognition sinking in.

Helen Wright, her voice now softer, added one final note, almost as an afterthought but with a twinkle of pride in her eyes. "By the way," she said quietly, leaning slightly forward as if to share a secret, "it comes with a $100,000 prize."

The table fell silent for a brief moment as the words sunk in, and then the congratulations came in earnest, everyone leaning in to pat Caleb on the back, shake his hand, or simply share in the moment. The room felt warmer, more intimate, as they basked in the glow of their collective success.

As the team settled back into their seats, the conversation picked up again, but the mood had shifted. There was a new energy in the air, a sense of anticipation for what lay ahead. For Caleb, the prospect of a month off suddenly seemed even sweeter, a chance to savor this victory, plan the next steps, and perhaps most importantly, spend more time with Emma—time that, until now, had been a rare luxury.

Dr. Wright had done what seemed impossible—she deftly reassigned the duties of every team member, except herself, to other astronomers scattered across the globe. Caleb marveled at her efficiency. It was one thing to manage a project of this magnitude, but it was another entirely to navigate the labyrinthine bureaucracies of both the university and the wider astronomical community with such finesse. Wright's ability to orchestrate this without missing a beat only deepened Caleb's respect for her. She had, once again, proven why she was at the helm of such a groundbreaking project.

The next morning, Caleb met up with Emma, their destination set for the famed North Shore, where the best surfing on Oahu could be found. The North Shore was a world apart from the tourist-heavy beaches of Diamond Head, where the waves were gentler, and the sand was softer, catering to beginners and casual surfers. In contrast, the North Shore was raw, wild, and untamed. The beaches here were framed by jagged rocks and lined with coarse, golden sand that met the powerful, thunderous waves with a roar. The water was a deeper blue, almost indigo, and the waves—massive and unforgiving—were the stuff of legends. Only the most skilled surfers dared to challenge them, and Emma was one of them.

She knew this coastline intimately, which was why she insisted on driving. "If we take your car, the locals might scratch it, or worse, puncture your tires," she warned with a knowing smile as they packed up their gear. "I'm a local, and they know me. The Edwin Powell Hubble Medal of Honor doesn't mean anything to them. But if you're with me, we'll get the good parking spots and the respect we deserve!"

Caleb couldn't argue with that. He knew enough to trust her judgment. As they loaded their boards onto her car, the difference between them was stark. Emma's surfboard was well-worn, its edges smoothed by years of use, yet it was still superior in every way. The board had a few nicks and scratches, each one a testament to her skill and the many waves she had conquered. The shape was sleek, perfectly designed for the kinds of waves they would encounter on the North Shore—sharp, fast, and responsive. It was clear that this board had seen many epic days on the water and had been expertly maintained despite its wear.

In contrast, Caleb's surfboard was a far cry from Emma's. It was a budget-friendly model he had picked up at a discount store, more out of convenience than any real consideration for quality. The board was functional, sure, but it lacked the finesse and craftsmanship of Emma's. The plastic fins were clearly mass-produced, and the wax job was haphazard at best. It was a board designed for the gentle waves of Diamond Head, not the ferocious breakers of the North Shore. Caleb could see the difference in their gear and felt a twinge of self-consciousness, but Emma didn't seem to mind.

As they drove along the winding coastal roads, the landscape changed dramatically. The high-rises and tourist traps of Honolulu gave way to lush, rolling hills and small, tight-knit communities. The ocean was never far from view, its vastness a constant companion as they traveled. When they finally reached the North Shore, the air was thick with the scent of salt and the sound of waves crashing against the shore.

They parked in a small, gravel lot nestled between a row of palm trees and a grassy dune, a prime spot that would have been out of the question without Emma's local clout. As they unloaded their boards, Caleb felt the tension of the last few weeks begin to melt away. Here, with the roar of the ocean and the sun beating down on his back, the stress of Alohanui, the media frenzy, and even the weight of his recent honor felt distant.

Emma led the way to the water's edge, her surfboard under her arm with the ease of someone who had done this countless times before. Caleb followed, his board feeling a bit heavier and less sure. The waves were massive, intimidating even, but there was a thrill in the air—a sense that this was where they were meant to be.

As they paddled out together, Caleb couldn't help but steal a glance at Emma. She was in her element, her eyes scanning the horizon, searching for the perfect wave. He realized then that this was exactly what he needed—not just the challenge of the surf, but the time with her, away from the pressures of their work, where they could simply be themselves.

The waves on the North Shore were as unforgiving as they were exhilarating. Caleb's first few attempts were rough, his board struggling to keep up with the power of the ocean. But Emma, with her well-worn board and effortless skill, glided over the water like she was born to it. She caught wave after wave with a grace that left Caleb both in awe and motivated to keep trying.

The day wore on, and as the sun began to set, casting the sky in shades of orange and pink, they finally headed back to shore. Exhausted but exhilarated, they collapsed onto the sand, their boards resting beside them.

Caleb looked over at Emma, her face glowing with the kind of happiness that only comes from doing something you truly love. "Thanks for bringing me here," he said, his voice filled with gratitude.

Emma smiled, her eyes reflecting the last light of the day. "Anytime, Caleb. I needed this as much as you did."

Caleb stood in the shade of a tall palm tree, its broad, emerald fronds swaying gently in the warm breeze. The late afternoon sun cast dappled patterns on the ground, creating a dance of light and shadow around him. He leaned against the rough, fibrous trunk, the coarse texture grounding him in the present moment, even as his thoughts drifted elsewhere. The weight of responsibility still hung heavy on his broad shoulders, despite being officially relieved of his duties. The month-long break he had been granted was supposed to be a time for rest, but Caleb knew that his mind would be far from restful.

At six feet tall with a lean, athletic build, Caleb usually carried himself with a relaxed, easy going demeanor, but today there was a tension in his posture that betrayed his inner turmoil. His sandy brown hair was tousled by the wind, and his hazel eyes, usually bright with curiosity, were clouded with concern. Even with the luxury of time off, he couldn't shake the sense that he was still the unofficial guardian of Alohanui. The responsibility felt like a mantle he had donned, one that he couldn't easily shrug off.

Being the spokesman for the team had come with its own set of challenges. In many ways, it had felt like he was speaking on behalf of Alohanui itself, defending it against the rampant sensationalism of the media. The journalists had latched onto the term "Borg Cube," drawing parallels to the ominous, fictional entity from *Star Trek*. Caleb knew the comparison was ridiculous, yet he couldn't help but take it personally. He had spent countless hours clarifying, correcting, and, in his own way, protecting the enigmatic object from the barrage of misinformation that swirled around it.

Emma approached him quietly, her presence as calming as the rustling leaves overhead. She was now out of her bikini and dressed casually, in a light, sleeveless top and comfortable jeans, her long, dark hair tied back in a loose ponytail. Her brown eyes, deep and warm, reflected both intelligence and empathy—qualities that Caleb had come to rely on more than he realized. Her surfboard, which leaned against the palm tree next to them, bore the marks of many adventures, its once vibrant colors now faded from years of exposure to the sun and sea. It was a testament to her skill and passion, much like the way she approached everything in life.

"You look like you're miles away," Emma said softly, leaning against the tree beside him.
Caleb smiled faintly, grateful for her presence. "I guess I am," he admitted, his voice tinged with a mix of exhaustion and resolve. "Even with a month off, I can't help but think about Alohanui. I've been defending it for so long, it feels like I'm responsible for it, like I'm its guardian."

Emma nodded, understanding. She knew how deeply Caleb had invested himself in this discovery. "It's hard to switch off, especially when it's something that important. But you deserve this break, Caleb. You've earned it."

He sighed, turning his gaze out to the horizon where the sun was beginning its slow descent. "What's been on my mind the most is how close Alohanui is going to come to Jupiter. The calculations are precise, but there's still a margin of error. There's a chance it could collide with Jupiter, and that would be... catastrophic. Alohanui could be destroyed, and that would be the end of this story we've only just begun to tell."

Emma listened quietly, her eyes never leaving his face as he continued. "Then there's the other possibility—a reverse slingshot. Alohanui could pass so close that it slows down, while Jupiter speeds up just a bit, though no one would notice. What would the media say about that? And what might happen to Juno if that takes place?"

He paused, lost in thought for a moment, before he continued. "I've been thinking I should reach out to NASA, talk to them about what might happen to Juno if Alohanui passes that close. But I'm not even sure who to talk to. Dr. Wright would know, of course. She always knows."

Emma smiled, a soft, understanding smile. "You're not alone in this, Caleb. You have a team that respects you and a partner who's here to help you through it. Take the time you need, but don't carry this burden by yourself."

Caleb looked at her, appreciating the calm reassurance in her words. "You're right. I just can't seem to let go of it completely. But maybe that's okay. I'll take this time, but I'll keep thinking about it, too. And when the month is up, I'll be ready to face whatever comes next."

Eighteen months. In just eighteen months, Alohanui would reach Jupiter, a monumental event that Caleb couldn't stop thinking about. The vast cube, hurtling through space, would most likely fly by the gas giant at such incredible speed that Juno, the spacecraft orbiting Jupiter, would only have time to capture a dozen or so images. Out of those, if they were lucky, maybe one or two would be truly breathtaking—images that would leave the world in awe.

The thought of what could be revealed in those fleeting moments preoccupied Caleb's mind. Eighteen months felt both like a lifetime and a blink of an eye. It was, after all, the same amount of time that had passed since he had graduated from university and thrown himself into the deep end of professional astronomy. So much had changed in those months, yet here he was, still caught in the gravitational pull of the mysterious Alohanui.

As he stood on the beautiful beach under the shade of a swaying palm tree, the setting sun casting golden hues across the waves, his thoughts drifted back to the object of his obsession. "Once we're back to work, I'd like to run more simulations of Alohanui's swing around the sun," Caleb mused internally. The fact that they hadn't known about Alohanui's perfectly flat, 18-mile-square face nagged at him. It had to have influenced the object's trajectory and the way it interacted with solar radiation. He felt an itch to dive back into the data, to re-run the models with this new information and see what secrets might be uncovered.

In this perfect setting, with the warm sand beneath his feet and the calming rhythm of the waves in his ears, Caleb should have felt completely at peace. But his mind was elsewhere, far away in the cold, distant reaches of space, pondering the intricacies of a mysterious interstellar visitor.

Emma, standing beside him, noticed the faraway look in his eyes. She knew that look well. It was the same look he got whenever he was lost in thought, turning over some complex problem in his mind. She smiled softly, though there was a hint of wistfulness in her expression. She had hoped that today, here on this beautiful beach, his thoughts might be more grounded, more present—with her.

Realizing that Caleb was once again deep in thought about Alohanui, Emma decided to gently pull him back to the here and now. "I think I'd like to take you back home," she said, her voice laced with playful mischief, a coy smile playing on her lips.

Caleb snapped back to the present, her words drawing him out of his reverie. "Great!" he replied, a grin spreading across his face. "I've never been to your place. Today was the first time I even saw where you live." He hoped he understood what she had in mind, the possibility sending a thrill through him.

Emma's smile widened as she saw the hopeful glint in his eyes, but she wasn't quite done yet. "You didn't let me finish," she teased, her tone soft and inviting. "I think I'd like to take you home to meet my parents."

Caleb blinked, momentarily taken aback. "Am I dressed appropriately for that?" he asked, looking down at his casual attire—board shorts, a simple T-shirt, and flip-flops, all of which seemed more suited for the beach than for meeting someone's parents.
Emma laughed, a light, melodious sound that Caleb loved to hear. "Don't worry, they're not formal people. They'll just be happy to meet you."

The idea of meeting Emma's parents stirred a mixture of excitement and nervousness in Caleb. It was a significant step, one that he hadn't quite expected today, but one that felt right. As he looked into Emma's eyes, the thoughts of Alohanui faded just a bit, replaced by the realization that this moment, here on the beach with her, was just as important—if not more so.

"Then let's go," he said, his voice steady and sure. "I'm ready."

Caleb, feeling a mix of anticipation and nerves, accompanied Emma to meet her parents, Ted and Star Kanoa. As they pulled up to the modest home, Caleb took in the surroundings. The house was a classic example of mid-20th century Hawaiian architecture, a wood-frame structure raised on piles to protect against flooding during the rainy season. Built in the 1960s, it had a weathered charm, with its sun-bleached siding and the soft creak of the wooden steps leading up to the lanai. The front yard was small but lush, bursting with vibrant tropical plants—hibiscus, plumeria, and a few spiky ti leaves, their rich greens and reds contrasting against the warm hues of the house.

As they approached the front door, it swung open, and Caleb found himself face-to-face with Emma's parents. Ted Kanoa was a robust man in his sixties, his skin bronzed by the sun and his hair, once jet black, now streaked with silver. He wore a loose-fitting aloha shirt adorned with a traditional floral pattern, the bright blues and greens echoing the ocean and foliage that surrounded their home. His shorts were simple and practical, showing off his sturdy legs, which spoke of a lifetime spent outdoors—fishing, surfing, and tending to his garden. Ted's eyes were sharp, yet warm, as he took in Caleb with a quick, appraising glance before breaking into a welcoming smile.

Beside him stood Star Kanoa, petite and graceful, her Chinese heritage evident in her delicate features and the soft, almond shape of her eyes. She had emigrated from Hong Kong with her parents in 1998 just before the British colony was returned to China, and though many years had passed, she still carried herself with the quiet elegance that was a hallmark of her upbringing. Her hair, long and glossy black with only a few strands of gray, was pulled back into a simple bun, and she wore a light, flowing dress in soft pastels that complemented her serene demeanor. The dress, adorned with intricate floral embroidery, seemed to sway gently with her movements, much like the fronds of the palms that surrounded their home. Star's smile was gentle, her gaze thoughtful and kind as she greeted Caleb with a nod that was both respectful and welcoming.

The interior of the house was cozy and inviting, filled with the comforting scent of something delicious simmering in the kitchen. The decor was a mix of Hawaiian and Chinese influences—a testament to the blending of two rich cultures. Wooden furniture, lovingly polished over the decades, was adorned with delicate Chinese ceramics and vibrant Hawaiian quilts. A large family portrait hung on the wall, capturing a younger Ted and Star with Emma as a child, all of them smiling against the backdrop of the Pacific Ocean.

Ted gestured for them to sit at the large, round dining table, which was covered with a simple, yet elegant, tablecloth that Star had embroidered herself. The table was set for dinner, with an assortment of dishes that reflected the couple's blended heritage—steamed fish with ginger and scallions, a plate of poke made with the freshest ahi tuna, and a colorful stir-fry of local vegetables.

As they sat down, Caleb felt a wave of calm wash over him. The house, with its warm wooden floors and the soft murmur of conversation, felt like a sanctuary from the world outside. Ted and Star made him feel at ease, their genuine warmth and hospitality shining through in every word and gesture.

"So, Caleb," Ted began, his voice deep and resonant, "Emma's told us a lot about you. We're glad to finally meet the man she's been spending so much time with."

Caleb smiled, feeling the tension in his shoulders ease slightly. "I'm honored to meet you both," he replied, his voice steady. "Emma's been wonderful to me, and I'm grateful for the chance to get to know her better—and now, to meet her family."

Star's eyes twinkled with amusement as she exchanged a glance with Ted. "Well, we're just happy that she's found someone who shares her passions," she said, her voice as soft and soothing as the gentle waves outside.

The evening unfolded in a comfortable rhythm, with stories exchanged over the delicious meal. Ted regaled them with tales of his surfing days on the North Shore, while Star spoke of her journey from Hong Kong to Hawaii, the challenges and triumphs she had experienced along the way. Caleb listened intently, feeling a deepening connection not only to Emma but to the rich tapestry of her family's history.

As the night wore on, Caleb realized that this was more than just a meeting of introductions. It was the beginning of something deeper, a blending of lives and stories that felt as natural as the ocean meeting the shore. And in that moment, surrounded by Emma's family, Caleb felt a profound sense of belonging—like he had found a new home, one built not just of wood and nails, but of love and shared experiences.

Two thoughts struck Caleb simultaneously: First, Emma hadn't met his parents yet. Second, he now had $100,000 sitting in the bank. The combination of these realizations stirred a sense of excitement in him, and the next day, after a trip to the North Shore, he turned to Emma.

"Would you like to meet my parents?" Caleb asked, his voice laced with hopeful anticipation.

"Of course," Emma replied without hesitation, though a flicker of uncertainty crossed her mind. The thought of visiting the American Southwest gave her pause, bringing with it a few reservations. She couldn't help but wonder, perhaps unnecessarily, if her skin might be a little too dark for the region. But she quickly brushed aside the thought, her smile warming as she looked into Caleb's eager eyes.

"Could you pack tonight and leave with me tomorrow?" he pressed, his excitement palpable.

"Of course," she echoed, though this time her voice carried a growing excitement of her own. The enthusiasm in Caleb's eyes was contagious, and she found herself looking forward to the adventure ahead. "But what about work? We're supposed to be back tomorrow."

"I cleared it with Dr. Wright already," he said, a hint of mischief in his grin. "Is that okay?"

"Yes, absolutely," Emma agreed, her reservations melting

away.

"Great," Caleb said, his smile widening as he quickly tapped a few buttons on his phone.

"Your ticket is on its way," he added, sending the boarding pass to her with a satisfied nod.

Emma's phone buzzed with the arrival of the boarding pass, and as she looked down at the screen, she felt a surge of excitement. This was more than just a trip—it was a step forward, an invitation into Caleb's world, and she was ready to embrace it fully.

The next morning, they found themselves at Daniel K. Inouye International Airport in Honolulu, the air thick with humidity as they navigated the bustling terminal. The airport was alive with the sounds of travelers—families heading out on vacation, business people making their way to meetings, and surfers with boards in tow, chasing the next big wave. The scent of tropical flowers mingled with the crisp, cool air conditioning as they made their way through the terminal, the large windows offering sweeping views of the tarmac against the backdrop of lush, green mountains.

Their flight to Oklahoma City would be long, but Caleb couldn't help but feel a sense of anticipation. The journey would take them from the vibrant, sun-soaked shores of Hawaii to the heartland of America, where the landscape would shift dramatically—from the turquoise waters of the Pacific to the endless plains of Oklahoma.

As they boarded the plane, Caleb noticed the contrast in Emma's expression—both excitement and a hint of apprehension. The flight was smooth, the hours passing quickly as they soared high above the Pacific Ocean, the blue expanse stretching out endlessly beneath them. Soon, they crossed over the continental United States, where the rugged terrain of the West gave way to the flat, sprawling plains of the SouthWest. The descent into Will Rogers World Airport in Oklahoma City offered a bird's-eye view of the vast, open land below, dotted with the occasional cluster of buildings and the winding paths of rivers cutting through the fields.

Will Rogers World Airport was much smaller than Honolulu's, with a quieter, more laid-back atmosphere. The terminal, with its rustic design elements—wood beams and brick accents—welcomed them with a sense of understated charm. The people moved at a slower pace, the urgency of the islands replaced by the easygoing rhythm of the SouthWest.

As they exited the airport and made their way through the city, the landscape around them began to change. The tall skyscrapers of downtown Oklahoma City eventually gave way to suburban neighborhoods, where wide streets were lined with neatly kept houses and well-manicured lawns. Trees, now in the full bloom of summer, shaded the sidewalks, and children played in the yards, their laughter echoing in the warm evening air.

Caleb's parents lived in a quiet, comfortable neighborhood that epitomized the American dream. The houses were all variations of the classic ranch style—single-story homes with wide porches, big windows, and driveways leading up to two-car garages. Caleb's parents' house was no different—a cozy, brick home with a large oak tree in the front yard, its branches providing ample shade. The lawn was lush and green, meticulously cared for by his father, who took pride in keeping it in perfect condition.

The house itself was warm and inviting, a place where Caleb had grown up surrounded by love and security. Inside, the decor was a blend of comfort and nostalgia—plush sofas, family photos lining the walls, and the faint scent of homemade apple pie wafting from the kitchen. The living room was dominated by a large, stone fireplace, its mantle decorated with keepsakes and mementos from family vacations and milestones.

Caleb's mother, Jean, a kind woman with silvering hair and a warm smile, greeted them at the door, pulling Emma into a hug as if she were already part of the family. His father, Jake, a sturdy man with a salt-and-pepper beard, followed suit, welcoming them both with a firm handshake and a hearty laugh.

As they settled in, the evening unfolded with the easy, unhurried pace that Caleb remembered from his childhood. They shared stories over a home-cooked meal, Caleb's parents asking Emma questions about her life in Hawaii, their genuine curiosity and warmth putting her at ease. The initial reservations she had felt began to melt away, replaced by a sense of belonging.

When Emma stepped into Caleb's childhood home, one detail immediately caught her attention—the plaques. Though small, they stood out, carefully placed in various rooms, each bearing a different scripture inscribed in elegant, flowing script. These quiet reminders of faith seemed woven into the fabric of the house, reflecting the beliefs that had shaped Caleb's upbringing.

One plaque in the living room particularly drew her in. Hanging above a side table adorned with family photos and fresh flowers, it read: "For God so loved the world, that He gave His only begotten Son, that whosoever believeth in Him should not perish but have everlasting life. John 3:16." Though familiar in passing, the verse struck Emma differently this time. Its simple yet profound message resonated with her, bridging intimacy and universality.

Emma reflected on her own upbringing, steeped in a blend of her mother's Buddhist spirituality and her father's Hawaiian traditions. Respect for nature, meditation, and ancestral reverence had shaped her worldview, leaving Christianity a foreign concept. The teachings, scriptures, and idea of a singular, all-encompassing God were uncharted territory for her.

Standing there, rereading the verse, Emma felt a stirring curiosity. This home, with its warmth and love, seemed built on these beliefs. She saw it in the way Caleb's parents interacted, their gentle respect for the world and others. It was a lived faith, quietly expressed yet deeply ingrained.

Throughout the evening, the verse lingered in her thoughts, prompting her to consider how it shaped Caleb's family. This visit, she realized, wasn't just about meeting his parents—it was about uncovering layers of his world and understanding the foundations of the man she cared for so deeply.

For Caleb, the plaques were simply part of the home he knew. For Emma, they opened a door to new understanding, offering insight into Caleb's life and the broader tapestry of faith, love, and family that shaped him.

As Jean guided Emma through the house, showing her the bedrooms and even the pantry, Emma noticed scripture plaques everywhere—even in unexpected places like the garage and storage rooms. Only the water heater closet, with its bare studs, was spared. Each plaque bore a thoughtfully chosen verse, reinforcing the pervasive yet understated faith within the home. Eventually, curiosity compelled her to turn to Caleb.

"Your house has a lot of Bible wall art. I guess your family is Christian, but you've never really talked about it," Emma said gently.

Caleb glanced at a familiar plaque and smiled. "No, I haven't. I was raised Christian—church three times a week, Sunday school, the works. But honestly, it never really stuck."

Intrigued, Emma asked, "What do you mean?"

Caleb leaned back, gathering his thoughts. "When I went to Caltech, it was a different world. Almost everyone—students and professors alike—was atheist. The emphasis on evidence, science, and logic made it hard to hold onto what I was taught growing up. Sunday school presented a literal interpretation of creation—six days, genealogies tracing from Adam to Jesus, suggesting a 6,000-year-old universe. But astronomy showed me a universe 13.8 billion years old. The science was clear, and reconciling it with my upbringing became impossible."

His voice softened. "I didn't abandon belief entirely—it just changed. I started seeing faith as more abstract, tied to the awe and wonder I feel when I study the cosmos. The literal interpretations no longer fit."

Emma listened intently. "So, you've redefined it?"

"Yeah," Caleb admitted. "I believe in something greater, but it's more about the mysteries of the universe than the teachings I grew up with."

Emma placed a hand on his arm. "I'm glad you shared this with me. It's important to explore, even without clear answers."

Caleb smiled, feeling a weight lift. They sat in reflective silence, the plaques around them taking on deeper meaning—symbols of Caleb's journey and his ongoing quest for understanding.

As the evening unfolded, Emma began to see this visit not just as meeting Caleb's family but as stepping into the roots of his life. Together, they sat on the porch, the Oklahoma night carrying the scent of fresh-cut grass. Caleb cherished the moment, where past and present converged, with Emma by his side.

Emma and Caleb spent two weeks at his parents' home, a time that felt both nostalgic and enlightening. Caleb settled into his old childhood bedroom, a space that had been lovingly preserved as if frozen in time since the day he left for Caltech. The room was a snapshot of his younger self, with posters of constellations and galaxies still taped to the walls, his high school trophies lined up on the dusty shelves, and his old desk cluttered with remnants of unfinished projects and notebooks filled with sketches and ideas. Sleeping in that room brought a flood of memories—of late-night study sessions, dreaming about the stars, and the innocence of youth before the complexities of the world had fully set in.

Emma, out of respect for his parents' beliefs, stayed in the guest room. The room was simple but cozy, with a neatly made bed covered in a quilt that Caleb's mother, Jean had sewn years ago. The walls were painted a soft, calming blue, and there was a small dresser topped with a vase of fresh flowers that Jean had placed there to make her feel welcome. Despite being a guest, Emma felt at home in the Jacobson household, surrounded by warmth and kindness.

The two weeks were a whirlwind of activities, filled with visits to all the tourist spots that Oklahoma City had to offer. They toured the Oklahoma City National Memorial and Museum, walked through the vibrant Bricktown District, and spent an afternoon at the Oklahoma City Zoo. Jake and Jean joined them for many of these outings, sharing stories and laughter along the way. The experience brought Emma closer to Caleb's world, allowing her to see the place and the people who had shaped him.

As the days passed, there was a growing sense of belonging for Emma, and a deepened appreciation for Caleb's roots. For Caleb, the visit was a bittersweet reminder of the passage of time and the journey he had taken from his small hometown to the vast reaches of space. It was grounding, in a way, to reconnect with his family and his past, even as he prepared to return to the life he had built in Honolulu.

When the time came to head back to Honolulu, there was a palpable sense of reluctance mixed with excitement. They had enjoyed their time in Oklahoma City, the warmth of family, and the slower pace of life. But the call of their work, and the mysteries yet to be uncovered, beckoned them back to Hawaii.

As they packed their bags and said their goodbyes, there was an unspoken understanding between them. This trip had been more than just a visit; it was a step forward in their relationship, a blending of their lives and their worlds. And as they boarded the plane back to Honolulu, they knew that while they were leaving one home behind, they were returning to another—a place where the stars awaited, and where the next chapter of their journey together would begin.

While Caleb and Emma were away, the world of astronomy continued to spin on, not slowing for a moment. In fact, the study of Alohanui seemed to gain momentum in their absence. Caleb's alma mater, CalTech, became a hive of activity as a group of astronomers took it upon themselves to delve deeper into the mysterious object's trajectory. Armed with the new data about Alohanui's shape and composition—specifically a perfectly flat, 18-mile by 18-mile highly reflective surface—they re-ran all the calculations for its swing behind the Sun.

Mark Hourigan handed Caleb a stack of papers, his eyes alight with excitement. "You won't believe it, Caleb," he said, almost breathless. "The CalTech team nailed it. They've confirmed that sunlight and solar wind alone can account for Alohanui's trajectory, including that mysterious course change behind the Sun. It's all there in the data, clear as day."

Caleb flipped through the papers, scanning the meticulous calculations and detailed graphs. His heart raced as the implications of the findings sank in. "Vindicated!" he exclaimed, a grin spreading across his face. "This will make future press conferences so much easier to handle. We can finally shut down the *Borg Cube* theory and, hopefully, put to rest any fears about assimilation."

Emma, standing beside him, shared in his relief. The burden of defending Alohanui against wild speculation had weighed heavily on both of them, but now they had solid, scientific answers to back them up. The room buzzed with a renewed sense of purpose, the energy almost palpable as their colleagues discussed the implications of the CalTech findings.

Dr. Wright, her face still glowing with pride, added, "This is a significant leap forward. Not only does it validate our approach, but it also establishes a new standard for how we tackle these kinds of discoveries in the future. We've shown that we can depend on the fundamental laws of physics to explain even the most extraordinary phenomena."

Caleb nodded in agreement, though inwardly, he couldn't help but acknowledge the irony. The truth was, the only reason he had managed to locate Alohanui after its swing behind the sun was because he had entertained the outlandish notion that it might be a spacecraft piloted by intelligent aliens heading toward Earth. It was a reckless assumption—one born out of desperation rather than logic. How foolish he had been, and yet, how incredibly lucky.

The *warm room*, filled with the hum of excitement and the rustle of papers, felt like a different place from the one they had left just a few weeks ago. The atmosphere was charged with anticipation, but this time, it was tempered with a sense of clarity and direction. They weren't chasing shadows anymore —they were on the cusp of real, tangible discovery.

Dr. Wright couldn't help but smile as she watched Caleb and Emma dive back into the work they had left behind. "It's good to have you both back," she said warmly. "The next phase of this study is going to be even more exciting, and we're going to need all hands on deck."

Caleb nodded, feeling a renewed sense of purpose. The time spent with his family in Oklahoma had been meaningful, grounding him in ways he hadn't anticipated. But now, standing in the midst of his team, surrounded by the tools of his trade and the people who shared his passion, he knew that this was where he belonged.

Emma, too, felt the pull of their work, the thrill of discovery that had first drawn her to astronomy. As they settled back into the rhythm of their research, both of them knew that Alohanui still held many mysteries—mysteries they were determined to uncover together.

After meeting each other's parents, Caleb felt a quiet certainty settle over him—both his and Emma's families would now be watching their relationship with growing expectations. He knew his own parents, Jake and Jean Jacobson, well enough to predict exactly what they would hope for. In their minds, the ideal progression was clear: Emma would convert to Christianity, he and Emma would get engaged, get married, buy a house, and eventually raise children who would be brought up as firm believers in the faith. The vision was so vivid in his mind that he could almost hear his mother's voice, gently nudging him toward that future.

But when it came to Emma's parents, Ted and Star Kanoa, Caleb wasn't as certain. He wondered what they might expect of him and their daughter. Would they be comfortable with the two of them moving in together, or would they, like his own parents, prefer that marriage come first? There was also the possibility that they had been so gracious and polite during his visit that they hadn't revealed their true feelings—perhaps they had reservations about him that they hadn't voiced, or maybe they were entirely accepting but simply more reserved in expressing their hopes.

Caleb found himself ensnared in a tangle of assumptions

and uncertainties, but one thing was clear: his parents were likely to be disappointed. "They know I'm a backslider," he thought, the term resonating from his upbringing yet feeling disconnected from the man he had become. He had long since drifted from the religious convictions of his youth and had no intention of imposing them on Emma, whose spiritual path was shaped by her own cultural and religious background.

"I won't let my parents force their beliefs on my partner," Caleb resolved, the thought crystallizing. He loved Emma for who she was, not for who she might become under the weight of his family's expectations. Their relationship thrived on mutual respect and understanding, and Caleb was determined to protect that, even if it meant disappointing the people who had raised him. The road ahead would be complicated, navigating the hopes and desires of two families from vastly different worlds. Yet Caleb was certain of one thing: their choices would remain true to who they were—individually and as a couple.

Other than the trip to Oklahoma, Caleb hadn't touched his $100,000 Edwin Powell Hubble Prize money. The balance had been sitting in his bank account, a symbol of both his recent achievement and the looming financial obligations that constantly weighed on his mind.

"I was planning on using it to pay off $80,000 of my $440,000 student loans," he said as they strolled through the university grounds during a break. The campus was alive with the usual hustle and bustle of student life, but Caleb's thoughts were focused elsewhere. "But then I started thinking… maybe we could use it as a down payment on a house. That way, we wouldn't have to keep paying rent."

Emma listened carefully, her eyes thoughtful as they wandered over the familiar paths of the campus. "I've lived rent-free with my parents my whole life, except when I was working on my doctorate at Washington State in Seattle," she began. "Even then, I stayed with my aunt and uncle in Kirkland, just across the lake from the campus. I didn't accumulate any debt getting my education—scholarships covered my undergrad at the University of Hawaii, and I earned about $20,000 a year as a TA at WSU. I've always had a part-time job from high school on. Mom's frugality rubbed off on me; she's the one who manages all the money at home."

Caleb couldn't help but feel a little envious of her situation. "Wow, we really are different," he admitted. "I mean, I worked through school and was a TA too, but no scholarships. And honestly, managing money has never been my strong suit."

Emma gave him a reassuring smile. "It's not easy, especially when you've got so much on your plate. But here's the thing—I think we can figure it out together. Maybe it's not the right time to buy a house. We could focus on what's more pressing right now."

Caleb looked at her, feeling a weight lift off his shoulders. "You're right," he said, after a moment of reflection. "I've been thinking about it, and maybe we should hold off on the house. I can use most of the prize money to make a dent in my student loans—$80,000 is a start. And with what's left, well... I was thinking I could get you something special."

Emma raised an eyebrow, curious. "What do you mean?"

"A ring," Caleb said, his voice softening. "A really nice engagement ring. I know we've talked about marriage before, but I want to make it official, even if the wedding is a ways off. We can wait until the debt is paid down and we've saved up for a down payment on a house. But in the meantime, I want you to know that I'm committed to our future."

Emma's eyes lit up with surprise and warmth. "Caleb, that sounds perfect. We don't need to rush into anything. We'll build our future one step at a time."

The very next day, Caleb and Emma set out on a mission to find the perfect engagement ring. Caleb's heart raced with a mixture of excitement and nerves, knowing this was a significant step in their relationship. They decided to start their search in downtown Honolulu, where the streets were lined with upscale jewelry stores, each window glittering with the promise of forever.

Their first stop was a well-known jeweler, its facade gleaming with polished marble and gold accents. The interior was equally opulent, with glass cases displaying rows upon rows of sparkling diamonds, sapphires, and emeralds. Caleb and Emma, in surfer attire, were greeted by a salesperson with a slick smile, his tailored suit and perfectly coiffed hair adding to his air of superiority.

"Good morning," the salesperson said, his tone overly formal. "How can I assist you today?"

Caleb felt a little out of his depth in the luxurious surroundings, but he squared his shoulders and replied, "We're looking for an engagement ring."

The salesperson's smile widened, though there was a hint of condescension in his eyes as he assessed them. "Of course," he said smoothly, leading them to a display case filled with the most extravagant rings in the store. "These are some of our finest pieces. Perhaps you'll find something suitable here."

Caleb and Emma exchanged a glance. The rings in front of them were stunning, but the prices were astronomical. Emma, always practical, could see the discomfort in Caleb's expression and squeezed his hand gently. "These are beautiful," she said politely, "but maybe we could look at something a bit simpler?"

The salesperson's smile faltered slightly, and Caleb noticed the subtle shift in his demeanor. "Of course," he said, his tone now laced with a hint of impatience. He led them to another case, this one filled with more modest rings, though still far beyond what Caleb had in mind. The entire experience left them both feeling uneasy, as though they were being judged for not meeting some unspoken standard.

After a few more awkward moments, Caleb thanked the salesperson and ushered Emma out of the store. "Well, that was... something," he said, trying to shake off the lingering feeling of inadequacy.

Emma laughed softly, trying to lighten the mood. "Maybe we should try somewhere else," she suggested. "Someplace that feels more... us."

They continued their search, visiting several more stores. At each stop, they encountered salespeople who either overwhelmed them with choices or looked down their noses at them for not being willing to spend tens of thousands of dollars. The entire process was exhausting, and by the end of the day, Caleb was beginning to feel disheartened. Finding the perfect ring for Emma was proving to be more challenging than he had anticipated.

Just as they were about to call it a day, they stumbled upon a small, unassuming jewelry store tucked away on a quiet side street. The shop's exterior was modest, with a simple wooden sign that read "Lani's Jewels." Inside, the atmosphere was warm and inviting, a stark contrast to the flashy stores they had visited earlier.

An older woman with kind eyes and a gentle smile greeted them as they entered. "Welcome," she said, her voice soft and genuine. "What can I help you with today?"

"We're looking for an engagement ring," Caleb said, his nerves finally starting to settle.

The woman, who introduced herself as Lani, nodded with understanding. "You've come to the right place," she said. "I believe the perfect ring is one that speaks to your heart, not just to your wallet."

Lani led them to a small display case filled with a carefully curated selection of rings. Each one was unique, with its own story and character. Caleb and Emma took their time, examining each piece carefully, until one ring caught Emma's eye. It was simple, yet elegant—a delicate band with a single, beautifully cut diamond that sparkled with understated brilliance.

"This one," Emma whispered, her voice filled with certainty.

Caleb looked at the ring and then at Emma, seeing the joy and love in her eyes. He knew instantly that this was the one. "We'll take it," he said, feeling a sense of relief and excitement wash over him.

Lani smiled warmly as she carefully packaged the ring. "Congratulations to both of you," she said. "I'm sure you'll have a beautiful life together."

With the ring safely in his pocket, Caleb knew exactly how he wanted to propose. The following weekend, he and Emma drove up to the North Shore, one of their favorite spots on the island. The sun was beginning to set, casting a golden glow over the water as the waves gently lapped against the shore. The beach was quiet, the only sounds coming from the rustling of palm leaves and the distant call of seabirds.

As they walked along the shoreline, Caleb's heart pounded in his chest. He led Emma to a secluded spot under a tall palm tree, its broad leaves providing a cool shade as the sun dipped lower on the horizon. The moment felt perfect, as if the universe itself was conspiring to make everything just right.

Caleb stopped walking and turned to face Emma, his hand slipping into his pocket to retrieve the ring. Taking a deep breath, he got down on one knee, his heart racing with both nerves and excitement.

"Emma," he began, his voice steady but filled with emotion, "I've known from the moment we met that you were someone special. You've brought so much love, joy, and meaning into my life. I can't imagine spending the rest of my life without you by my side. Will you marry me?"

Emma's eyes filled with tears of happiness as she looked down at Caleb, her heart swelling with love. "Yes, Caleb," she said, her voice trembling with emotion. "Yes, of course I'll marry you!"

Caleb slipped the ring onto her finger, and they both stood up, embracing each other tightly as the waves crashed softly against the shore. The world seemed to melt away, leaving only the two of them in their perfect moment.

After a few moments of holding each other, Emma pulled back slightly, her lips curling into a playful smile. "I have something for you, too," she said, reaching into her backpack. With a flourish, she pulled out a brand-new toothbrush, holding it up with a twinkle in her eye.

"So, do you have a place for my toothbrush somewhere in your apartment?" she asked, her tone teasing but full of warmth.

Caleb burst into laughter, his heart swelling with joy at the gesture. "If I do a major cleanup, I think I might just be able to make enough room," he replied, grinning. "I just have to throw out a couple of surfboards."

He paused for a moment, considering, then added with a chuckle, "Maybe I'll just hide them under a table in the *warm room*."

But Caleb knew that the toothbrush meant so much more. It was a symbolic exchange, a subtle choreography of commitment. He had given her a ring, she had given him a toothbrush—next would be a key to his apartment. It was an unspoken agreement, a dance of love where they gradually intertwined their lives without flaunting it. They wouldn't need to announce to his parents that they were sharing a bed; it was understood, even if unspoken.

Caleb, back at his apartment, was laying on his couch, just about to doze off, when his phone buzzed. Seeing "Mom" flash on the screen, he smiled and answered, leaning back into the cushions.

"Hi, Mom. How's it going?"

"Caleb, honey! Your dad and I have some exciting news," Jean Jacobson's voice bubbled with enthusiasm. "We've decided to finally make that trip to the Holy Land! We're going next month."

Caleb's smile faded slightly as he processed the information. "Next month? That's pretty soon. Are you sure it's safe?"

"We've been hoping to do this for years, Caleb," Jake Jacobson chimed in, his deep voice steady and resolved. "We feel that now is the right time. We don't want to wait any longer."

"But... isn't it a little dangerous right now?" Caleb asked, concern creeping into his voice. "I mean, with everything going on over there—there's been unrest, and it's not exactly a vacation spot."

"That's why we're calling you," Jean said, her voice softening. "We wanted to invite you and Emma to join us. It would mean so much to have you both there with us, sharing this special experience."

Caleb hesitated, torn between his love for his parents and the reality of his current situation. "Mom, I'd love to, but I can't afford to take time off. I've used up all my vacation days, and with everything going on here... It's just not possible. Plus, I really think it's too dangerous for you and Dad to go right now."

"Caleb, we understand," Jake said, his tone calm but unwavering. "But your mother and I feel that this might be our last chance to make this pilgrimage. We're not getting any younger, and we've always wanted to walk where Jesus walked, to see the places we've read about our whole lives. Besides, the tour guide says we won't be going anywhere near the unrest and besides that, the State Department hasn't issued any advisories."

Jean's voice broke in, filled with quiet conviction. "We believe God will protect us, Caleb. This is something we feel called to do. We know it's not easy for you to take time off, and we don't want you to worry. But we'd be so happy if you could find a way."

Caleb rubbed his forehead, feeling a headache coming on. He understood how much this meant to them, but the thought of them going to a potentially dangerous place made him uneasy. "I know how important this is to you both, but I just can't shake the feeling that it's risky. Are you sure you don't want to wait until things calm down?"

"We've prayed about this," Jake replied, his voice steady. "We feel this is the right time for us. We know you're busy with your work, and we respect that. But please don't worry about us. We're in God's hands."

Caleb sighed, knowing there was little he could say to change their minds. "Alright, Dad. Just promise me you'll be careful. I wish I could go with you, but I'll be here, praying for your safe return."

Caleb felt a little guilty about the last part, he hadn't prayed in years and didn't expect to start. *Maybe I'll get Emma to burn some incense. Then again, maybe not.*

"Thank you, son," Jean said warmly. "We'll send you pictures and keep you updated. And who knows, maybe one day you and Emma can take this trip together. It would be wonderful."

"Yeah, maybe," Caleb said, trying to keep his tone light. "Take care, okay? And keep in touch."

"We will, Caleb," Jake said. "Take care of yourself, and give our love to Emma."

"I will. Love you both," Caleb said, feeling a mixture of relief and lingering concern as the call ended. He set his phone down, staring at the ceiling as he mulled over their conversation.

While he respected their faith and desire to make the pilgrimage, he couldn't shake the worry gnawing at the back of his mind. But he knew his parents, and when they set their minds to something, there was little he could do to change it.

With a sigh, Caleb pushed the thoughts aside and refocused on the task at hand. There was still work to be done, and worrying wouldn't help anyone.

Back at work, Caleb found himself plunged into the center of something far more intense. Out of deep respect for the astronomer who first discovered Alohanui, Caleb was discreetly invited to join a highly encrypted ZOOM meeting—the inaugural session of a select, unofficial liaison committee. This group, comprising some of the brightest minds from the Institute for Astronomy (IfA), NASA, and the Jet Propulsion Laboratory (JPL), was tasked with coordinating efforts to determine, with the highest possible accuracy, the trajectory of Alohanui as it approached its rendezvous with Jupiter. The stakes couldn't have been higher, and as Caleb's computer screen filled with the faces of seasoned astronomers and engineers, the gravity of the situation settled over him.

Thanks to the radar telescopes that had tracked Alohanui during its closest approach to Earth—roughly 10 million miles away—NASA and JPL had calculated its trajectory with astonishing precision. The data was so detailed that they could predict with a 50% probability that Alohanui would execute a reverse slingshot maneuver around Jupiter. This wasn't some maneuver pulled off by advanced extraterrestrial technology; it was pure physics. Alohanui was following a ballistic trajectory, like a stone tossed into a river or the moon orbiting the Earth.

It was a cosmic coin toss. Heads: Alohanui would pass so close to Jupiter that it would lose about half its momentum to the gas giant, slowing down just enough to be captured by the Sun's gravity, becoming a permanent resident of our solar system. Tails: the object would be deflected by Jupiter's gravity, but would continue on its path, eventually slipping back into the vastness of interstellar space.

The committee faced an immense challenge: devising the optimal orbit for the Juno spacecraft to gather as much data as possible on Alohanui during its approach. The situation was further complicated by the fact that Juno was nearing the end of its mission. The spacecraft was running critically low on hydrazine, the fuel necessary for its thrusters, and was scheduled for decommissioning in just a month—four months before Alohanui's closest approach to Jupiter.

As the discussion intensified, another potential complication emerged. If Alohanui did indeed perform the slingshot maneuver, there was a chance it might cross paths with NASA's long-dormant spacecraft, Dawn. Dawn had been a trailblazer, the first spacecraft to orbit two extraterrestrial destinations—the protoplanet Vesta and the dwarf planet Ceres, both located in the asteroid belt beyond Mars. However, after exhausting its hydrazine reserves, Dawn lost its ability to adjust its orientation, leading to a loss of communication with Earth.

Despite the silence from Dawn, NASA's Deep Space Network (DSN) had continued to listen for any signal, though none had come. The possibility that Alohanui might pass close enough to Dawn to disrupt—or even interact with—the derelict spacecraft added a new layer of complexity to their calculations. Now, the team wasn't just tasked with studying Alohanui; they also had the chance, however slim, to gain unexpected insights from a long-lost NASA mission if their paths intersected.

The gravity of the situation was clear to everyone in the meeting. Caleb listened intently as the team debated potential strategies, the tension palpable through the virtual connection. The decisions they made in the coming weeks could shape the future of space exploration and significantly deepen humanity's understanding of the universe.

As the discussion continued, it became evident that they were racing against time. Juno's remaining fuel would need to be conserved with meticulous care, and its orbit adjusted with surgical precision to ensure it could gather the most critical data on Alohanui. The possibility of extending Juno's mission, even by a few months, was considered, but the feasibility was uncertain given the spacecraft's dwindling resources.

For Caleb, the weight of responsibility was immense. The outcome of these deliberations could mean the difference between capturing groundbreaking data or missing a once-in-a-lifetime opportunity.

The thought of Dawn, a state-of-the-art space probe, drifting silently through the endless void of space, was haunting. It was a fully functional marvel of engineering, packed with instruments and sensors designed to unravel the mysteries of the cosmos. Yet, despite its potential, it had become a silent sentinel, unreachable and unable to fulfill its mission, all because it had run out of fuel—a mere shortage of hydrazine. The thought was maddeningly frustrating. Here was a spacecraft that had already made history by orbiting two extraterrestrial bodies, poised to deliver even more groundbreaking data. But now, it was rendered impotent, floating aimlessly in the darkness, its wealth of knowledge locked away, just out of reach. The irony was bitter—so much investment, so much promise, and all of it cut short because of something as mundane as running out of gas. For the scientific community, and indeed all of humanity, Dawn was a poignant reminder of how fragile and fleeting our grasp on the cosmos can be, even with the most advanced technology at our fingertips.

As the meeting drew to a close, Caleb felt a mix of awe and apprehension. The challenges ahead were daunting, but the potential rewards were beyond imagination. They stood on the brink of something extraordinary—if only they could navigate the intricate dance of celestial mechanics in time.

CHAPTER 4 JUNO

Juno was retasked, its instruments pivoting away from Jupiter and its moons to focus back toward the sun. "Please, please show us Alohanui," the astronomers silently pleaded, fully aware of how critical these next images could be.

Juno complied, capturing frame after frame of the region where Alohanui was expected to be and transmitting them back to NASA's Deep Space Network. Then, just as they had hoped—there it was—right on target, exactly as predicted.

"We nailed it," the trajectory team at JPL announced to the unofficial liaison committee during their encrypted Zoom meeting, their voices a mix of relief and triumph. "Alohanui is exactly where we expected it to be, no surprises this time—unlike when it changed course behind the sun. And by the way, the probability of a reverse slingshot maneuver now stands at 99.93%."

With the discovery confirmed, it was time for another press conference. Caleb had almost forgotten how much he loathed these events. Once again, he was the face of astronomy—the chosen one to communicate these findings to the world. Why risk confusing the public by letting someone from JPL, Caltech, or NASA take the lead? Caleb was trusted, and when cleaned up for the cameras, he had the kind of approachable appearance that TV loved. His genuine, slightly awkward authenticity set him apart from many other researchers; it was something the media—and the public—could connect with.

As Caleb stepped into the hall, it was already buzzing with activity. Reporters and some of his coworkers were filling the seats, their anticipation palpable. The air was thick with the familiar scent of coffee and the low hum of quiet conversations. The walls were adorned with framed photographs of famous astronomers, prominent University of Hawaii professors, constellations, and telescopes perched on mountaintops, all seeming to echo the weight of history. The lights were bright—almost blinding for someone who worked mostly in the dark—casting sharp shadows and making Caleb squint as he took his place at the podium.

He cleared his throat, blinking against the glare as he focused on the notes in front of him. "I want to read a statement first, and then I'll take questions," Caleb began, his voice steady but heavy with the significance of the moment. For a brief second, he considered how much easier this would be with a teleprompter, but quickly dismissed the thought. This was part of the job, part of what it meant to be the public face of such a monumental discovery.

"Yesterday, the NASA spacecraft Juno furnished us with new images of Alohanui," Caleb began, and the room instantly fell into a hush. "The pictures, which are being uploaded to NASA's website as we speak, show a single bright pixel on each frame—exactly where Alohanui was predicted to be by a team of astrophysicists from Caltech, JPL, and NASA."

He paused, letting the weight of the data sink in before continuing. "This confirmation allowed the NASA-Caltech-JPL team to conclude beyond a doubt that Alohanui will not be leaving the solar system, as was previously expected. As Alohanui approaches Jupiter, it will pass extremely close to the planet, moving in the opposite direction of Jupiter's orbit around the Sun. When this happens, a transfer of momentum will occur due to the gravitational interaction between the two bodies. Jupiter will gain an infinitesimal amount of speed, while Alohanui will slow down enough to be captured by the Sun's gravity and become a permanent part of our solar system."

Caleb carefully chose his words, consciously avoiding the term "reverse slingshot maneuver." He felt that "maneuver" implied a level of control or intent, as if an intelligent being were steering Alohanui, much like "maneuvering in traffic" implies a driver. The phrase also sounds more like a stock trading strategy than a concept in astrophysics.

For a brief moment, the room was silent, the gravity of his announcement settling over the crowd. Then, almost in unison, the buzz of excitement surged back to life. Reporters furiously scribbled notes, cameras flashed, and a wave of murmurs rippled through the audience as they began to grasp the full implications of what Caleb had just revealed.

Caleb could feel the intensity of the moment, the collective realization that they were witnessing something truly extraordinary. He braced himself for the inevitable barrage of questions, knowing that each one would bring them closer to unraveling the mysteries of Alohanui.

As the first hands shot up in the audience, Caleb took a deep breath, preparing to navigate the flood of inquiries with the poise and clarity that had earned him the trust of the public. This was his moment, and he was determined to make every word count.

"Will Alohanui hit Earth?" asked one of the reporters, a question Caleb had anticipated and prepared for.

"I can confidently say no," Caleb responded. "The NASA-

Caltech-JPL team has not completed the trajectory calculations much beyond the encounter with Jupiter because Alohanui will be entering the asteroid belt, where its path could be influenced by asteroids. Most likely, it won't be affected much—after all, the asteroid belt is mostly empty space, and encounters are rare. Our initial calculations suggest that Alohanui will settle into an eccentric orbit within our solar system, with its closest approach to the Sun being just outside Mars' orbit and its farthest point just inside Jupiter's orbit."

A student in the front of the auditorium raised his hand. "So, Alohanui is approaching Jupiter from the opposite direction of its orbit around the Sun. Does that mean it will be like driving into oncoming traffic in the asteroid belt?"

"No, not at all," Caleb explained. "Once Alohanui swings around Jupiter, it will end up traveling in the same direction as Jupiter, just a little slower and closer to the sun. When it moves through the asteroid belt, it will be traveling at a similar speed to the asteroids it's moving through."

"How soon will we get close-ups of Alohanui?" a reporter shouted from the back of the room, his voice cutting through the buzz of anticipation.

Caleb took a moment before responding, choosing his words carefully. "Well, we're not exactly getting close-ups in the way you might imagine," he clarified. "The images we'll receive will be from about a quarter of a million miles away—the same distance as the moon is from Earth—of an object that's roughly 18 miles wide. To give you some perspective, have you ever seen the Apollo 11 lunar lander?"

From the middle of the crowd, someone called out, "Sure, it's in the Smithsonian." A ripple of laughter spread through the room.

Caleb smiled but pressed on. "What I meant was, have you

ever seen a picture of the lunar lander sitting on the moon's surface?"

The reporter hesitated before replying, "Well, I suppose so—I must have seen a photo, but I can't recall it clearly."

"That's understandable," Caleb said, nodding. "Let me explain. The Very Large Telescope in the Atacama Desert of northern Chile is one of the most powerful optical telescopes on Earth. It consists of four telescopes, each with a 27-foot-diameter mirror. These telescopes can be combined to achieve an incredibly high resolution. Back in 2002, astronomers tested the Very Large Telescope by photographing the Apollo landing sites. The telescope provided a resolution of about 400 feet. But even with that level of detail, it wasn't enough to see the 14-foot-wide lunar lander or its shadow on the moon's surface. So, despite the capabilities of the telescope, we still couldn't offer definitive, independent proof to those who still, somehow, believe the moon landing was a hoax."

Caleb paused briefly before getting back to the point. "Now, Juno's resolution for Alohanui won't be quite as sharp as that. We're looking at something closer to 1,000 feet per pixel. But here's the exciting part: Alohanui is 18 miles wide, so the images we're expecting will be about 660 pixels across by 660 pixels high. That's a pretty significant improvement, though it means we won't be able to pick out anything smaller than 1,000 feet in size."

The room was silent for a moment as the audience digested this information. While it wasn't the detailed close-up that some might have hoped for, the potential to see Alohanui in such unprecedented clarity was still thrilling. Caleb could sense the reporters' excitement, even if tempered by the limitations of the technology. They were on the brink of seeing something truly extraordinary, even if the images wouldn't reveal every detail.

Juno continued to send back daily images of Alohanui, except for the brief periods when the object was obscured behind Jupiter. The images started with a single pixel, then grew to 2 pixels, then 4, and so on, gradually revealing more detail as Alohanui neared its closest approach to both Jupiter and the spacecraft. As promised, the relatively high-resolution images began streaming in, faster and more detailed with each passing day. Alohanui seemed almost to indulge the camera, rotating slowly as if to offer a full view of every side, revealing itself in all its enigmatic glory.

Under mounting pressure from the President and Congress, NASA made the difficult decision to sacrifice the remaining hydrazine in Juno's tanks, effectively bringing an early end to the spacecraft's primary mission of studying Jupiter and its moons. The decision was not made lightly, as Juno had been providing invaluable data about the gas giant's atmosphere, magnetic field, and the intricate dance of its many moons. However, the opportunity presented by Alohanui was too extraordinary to pass up. The mysterious object had captivated the world's attention, and the potential to gather unprecedented data on it became a national priority.

In response, NASA sent a series of commands to Juno, instructing the spacecraft to leave its stable polar orbit around Jupiter—a trajectory that had allowed it to make detailed observations of the planet's poles and auroras—and instead, transition into an equatorial elliptical orbit. This new path was calculated to bring Juno as close as possible to Alohanui, effectively enabling an almost-rendezvous with the enigmatic interstellar visitor.

The move was both bold and risky. By abandoning its polar orbit, Juno would no longer be able to carry out its planned studies of Jupiter's magnetosphere or its complex atmospheric dynamics. The shift to an equatorial elliptical orbit meant that Juno's remaining fuel would be consumed at a much faster rate, leaving the spacecraft with only limited time to capture detailed images and data of Alohanui before its mission would inevitably end.

But the potential payoff was immense. The equatorial elliptical orbit would allow Juno to match Alohanui's trajectory as closely as possible, giving the spacecraft the best chance to capture high-resolution images and other critical data from multiple angles. This new orbit would bring Juno closer to Alohanui than any other spacecraft had ever come to an interstellar object, offering an unprecedented opportunity to study its structure, composition, and behavior.

The shift in mission focus also symbolized the growing importance of Alohanui in the eyes of the scientific community and the public. It underscored the global fascination with this mysterious object and the lengths to which humanity was willing to go to unlock its secrets. The decision to prioritize Alohanui over Jupiter's moons was a testament to the object's potential to reshape our understanding of the universe.

NASA was, of course, the entity in charge of the Juno mission. It made perfect sense to them that they should be the ones addressing questions about Juno, given their deep expertise and the complexity of the mission. From their perspective, it was only logical that the responsibility for public communication about the spacecraft should fall to their team. However, it might have been considerate—if not professional—for NASA to at least inform Dr. Wright, and perhaps even Caleb himself, that they were planning to take over the narrative. Instead, NASA unilaterally decided that all future press conferences would be held at the Kennedy Space Center, specifically at the NASA News Center located at Launch Complex 39.

This facility was fully equipped for high-profile briefings:

it boasted a web studio, multimedia libraries, a television production studio with a 100-seat auditorium for press conferences and social media briefings, and comprehensive facilities for local media and television networks. It even had a digital countdown clock to mark significant moments. NASA's plan was to replace the single, familiar face of Alohanui—Caleb—with a rotating cast of experts who could speak to every facet of the mission with precision and authority.

What they didn't plan for, however, was including Caleb or any member of the IfA team in these press briefings. Caleb, who had become the public's go-to voice on Alohanui, was left out of the loop entirely.

"Did I offend NASA somehow?" Caleb wondered, feeling an uncomfortable mix of confusion and disappointment. It seemed they had been quietly sidelined, their contributions to the discovery of Alohanui overshadowed by NASA's desire to control the conversation.

As Juno's engines fired for the last time, adjusting its orbit to bring it in line with Alohanui's path, the world held its breath. The spacecraft was now on a new trajectory, one that would take it closer to the interstellar visitor than anyone had dared to hope. The mission had changed course, quite literally, but the new direction held the promise of discoveries that could be as monumental as any ever made in the exploration of space.

Due to the vast distance between Earth and Jupiter, the time delay for commands sent to Juno was approximately 50 minutes each way. This meant that every instruction NASA sent to the spacecraft had to be carefully planned and executed with precision—there was no room for error or second-guessing. NASA's engineers and mission planners knew they had to get their ducks in a row quickly. The window for optimal data collection on Alohanui was rapidly closing, and every second counted.

The team at NASA worked feverishly to determine the best possible orientation for Juno's cameras and scientific instruments. With the spacecraft now on its final trajectory, having fired its rocket engine for the last time, the priority was to maximize the quality and quantity of data they could gather on Alohanui. The spacecraft's imaging systems and detectors needed to be pointed at exactly the right angles to capture detailed images and measurements as Alohanui drew closer.

But there was an additional challenge. While Juno's main rocket engine was no longer operational, the spacecraft still had to reserve enough hydrazine fuel to power its thrusters. These thrusters were crucial for maintaining Juno's orientation, ensuring that its high-gain antenna remained locked on Earth. Without this precise orientation, the precious data collected on Alohanui would never make it back to NASA's Deep Space Network, rendering the entire endeavor futile.

The mission team calculated the spacecraft's remaining fuel reserves, balancing the need to maneuver Juno for the best possible observations with the imperative to keep the antenna pointed toward Earth. Every command had to be executed with tactical precision, factoring in the 50-minute communication delay. If Juno's orientation drifted even slightly, it could lose its connection with Earth, and with it, the chance to transmit the final, critical data on Alohanui.

The pressure was immense. This was a one-shot deal—an opportunity that might never come again. Alohanui was an enigma, a visitor from the depths of space, and the data Juno could send back might hold answers to questions that humanity hadn't even thought to ask yet. The stakes were as high as they had ever been in space exploration.

As the team at NASA sent the final set of commands to Juno, they knew that the next few hours would be critical. The spacecraft was now on its final approach, its instruments trained on Alohanui, its thrusters carefully rationed to ensure the last bits of data could be transmitted across the vast gulf of space. All they could do now was wait, hoping that everything had been calculated correctly and that Juno's last mission would yield the insights they so desperately sought.

But Juno was the very definition of a multitasker, a spacecraft designed to juggle a myriad of complex tasks simultaneously. Even as it executed engine burns and intricate orbital maneuvers, Juno continued to snap pictures and transmit a constant stream of data back to Earth. These images, many of which quickly became favorites with the media, provided the public with glimpses of Alohanui, a tiny black dot on a background of Jupiter's swirling clouds and moons Io, Europa, Ganymede, and Callisto. But there was more to Juno's mission than just capturing stunning visuals. Every bit of data it sent back was a treasure trove for scientists, each piece contributing to our understanding of the gas giant and the mysteries of the cosmos.

As anticipated, the hydrazine fuel that powered its thrusters was almost gone yet not completely, carefully rationed to ensure the spacecraft could maintain its precise orientation. As if that weren't enough, Juno's battery—never fully charged due to the feeble sunlight so far from the sun—was also nearly empty.

Mission planners at NASA had calculated that the hydrazine and the battery would likely run out at almost the same time, a synchronized finale to Juno's long and fruitful journey. It was as if the spacecraft itself knew that its final act was approaching and was determined to make the most of every remaining moment. The timing was both poetic and practical: as long as Juno could keep its thrusters firing, it could maintain its orientation, keep its solar panels aligned, and continue transmitting data right up until the very end.

Almost paradoxically, NASA was delaying the release of Juno's images to the public by at least 24 hours. This decision raised eyebrows and sparked speculation. Was NASA strategically pacing the release of these images to maintain public interest, ensuring that the world remained captivated by the unfolding mystery for as long as possible? Or was there something more ominous at play—perhaps a hesitation borne out of fear about what the public might see?

The agency's timing seemed to be a delicate balancing act. On one hand, they were acutely aware of the need to keep the narrative alive, to sustain the global fascination with Alohanui. Drip-feeding the images allowed NASA to control the flow of information, each new picture reigniting public curiosity and fueling the media frenzy. The slow reveal kept people on the edge of their seats, speculating about the next piece of the puzzle that would be unveiled.

On the other hand, there was a certain unease within NASA. The images Juno was sending back were unlike anything seen before—cryptic and, at times, difficult to interpret. What if there was something in those images that the public wasn't ready for? Something that could trigger panic or misinterpretation? NASA's scientists and engineers were tasked with making sense of these images, deciphering the data before it was released into the wild where it could take on a life of its own.

In truth, the delay was likely a bit of both—caution and strategy intertwined. The need to carefully analyze each image before making it public was paramount. Scientists wanted to ensure that they fully understood what they were seeing before the world got its first look. But at the same time, NASA understood the power of anticipation. By controlling the narrative, they could keep the world engaged, maintain the momentum of the discovery, and perhaps soften the impact of any unsettling revelations that might emerge.

The situation gnawed at Caleb, Emma, Helen, Mark, and the rest of the team at the Institute for Astronomy (IfA). They had been at the forefront of the Alohanui discovery—doing the heavy lifting, as it were. They were the ones who spotted the object, analyzed the data, held the press conferences, and kept the public informed. Now, they found themselves relegated to the back of the line, forced to wait, just like everyone else, for NASA to release the new data and images. It was a long, slow wait, and it stung. They were scientists, not spectators, and the delay felt like a betrayal of sorts.

When the first high-resolution image of Alohanui finally made its way into their hands, the entire team gathered around in eager anticipation. What they saw was intriguing—not for its detail, but for its sheer simplicity. The image displayed a large, bright white square. There were no intricate patterns or textures, just a stark, perfect square. The shape alone was enough to spark a flurry of speculation and excitement. A square of that size in the cosmos? It was unheard of.

NASA quickly identified the material as quartz, a common mineral in our solar system, but this quartz was different—unusually white and highly reflective. The reflective properties suggested that the quartz might provide significant protection against the intense sunlight Alohanui had experienced while transiting the far side of the sun. Some scientists hypothesized that this highly reflective surface could be a protective measure, shielding the object from solar radiation in a way that had never been seen before.

As NASA spaced out the release of subsequent images, each one unveiled more details about Alohanui, keeping the public and the scientific community on tenterhooks. The images, released one at a time, allowed viewers to metaphorically "see around the corners" of the object, revealing more of its mysterious structure. It became clear that the perfect square was a massive 18 miles by 18 miles. But what really caught everyone's attention was the realization that the sides of this square were incredibly narrow—about 2800 feet wide, forming elongated rectangles that stretched 2800 feet by 18 miles. The bizarre geometry was perplexing, to say the least.

Even stranger, these narrow sides appeared to be composed of two distinct materials. The primary material was the same white quartz as the square face, but interspersed within were three extremely smooth, perfectly circular—possibly spherical—calcium carbonate inclusions. These inclusions were evenly spaced, further adding to the puzzle. The combination of materials and shapes was like nothing the team had ever encountered, and the implications were as vast as they were confounding.

For perhaps the first time, the average person began to pay close attention to what the exogeologists had to say. The public's curiosity was piqued not just by the alien nature of the object but by the possibility that this was something truly extraordinary—something that could change our understanding of the universe. The shape, the materials, the strange inclusions—each new detail added another layer to the mystery of Alohanui, drawing in not just scientists, but people from all walks of life, eager to see what would be revealed next.

Once again, Caleb found himself feeling like Dr. Eleanor Arroway, the character played by Jodie Foster in the movie *Contact*—hoping, almost desperately, that he could find a way to get dealt back into the game. The analogy wasn't lost on him; after all, just like Arroway, he was facing the challenge of proving his worth in a field dominated by the powers that be, where every new discovery seemed to slip further from his grasp.

But there was a silver lining. Caleb couldn't help but get a kick out of having a fiancée—one who was not only incredibly intelligent but also eager to dive into the complexities of their work. Emma Kanoa was arguably smarter than he was, and her enthusiasm for the work they were doing together was infectious. It occurred to Caleb that maybe, just maybe, Emma could help them both get dealt back into the game. After all, no one had yet mentioned the rate and plane of rotation of Alohanui, and as far as he could tell, NASA hadn't published anything on the subject.

"Emma," Caleb called out from the table in the warm room, right next to hers, "have you ever heard that old saying that if you want something done fast, you should ask the busiest man in town?"

Emma looked up with a playful smile. "Why yes, Caleb, my one true love, I think I've heard something like that. The idea being that if he's really the busiest man in town, he must be incredibly efficient. So, what's on your mind?"

"Could you determine from NASA's photos the rate and plane of rotation of Alohanui?" Caleb asked, his voice carrying a mix of hope and anticipation.

"Yes, my Aloha Nui," Emma replied with a wink, already pulling up the images on her screen.

"I'm going to see how it compares to the rate of rotation from that radar data we were analyzing earlier," Caleb added. "Now that we know the exact shape of Alohanui, I want to see if I can determine its plane of rotation from the signal. Let's compare notes in about three hours."

Three hours later, Emma was practically bursting with excitement. She couldn't wait to share what she had discovered, but she knew they needed to be discreet.

"Let's go for a walk," she suggested, putting a finger to her lips as if to say, *not here, not now.*

Once they were outside in the University Garden, safely away from prying eyes and ears, Emma leaned in close, her voice barely above a whisper. "The timestamps are wrong," she said, her tone laced with urgency. "Some of the minor asteroids are out of place. It's as if they deliberately assigned almost-but-not-quite-right timestamps to the images, making it incredibly difficult to do what you wanted."

Caleb's eyes widened in surprise. "And?" he whispered back, his heart beginning to pound in his chest.

"It's unbelievable," Emma continued, her voice a mix of awe and disbelief. "Alohanui's rotation period could be matching a sidereal day. And the plane of rotation? It's parallel to the ecliptic plane, but with a slight offset."

Caleb stared at her, struggling to process the implications of what she was saying. "That's... I don't even know what to say," he finally managed. After a pause, he asked, "How precisely were you able to calculate the rate of rotation?"

Emma shrugged, though her expression remained serious. "The error bars leave room for a 24-hour period, but my calculations came out to 23 hours and 55 minutes—closer to a sidereal day than a solar day. It's almost too precise to be a coincidence. So, what did you figure out?"

Caleb grinned sheepishly. "Oh, I just took a nap because I knew you were on top of the problem."

Emma laughed, but the uneasiness remained palpable. The perfect alignment of Alohanui's rotation with Earth's sidereal day couldn't be dismissed as mere chance. It suggested something deliberate, something that defied the random chaos of celestial mechanics.

"Honestly, I only had three days' worth of radar data to work with," Caleb admitted, his voice serious now. "It was difficult to calculate the rotation period down to the hour, let alone the minute, especially when working from a wiggly line that kept attenuating. I guessed the radar signal repeated with the periodicity of a solar day, but if it was matching Earth exactly, it would, of course, align with a sidereal day." said Caleb. Then with a smile he added, " It was a good idea to ask for your help!"

As they walked through the garden, Caleb's mind raced, his thoughts spinning with the implications of their discoveries. "Why would someone—or something—go to such lengths to synchronize Alohanui's rotation with Earth's?" he whispered, more to himself than to Emma. "Is it a signal, a message, or some kind of deliberate alignment designed to catch our attention? And what about the tampered timestamps? What could NASA be hiding, and why are they making it so difficult for us to uncover the truth? And... Why am I suddenly paranoid?"

For the first time since the discovery of Alohanui, Caleb felt a deep, unsettling concern. This wasn't just an interstellar object passing through the solar system; it was something more, something that might be connected to Earth in ways they had never imagined. The thought sent a chill down his spine—it was both thrilling and terrifying to consider.

Emma looked at him, her expression serious. "I think it's time we consider the possibility there's extraterrestrial intelligence involved," she said quietly. "Whether they're piloting Alohanui, remotely controlling it, or—like we do with our own probes—they preprogrammed it for some specific mission, we can't ignore the signs any longer."

The gravity of her words hung in the air between them. Caleb nodded slowly, knowing that this was no longer just a scientific mystery. They were on the edge of something much larger—something that could redefine humanity's understanding of the universe and its place within it. The question was, were they ready for what they might find?

Alohanui seemed determined to make a liar out of Caleb. Back when he was the "Voice of Alohanui" he had assured the public that the asteroid belt was practically empty and that Alohanui would not likely encounter any asteroids. That turned out not to be true.

Caleb was conflicted. On one hand, he felt a wave of relief that NASA had taken the lead, stepping in to handle the press conferences. The constant pressure of being the face of Alohanui had been exhausting, and a part of him was grateful to step out of the spotlight. But on the other hand, he couldn't deny the pang of disappointment he felt. He actually missed the attention, the sense of importance that came with being the public voice of such a monumental discovery.

However, as it turned out, NASA had only taken one press conference away from Caleb. Once Juno had run out of fuel, NASA was no longer in the driver's seat. But that didn't mean Caleb was back in control either—far from it. In hindsight, it made sense to Caleb. NASA had withheld so much information from him and his team, but there was no way they could withhold it from the White House.

So, when the time came for the next press conference, it wasn't NASA calling the shots—it was the White House. More control of the narrative was required, and there was no better place to do that than the James S. Brady Press Briefing Room. This small theater in the West Wing of the White House was where the press secretary briefed the media, and where, on occasion, the President of the United States addressed the press and the nation.

The shift in venue made it clear that Alohanui was no longer just a scientific curiosity—it was now a matter of national, perhaps even global, significance. Caleb understood why the reins had been taken from his hands, but the sting of being sidelined once again was undeniable. The narrative was slipping further away from him, and as much as he tried to convince himself that he was relieved, he couldn't shake the feeling of loss that came with it. The discovery that had once felt so personal was now a political tool, shaped and controlled by forces far beyond his influence.

CHAPTER 5
KAʻEPAOKAʻĀWELA

Dr. Wright joined the team at the Gateway Café once more, and, in her signature move, climbed onto the table to address everyone. The familiar sight made the group pause their conversations, turning their attention to her.

"It's time to refocus on our purpose here," she began, her voice steady but firm. "Nowhere is it written that we are looking for interstellar visitors. Nobody minds when we find one, but our job—our stated purpose—is planetary defense. Pan-STARRS is designed to find asteroids that may pose a danger to Earth, and of course, we have to study and catalog everything we find so we don't end up discovering the same rocks over and over again."

She looked around the table, making eye contact with each team member, her expression serious. "Sorry to put too fine a point on it, but studying Alohanui is not our job. It's clear to me that NASA is taking the lead on this under the White House's oversight, and that we should get back to looking for new rocks, not studying the old ones. Sorry to be a wet rag, but tonight I want everybody back doing the jobs they were hired to do. Clear?"

The room was silent for a moment, the weight of her words sinking in. Then, Dr. Wright repeated, "Am I clear?"

"Crystal!" Mark responded with a grin, mimicking Tom Cruise's iconic line from *A Few Good Men*.

Polite, subdued laughter rippled through the group, easing some of the tension.

"OK, I'm going to get back to work," Dr. Wright said, climbing down from the table. "Please finish your 'lunch'—no need to rush. Pan-STARRS won't be online for an hour, so take your time."

The Gateway Café was a cozy, unassuming spot, tucked away from the main campus thoroughfares. Its wooden tables were well-worn from years of use, their surfaces etched with the faint traces of countless conversations and hurried meals. The team's usual table, a large, round one near the back, had become something of a headquarters for them—a place where ideas flowed as freely as the coffee. The air was thick with the rich aroma of freshly brewed coffee, mingling with the scent of warm pastries and grilled sandwiches. The soft murmur of conversation from other patrons blended with the occasional clatter of dishes from the kitchen, creating a comforting background hum that made the café feel like a refuge from the intensity of their work.

As Dr. Wright climbed down from the table, the team remained seated, the gravity of her words still hanging in the air. The table, strewn with coffee cups, half-eaten plates of food, and the occasional notebook or tablet, felt like the center of their world—where everything had happened, and where everything was now shifting.

Emma leaned in closer to Caleb, her voice low. "Do you think that came directly from someone in NASA, or is she just reading the writing on the wall?"

Caleb glanced at Dr. Wright as she made her way out of the café, then back at Emma. "Well, NASA couldn't have made it any clearer. A phone call would have been unnecessary. But it would have been nice if someone from NASA had called Helen and thanked her for her and the team's service while making it clear that no further service was required."

The café's familiar sounds and scents seemed to fade as the weight of their new reality settled in. The hum of the espresso machine, the soft clinking of silverware, even the laughter from a nearby table—all of it felt distant, almost irrelevant. They had been so deeply involved in the excitement surrounding Alohanui, and now, suddenly, they were being reminded of their original purpose, a purpose that now felt strangely mundane.

The team members exchanged glances, each of them processing the shift in their own way. The café, which had once been a place of lively debate and shared discovery, now felt quieter, as if the energy had been drained from the room. Even the comforting warmth of the coffee and the inviting smell of freshly baked goods couldn't fully chase away the sense of loss that came with being sidelined from the adventure they had all been so passionately pursuing.

The team left and headed back to the Institute. As usual, Caleb and Emma walked together but far away from the other members of the team.

The night was thick with humidity, the air heavy with the scent of salt from the nearby ocean, mingling with the earthy aroma of the tropical foliage. The sounds of the island night surrounded them—the distant crash of waves against the shore, the rustle of palm fronds in the gentle breeze, and the low hum of insects hidden in the shadows. The campus was quieter now, the usual daytime bustle replaced by the soft murmurs of students heading back to their dorms and the occasional echo of laughter carried on the warm night air.

As they walked back toward the warm room, Emma suddenly pulled Caleb aside, leading him behind a towering palm tree that stood like a sentinel in the moonlight. The rough bark of the tree pressed against Caleb's back as he looked at her, half-expecting a playful kiss for luck.

Is Emma gonna give me a kiss for luck? he wondered, his thoughts momentarily distracted by the softness in her eyes.

But Emma's expression was serious, her voice intense as she whispered, "You know that 90% of our funding comes from NASA, right?"

"Of course, I do," Caleb replied, his curiosity piqued by her tone.

"Well, don't mess it up," she requested, her words carrying a weight that made Caleb's heart skip a beat.

"So, this little duck behind a palm tree is more of a word to the wise than a kiss for luck?" Caleb said, trying to keep the mood light, though he could feel the tension in the air.

Emma leaned in closer, her breath warm against his ear. "What I'm saying is if you're going to try to find out what NASA knows about Aloha Nui that you don't, don't do it at work," she whispered directly into his ear. "And not even at your apartment, or in your car, or with your phone or laptop."

The words sent a shiver down Caleb's spine, the implications settling in like the sticky humidity clinging to his skin. Before he could respond, Emma pulled back slightly, only to press her lips against his in a long, intense kiss, her hands gently cupping his face.

When they finally parted, she looked into his eyes and said, "In case someone is watching."

The kiss lingered in Caleb's mind as they continued their

walk, the sounds of the night fading into the background. The weight of her warning hung between them, a silent reminder that the stakes were higher than he had realized. The palm trees swayed gently above them, their rustling leaves whispering secrets to the night, as Caleb contemplated the subtle but profound shift in their world.

After work, as the sun began to rise, Caleb and Emma walked together back to Caleb's place. The campus was serene in the early morning light, the first rays of the sun casting a warm, golden hue over the lush greenery that surrounded the university. The palm trees, their fronds swaying gently in the breeze, lined the pathways like silent guardians, and the distant sound of waves crashing against the shore provided a soothing backdrop to their conversation.

The university was nestled in a picturesque area, with the ocean just a short walk away. The air was thick with the scent of saltwater and blooming hibiscus, a fragrant reminder of their tropical surroundings. As they walked, the sounds of the early morning—a few birds chirping, the rustle of leaves, and the occasional hum of a distant car—created a peaceful, almost dreamlike atmosphere.

"If an invasion was imminent, would you want to know? Or if an asteroid was about to hit the Earth…" Caleb's voice trailed off as he contemplated the weight of such knowledge. Then, with a playful yet serious tone, he continued, "OK, Dr. Kanoa, here's a pop quiz. If and when Pan-STARRS identifies a PHO, a Potentially Hazardous Object, but it's too close—not enough time to launch DART and deflect it—what would we, the guardians of Pan-STARR, know?"

Emma glanced at him, the corners of her mouth curving into a slight smile as she considered the question. The path they walked on wound through a grove of towering palms, their shadows stretching long across the dewy grass. "OK, Professor

Jacobson, I guess I need to answer. We would almost certainly know where it would hit before it actually struck. If it was a small asteroid, you could possibly evacuate a town, save a lot of lives. But if it's a planet killer and it's headed for, say, Washington DC—as it always seems to be in these scenarios—you'd have to evacuate to the exact opposite point on the planet. If I remember right, that would be in the middle of the Indian Ocean."

Caleb nodded, the weight of her words sinking in as they continued their walk. The path led them toward a small park on the edge of campus, where the scent of damp earth and morning blossoms filled the air. The ocean breeze rustled through the trees, carrying with it a faint mist that cooled their skin.

"This is where it comes in handy to be a surfer as well as an astronomer," Emma added with a wry smile. "An asteroid strike on Washington DC would cause a tsunami that could damage every coastline on the planet. But here's something a surfer might know that others don't: if you're far enough from the shore, you might not even notice the tidal wave. It makes you wonder if there are floating bunkers in the middle of the oceans where the rich and mighty will go to escape the apocalypse."

"Hey," Caleb said, a hint of amusement in his voice, "maybe that's why there are so many massive cruise liners—those floating cities with 6,000 guests and 3,000 staff on board. They could be the bunkers we've been talking about, hidden in plain sight. Of course, there'd also be the more conventional bunkers, the underground fortresses reserved for the rich and powerful."

As they continued to walk, Caleb couldn't help but reflect on the irony of the moment. "Here I am, in the most beautiful place on Earth, with the most beautiful woman on Earth, and we're talking about the apocalypse," he thought, a mix of wonder and melancholy washing over him. The early morning light played on Emma's face, highlighting her features with a soft glow, making the surreal nature of their conversation all the more poignant.

"But honestly," he continued, his tone becoming more serious, "I don't think this is about an asteroid strike. NASA has too much of a head start on Alohanui—they have plenty of time to launch a DART mission, rendezvous, and deflect it if necessary. So what are they trying to hide?"

Caleb's mind raced as he tried to piece together the puzzle. The secrecy, the unusual behavior from NASA, the sudden shift in control—all of it pointed to something bigger than just a potential impact event. As they walked through the quiet, sun-dappled campus, the beauty of their surroundings contrasted sharply with the dark thoughts swirling in Caleb's mind. What was NASA hiding, and why did it feel like they were on the brink of something far more significant than they had ever imagined?

"OK, so it's an invasion then," Emma said, her voice tinged with a mix of sarcasm and genuine concern. "They must have seen something in one of the images that convinced them Alohanui is under intelligent control. It's clear they tried to obscure its rate of rotation—maybe it's as simple as that."

Caleb nodded thoughtfully, the gears in his mind turning. "I took the CalTech team's word for it," he admitted. "But maybe the trajectory of Alohanui's swing behind the sun can't be explained by solar wind and sunlight acting on that huge, perfectly polished square of quartz. I bet it wasn't. I mean, think about it—an interstellar object with one face that's a perfect square? Who could believe that it isn't a spacecraft? Maybe they even have pictures of the occupants—an invading army."

The idea, once spoken aloud, hung heavily between them. The possibility that Alohanui was more than just a natural phenomenon was both terrifying and fascinating. Caleb's mind raced through the implications. If Alohanui were a spacecraft, what was its purpose? Was it an exploratory vessel, a harbinger of a peaceful contact, or something more sinister? The secrecy surrounding it suddenly made sense if NASA had indeed discovered evidence of intelligent life aboard the object.

Emma's eyes searched Caleb's face, trying to gauge his reaction. "If that's true, it's no wonder they're being so secretive. They'd want to control the narrative completely, to prevent panic or mass hysteria. And we're not just talking about a few fuzzy images. If they have definitive proof—images of the occupants or signs of technology—then this is a game-changer, Caleb. It would shift everything we know, everything we believe about our place in the universe."

Caleb nodded slowly, the enormity of the situation sinking in. "And we're caught in the middle of it. I knew there was something off about the way they've been handling this, but this... this is bigger than I ever imagined." He paused, his thoughts a jumble of fear, excitement, and curiosity. "If they're hiding something this monumental, we need to be careful. We're dealing with forces—both cosmic and political—that are way beyond our control."

As they continued their walk, the early morning light casting long shadows around them, the reality of their situation weighed heavily on them both. What had started as an incredible scientific discovery was now spiraling into something far more complex and dangerous. They were no longer just scientists studying an interstellar object; they were potentially on the front lines of humanity's first contact with an intelligent extraterrestrial civilization. And with that realization came a chilling question: what did Alohanui want, and what role would they play in the events to come?

"OK, it's decision time," Caleb said, his voice laced with a mixture of resignation and resolve. "Do we really want to dig deeper into this? What can we do about it, anyway? Speaking just for myself, I'm sure there are far better minds than mine working on whatever's happening. I'm curious about the truth, and it pisses me off that our government might be lying to us, but I don't see how I can actually make a difference. On the other hand, it's not like I have anything else pressing to do—aside from looking for potentially hazardous objects at work and enjoying the company of the most wonderful woman on the planet."

Emma leaned in closer, her breath warm against his ear as she whispered, "Let's grab our boards and head for the North Shore. I won't be able to sleep and I don't think you will be able to either, but maybe a little exercise will tire us out and help us to relax."

The decision was made. They quickly gathered their things and headed out, the night still clinging to the early morning hours. The drive to the North Shore was always a bit of an escape, a chance to leave behind the concerns of their work and immerse themselves in the raw beauty of Oahu's northern coastline.

As they left the city behind, the landscape began to change. The buildings and streetlights gave way to winding roads bordered by dense, lush foliage. Towering banyan trees with their sprawling roots created canopies overhead, casting dappled shadows on the pavement as Caleb navigated the twists and turns. The scent of damp earth and fresh leaves filled the car, mingling with the faint saltiness of the ocean carried on the wind.

The sky above them continued to lighten, a soft gradient of purples and blues hinting at the approaching dawn. As they drove further north, the road opened up, and the vast expanse of the Pacific Ocean came into view, its dark waters reflecting the first hints of morning light. The rhythmic sound of waves crashing against the shore could be heard in the distance, a constant, soothing reminder of the power and serenity of the ocean.

Emma rolled down the window, letting the cool, salty breeze wash over them. The tension from their earlier conversation seemed to lift, replaced by the anticipation of the surf and the peacefulness of the North Shore. The road took them past fields of sugarcane and pineapple, the air occasionally carrying the sweet, earthy scent of the crops.

As they neared their destination, the iconic surf spots of the North Shore began to appear—Waimea Bay, with its massive waves, and the Banzai Pipeline, legendary among surfers for its perfect, barreling waves. The beaches were still quiet, with only a few early risers out on the sand, their silhouettes outlined against the rising sun.

Caleb pulled the car into a small, sandy parking lot near their favorite spot. The sound of the ocean was louder now, the waves crashing rhythmically against the shore, calling them to the water. They got out of the car, grabbing their surfboards from the back, and made their way down to the beach. The sand was cool beneath their feet, and the air was filled with the scent of saltwater and the promise of a perfect morning on the waves.

For a moment, as they stood on the edge of the shore, the worries about Alohanui, NASA, and everything else seemed to fade into the background. It was just them, the ocean, and the surf—a reminder that, no matter what mysteries or challenges lay ahead, there were still moments of pure, simple joy to be found.

Their surfing session was shorter than usual, the waves

not holding the same allure as they often did. After a few good rides, Emma signaled that she was heading for a more secluded part of the beach, and Caleb followed without hesitation. The sun was climbing higher now, casting long shadows across the sand, and the beach was still mostly deserted, offering them the privacy they needed.

"Do you see any bugs on me?" Emma asked with a playful smile, her tone light, but her eyes serious.

Caleb paused, unsure if she was joking, but he didn't take any chances. He stepped closer, examining her carefully, his fingers brushing lightly over her skin as he checked for anything unusual. Whether or not the real purpose was to find electronic listening devices, he didn't mind the task at all. He ran his fingers along the folded and sewn edges of her bikini, the only places where a bug might realistically be hidden. He checked the towels they had brought with them, even the logo on her swimsuit, scrutinizing every detail.

"Now you," said Emma, and then she returned the favor.

"Clean as a whistle," she said.

Satisfied, Caleb and Emma glanced around. The beach was quiet, the sound of the waves the only thing filling the air. There was no one nearby, no suspicious figures lurking in the distance, and their cell phones were locked securely in the glove compartment of the car.

"All clear as far as I can tell," Caleb said, his voice reassuring.

Emma nodded, her smile returning, but a seriousness lingered in her gaze. "So, what are you going to do?" she asked, her tone a blend of curiosity and concern.

Caleb took a deep breath, his mind already working through the details. "First, I'm going to get an old, used laptop—something that's completely off the grid. I'll reformat the hard drive and install Ubuntu, making sure to keep it clean from any traceable software. Then I'll either find or build a directional Wi-Fi antenna, so I can tap into the free Wi-Fi from any number of coffee shops, barbers, or hotels around town. After that, I'll set up a VPN account, but I'll be careful about it. Free accounts aren't secure, so I'll need to go with a reputable paid service. But I can't use a credit card—that's too easy to trace. I'll have to look into alternative payment methods. Maybe bitcoin or another cryptocurrency."

He paused for a moment, gauging Emma's reaction as he laid out his plan. She listened intently, her expression serious but supportive.

"Once that's set up," Caleb continued, "I'll install Astropy and start downloading images from NASA's public site. From there, I'll work on accessing their firewalled and encrypted server. The goal is to compare the images—see what they've released publicly versus what they're keeping hidden. I'll analyze them, figure out what's missing, and try to uncover whatever it is they might be hiding."

Emma's eyes narrowed slightly as she considered his words, her mind clearly turning over the possibilities. She knew Caleb was diving into something potentially dangerous, but she also knew that his curiosity and determination wouldn't let him walk away from this.

"Just be careful," she said quietly, her concern evident in her tone. "This isn't just about the science anymore. If they're hiding something, they'll go to great lengths to keep it that way."

Caleb nodded, fully aware of the risks involved. But now that he had a plan, he felt a renewed sense of purpose. It wasn't just about getting answers for himself—it was about uncovering the truth, no matter how deeply it was buried. And with Emma by his side, he knew he wasn't alone in this. Together, they would push forward, navigating the murky waters of secrecy and surveillance, determined to find out what NASA—and perhaps others—didn't want them to know.

Emma listened intently, her expression thoughtful. "You know this is risky," she said softly. "If they're watching, they'll notice any unusual activity."

"I know," Caleb replied, his voice steady. "But I can't just let this go. There's something they're not telling us, something we need to know. If there's any chance we can figure it out, I have to try."

The weight of their conversation hung between them, the implications of Caleb's plan settling in. The secluded beach, with its gentle waves and peaceful surroundings, seemed almost surreal in contrast to the tension that had built up over the past few days. But beneath the calm exterior, they both knew they were venturing into dangerous territory, where the stakes were higher than ever before.

For now, though, they were alone on the beach, with nothing but the sound of the ocean and the warmth of the sun to keep them company. The world outside might be filled with secrets and uncertainties, but here, in this quiet moment, they had each other—and that was enough.

Emma and Caleb fell into a comfortable routine. Every morning, they would meet up at Diamond Head for a bit of unchallenging surfing. The gentle waves weren't exactly thrilling, but they were enough to keep them in shape and to clear the brain fog that came from nights spent scanning the skies for potentially hazardous objects. It became their ritual —an anchor to their day. Most mornings, after a long night's work, Emma would head back to her house for some much-needed sleep, while Caleb would return to his apartment. But Ted and Star Kanoa soon learned not to expect to see Emma on Saturdays or Sundays. Those were the days she and Caleb dedicated entirely to each other.

Caleb had thought a lot about surveillance. If someone was watching you, he reasoned, it was in your best interest to make it as easy for them as possible. What made it easy for them? A routine. Routines are predictable, easy to follow, and don't require a large team to monitor. Even better was limiting your movements to just two locations—work and home.

Caleb had thought it through. If you make it simple enough for just two or three watchers to cover your movements, they might feel satisfied that their job is under control. But complicate things—make them spread thin by requiring more personnel, more resources—and you risk provoking them. It might occur to the watchers that their task would be much simpler if you were eliminated entirely. Why expend unnecessary resources when you could just remove the target? And so, Caleb lived by the logic that what seems better for them may be better for his own survival. It was a cynical, almost paranoid calculation, but one that he felt had kept him safe.

As they continued their routine, Emma might have sensed Caleb's unspoken concerns, though she never pressed him on it. There was an unspoken understanding between them—a shared awareness of the larger game they were now a part of. While they might have preferred a life of simple pleasures and scientific discovery, they knew that the reality they were living in was far more complex, and far more dangerous.

So, they surfed. They worked. They loved. And they kept their routine, hoping it would be enough to keep the darker forces at bay.

There's no place easier to buy a used laptop than a university, Caleb thought. And, if he was being honest, there's probably no place easier to buy a stolen one, either. The campus was teeming with students who were always in need of quick cash, and laptops were one of the quickest ways to get it. Caleb briefly considered asking his teammates if anyone had an old laptop they wanted to sell, but he quickly dismissed the idea. If someone was watching him, there was a good chance they were watching the entire team. All the computers in the warm room, along with every laptop and home computer his colleagues used, were likely being monitored.

No, Caleb needed something off the grid—something that hadn't been flagged or tagged by the ever-watchful eyes of NASA or anyone else who might be keeping tabs on them. He figured a 15-year-old laptop would do the trick—old enough to be considered obsolete, but still functional enough for his purposes.

His search led him to the chemistry student study area, where he found exactly what he was looking for: a real geek, complete with thick glasses and a perpetually disheveled appearance, who was willing to part with a battered old laptop for an unreasonably high price. The kid was a born haggler, and Caleb quickly realized he was outmatched.

That's when it hit him—Emma. Not only was she less likely to be under surveillance, but she also had a knack for bargaining. Emma could probably get the price down and, more importantly, make the purchase without drawing too much attention.

When Caleb suggested the idea, Emma was more than happy to help. She had a way of blending in, of making herself seem inconspicuous, and within an hour, she returned with the laptop in hand, having secured it for half the asking price. Caleb couldn't help but feel a surge of admiration—and gratitude. Emma was the perfect partner in every sense, and now, with her help, he had taken the first step toward turning the tables on NASA.

As Caleb looked down at the old laptop, he felt a spark of

determination. It wasn't much to look at—its plastic casing was scratched and worn, and the keyboard was missing a few keys—but it was exactly what he needed. With this, he could start his own investigation, free from the prying eyes that were likely fixed on every official device he had access to. This was his way to push back, to take control of the situation that had spiraled so far beyond his reach.

Caleb's first task was to find a Wi-Fi adapter for his newly acquired, yet decidedly ancient, laptop. The machine was so old it didn't even come equipped with built-in Wi-Fi capability —a fact that would be a hindrance for most, but for Caleb, it was perfect. The lack of modern connectivity meant fewer vulnerabilities and a greater level of anonymity for what he had planned.

This wasn't Caleb's first foray into tapping into free Wi-Fi networks. Back in his undergraduate days, he had become something of an expert in the art of accessing wireless internet without paying a dime. It wasn't that he couldn't afford it; he simply saw no reason to spend money on something that was freely available all around him. Sure, he could have been content to sit in a crowded Starbucks, sipping overpriced coffee while checking his emails and browsing news feeds. But Caleb had always been resourceful and a bit more inventive than that.

During those simpler times, he had crafted a makeshift directional antenna for his Wi-Fi adapter—a small, unassuming device measuring just two and a half inches square and a mere sixteenth of an inch thick. Affixed to the single window of his cramped dorm room, the antenna had the remarkable ability to latch onto the Starbucks Wi-Fi signal from over a thousand feet away. It was a humble setup, but it served him well, allowing him to study, game, and surf the web from the comfort of his own space without any extra expense.

As he reminisced about his college exploits, a thought sparked in his mind. *Could that old antenna and adapter still be around?* Given his tendency to hold onto things—much to Emma's occasional chagrin—it was entirely possible he had stashed them away somewhere. The challenge was figuring out where.

After a moment of contemplation, he recalled the storage locker assigned to him on the ground floor of his apartment complex, right next to his designated parking spot. It was a small, cluttered space filled with forgotten boxes and relics of his past—an organized chaos that only Caleb could navigate.

Determined, he made his way down to the storage area, the fluorescent lights casting a cold glow over rows of identical lockers. The air was tinged with a slight mustiness, a mix of dust and aged cardboard. Unlocking his unit, he was greeted by stacks of boxes piled haphazardly, each labeled in his scrawled handwriting.

He rummaged through a few containers before his eyes landed on a worn-out banker's box tucked away in the corner. The box was sagging, its edges warped from apparent water damage, but something told him this was the one. He carefully dragged it out into the open corridor and lifted the flimsy lid.

Inside, amid a tangle of outdated cables and obsolete gadgets, lay the prized Wi-Fi adapter and its companion directional antenna. A grin spread across Caleb's face as he picked them up, memories flooding back of online gaming marathons.

"Gotcha," he muttered to himself, feeling a surge of satisfaction wash over him. The devices were a bit dusty but appeared to be in working condition—a testament to the durability of older tech.

But Caleb knew he couldn't just waltz back upstairs with the gear without raising potential suspicions. If anyone was indeed monitoring his movements, a sudden trip to his storage locker could seem out of the ordinary. He needed a plausible cover story.

Scanning the contents of his cluttered locker, an idea formed. He decided to turn this into a spontaneous cleaning and organizing session—a perfectly mundane activity that wouldn't raise any eyebrows. He began sorting through the various boxes, consolidating items, and setting aside things he no longer needed.

He found an empty, sturdier box and began transferring items from the damaged one, carefully arranging them in a neat, compact fashion. Old textbooks, forgotten knick-knacks, and obsolete electronics were either packed away or set aside for disposal. The Wi-Fi adapter and antenna were casually slipped into his jacket pocket amid the reorganization.

After about an hour of sorting and stacking, Caleb emerged from the storage area carrying a small pile of items destined for the dumpster. As he approached the large metal bin behind the building, he couldn't help but chuckle at the thought of some overzealous agent sifting through his discarded junk, hoping to find incriminating evidence in outdated manuals and broken calculators.

With a satisfying thud, he tossed the unwanted items into the dumpster, dusted off his hands, and headed back toward the building. The morning sun was just beginning to peek over the horizon, casting a golden hue across the parking lot and signaling the end of another long night.

Back in his apartment, Caleb laid out his recovered treasures on the kitchen table. He examined them closely, checking for any signs of damage or wear that might impede their functionality. Satisfied, he began the process of configuring his setup, his mind already several steps ahead, plotting the next moves in his plan to uncover what NASA was keeping hidden.

As he worked, the aroma of freshly brewed coffee filled the room, mingling with the soft sounds of morning traffic filtering in through the open window. It was moments like these—quiet, purposeful, and filled with the thrill of discovery—that reminded Caleb why he loved his work, and why he couldn't just let this mystery go.

Hours later, as the sun climbed higher and the day grew warmer, Caleb leaned back in his chair, stretching his arms above his head. The old laptop hummed quietly beside him, its screen displaying lines of code and network configurations. Progress was being made, slowly but surely.

He reached for his phone and texted out a quick message to Emma: *"Lunch later?"*

A few moments passed before his phone buzzed with her reply: *"Sushi at our spot?"*

Caleb smiled, feeling a warmth spread through him that had nothing to do with the morning sun. *"Perfect. See you then."*

Caleb approached the task of collecting and using Wi-Fi passwords with the same meticulous care he applied to his research. He knew that blending in was key, so he made sure every interaction was unremarkable. Whenever he asked for a password, whether it was written on a sign or required him to speak with someone, he always made a purchase—a pastry, a bottle of water, or even a newspaper, though he hadn't actually read one in years. His news came from his phone, but the act of buying a paper made him look like any other customer.

He was careful never to appear out of place. Each visit to a coffee shop, convenience store, or restaurant was calculated. He limited himself to obtaining one password per day, ensuring that he never overused any one location. To add an extra layer of randomness to his routine, Caleb kept a die near his laptop. Each morning, he would roll it to determine which shop's Wi-Fi he would connect to that day. It was a simple trick, but it helped him avoid any predictable patterns that might draw unwanted attention.

Caleb was aware that, in this game of cat and mouse, it was the little details that mattered. By maintaining an air of normalcy, he ensured that nothing about his behavior stood out. He never connected to the same shop's Wi-Fi two days in a row, and he never lingered longer than necessary. Once he had the password, he would discreetly connect, do what he needed to do, and then move on.

This cautious approach gave Caleb a sense of security, a buffer between him and any prying eyes that might be watching. Each step, each roll of the die, was part of a broader strategy to stay under the radar while he pursued the truth about Alohanui. And as he navigated this digital landscape, he knew that every move he made brought him one step closer to uncovering whatever it was that NASA—or perhaps something even larger—was trying so desperately to keep hidden.

Caleb and Emma met for sushi at their favorite spot, just as they had planned. The restaurant was a cozy little place tucked away on a quiet street, its minimalist decor and soft lighting providing the perfect atmosphere for their regular get-togethers. Emma loved everything about sushi—the delicate flavors, the artistry of the presentation, the freshness of the ingredients. Caleb, on the other hand, couldn't stand fish, let alone raw fish. But he adored Emma, and that made all the difference.

Whenever they dined there, Emma would enthusiastically order a variety of sushi and sashimi, eager to share her favorites with Caleb. Despite his aversion, Caleb would always try a little of everything she offered him, even though it sometimes took all his willpower not to gag. The slippery texture of the raw fish and the briny taste of the seaweed were almost too much for him, but he forced a smile and took small bites, more focused on the joy in Emma's eyes than on the food itself.

To make the meal more bearable, Caleb always ordered a California roll. It was his go-to—a safe option made with raw vegetables, avocado, and seaweed, something he could handle without much effort. The familiar flavors of the California roll grounded him as he ventured into the more challenging dishes Emma placed in front of him.

As they sat together, Emma's chopsticks deftly picking up pieces of sushi and offering them to him with a playful smile, Caleb couldn't help but feel a deep affection for her. The way she lit up when she talked about her favorite dishes, the care she took in explaining the subtle differences between types of fish, and the way she teased him for his reluctance—it all made the experience worthwhile.

Even though sushi wasn't his thing, these meals were a ritual he cherished. They were a reminder of how much he cared for Emma and how he was willing to step outside his comfort zone for her. And, in a way, it was also symbolic of their partnership—two people from different worlds coming together, sharing experiences, and finding joy in each other's company, even when the road wasn't always smooth.

The North Shore was Caleb's sanctuary, the one place where he felt secure enough to talk openly about his attempts to uncover what NASA might be hiding. The coastline, with its rugged beauty and vast stretches of sand, offered a sense of isolation that was hard to find elsewhere. Here, the sea seemed endless, its deep blue waters crashing rhythmically against the shore, while the sky above stretched out in an uninterrupted dome of brilliant azure. The sun hung low on the horizon, casting long, golden rays that bathed everything in a warm, amber glow.

After an hour of intense surfing, Caleb and Emma retreated to a secluded part of the beach, far from the prying eyes of other beachgoers. The area was shielded by tall, windswept palms and dense vegetation, creating a natural barrier that ensured their privacy. The sand beneath their feet was soft and cool, a stark contrast to the intense heat of the day. As they sat down, the sound of the waves provided a soothing backdrop, allowing Caleb to gather his thoughts before bringing Emma up to speed.

Caleb, with his tousled hair still damp from the ocean and a few grains of sand clinging to his skin, spoke with a mix of frustration and determination. "I haven't got a clue how to hack into NASA. But it's clear the closeup images of Alohanui that they're circulating publicly are manipulated," he said, pausing as he looked out at the sea, the water shimmering under the fading light.

Emma, sitting next to him, her dark hair still wet and clinging to her back, listened intently. Her deep brown eyes reflected the colors of the ocean, a mix of curiosity and concern evident on her face. The breeze played with the strands of her hair, lifting them gently as she considered Caleb's words.

"Something just occurred to me," Caleb continued, his voice more animated. "They're sanitizing the images. NASA doesn't want us to know Alohanui's actual location and trajectory. But it's so simple for them, trivial really! Pan-STARRS1, Pan-STARRS2, and every other NASA-controlled telescope has a database of satellites—both the ones everyone knows about and the classified ones, only known to the military-industrial complex. Alohanui is just a single pixel while it's in the asteroid belt; it would have to get much closer to Earth before it's more than that. So if NASA, who has full access to Pan-STARRS, wants to prevent anyone from determining its trajectory, all they have to do is add it to the satellite database."

Emma nodded, her gaze fixed on the horizon. "Sure," she said thoughtfully. "I'm sure that was the first thing they did, many weeks ago. And no one has ever complained about them redacting satellites and secret space force missions because it makes it easier to find PHOs—potentially hazardous objects."

"And it's going to make finding Alohanui easier too," Caleb added, excitement creeping into his voice. "I just need to program the laptop to search for pure black pixels in the images—starting with Alohanui's last known location. That's half the job done. The other half is getting the close-up images that Juno took, the ones NASA doesn't want the world to see. But I have no idea how to do that."

Emma turned to him, her eyes narrowing as she considered the problem. "Isn't the data stream from every NASA satellite, including Juno—may she rest in peace—directed first to JPL and then forwarded to NASA? If everyone thinks NASA is sharing everything, maybe they aren't too worried about the security of JPL's server."

Caleb's eyes widened with the realization. "Well, hacking into a less secure server is still not something I have the slightest clue how to do. But wow, I love where you're going with this. There's bound to be some proud Juno team members who might want to distribute some of those images. And maybe, instead of downloading them from NASA's website, they might grab them directly from JPL's server. Perhaps just out of habit, or because they're not aware that they're being lied to and manipulated."

He leaned back, staring up at the sky as it transitioned into shades of pink and orange. "What would be wrong morally with downloading an image from your own server that's already been approved for public distribution? Sure, it might violate some tiny technical rule, but most of the Juno team probably wouldn't even know about that. And you know NASA wouldn't caution JPL's members not to talk about Juno—that would just fuel conspiracy theories."

As the last light of the day faded and the first stars began to twinkle in the sky, Caleb and Emma sat in comfortable silence, the weight of their conversation lingering between them. The sea breeze carried the scent of salt and damp earth, and the rhythmic sound of the waves continued to provide a calming presence.

In this secluded spot, away from the world and its watching eyes, they felt a sense of clarity. They knew they were onto something, something bigger than either of them had initially imagined. The pieces were starting to fall into place, and while the path ahead was uncertain, they were ready to take the next steps together.

The following weekend, Caleb and Emma returned to the North Shore, their usual sanctuary away from the prying eyes of the world. As they unloaded their surfboards, Emma noticed that Caleb looked more exhausted than usual. His eyes were shadowed with fatigue, and his movements were a bit slower, the result of burning the candle at both ends. Despite this, they enjoyed a great, albeit shorter, surfing session before setting off to find another secluded spot where they could talk in peace.

Once they were settled, Caleb took a careful look around to ensure they were alone before speaking. "No close-ups of Alohanui yet, but I know where she is and where she's headed," he said, his voice tinged with both frustration and determination.

Emma's eyes narrowed thoughtfully. "Remember Kaʻepaokaʻāwela?" Caleb asked.

"Jupiter's mischief," Emma replied, recognizing the name immediately. It was a retrograde asteroid, meaning it travels around the solar system in the opposite direction to all the planets—a rarity in itself.

"Exactly," Caleb continued. "It shares Jupiter's orbit pretty closely except it travels clockwise around the solar system instead of counterclockwise like all the planets. Many of our colleagues believe it's as old as the solar system itself—about 4.5 billion years. And here's the kicker: it's also an interstellar object, just like 'Oumuamua and Alohanui. Strange that it doesn't get any press. Maybe the name is too hard to pronounce."

Emma chuckled, a sound that mingled with the rustle of palm fronds and the distant crash of waves. "I know a bit about it. It's not just the name; it's too expensive."

"What do you mean?" Caleb asked, laughing at the unexpected answer.

"It's here in our solar system, and in theory, we could send a Juno-like probe to visit it," Emma explained. "But the problem is its retrograde orbit. Even if we still had Saturn V rockets, they couldn't get us there."

"In simple terms," she continued, "you don't just have to reach it; you have to be traveling at 60,000 miles per hour in the wrong direction when you arrive. That's a lot of energy, and it makes the mission nearly impossible."

Caleb nodded, impressed. "That's why they call you *Doctor* Kanoa."

"That's right," Emma said with a grin, "but no one actually calls me Dr. Kanoa. So, what about Ka'epaoka'āwela?" The name rolled effortlessly off her tongue, a testament to her Hawaiian heritage and her work with Pan-STARRS.

Caleb's expression turned serious. "Head-on collision," he said quietly. "At, as you say, 60,000 miles per hour."

Emma's eyes widened as she considered the implications. "They'll both be vaporized," she said, then quickly added, "No, wait—Kaʻepaokaʻāwela will be vaporized. It's only about two miles in diameter, compared to Alohanui's 18 miles. Alohanui is way bigger and probably much heavier. I don't know what will happen to Alohanui."

"Well, I think I might have an idea," Caleb replied. "I've been studying how Alohanui perturbs the orbits of other asteroids it's encountered since it left Jupiter. It is bigger and has more mass than Kaʻepaokaʻāwela, but I think it's mostly hollow. Kaʻepaokaʻāwela is around 78 billion tons, while Alohanui seems to be about 130 billion tons. If their center-of-mass trajectories are perfectly aligned, Kaʻepaokaʻāwela will be pulverized, and Alohanui will lose about two-thirds of its velocity."

He paused, letting the weight of his words sink in. "As a result, Alohanui will likely start moving into the inner solar system in a highly elliptical orbit. But without access to NASA's Aitken supercomputer, I can't calculate its precise trajectory. I've hit a dead end with tracking its path. I'll keep monitoring it, but I won't be able to project its course any significant distance."

Emma listened, her expression a mix of concern and admiration for Caleb's dedication.

"So, what's your next move?" she asked.

Caleb sighed, a hint of frustration in his voice. "I'm going to shift my focus and try to find the unmanipulated close-up images of Alohanui taken by Juno. If we can get those, we might be able to figure out what else NASA is hiding."

Emma nodded, understanding the gravity of their situation. The secluded beach, with its calming waves and the scent of salt and sun-warmed sand, was a stark contrast to the tension that had built up between them. They were standing on the edge of something monumental, something that could change everything.

"Oh, I forgot to ask—when will Alohanui and Kaʻepaokaʻāwela collide?" Emma inquired, her curiosity piqued.

Caleb instinctively reached for his phone, only to remember that they had hidden their phones in the car to ensure their conversation remained private. He paused for a moment, then turned to Emma with a grin. "Hey, what time is sunset today?" he asked.

"6:47 local time," she replied without missing a beat. Caleb couldn't help but smile at how she always seemed to have astronomical and meteorological fun facts like that at the ready, a small but endearing quirk that he loved.

He glanced out over the water, watching the sun inch closer to the horizon. The sky was beginning to blush with the soft hues of twilight, and he mentally calculated the time left until the sun would disappear completely. Estimating the sun's angular distance from the horizon, he let out a slow breath.

"If all my calculations, approximations, and estimates are right, it just happened," he said, his voice tinged with a mix of awe and melancholy. "Kaʻepaokaʻāwela was just destroyed. After four and a half billion years of traveling the wrong way on a one-way street, it just got blasted by another newly arrived interstellar visitor."

Emma's eyes widened as she absorbed the weight of his words. The realization that something so ancient, so timeless, had met its end at this very moment was staggering. The soft sound of the waves lapping against the shore seemed to underscore the finality of it all.

"Wow," Emma whispered, her gaze fixed on the horizon where the sun was slowly dipping into the ocean. "To think that we were here, talking about it, while it happened—it's surreal."

Caleb nodded, feeling a deep sense of connection to the vastness of the cosmos, as if he were somehow a witness to the collision. "Yeah, it's mind-blowing. Two objects from two different systems, on a collision course for billions and billions of years, and here we are, sitting on a beach, no flash, no crash, and yet we are aware of it all."

They sat in silence for a moment, both lost in thought as the sun continued its descent, painting the sky in shades of orange, pink, and purple. The sheer scale of the universe, the countless years these celestial bodies had traveled, and the randomness of their fateful encounter—it was all unfathomable.

"Do you think Alohanui is still intact?" Emma finally asked, her voice soft.

Caleb shrugged, his eyes still on the horizon. "I think so. It's bigger, more massive, and if it's what we suspect, vastly superior alien technology, then it survived. But it's going to be interesting to see what happens next. Alohanui's trajectory will change, and who knows where it will go from here."

As they sat in silence, watching the sun dip lower in the sky, they both knew that whatever came next, they would face it together. The North Shore, their private retreat, had become the backdrop to a mystery that was growing deeper with every discovery. And while the road ahead was uncertain, Caleb and Emma were determined to uncover the truth, no matter the cost.

CHAPTER 6 ARRIVAL

Jake and Jean Jacobson, Caleb's parents, had been eagerly anticipating their pilgrimage to the Holy Land for years. The day finally arrived, and their excitement was palpable as they prepared to leave. Bethany, Caleb's sister, who also lived in Oklahoma City, had taken the day off work to drive them to the airport. The early morning air was crisp, and the sky was just beginning to lighten with the first hints of dawn as Bethany pulled up in front of their modest home.

Bethany watched as her parents, both in their early seventies but still spry, double-checked their luggage one last time. Jake, with his graying hair and broad shoulders, was still every bit the rock of the family. Jean, with her warm smile and ever-present kindness, was the heart. They shared a quiet prayer before heading out the door, their hands clasped tightly together.

As they loaded their bags into the trunk of Bethany's car, she noticed how her mother had tucked a small, well-worn Bible into her carry-on bag, a symbol of the faith that had guided her through life. Jean caught Bethany's eye and gave her a reassuring smile. "God will take care of us," she said softly, sensing her daughter's unspoken worries.

The drive to the airport was filled with light conversation, Jake and Jean reminiscing about their years together, their excitement for the trip, and how much they looked forward to walking in the footsteps of their faith. Bethany, though trying to share in their enthusiasm, couldn't shake a nagging feeling of unease. She glanced at them occasionally in the rearview mirror, forcing herself to smile back whenever her father caught her eye.

At the airport, they said their goodbyes. Bethany hugged them both tightly, lingering a little longer in their embrace than usual. "I'll be praying for you both," she whispered, her voice catching slightly as she tried to hold back tears. Jake and Jean reassured her, promising to call as soon as they landed. With a final wave, they disappeared into the bustling crowd of travelers.

Hours later, the world as Bethany, Caleb, and their entire family knew it changed forever.

The plane that Jake and Jean were on—a transatlantic flight to Tel Aviv—never reached its destination. Somewhere over the middle of the Atlantic Ocean, the plane disappeared from radar. Initial reports were vague, and for agonizing hours, Caleb and Bethany clung to hope. But then came the devastating news: the plane had crashed, and while some wreckage and a few bodies were recovered, the vast majority of the passengers, including Jake and Jean, were lost to the sea. Their bodies were never found.

For Caleb, the loss was almost too much to bear. Grief weighed heavily on him, mingled with a growing sense of dread as he continued his work. His attempts to access the raw data from Juno's archives had been frustratingly unsuccessful and time-consuming. Despite his best efforts, he found himself hitting wall after wall, his every attempt thwarted by layers of security and obfuscation.

Long discussions with Emma became his refuge, a way to make sense of the turmoil within him. Emma, with her steady presence and sharp mind, helped him navigate the maze of emotions and technical challenges. Eventually, Caleb made the difficult decision to be satisfied with tracking what he believed was Alohanui, even as NASA and Pan-STARRS reported a different trajectory—one that kept Alohanui far from Earth and far from any of NASA's other spacecraft.

But Caleb's own calculations told a different story. According to his projections, Alohanui would eventually enter near-Earth space in about a year. The weight of this knowledge pressed down on him like a physical burden. He couldn't shake the feeling that something monumental was coming, something that could change the course of human history. And yet, with his parents gone, the personal cost of this burden seemed even greater.

Bethany, devastated by the loss of their parents, leaned heavily on Caleb for support, despite the distance between them. She struggled to come to terms with the suddenness of their death, the emptiness left in the wake of their absence. Caleb, though grappling with his own grief, took on the role of comforter, speaking to her for hours on the phone, offering what solace he could. He listened as she cried, as she raged, as she tried to make sense of the senseless. And each time they spoke, Caleb's heart broke a little more, knowing that he couldn't be there in person to hold her, to grieve with her in the way they both needed.

Despite the immense sorrow, Caleb felt the need to press on with his work. The knowledge he carried about Alohanui felt like a secret too heavy to keep, yet too dangerous to share. He was caught between worlds—the personal tragedy of losing his parents and the professional responsibility of uncovering the truth about an interstellar visitor that might soon pose an unprecedented threat to Earth.

As the weeks passed, Caleb found himself more and more

consumed by his work, using it as a way to keep the grief at bay. But no matter how much he threw himself into his calculations and research, the loss of Jake and Jean was a wound that refused to heal. Their faith had sustained them, but now Caleb found himself questioning everything—his purpose, his beliefs, and the path that lay ahead.

Would he find the answers he was looking for? And if he did, would they bring him peace—or would they only deepen the sense of loss and uncertainty that now defined his life?

Tracking Alohanui had become almost routine for Caleb. It required only a few minutes of his day, and even that was more out of habit than necessity. If he had been willing to leave the old laptop running and connected to Wi-Fi 24 hours a day, the programs he'd meticulously crafted—along with the scripts he'd written—would have handled everything automatically. The algorithms were precise, the data flows uninterrupted, and the entire process was as seamless as it was efficient.

The truth was, Caleb didn't need to be so hands-on anymore. The only real task left for him was to roll the dice each day, a small ritual to determine which Wi-Fi network to connect to, and then adjust the directional antenna accordingly. It was almost absurdly simple, a task so mundane it felt like a game—though the stakes were anything but trivial.

This small daily ritual was perhaps the only thing grounding Caleb in the midst of everything else that had spun out of control. Each morning, he would take out the die, its edges worn smooth from use, and let it clatter across the table. The number that came up dictated his next move, a seemingly random decision that added a layer of unpredictability to a process otherwise governed by logic and code.

Caleb would then position the antenna, a device cobbled together with the remnants of his undergrad ingenuity, and watch as the laptop connected to a new network. The scripts would kick in, downloading and analyzing the data from the Pan-STARRS images. The process was almost entirely automated, but Caleb still felt a strange sense of satisfaction every time the data rolled in, confirming that Alohanui was still on course—his course, not the one NASA and Pan-STARRS publicly reported.

These moments of quiet routine were a stark contrast to the emotional turmoil Caleb was going through. The simplicity of the task offered a brief escape, a few minutes where he could focus solely on the technical, on the tangible. It was a respite from the constant undercurrent of grief, the weight of loss, and the gnawing anxiety about what might be coming.

In these moments, Caleb felt like he was holding onto the last vestiges of control in a world that had become increasingly uncertain. The quiet hum of the old laptop, the soft click of the die, the precise angle of the antenna—it was all a small rebellion against the chaos that threatened to overwhelm him.

But deep down, he knew that the real challenge lay ahead. Tracking Alohanui was the easy part. What would happen when it finally reached near-Earth space? What would he do then, armed with knowledge that no one else seemed to share —or, if they did, were keeping from the world?

For now, though, Caleb let the ritual soothe him. The die was rolled, the antenna adjusted, and the data flowed. And for those few minutes each day, he could almost convince himself that everything was under control.

Unrest in the Middle East had escalated in the weeks following Caleb's parents' tragic plane crash. The region, already a powder keg, had become even more volatile, with reports of violence and terror attacks dominating the news. Then, one day, a headline caught Caleb's eye that made his blood run cold —a tour bus from the same company his parents had booked with was blown up in a terrorist attack. It was the exact same bus, scheduled at the same time and place that Jake and Jean Jacobson would have been on, had they made it to the Holy Land.

Caleb stared at the news in disbelief, his mind struggling to process the cruel twist of fate. His parents had died in a plane crash over the Atlantic, and now this—a bus that should have carried them on their pilgrimage was reduced to twisted metal and smoke. He couldn't help but wonder, was this some kind of divine contingency plan? Was their plane crash merely the first act in a script written by a God determined to take them, one way or another?

The thought sickened him. Caleb had long struggled with his faith, the beliefs instilled in him during childhood eroded by years of scientific study and personal tragedy. But this—this was something else entirely. The idea that a higher power might be orchestrating such horrific events to fulfill some inscrutable plan was more than he could bear.

"Is this how God works?" Caleb muttered bitterly to himself. "If the plane hadn't gone down, they would have been blown up on a bus instead? That's another reason I don't believe in God."

He said the words aloud, almost daring himself to challenge the anger that simmered just beneath the surface. For years, he had wrestled with the dissonance between the faith of his upbringing and the cold, hard facts of the universe he had come to understand through his work. And now, with this latest blow, any remaining threads of belief seemed to snap.

Caleb found himself spiraling into a dark reflection on the nature of life, death, and the universe. The idea that his parents were somehow destined to die on this trip—whether by plane crash or terrorist attack—was too much. It felt as though the universe was mocking him, as if all the logic and reason he had clung to could offer no protection against the randomness of fate.

He thought of Emma, of the quiet strength she had shown as they navigated their way through grief and uncertainty. He thought of the work they were doing, the mystery of Alohanui that consumed their days. Everything seemed so fragile, so precarious, as if any moment could be their last.

But more than anything, Caleb was angry. Angry at the world, at the senselessness of it all, and, though he barely admitted it to himself, angry at a God he no longer believed in. If there was a divine plan, it was a cruel and heartless one.

Caleb's thoughts darkened further as he pondered the implications. If his parents were meant to die on this pilgrimage, what did that say about the rest of their lives? About the choices they made, the faith they held onto so dearly? Were they just pawns in some cosmic game, their deaths an inevitable outcome regardless of the path they took?

The questions haunted him, gnawing at the edges of his mind as he tried to focus on his work, on the life he was trying to build with Emma. But no matter how hard he tried to push them away, they kept coming back, each one more relentless than the last.

As Caleb sat alone in his apartment, staring at the wall, he realized that he wasn't just grieving for his parents. He was grieving for the loss of something deeper—the belief that there was any sense or order to the universe at all. And that, more than anything, left him feeling hollow and lost.

A drive to the north coast was exactly what Caleb needed—a way to escape the heaviness that had settled over him in the past few months.
The cityscape of Honolulu gradually gave way to the more rugged, untamed beauty of Oahu's northern shores. The roads wound through dense forests, with trees that formed a canopy overhead, their leaves rustling softly in the breeze. The air

grew fresher, carrying the scent of salt and damp earth, as the ocean drew nearer.

Before they set out, Caleb had taken extra precautions, fully embracing the paranoia that had been creeping into his life. His apartment, small and cluttered but comfortable, had become a fortress of sorts. The kitchen was filled with mismatched furniture and appliances, a testament to Caleb's indifference toward domestic life. The aluminum foil he used was stored in a drawer next to the sink. Caleb took the roll and meticulously wrapped their phones, sealing them in the foil like precious artifacts. He then grounded the foil by removing a register and placing the phones in the cold, galvanized steel A/C ductwork beneath—a makeshift Faraday cage.

"Now if I get lost or in an accident, we're screwed," Caleb said to Emma with a wry smile. "Paranoia makes life a lot more difficult!"

Emma chuckled, though she shared some of his unease. But as they drove farther from Honolulu, the tension began to ease. The hum of the city was replaced by the sounds of nature—the distant crash of waves, the rustle of palm fronds, and the occasional cry of a seabird. The farther they got, the safer and calmer Caleb felt, as though the physical distance was putting miles between him and the worries that had plagued him.

Emma led him to a secret spot, a secluded cove she had never shared with him before. The trail to the beach was narrow, overgrown with tropical plants and shaded by tall trees that filtered the sunlight into dappled patterns on the ground. The air was thick with the scent of hibiscus and the faint, briny smell of the ocean. As they emerged from the trail, the cove opened up before them—a crescent of white sand bordered by jagged rocks on either side, the waves gently lapping at the shore. The sky above was a brilliant blue, streaked with wisps of white clouds, and the ocean stretched out endlessly, its surface sparkling in the late afternoon sun.

They surfed for what felt like hours, the rhythm of the waves and the physical exertion gradually clearing Caleb's mind. The ocean was a deep, rich blue, darker than the sky above, and the waves were perfect—smooth and steady, carrying them effortlessly along. Caleb felt the tension in his muscles slowly dissolve with each ride, the water washing away the last remnants of his worries.

Afterward, they made their way to a totally private part of the beach, a small, hidden alcove nestled between the rocks. The sand was warm beneath their feet, and the only sounds were the gentle whisper of the waves and the distant call of seabirds. The sky had begun to change, the sun dipping lower toward the horizon, casting a golden glow over everything.

Emma turned to Caleb with a playful smile, twirling slowly in the sand. "Any bugs on me?" she asked, her voice light and teasing.

Caleb couldn't help but smile as he watched her, her dark hair catching the light, her skin glowing in the soft sunlight. But as she turned, something caught his eye—something small, barely noticeable, just under her suit on her right side just below the rib cage.

"What's that?" he asked, his tone shifting from playful to curious.

Emma paused, reaching down to feel the spot he had noticed. Her brow furrowed slightly as she examined it. "It's me, but I've never noticed it before. Have you ever noticed it?"

Caleb considered making a joke, a dozen witty replies running through his mind, but he wasn't in the mood. The day had been too heavy, too filled with thoughts of what might be watching them, what might be hidden. So he simply shook his head, answering with a quiet, "No."

They stood there for a moment, the waves gently rolling in behind them, the sky beginning to turn shades of pink and orange as the sun set. The peaceful surroundings contrasted sharply with the unease that was starting to creep back into Caleb's mind. So many things weren't right—he could feel it. But for now, in this secluded paradise, they had each other, and that was enough to keep the darkness at bay, if only for a little while longer.

On the drive back, Caleb couldn't shake the image of the small, unfamiliar bump they had noticed earlier. "You'll get that checked out, right? See your doctor?" he asked, trying to keep his tone casual.

Emma sighed, "Yes, but I don't really have a doctor. The walk-in clinic at UH is awesome though, and it's free. Plus, as employees of the Institute, we've got that excellent health care plan from the University of Hawaii."

Caleb nodded. "You want to drop by there now?"

"Of course not, but I'm gonna," Emma replied, determination in her voice. "But we better pick up our phones first. My medical plan information is on my phone."

After a quick detour to retrieve their phones from Caleb's makeshift Faraday cage, they headed to the University Health Clinic. By the time they arrived, it was around 6 p.m., and the waiting room was busy but not packed to the point of being uncomfortable. The fluorescent lighting bathed the room in a sterile, slightly too-bright glow, and the hum of conversation filled the air.

The waiting room was a blend of neutral tones, with worn-out chairs upholstered in muted grays and blues. A few outdated magazines were scattered on a low table, mostly untouched. The walls were adorned with posters promoting various health initiatives—flu shots, mental health awareness, and STD prevention. A television mounted in the corner played a local news channel on mute, the closed captions struggling to keep up with the anchor's rapid speech.

Despite the number of people, Caleb noticed that half the crowd seemed to be there more for moral support than for medical attention. Conversations, half heard over the murmur of the room, revealed that most were there seeking contraceptives or treatment for an STD. The air was tinged with the faint scent of antiseptic, a reminder that this was a place of healing, albeit an impersonal one.

After waiting for what felt like an eternity, but was really just under two hours, Emma's name was finally called. A triage nurse, efficient and brisk in her manner, escorted them in. The nurse was in her mid-40s, her face lined with the fatigue of someone who had seen too much and worked too many shifts. Her scrubs were a faded blue, and a stethoscope hung loosely around her neck. She checked Emma's vitals with practiced precision, noting everything down on a tablet before leading them to the examination room.

The examination room was small, with just enough space for the essential medical equipment. A stark white examination bed with crinkled paper stretched across it dominated the room. The walls were painted a bland, unassuming beige, interrupted only by a few educational posters on human anatomy. A blood pressure monitor and various other instruments sat on a counter beside the sink, and a faint smell of disinfectant lingered in the air. The atmosphere was clinical, almost detached, as if to remind the patients that this was a place for facts and figures, not emotions.

A few minutes later, Dr. Smith entered—a woman in her late 30s with a no-nonsense demeanor. Her white coat was crisp, her hair pulled back into a tight bun. She greeted Emma with a professional smile and got straight to the point, asking about the bump they'd discovered.

She examined Emma, her hands pressing gently but firmly on Emma's abdomen, her face betraying no emotion as she worked. "Well, it could be anything or nothing at all," the doctor finally said, her tone carefully neutral. "I'm going to put you on the urgent ultrasound list, just to be sure. Someone will call you with an appointment. In the meantime, try not to worry."

With that, she gave Emma a reassuring nod and sent them on their way. Emma and Caleb walked back through the waiting room, which had thinned out considerably since their arrival. The overhead lights still buzzed softly, and the muted television continued to display the day's headlines. As they stepped out into the cool evening air, the clinic doors closing behind them, the weight of uncertainty hung between them.

Emma had waited three agonizing weeks for the phone call from the University of Hawaii Health Services Urgent Ultrasound Department, all the while trying to push the looming sense of dread from her mind. Fortunately, when the call finally came, the appointment was scheduled for just three days later, on a Friday. It wasn't ideal, but at least she wouldn't have to wait much longer.

She was instructed to fast for the procedure—something that seemed odd to her. Why would she need to fast for an ultrasound? After some brief research, she learned that fasting could improve the clarity of the images, especially for abdominal ultrasounds, by reducing the amount of gas in the intestines that could obscure the view of the kidneys.

Her appointment was set for 8 a.m., which was conveniently just after her shift at the Institute of Astronomy. Afterward, she planned to head home to rest and hopefully sleep through the stress of waiting for the results. The clinic itself had been much like the other medical facilities she had visited—sterile, with soft lighting and the distant hum of medical machinery. She was ushered into a small room where the ultrasound technician, a woman with kind eyes and a reassuring smile, explained the procedure. Emma was asked to lie down, her abdomen coated in cool gel as the ultrasound wand glided over her skin. The technician's calm demeanor did little to soothe Emma's nerves, but at least the process was painless.

After the appointment, Emma returned home, her body and mind weighed down by exhaustion. The combination of sleepless nights and the mental strain of waiting for answers had drained her. She collapsed onto her bed, hoping that sleep might offer some escape from the relentless anxiety. It was late into the morning when she finally stirred, the warm afternoon light filtering softly through her bedroom window. As she began to get ready for her usual surfing session with Caleb at Diamond Head, her phone rang.

"Dr. Smith here. Is this Emma?" The voice on the other end was calm but carried a gravity that made Emma's stomach tighten instantly.

"Yes, it's Emma," she replied, her heart pounding as if it already knew what was coming.

"The radiologist reviewed your ultrasound, and unfortunately, the results don't look good. I'm going to refer you to a surgeon. Their medical office assistant will contact you to schedule a consultation and surgery."

The words hit Emma like a punch to the gut. She had been trying to prepare herself for bad news, but hearing it confirmed was a different kind of blow. Her mind raced, a whirlwind of questions and fears. Surgery? What did "not good" mean? How serious was this?

Dr. Smith's voice continued, but Emma barely registered the words until she heard the familiar ping of a text message.

Dr. Smith had followed up with a message that detailed what might come next if the mass is determined to be liver cancer:

> "Emma, here's some information that might be useful about what could come next if the mass is determined to be liver cancer. Here are a few typical procedures and protocols:
>
> 1. Advanced Imaging to gather more detailed information about the liver lesion such as Contrast-Enhanced CT Scan, MRI or PET Scan (Positron Emission Tomography)
>
> 2. Blood Tests
>
> Alpha-Fetoprotein (AFP):
>
> Elevated levels of AFP are often associated with hepatocellular carcinoma (HCC) but are not definitive.
>
> Liver Function Tests (LFTs):
>
> Assess overall liver health, which is critical for treatment planning. These include bilirubin, albumin, and clotting factors.
>
> Viral Markers:
>
> Testing for hepatitis B and C, which are risk factors for liver cancer.
>
> Complete Blood Count (CBC):
>
> Evaluates general health and checks for anemia or signs of infection.
>
> Kidney Function Tests:
>
> To ensure kidney health, especially if certain imaging or treatment requires nephrotoxic agents.
>
> 3. Biopsy (If Needed)
>
> Liver Biopsy:

Not always required if imaging and AFP levels strongly suggest liver cancer.

If performed, a needle biopsy is typically guided by ultrasound or CT to sample the suspicious lesion.

Pathologists confirm whether the tissue is cancerous and determine the tumor type.

4. Staging Workup

Tumor Staging (TNM or BCLC):

Imaging and biopsy results help determine the size of the tumor (T), lymph node involvement (N), and distant metastasis (M).

Assessment for Metastasis:

Imaging of the lungs (chest X-ray or CT) to check for metastases.

5. Treatment Planning

Based on staging, liver health, and patient factors, treatment options include:

Curative Options:

Surgery: Resection of the tumor or liver transplant for eligible patients.

Ablative Therapies: Radiofrequency ablation (RFA) or microwave ablation for localized tumors.

Immunotherapy: Checkpoint inhibitors (e.g., atezolizumab with bevacizumab).

Radiotherapy: Stereotactic body radiation therapy (SBRT) or radioembolization.

6. Monitoring and Follow-Up

If treatment is initiated, regular monitoring is essential:

Imaging every 3–6 months to track tumor response.

Blood tests, including AFP and liver function, to evaluate treatment effectiveness and liver health.

Here are some things to know about chemotherapy for liver cancer:

Effectiveness: Most chemotherapy drugs are not very effective against liver cancer, and even a combination of drugs may only shrink a small number of tumors.

Chemoembolization: Chemotherapy is often used in combination with chemoembolization, a treatment that blocks the blood supply to the tumor.

Hepatic artery infusion (HAI): A form of chemotherapy that involves putting drugs directly into the hepatic artery, often more effective than traditional chemotherapy.

Adjuvant therapy: Chemotherapy can be used before surgery to shrink a liver tumor.

Neoadjuvant therapy: Chemotherapy can be used to lower the risk of the cancer returning.

Monoclonal antibodies: These man-made proteins are designed to attach to a specific target, affecting the tumor's ability to form new blood vessels.
Each step is tailored to the patient's overall health, liver function, and stage of cancer.

Early detection: People with small, resectable tumors that are removed and who do not have other serious health problems can have a 5-year survival rate of over 50%.

Liver transplants: People with early-stage liver cancer

who are able to have a liver transplant can have a 5-year survival rate of 60% to 70%.

Age: Younger patients have an increased 5-year survival rate across several subgroups.

Sorry to dump all this on you in a text but I've found that patients take home the brochure on liver cancer from my office but rarely read it. This way it's in your phone for anytime you are ready to read and perhaps process it and, *only* if you wish, you can forward it to loved ones."

Emma took a deep breath, trying to steady herself as the weight of the unknown settled over her like a heavy blanket. She had a basic understanding of what might lie ahead, but the thought of surgery, the potential for chemotherapy, and the sheer uncertainty of it all made her feel suddenly small and vulnerable.

She knew Caleb would support her, but she hadn't yet told him about the appointment or the call from Dr. Smith. As she put down the phone, a wave of fatigue washed over her, not just from the day but from the emotional toll of processing this new reality. The waves at Diamond Head could wait. Surfing, which had always been a source of solace, felt distant and unimportant right now.

For now, Emma needed time—time to process, time to gather her thoughts, and time to figure out how to tell Caleb. She knew he would be there for her when she was ready, but this moment was hers alone. She reached for her phone and quickly typed out a message to Caleb: "Have to stand you up. I'll explain later."

She sent the message and then sat there for a moment, letting the reality of the situation sink in. The road ahead was uncertain, and the only thing she was sure of was that it would be a difficult journey. But she also knew she wouldn't be facing it alone.

Caleb received Emma's text before he even left his apartment. His surfboard was leaning against the wall, ready for another day of escaping into the waves, but her message made him pause. "Have to stand you up. I'll explain later." Something wasn't right, and Caleb immediately decided to skip his usual surfing session. He could feel the weight of uncertainty pressing on his chest, though he wasn't sure what had caused Emma to cancel.

Instead of heading out, Caleb sat down at his desk and resumed his investigation. He'd been diving deep into the rabbit holes of the internet, searching for anything related to Alohanui—though not the dark web. He knew better than to touch that. The U.S. government would have eyes everywhere, ready to shut down any unapproved publication of images or information about Alohanui. No, Caleb was combing through the more obscure corners of the web—those algorithm-driven news feeds that churned out clickbait stories like "The doctor looks at the baby and turns pale," or "The vet looks at the puppy and turns pale."

Today, he stumbled upon a story titled: "Scientist Looks at Image and Turns Pale." At first, he dismissed it as more nonsense, but something about it caught his attention. Clicking the link, he expected some fabricated tale of sensationalism. But what he found left him stunned.

The article contained close-up images of Alohanui—images that NASA had officially released—but these were different. Unlike the carefully sanitized photos that had been distributed to the public, these images showed something new, something disturbing. Symbols. Carved into the surface of the calcium carbonate inclusions on the 18-mile by 200-foot faces of Alohanui were strange symbols, etched deeply and with clear intent. Many of the images also showed other symbols scattered across the rest of its vast face.

Caleb leaned in closer to the screen, his breath catching in his throat. The symbols looked like nothing he had ever seen, but there was something familiar about them, too. Some of them resembled stylized Hebrew characters but he didn't know any Hebrew or even any names of any of the characters. Others, though, were unmistakably Greek—sigma, iota, mu, omega, nu, those he recognized. His mind raced as he tried to make sense of it all. What could this mean? Were these symbols ancient, extraterrestrial, or some kind of cosmic graffiti?

He realized, with a creeping sense of dread, that these weren't just random markings. There was a pattern, a purpose behind them. Whoever—or whatever—had created them had a message to convey. Caleb's hands trembled slightly as he scrolled through the images, each one more bizarre than the last.

It was only after a few minutes that he realized how fast his heart was racing. He felt a cold sweat forming on the back of his neck, and though he couldn't see himself, he was certain that his face had drained of color. Caleb wasn't one to scare easily, but something about these symbols, something about NASA deliberately hiding them, unsettled him deeply.

He pulled his chair back from the desk, his mind spinning with questions. Why hadn't these symbols been released to the public? And more importantly, what did they mean? He had no doubt that this information was being deliberately concealed —and not just from the public, but from him and his team at IfA as well.

Caleb took a deep breath, trying to steady himself. This wasn't the time to panic. He needed to think clearly, to figure out the next step. Should he confront NASA? Should he tell Emma? Or should he keep digging, quietly, until he understood more?

Then it dawned on him.

"Shit! I'm looking at clickbait!" Caleb muttered under his breath, a wave of frustration and embarrassment washing over him. How had he fallen for something so obvious? His mind raced, trying to piece together the implications. *Think! Think! What does this mean?*

Then it hit him like a cold shock: *Bait*. It was bait—deliberately planted, maybe even targeted at him. His instincts kicked in, a deep-seated sense of paranoia bubbling up.

Shut off your laptop.

The thought came to him like a command from somewhere deep in his subconscious. No downside, right? Without hesitating, Caleb moved swiftly across the room. He unplugged the laptop, shut it off, yanked out the battery, and unplugged the directional antenna. His heart pounded as he gathered the pieces and walked to the kitchen. He opened the oven, placed the laptop inside, and then closed the door firmly. Grabbing a roll of aluminum foil from the drawer, he quickly taped it over the glass of the oven door, sealing off any chance of a signal leaking in or out.

Another improvised Faraday cage. Another layer of protection against whatever—or whoever—was baiting him.

NASA? Certainly, but also something bigger, *The Whole U.S. Government!*

His mind was spinning in a thousand different directions, each more paranoid than the last. But there was one constant in his thoughts: *Emma*. He needed to talk to her. She was the only one who could help him think straight, the only one he trusted completely.

Emma, I need to talk to Emma.

Caleb grabbed his phone from the counter, swiping to unlock it. He started typing a message, then stopped. If they were being watched, if they were being baited, this wasn't something he could talk about over the phone. He deleted the text before sending it.

This has to be face-to-face.

Caleb took a deep breath, grabbed his keys, and bolted out the door. He knew Emma would understand the gravity of the situation, and more importantly, she'd help him figure out the next steps. But as the door closed behind him and the cool evening air hit his face, he made an impulsive decision—he'd walk. He wasn't in the right headspace to drive, and the walk might help him clear his mind.

With each step, the tension in his chest loosened just a bit. The familiar sounds of the city—cars in the distance, people laughing as they passed, the gentle rustling of palm trees—began to pull him out of his spiraling thoughts. He felt the rhythm of the sidewalk beneath his feet, each step a reminder to breathe. Slowly, the fog in his brain started to lift.

As Caleb walked, his thoughts shifted to the concept of elegance. Elegance, he mused, had one meaning to the general public and an entirely different one to scientists. To most people, elegance meant something graceful, dignified, even beautiful. But to a scientist, elegance wasn't about appearance. It was about function—something that could serve multiple purposes, efficiently and effectively. A kidney, for instance, cleans the blood but also regulates blood pressure. To a biologist, that was elegant.

He wondered if the trap designed and built for him could also be described as "elegant." What if the deep state wasn't just trying to catch him but was also testing the waters? Perhaps they were gauging how the public might react to the revelation that a massive interstellar object that entered our solar system was guided by some kind of intelligence. What if those symbols—those ancient, Greek and Hebrew-like carvings—were bait, a carefully crafted way to see how people would wrap their minds around the idea that something like Alohanui existed?

The best minds in astronomy had already concluded that Alohanui came from another star system, a journey that had taken at least 75,000 years. If that was true, then Alohanui had been traveling long before either the Hebrew or Greek languages even existed. So what could those symbols really mean? How would the average citizen process the fact that an object, likely older than human civilization itself, bore markings that seemed eerily familiar?

Caleb stopped walking for a moment and looked up at the sky, where the first few stars had started to flicker into view. *How would anyone make sense of that?*

The question gnawed at him. He wasn't just worried about the scientific implications anymore—he was beginning to fear the societal ones. What would happen if the public saw those images and believed them? Would there be panic? Would people assume that some ancient intelligence, possibly even divine, had been steering Alohanui toward Earth for millennia? Would they see it as a sign, a message, or worse—an invasion?

Caleb shook his head, trying to clear away the darker thoughts. He needed to get to Emma. She'd know how to bring him back down to Earth, how to help him sort through the noise. And right now, more than ever, he needed her level-headedness.

When Caleb arrived at Emma's place, he immediately noticed something unusual. Emma, her mother Star, and her father Ted were huddled around their old television, the screen flickering in the dimly lit living room. The TV itself seemed out of place, a dusty relic from the past, its bulky frame sitting in the corner as though forgotten. It was strange because Emma's family hardly ever watched TV. Star preferred the radio, often listening to Hawaiian music or news while cooking or cleaning, but tonight was different.

The room smelled faintly of incense, as it always did, and the low hum of the TV's static mixed awkwardly with the serene energy the house usually held. A single lamp cast a warm, golden glow over the modest living room, with its soft, worn furniture and the bamboo accents that Star had carefully curated over the years. The television's blue-tinted light flickered against the walls, contrasting with the cozy, earthy tones of the space.

Star turned on the TV after hearing a news flash on the radio. The room fell into a tense stillness as everyone stood watching, seemingly frozen in time. Emma's eyes flicked to the door just as Caleb walked in. Her face crumpled, and she ran to him, sobbing uncontrollably. She collapsed into his arms, her body trembling with raw emotion.

At first, Caleb thought her tears were solely about the bad news from her ultrasound—and he was mostly right. But the full weight of the situation hit him like a wave, overwhelming him. Tears began to stream down his face as his chest tightened, the room seeming to spin around him. Fear, uncertainty, and love collided in a moment too intense to bear.

Star, who had always been the strong one, felt her own composure break as she watched her daughter and Caleb in tears. Tears welled in her eyes, and soon she was crying too, her hands trembling as she instinctively tried to comfort Emma but felt utterly helpless in the face of her daughter's heartbreak.

Ted stood nearby, his brow furrowed, unsure of how to react to the storm of emotions engulfing the room. He rested a hand awkwardly on Star's shoulder, his own feelings buried beneath the suffocating weight of the moment. The flickering television became an irrelevant backdrop, a faint hum in a room filled with unspoken fears and overwhelming grief.

After what felt like an eternity of shared tears, Emma's sobs finally subsided. She took deep, shuddering breaths and slowly pulled away from Caleb's embrace, wiping her tear-streaked face. The room grew quiet, save for the faint hum of the TV.

"I don't know where to start," Emma said softly, her voice barely above a whisper. "I found a bump on my abdomen a while ago. I didn't tell you because... I thought it might be nothing. But I had an ultrasound, and it looks like liver cancer. I'm scheduled for a consultation with the surgeon next week."

Her words hung heavily in the air, like an unbearable weight pressing down on everyone. Star gasped, her hand flying to her mouth as her eyes widened in disbelief. Ted stood frozen, his face pale and etched with shock. For a moment, neither spoke, their minds racing to comprehend the news that had shattered the fragile calm of the evening.

Star was the first to move. She stepped toward Emma, her voice trembling with emotion. "Oh, my baby girl... why didn't you tell us sooner?" She pulled Emma into her arms, holding her tightly as though she could shield her from the pain. "We could've been here for you. We *are* here for you."

Ted, ever the quiet one, placed a firm hand on Emma's shoulder. His voice, though steady, brimmed with emotion. "You're strong, Emma. We'll get through this. We're with you every step of the way. You're not going through this alone."

Emma took a deep, steadying breath, her parents' words giving her strength. Then she said something that made the air shift again. "Caleb knows all this, but there's more. Alohanui has arrived."

The mood shifted. Star and Ted exchanged confused glances, unsure what to make of the sudden change in subject. The gravity of Emma's diagnosis still consumed the room, but now she had introduced something else.

"Alohanui?" Ted asked, frowning. "What's that?"

Emma wiped her eyes and looked at Caleb for encouragement. He gave her a small nod. "It's the interstellar object Caleb and his team have been tracking," she explained. "It's not just a rock in space. There's been a lot going on, and now it's here—closer than anyone expected. It's… complicated."

Star frowned, sensing the importance in Emma's tone despite not fully grasping the context. "So, you're not just worried about your health. There's more."

Emma nodded, her voice steady now. "There's always more. But right now, this cancer… it's real, and I don't know what the future holds."

Star hugged her again, tears welling anew. "We'll take it one step at a time. Whatever's happening out there, you come first. Your health, your happiness. We'll face everything else when we need to."

Ted nodded in agreement. "We've got you, Em."

Emma smiled faintly, a small flicker of relief breaking through. "I know you do."

After a moment, she took another deep breath, ready to shift the conversation. "There's something else you need to know about Alohanui," she said, addressing her parents. "That asteroid they mentioned on the news—the one now in orbit around Earth—that's Alohanui. Caleb discovered it."

Star's hand flew to her chest. "Wait, so the asteroid they're talking about on the news—that's *your* asteroid?"

"Yes," Emma confirmed. "And it's not just an asteroid. There's more to it than anyone knows."

Caleb placed a steadying hand on Emma's shoulder. "But right now, none of that matters. All the secrets, all the discoveries—they're secondary. The only thing I care about is Emma." His voice wavered with sincerity. "I've wasted too much time chasing answers, thinking they were the most important thing. But they're not. This—being here with the people I love—is what matters most."

For a long moment, the room was silent, save for the faint hum of the TV and the beating of four hearts bound by love, fear, and a shared determination to face whatever lay ahead together.

Caleb was determined to attend the consultation with Emma, his presence a steadying force by her side. As they sat across from Dr. McCormick in the sterile, bright room, the tension in the air was palpable. The surgeon, a kind but direct woman in her fifties, leaned forward with a reassuring smile.

"We caught it very early," Dr. McCormick began, her voice calm but filled with the gravity of the situation. "That's a good sign."

Emma nodded again, her grip on Caleb's hand tightening.

"What does this mean with respect to having a family?"

She paused, her eyes softening as she turned her focus back to Emma. "I strongly recommend you consider harvesting and freezing your eggs before we proceed. It's an option that gives you more control over your future, especially if we need to use chemotherapy after the surgery."

Emma's eyes widened slightly. "How long does that process take?"

"It can usually be done in as little as two weeks, though in that time you'll likely get fewer eggs than with a longer treatment cycle. You'd start hormone injections to stimulate your ovaries to produce more eggs than usual, and we'd monitor you with ultrasounds and blood tests to see how they're developing.

Once we have enough mature eggs, they will be retrieved in a minor procedure."

Dr. McCormick continued, her voice steady but empathetic. "The timing would be tight, but if fertility is a priority for you, it's worth considering. There are risks involved, as always, but it's a way to ensure that you'd still have the chance to have a child later."

Emma looked at Caleb, uncertainty flickering in her eyes. Caleb squeezed her hand gently. "It's your decision, Em. But if this gives you more options down the road…"

Emma took a deep breath, the weight of the decision pressing on her. "Two weeks," she whispered, nodding slowly. "I'll do it. Let's freeze the eggs before the surgery."

Dr. McCormick smiled, a small but supportive gesture. "We'll get the ball rolling on that immediately. It's a lot to take in, but you're making a smart choice."

Caleb squeezed her hand, his heart aching at the crossroads they were facing. He wanted her to be safe more than anything, but he understood the weight of her words—the possibility of a future they hadn't yet talked about. "I just want you healthy, Em," he said quietly, his voice thick with emotion. "But whatever you and Dr. McCormick decide, I want you here with me."

Emma exhaled, feeling the weight of Caleb's love and the difficult choice ahead. "Thank you, Dr. McCormick," she said, her voice steady but filled with uncertainty. She glanced at Caleb, who gave her a small, reassuring smile. They had a lot to think about.

The waiting room was far from welcoming. Harsh fluorescent lights cast an unforgiving glow on the dated furniture—vinyl chairs that squeaked every time you shifted and tables stacked with months-old magazines that no one ever seemed to read. The air smelled faintly of antiseptic, layered with the occasional waft of burnt coffee from a nearby vending machine. A muted hum of activity drifted through the space, punctuated by the beeping of distant medical monitors and the occasional murmur of hushed conversations between anxious families.

Ted and Star sat beside Caleb, their quiet anxiety evident in their body language. Ted, usually so grounded and strong, rubbed his hands together absentmindedly, staring at the floor as if lost in thought. Star sat stiffly, her arms crossed tightly across her chest, her lips pressed into a thin line. She was a woman of deep conviction, and in moments of uncertainty like this, her belief usually steadied her. But today, the gravity of their daughter's surgery weighed heavily on her. Occasionally, she would look at Caleb as though searching for reassurance but would quickly avert her eyes, afraid of what she might see.

In the background, the television mounted on the wall blared on, though the volume was low enough to keep it from being too intrusive. The news channel was, of course, covering the same story that had been dominating headlines for weeks: Alohanui. Caleb had promised himself to stay focused on Emma, but the gravitational pull of the story was too much to resist. He couldn't help but glance at the screen.

"The asteroid is using light pressure against its 18-mile-square base to achieve a geostationary orbit," the anchor was saying. Caleb's attention was immediately captured, despite everything. "But it's not the kind of geostationary orbit we're used to seeing. It's offset. Rather than being directly above the equator, this orbit seems to place Alohanui above 32 degrees North latitude—the same latitude as Odessa, Texas, and Savannah, Georgia and many other cities. No one knows which part of Earth it'll end up directly above"

Images of Alohanui flashed across the screen—satellite shots showing its massive, imposing structure from various angles. "Here's more images of Alohanui from satellites, typically used to look down, and are now forced to look up. And this one, just released, is from the International Space Station when Alohanui was at its perigee—the lowest point in its orbit."

As the news continued, the anchor introduced Dr. Eric Apostoli, a professor from the School of Architecture at the University of Hawaii. Caleb barely noticed the split screen that appeared on the television, with the anchor on one side and Dr. Apostoli on the other.

"Welcome, Dr. Apostoli," the anchor said.

"Thanks for having me, Ed," replied Dr. Apostoli, nodding. "I should clarify for the audience that I'm not an expert on spacecraft or exobiology. My expertise lies only in ancient Greek architecture, which I think can give us a useful vocabulary for describing what we're seeing."

Caleb leaned forward, utterly engrossed as Dr. Apostoli continued. "Now, in space, of course, there is no up or down. But for our purposes, I suggest that we imagine the large square base of Alohanui as the 'bottom' of the structure. When you look at it from the side—any side, really, since all four elevations appear identical—it resembles a staircase. I would describe these steps using the language of ancient Greek architecture. The lower twelve steps, or layers, could be referred to as the 'stereobate,' with the top layer being the 'stylobate.' Although they look like steps, they're actually foundation layers. So you can get the feel of the size of this, imagine a stairway 18 miles wide of twelve steps where each *step* is about 200 feet thick and 200 feet deep."

Dr. Apostoli paused as more images filled the screen, showcasing the bizarre, alien-like structure in even more detail. "NASA has told us that these layers are made from different materials, though most are chemically similar to quartz—silicon dioxide, with various additives. You can think of them like quartz countertops, available in different colors and patterns. Each layer has its unique composition."

Caleb couldn't pull his gaze away from the television. The anchor was still speaking, but his words barely registered. Caleb's mind raced with thoughts of Alohanui, of its strange architecture, and of the unanswered questions that still lingered. He had promised Emma that Alohanui didn't matter right now, but seeing the images on the screen brought all his curiosity and concern flooding back. What was it? Why was it here?

He had momentarily forgotten about Ted and Star sitting beside him, their own anxiety mirrored in the quiet glances they exchanged. He had forgotten, too, about the reason they were there in the first place—Emma, in surgery, fighting for her life.

Caleb shook himself out of his trance, guilt gnawing at him for letting his mind wander to Alohanui while Emma lay in the operating room. He reached over and squeezed Star's hand, offering a small smile of reassurance, though inside, his thoughts continued to whirl, torn between the woman he loved and the mystery he couldn't let go of.

Dr. McCormick entered the waiting room still in her scrubs, her face showing the wear of a long surgery but with a glimmer of relief. She headed directly for Caleb, who immediately stood up, his heart pounding. Star and Ted Kenoa, Emma's parents, watched anxiously from their seats.

"Dr. McCormick, these are Emma's parents, Star and Ted Kenoa," Caleb said, his voice steady but laced with tension. "You can speak freely in front of them."

Dr. McCormick gave a brief nod of acknowledgement before addressing the group. "We caught it early," she began, her tone measured but reassuring. "I'm estimating it's stage 1a, but of course, we'll need to wait for the pathology report and the oncologist's final assessment."

She paused, letting the news sink in. Caleb exhaled softly, a wave of relief washing over him. Star clasped her hands tightly, while Ted leaned forward in his seat, listening intently.

"I'm not the oncologist," Dr. McCormick clarified, likely for Star and Ted's benefit as they absorbed the medical terminology. "But based on what we've seen, I would expect Emma to go through about six courses of chemotherapy spaced roughly three weeks apart, most of my patients think of it as a way of way of killing any stray cancer cells that might have been released from the liver before and during the surgery and, of course, we will get her on the waiting list for a new liver."

Ted, though he looked calm, couldn't hide the tension in his jaw.

Star nodded slowly, her face tight with concern but grateful for the clarity. "I don't remember hearing anything about a liver transplant. Has Emma's liver stopped working?"

"Her liver is working but a liver transplant provides for the best possible prognosis," said the surgeon.

Caleb, still processing the information, felt a flicker of hope but knew the road ahead would still be challenging. "Thank you, Dr. McCormick," he said, his voice soft but sincere.

"We'll wait for the pathology report to confirm everything," she added, her gaze shifting to Star and Ted with a comforting smile. "But for now, she's stable and in recovery. You'll be able to see her soon."

Emma spent a couple of days in the hospital recovering from

surgery. Caleb made sure to be by her side as much as possible, but the hospital rules meant he couldn't stay overnight. He'd taken a few days off work to help out once she got home, though deep down he knew Star would likely handle most of the care. Still, he wanted to make sure Star and Ted knew he was there, ready to assist in any way they needed. But now, it was all a waiting game.

The weight of Emma's condition pressed down on him, but so did something else—something he couldn't shake. Caleb had been convinced for weeks that the government, NASA, or whatever deep state organization might exist, had no more secrets left to hide about Alohanui. The truth, in his mind, had to be out by now. Surely, at this point, all that was left was the ugly admission that they had lied and misled the public. Still, he couldn't let go of the nagging thought that maybe, just maybe, they weren't done yet.

After returning from the hospital, Caleb dug out the old laptop and the directional Wi-Fi antenna he'd been hiding. He set everything up and powered it on, half expecting to find nothing. But to his surprise, the laptop was still tracking Alohanui. More surprising was the fact that, according to his tracking, Alohanui was nowhere near Earth.

For a moment, he was dumbfounded. Then it clicked—the simplicity of the deception. It was almost… elegant.

Caleb's suspicions had been right all along. NASA, or whoever was controlling the narrative, had input the actual trajectory of Alohanui into Pan-STARRS' Moving Object Processing System (MOPS)—a powerful system designed to track the orbits of all solar system objects. What Caleb hadn't fully realized was that MOPS housed not just the open database for tracking known objects like satellites and space debris, but also a secret database containing classified objects. This included the US spy satellites, top-secret spacecraft, and now, Alohanui.

The system was designed to keep these classified objects out of publicly available Pan-STARRS images, which could potentially fall into the hands of U.S. adversaries. For ordinary objects, like weather satellites or communication arrays, Pan-STARRS simply blacked them out with a solid black pixel. But for top-secret objects, like Alohanui had become, the redaction was far more subtle—the system seamlessly matched the object's surroundings, making it virtually impossible to detect.

Caleb had been wrong in assuming that all redactions were done with pure black pixels. No—only the non-secret objects were handled that way. And for something as high-priority as Alohanui, they had provided it with a phantom trajectory, one that appeared in the public database showing the asteroid hurtling away from Earth, giving Caleb the false impression that Alohanui was no longer a threat.

All this time, Caleb had been following a breadcrumb trail, unknowingly tracking a decoy. The real Alohanui had been masked, hidden in plain sight by a classified application hidden in Pan-STARRS data processing system that he hadn't accounted for. The trajectory he had been tracing was a misdirection, part of an elaborate scheme to send anyone snooping after Alohanui on a wild goose chase.

He leaned back in his chair, staring at the screen. It was a stroke of brilliance on their part—a perfect blend of technological sophistication and misdirection. But now, he understood the game they were playing.

"The breadcrumbs led me straight into the woods," Caleb muttered to himself. "Right to the witch's cabin."

CHAPTER 7 WHITE

NASA's orbital mechanics team estimated that Alohanui would require a minimum of ten years to achieve geostationary orbit using nothing but the subtle forces of sunlight, solar wind, and the immense surface area of its 18-mile-square base functioning as a solar sail. From a scientific perspective, the gradual, methodical drift of such an enormous object toward a stable orbit was a marvel. Yet, its silent presence near Earth was an unrelenting source of dread. Suspended in the sky like an uninvited guest, it defied straightforward explanation, amplifying public unease despite NASA's assurances that it posed no immediate threat. Alohanui's sheer size and unknown purpose loomed ominously in the global psyche, a symbol of unease amid mounting chaos.

The world, meanwhile, teetered on the edge of catastrophe. Political tensions in the Middle East erupted into full-scale conflict, dragging more nations into an escalating spiral of violence. Fragile governments crumbled, alliances strained to breaking points, and whispers of global war became deafening. Alohanui, drifting in near-Earth space like a cosmic harbinger, fueled the flames of fear and speculation. Conspiracy theories spread like wildfire, countered by feeble reassurances from official channels.

But fear turned to terror when the unimaginable occurred.

Caleb found himself in a doctor's waiting room with Emma and her parents, listening to a NASA spokesperson on the television. The spokesperson's voice, calm but urgent, explained the mechanics of Alohanui's maneuvers.

"To alter its trajectory, Alohanui periodically adjusts its base's orientation to the sun, varying angles to optimize thrust. These adjustments cause it to accelerate or decelerate as it seeks a perfect circular orbit. During such maneuvers, sunlight reflecting off its vast surface can occasionally strike the Earth. On the night side, the effect is startling—a sudden blaze of light illuminating over a thousand square miles of darkness. But when these reflections strike the day side, the sunlight's intensity doubles in a targeted area. The result? Exposed skin burns instantaneously."

The screen cut to graphic footage. People writhed in agony, their clothing incinerated, their bodies reduced to charred remnants as they succumbed to the searing intensity. Caleb turned away, his stomach churning, but the haunting images were already seared into his mind.

The room fell silent, the reality too horrific to process. A celestial phenomenon, once regarded with scientific curiosity, had become an apocalyptic threat. Alohanui's presence no longer symbolized mystery—it heralded destruction.

"Apologies, apologies," the announcer stammered, his voice unsteady as he addressed the audience. "It seems we mistakenly aired some raw, unreviewed footage instead of the prepared clip. We deeply regret that our viewers had to witness such distressing content. Please allow us to correct this with the intended segment."

Before the broadcast could continue, Caleb strode over to the television and pressed the power button, cutting the screen to black. The faint hum of the powered-down TV was the only sound in the room for a moment. He turned to face Emma and her parents, his expression soft but resolute.

"I hope you don't mind," he said gently. "Maybe it's better if we just talk to each other for a while."

Soon after, Caleb, Emma, Star, and Ted were guided into the oncologist's office by a kind but efficient nurse. The room was a blend of clinical precision and an attempt at warmth, designed to offer a measure of comfort amidst the weighty discussions that often unfolded within its walls.

Soft, neutral tones dominated the space, with pale gray walls accented by framed prints of serene landscapes—a forest at sunrise, a calm beach, and a mountain lake reflecting a cloudless sky. A tall bookshelf lined one side of the room, filled with medical reference texts, neatly arranged binders, and a scattering of patient-centered materials about coping with cancer.

"Emma, I've reviewed your medical records thoroughly," Dr. Solis began, her tone calm but firm, radiating both empathy and authority. "The good news is that your doctors caught this early, which gives us a significant advantage. However, liver cancer can be unpredictable, so we need to act decisively. I recommend starting you on a six-cycle chemotherapy regimen as your team in Hawaii suggested, but that treatment hasn't started yet.

"We'll use GEMOX—a combination of gemcitabine and oxaliplatin—which is often the best choice for patients in good overall health who can tolerate a dual-drug protocol. I believe this regimen is the most effective option for you."

Dr. Solis paused, letting her words sink in before continuing. "To remain on the transplant list, it's critical that you achieve complete remission. Chemotherapy is our best—and sometimes only—tool to get there. The transplant committee won't even consider you for candidacy until you've completed at least one full course of treatment. Each course includes six cycles, so we'll take it step by step, keeping a close eye on your progress."

were rampant—was this massive object a weapon sent by an advanced alien race, a sign of impending doom, or some unknown piece of interstellar debris with hidden powers?

As the violence in the Middle East spread, drawing in more and more nations, the tension reached a boiling point. The sight of Alohanui in the sky became a symbol of both awe and fear. Some people speculated that its presence was triggering the unrest, while others saw it as a sign of divine intervention, a cosmic wake-up call. Social media was flooded with speculation and wild theories, from religious prophecies to claims of government cover-ups. The world seemed caught in a fragile balance, with Alohanui casting a long shadow over humanity's future.

Governments struggled to maintain control as civil unrest grew in many nations, fueled by fear and uncertainty. The presence of a massive object in the heavens—something far beyond human creation—only seemed to push tensions further. Military forces were on high alert, and some nations began to quietly prepare for the worst.

Emma's battle was on another front entirely. Dr. McCormick had been right—six rounds of chemotherapy, each spaced three weeks apart, and each one more grueling than the last. Emma faced not only relentless nausea but also painful mouth sores, and she had lost so much weight that she barely resembled her former self. Always slender, she now seemed fragile, and Caleb could hardly bear to see the toll it was taking.

Her decision to harvest and freeze her eggs before the surgery now seemed prescient. The chemotherapy, with all its life-saving potential, was also damaging her ovaries, robbing her of the hope of ever conceiving naturally.

Through it all, she maintained a quiet strength, though it pained her to see her once-glorious hair, which she had taken for granted, fall out in clumps. Emma wasn't vain, but her thick, wavy locks had always been part of her identity. Now she wore a wig in public, but even that made her look pale and sickly. Her eyes, once sparkling with life, seemed dull, shadowed by fatigue and the relentless fight against her own body.

Caleb, too, was at his breaking point. He had devoted every waking moment to caring for Emma, but there was only so much he could do. The chemo made her withdrawn, and on the worst days, she barely had the energy to speak. On top of the emotional toll, Caleb's connection to Alohanui had brought unwelcome attention. Some people, in the dark corners of social media like Facebook and X, had started blaming him, absurdly claiming that he was responsible for bringing Alohanui into near-Earth space. The accusations were baseless, but the harassment became real when someone threw a Molotov cocktail through the window of his apartment.

Caleb had no choice but to move, but the damage had been done. He was living in fear, not just for Emma's health but for their safety. His new apartment was smaller, more anonymous, and much farther from their usual haunts. He tried to stay off social media, but the threats still found their way to him through other channels. The once exciting mystery of Alohanui had turned into a nightmare.

Sitting by Emma's bedside, Caleb could hardly recognize the vibrant, sharp-witted woman he had fallen in love with. Her battle with cancer had sapped her strength, and the once-optimistic light in her eyes had dimmed. The joy they used to find in each other's company had been replaced with the grim reality of survival. Caleb was terrified—terrified of losing her, terrified of the unknown forces they seemed to be up against, and most of all, terrified of a future without her.

When the chemotherapy finally ended, Emma's doctors, with cautious optimism, proclaimed her "in remission." Caleb, ever the optimist, naively wondered how soon she could go surfing again. He imagined the two of them back at the North Shore, catching waves and laughing like they used to. Emma, however, wasn't so sure. She wondered if she'd ever find the strength—or the joy—to surf again. Even though the doctors had caught the cancer early, there was an unshakable feeling inside her that it might come back. The remission felt fragile, like a brief reprieve rather than a full victory.

Ted and Star Kanoa, Emma's parents, had suffered greatly alongside her during the grueling months of chemo. On the days she had to endure an IV drip, Emma would stay at her parents' home, where Star doted on her with quiet, unwavering support. Ted tried to stay strong, hiding his tears whenever Emma was too weak to notice. After one of the earlier rounds, she had tried staying with Caleb, thinking it might be easier for both of them. It had worked the first time—Caleb doing his best to take care of her, hovering just enough without smothering—but the following treatments hit her harder, and she found herself craving the familiar comfort of her parents' house. Their presence was calming in a way that Caleb, for all his love and good intentions, simply couldn't replicate.

Caleb and Emma would reminisce about the weekends they used to spend together before everything changed. Back then, life had felt so light, so effortless, like they had all the time in the world. The memory of carefree mornings at Diamond Head, surfing with the sun rising over the horizon, seemed like a distant dream. Neither of them could quite believe how easy life had once been—how unburdened by sickness, by fear.

During the four months of treatment, and for months afterward, Emma withdrew from the outside world. She had no interest in the news—none of it seemed to matter in the face of her own battle. Alohanui, once the focus of her work and so much of her life, now seemed irrelevant. Global events, once discussed with curiosity, now felt like noise. Her world had shrunk to survival, to getting through each day.

Emma knew all too well, from both her doctors and the countless hours spent scouring medical websites, that a liver transplant could completely change her prognosis. She imagined the life it could give her—a chance to surf with Caleb again, to cradle a baby in her arms, to reclaim the future she once dreamed of. A new liver could mean the difference between despair and hope.

But the harsh reality loomed over her like a dark cloud: the odds of climbing to the top of the transplant list and finding a compatible donor were painfully slim. It felt like betting on a lottery with impossibly long odds, where the prize was her very life—a jackpot that, despite its immeasurable value, seemed heartbreakingly out of reach.

For Caleb, though, the outside world seemed to be falling apart just as much as his personal one. Every time he turned on the television or checked his phone, the news was grim—wars escalating, protests turning violent, and Alohanui casting its long shadow over Earth. It was as though the entire planet had become infected with the same sense of unease, the same fear of the unknown that had plagued his and Emma's life for months.

Caleb found it hard to imagine a world worse than the one they were living in now. With Emma's health so precarious, the planet on edge, and Alohanui still hanging in the sky as a constant reminder of humanity's fragility, he felt overwhelmed by the sheer magnitude of it all. How had things unraveled so quickly? How had the future become so uncertain, both for Emma and for the world itself?

Apart from the Molotov cocktail incident, which had shaken Caleb to his core and felt like an anomaly in their otherwise peaceful existence, life in Hawaii remained remarkably untouched by the escalating wars and violence engulfing much of the world. The islands, with their serene beaches, swaying palm trees, and steady trade winds, felt like a sanctuary, almost as if they were insulated from the chaos beyond the Pacific. The locals went about their daily routines, tourists still flocked to the beaches, and the warm, humid air carried the scent of plumeria and saltwater, not fear.

In many ways, Hawaii seemed to exist in its own bubble, disconnected from the tensions brewing across the globe. The tranquility of the islands persisted, even as headlines screamed of unrest in the Middle East, political instability, and the looming presence of Alohanui. Life continued at its own unhurried pace—surfers catching waves, families enjoying barbecues, and Caleb and Emma trying to find moments of normalcy amid the storm of their personal and professional lives. The contrast between the peaceful rhythms of Hawaii and the turmoil unfolding elsewhere only heightened the surreal nature of it all, leaving Caleb feeling both grateful for the calm and uneasy about how long it would last.

How long would it last? Not long.

Caleb kept working, throwing himself into his research, while Emma, after weeks of recovering from chemotherapy, finally felt ready to return to work, albeit on a reduced schedule. She had missed the routine, the comfort of familiar faces, and the focus her work had always provided. But nothing could have prepared her for the shock of her first day back.

The moment she arrived at the IfA building, she froze in

disbelief. Huge, menacing letters scrawled across the once-pristine walls in thick black paint screamed, "YOU BROUGHT IT ON US. YOU DEFILE THE SACRED MOUNTAIN." The sight hit her like a punch to the gut. Her breath caught, her vision blurred, and before she knew it, tears welled up in her eyes. The hateful message, so stark and raw against the backdrop of the institute, felt like a personal attack, a cruel twist to everything she had been through.

Caleb had warned her about the tensions, about the growing unrest from those who viewed the observatories on Mauna Kea as a violation of the sacred land, but seeing the graffiti, she realized just how deep the anger ran. She wished she hadn't come in early, wished the darkness of the pre-dawn morning could have hidden the words from her. The sunrise, usually a source of beauty and hope, only illuminated the ugliness of the world around her.

Workers, just finishing up removing graffiti from other parts of the building, noticed her standing there, stricken, and rushed over. They immediately set to work, grabbing paint rollers and applying the first coat over the hateful words, trying to erase the insult as quickly as possible. But the damage was done. The words had left their mark, not just on the walls, but on Emma's heart.

She hadn't expected this. As a native Hawaiian, Emma knew the sacredness of Mauna Kea—its cultural and spiritual significance to her ancestors. But as a scientist, she also understood the critical importance of the observatories, their telescopes scanning the heavens to protect mankind from potential threats like planet-killing asteroids. The juxtaposition of these two truths had always lived within her, a balancing act of reverence for her heritage and dedication to the advancement of human knowledge.

But to see this, the hostility in those words, aimed not just at the building but at people like her and Caleb, was devastating. It was a reminder that some saw the work they did as a betrayal of the land and its people.

Just as she began to collect herself, the newly heightened security detail arrived, asking for her ID before admitting her inside. The rigid procedure felt almost cold in contrast to the compassion of the workers. It was a new reality—one in which both their work and their very presence at IfA were seen as a threat.

Caleb, arriving shortly after, found her sitting in the lobby, her face streaked with tears but her posture straight, her hands clenched. He sat down beside her without a word, placing a hand on her back, feeling her tense muscles beneath his fingers.

"I wish you hadn't seen that," he whispered, guilt weighing heavily in his voice. "You don't deserve any of this."

Emma shook her head, wiping away her tears. "We knew this might happen. Mauna Kea is sacred… but so is the work we're doing. It's to protect everyone. Why can't they see that?"

Caleb didn't have an answer. Neither did Emma. All they could do was keep moving forward, even as the world around them seemed to unravel in ways they hadn't anticipated.

It should have come as no surprise that Alohanui, in its slow and deliberate journey toward geosynchronous orbit, would encounter satellites and space debris along the way. As it moved, scientists and space agencies scrambled to adjust the orbits of spacecraft and expensive satellites for the most part successfully, a testament to the precision and coordination between international space agencies.

Alohanui also exhibited a remarkable effect on the seemingly endless swarm of space junk that clutters Earth's orbital space. As debris collided with the massive cube or entered its mysterious force field, the orbits of these fragments were altered. What had once been relatively stable, circular orbits were now transformed into highly elliptical trajectories. These altered paths would fling the debris farther away from Earth before pulling them back, closer to the atmosphere where they encountered drag from the planet's thin outer layers. This drag hastened their inevitable reentry, causing many pieces to burn up in the atmosphere, essentially cleaning up Earth's orbital space.

In a strange and unexpected way, Alohanui was doing the Earth a favor, systematically accelerating the removal of space junk. What was once a long-term hazard was now becoming a spectacle, as these pieces of debris reentered the atmosphere, igniting into fiery trails across the sky. It was an unusual sight—an artificial shooting star streaking across the night, burning up in a blaze of light. People around the world, unaware of the larger cosmic forces at play, made wishes on these dazzling streaks.

And these encounters revealed far more about Alohanui than anyone had previously known. For one, it was confirmed beyond doubt that Alohanui was a perfect cube—18 miles by 18 miles by 18 miles. But despite this new understanding, one thing remained baffling: the only part visible to Earth-based observers was what they had long assumed was the "bottom," the massive base that acted like a solar sail. Its other sides, including what should have been towering vertical faces, remained hidden or undetectable, shrouded in an impenetrable mystery.

The real shock came when space debris and smaller, undetected satellites strayed too close to Alohanui. Anything that ventured within 18 miles of its base seemed to encounter an invisible barrier. Rather than simply bouncing off or scraping against a solid surface, these objects were crushed, as if they had collided with a force field or an impenetrable, transparent wall. To those monitoring the event, it was as though Alohanui was shielded by some kind of unseen, but incredibly powerful, energy barrier.

This new information changed everything. If Alohanui wasn't just a solid mass but also had the ability to manipulate its environment—to crush incoming objects without ever touching them—then the implications were staggering. What technology could create such a field? What kind of intelligence, if any, was behind this?

At great expense, the CIA retasked one of its spy satellites to mirror Alohanui's highly eccentric geostationary transfer orbit. A satellite originally designed for decades of service was now burning through nearly all of its hydralazine fuel, struggling to keep pace with Alohanui's unpredictable, shifting trajectory. The decision had cost the agency dearly—what was intended to be a long-term asset in space was being sacrificed in the urgent effort to track the enigmatic object's every move.

Since Alohanui's encounter with Jupiter, NASA had been secretly sending a variety of signals toward the interstellar object—radio waves, microwaves, even lasers. They had been hoping for any kind of response, but for months, there was nothing. Alohanui remained silent, unmoving, and enigmatic.

Then, seemingly out of nowhere, something stirred. One of the massive, round calcium carbonate inclusions, previously dismissed by NASA as mere exogeological formations, began to move. It opened in a manner startlingly similar to a ball valve—a precise and mechanical motion. "Look at that," commented a voice from the television, excitement rising."The gate is a perfectly polished sphere that rotates exactly 90 degrees to open and close, just like a ball valve mechanism. I'd bet it's completely airtight—like an advanced airlock system." The eerie, technical precision with which the spherical gate turned was unsettling—suggesting not only intelligent design but advanced engineering far beyond anything they had expected.

As the gate fully rotated open, the world held its collective breath. From the newly revealed cavity emerged a white spacecraft, sleek and gleaming in the reflected light of the sun. It was something out of science fiction, resembling a cross between a futuristic Sea-Doo and a Transformer toy. Its design was both angular and fluid, sleek yet menacing in its precision. It accelerated gracefully, larger and faster than any human jet ski, its surface polished to a gleaming white that seemed to absorb and reflect light in a way that was almost unnatural.

Every satellite, camera, and telescope pointed at Alohanui instantly focused on this strange vehicle, capturing its every move in high definition. It moved effortlessly, defying all known physics, and carried a single passenger—a humanoid figure, with two arms, two legs, a torso, and a head. The figure sat atop the craft as if riding it like a mechanical steed, but from the current distance, no one could tell if it matched the size or proportions of a human being. Around the figure's head was a shimmering ring, a kind of halo that only added to its otherworldly appearance.

The TV commentator's voice crackled with astonishment. "We are witnessing something unprecedented. That craft, and its rider, have just emerged from within Alohanui. The engineering precision of that spherical gate alone is mind-blowing, and now—this. Who—or what—could be controlling it?"

As the footage beamed across screens worldwide, Caleb felt a chill run down his spine. The figure on the craft was purely alien. The sight was both awe-inspiring and terrifying.

Caleb's phone buzzed, drawing his attention away from the screen. It was a direct message, and when he opened it, the words made his heart sink:

"Caleb Jacobson, you traitor! We're coming for you. You lied to us—we could have prepared."

It was from Citizens Against Alohanui, the increasingly hostile fringe group that had been targeting anyone associated with the study of the interstellar object. Caleb's chest tightened. He knew the risks, but now it felt personal. They blamed him—someone who had spent his career unraveling the mysteries of space—for the arrival of something that even he had never imagined.

The message felt ominous, and after all the threats, graffiti, and even the molotov cocktail incident, Caleb couldn't help but feel that things were about to escalate.

As the white craft approached the edge of Earth's atmosphere, the tension across the globe skyrocketed. Every news outlet in the world was tuned in, watching the sleek, alien vehicle as it made its steady descent from space.

"Not the White House?" the TV commentator exclaimed, the confusion clear in his voice. "Why inject yourself into an active battle zone? We keep speculating about intelligent extraterrestrials, but this doesn't feel like a move made by something intelligent. Why fly straight into chaos?"

The craft, which had moved with unbelievable speed through the vacuum of space, began to slow dramatically as it neared the denser layers of the atmosphere. "Now that it's near the edge of the atmosphere," the commentator continued, "it's slowed down significantly. The pilot seems to be taking it slow now, according to NASA. They're saying it's well below Mach 1, subsonic flight levels. So if the craft continues on its current course—which, from all calculations, is pointed straight toward Baghdad—it's going to take roughly three hours to get there."

The news of the craft heading toward the Middle East, a region already gripped by war, sent shockwaves across the world. Caleb sat, frozen in front of the TV, his mind racing. What could the pilot want there? He had assumed the craft would make a beeline for the U.S. capital or some other seat of global power, but this—this was unexpected.

His phone buzzed incessantly with news updates, but he ignored them, his thoughts spiraling. The white craft's rider, an alien or whatever it was, was making its first move on Earth. Was it coming to observe humanity's violence? Or something worse?

Emma, pale but steady from her recent battles with cancer, had walked up behind Caleb. She placed a hand on his shoulder, her fingers cold against his skin. "What do you think is going to happen, Caleb? Why Baghdad?"

"I don't know," Caleb whispered, his voice thick with uncertainty. "Maybe it wants to understand us—or maybe it's here to make a statement. But flying straight into a war zone doesn't seem like the act of a species trying to be peaceful."

Emma's eyes remained glued to the screen. "Do you think it's here to help? To stop the violence?"

"I want to believe that," Caleb said, shaking his head, "but there's no way to know. Aliens or not, everything they've done so far is beyond anything we can comprehend."

The global tension was palpable, the world hanging in the balance as the craft slowly glided toward its target. War-torn cities, civilian casualties, political unrest—it was the worst possible place for a first encounter with an intelligent species.

"Three hours," Emma whispered. "NASA's got three hours to find out what it really wants."

Caleb hesitated for a moment, staring at the menacing

message on his screen. The direct message had rattled him, but it was Emma's reaction—her tears, her panic—that convinced him to take it seriously.

"Let me see it," she demanded.

Against his better judgment, he handed her the phone, letting her read the chilling words.

"You traitor!" the message had said. "We're coming for you. You lied to us. We could've prepared."

Emma's face paled as she read it. She looked at him, her voice trembling. "You've got to call the police, Caleb. Show them this—this is a threat! You can't ignore it."

Caleb nodded, feeling the weight of her concern settle on him. Emma was usually right, and deep down he knew this was serious. He grabbed his phone, hands shaking slightly, and dialed 9-1-1.

The phone rang once, then beeped. A pre-recorded voice came on the line. "All circuits are busy. Please try your call again."

Caleb blinked, trying to process what had just happened. He looked at Emma, her tears still falling, her face tense with worry. "It's busy," he said, his voice flat with disbelief. "The 9-1-1 line is busy."

Emma gasped, her eyes wide with shock. "What do we do now? We have to report this. Caleb, they threatened you! And what if it's not just you? What if it's the whole Institute for Astronomy? Those are all our friends."

Caleb ran a hand through his hair, trying to keep calm. "It's gotta be because of Alohanui," he muttered, thinking out loud. "The whole world's on edge. The police are probably overwhelmed right now, dealing with who knows what. Panic, riots, people losing their minds."

He grabbed her hands, pulling her closer, trying to steady her. "Okay, listen. We can't wait on 9-1-1 right now. First, we need to make sure we're safe. We'll lock everything down here, get the place secure. I'll keep trying the police, but if it's too chaotic, we'll figure out another way."

Emma nodded, still shaken but trusting his judgment. "But Caleb... this isn't just panic. Someone—someone really wants to hurt you. Because of Alohanui."

"I know," Caleb said quietly. "And we'll deal with it. But right now, we need to stay calm and get a plan together."

Caleb's pulse quickened as the weight of the situation sank in. All phone lines, even the cellular network, were jammed. The internet had slowed to a crawl, overloaded with millions of people trying to stream live footage of Alohanui. Email servers were crashing under the strain.

It's hard for the younger generations to believe, but in the chaos that unfolded, television turned out to be the most reliable source of news. People have come to expect that in a disaster, their cellular phones will be their lifeline, but what many didn't realize is how fragile that connection truly is. A cellular call travels by radio only as far as the nearest cell tower, and from there, it's routed through the internet, which was already buckling under the weight of millions of users.

Facetime calls, Zoom meetings, and constant video streaming bogged down the system when, ironically, simpler SMS texts would have been the fastest, most efficient way to communicate. But old habits die hard, and people clung to what they were used to, pushing Hawaii's already struggling internet infrastructure to its limit. Ranked 42nd among states for internet coverage, speed, and availability, the system was simply not built to handle the flood of digital communication all at once.

Calling the police, or anyone for that matter, was an option he didn't have.

But Emma's words stuck with him—this wasn't just about him anymore. The entire Institute of Astronomy, maybe even the whole University, could be in danger. Someone, or some group, had targeted him, and if they were willing to take it that far, others could be at risk too.

He glanced at Emma, her fingers flying over the screen of her phone. She was already ahead of him. "Dr. Wright needs to know," he muttered, thinking out loud. "She'll know what to do."

"I'm texting her now," Emma replied, focused. "We'll use SMS, not RCS—just pure text. It might slip through the mess." She kept typing, her brow furrowed with concentration.

Caleb grabbed his phone, deciding to do the same. Short, direct, nothing fancy. "SMS might be our best shot," he said, his mind racing. "I'll send her something too. Better chance one of us gets through."

Emma pressed send and handed Caleb her phone so he could see the message. "Caleb got a DM: 'Caleb Jacobson, you traitor! We're coming for you. You lied to us—we could have prepared.' It was from Citizens Against Alohanui. Worried the whole institute might be in danger."

Caleb glanced at Emma's message, then back at his own phone. "Good. Now let's hope one of these gets through."

The gravity of it all settled in his chest like a weight. They had always known that studying Alohanui would draw attention, but this—this felt personal, dangerous. He sent his own message to Dr. Wright: "Threat from Citizens Against Alohanui. Institute might be in danger. Urgent."

Emma stared at her phone, waiting for any sign that the

message had gone through. The seconds stretched out, feeling like hours.

Fortunately, Dr. Helen Wright had experience dealing with crises, and she knew exactly where to turn. Deep within the University's emergency protocols was a Disaster Incident Response Emergency Communications Terminal (DIRECT), which she accessed without hesitation. Her fingers moved swiftly across the keys, relaying the threat to the National Guard. The situation was urgent, but Helen kept her message clear and to the point. Along with her request for protection, she added a note about the ongoing threats aimed at Caleb and the Institute.

As expected, her request joined dozens of others—people all over the region were panicking, with military forces stretched thin. Still, Dr. Wright's persistence paid off. She received a favorable response sooner than expected, confirming that a National Guard unit had been dispatched to set up a security post beside the Institute of Astronomy.

Helen wasted no time sending Emma and Caleb a message: "Meet at the Institute. I've arranged for the National Guard to set up a post just beside us. It's probably the safest place to be right now."

Emma read the message first and quickly showed it to Caleb, who nodded in agreement. The relief was palpable between them—having the National Guard nearby meant they'd be safer, at least for the time being. But the urgency hadn't left their faces.

"We should go now," Caleb said, grabbing his bag and checking for anything they might need. "The streets might be a mess."

Emma didn't need convincing. She stuffed her phone into her pocket and looked Caleb in the eye. "We stick together, okay? Let's get to the Institute and figure out our next move once we're there."

With a final glance around the apartment, they headed out, the weight of the threat still pressing on them, but with a newfound sense of direction. They were heading to where they'd be safest—under the watchful eyes of the National Guard, with Dr. Wright and their colleagues by their side.

In the midst of the chaos, television remained the rare lifeline, cutting through the digital overload that had paralyzed phone lines and internet connections. Local stations broadcast news with a clarity and immediacy that the overwhelmed internet simply couldn't match. Some resourceful radio astronomers rigged up an old antenna to catch the signal, bringing much-needed updates to the team.

The astronomers on duty were gathered in the warm room, busy monitoring their instruments, while those off duty, along with their families, huddled in the nearby auditorium. The atmosphere was a strange mix of tense and casual—some people were visiting, sharing food, keeping their spirits up, while others stood at the front, transfixed by the continuous Alohanui news coverage.

Onscreen, the US Air Force's high-altitude drone hovered over the projected landing site of the white spacecraft, its steady, almost surreal video feed being shared with the television networks. It was no surprise the government would want to monitor such a significant event, but it was odd that they had chosen to share the footage so openly with the public. Caleb found it hard to believe that the same government which had been so secretive about Alohanui for months was suddenly taking this "full transparency" approach.

"Why be open and honest now?" Caleb muttered under his breath, as he and Emma watched the feed.

The drone, gliding silently through the sky, had become more than just an eye in the sky—it was now an actor in the escalating tension on Earth. It had no offensive mission, or so it seemed. Its role was purely observational, but as missiles were launched from the combatants below, the drone was forced to defend itself, periodically neutralizing the threats with clinical precision. Each time it did, a ripple of tension ran through the auditorium.

Caleb glanced at Emma, her attention fixed on the screen. She was looking stronger than she had in months, but her short hair, still growing back after chemo, wasn't as dark as it used to be. It was a stark reminder of everything she had been through.

He studied her face for a moment, wondering. *Does she need to watch this?* he thought, feeling protective. He knew the strain she had been under, and he wasn't sure if this constant stream of uncertainty and potential danger would help or harm her in her fragile state of recovery.

Emma must have sensed Caleb's gaze. She turned to him with a soft smile, reading his concern. "I'm fine," she said quietly, her eyes fixated on the screen.

The radio astronomers, ever resourceful, decided to give the gathering in the auditorium more options for distraction and information. They set up another TV in the opposite corner, this one tuned to CNN. Now, anyone who preferred the 24-hour cycle of political analysis and breaking news could tune into it. The tension in the room was palpable, and the crowd was clearly divided between those wanting to focus on the unfolding Alohanui crisis and others just seeking a mental escape from the constant barrage of grim updates.

Not stopping at two, they soon set up a third TV in another corner, this time connected to a Blu-ray player that played a loop of Disney cartoons. The familiar, whimsical characters brought a much-needed breath of levity to the room. Children, who had grown restless with all the adult chatter, gathered in front of the screen, their eyes wide with wonder, temporarily forgetting the chaos outside.

As if driven by a need to restore some normalcy to the strange situation, the astronomers decided to complete the transformation of the room. In the last remaining corner, they connected yet another Blu-ray player, this one loaded with a reel of old black-and-white movies. The flickering images of classic cinema transported the few who gathered around it to a simpler time—an escape from the unknown, the fear, and the uncertainty.

Now, the auditorium was divided into distinct pockets. At one end, the anxious watched the government's live updates, focusing on the drone's flight and slow descent into Earth's atmosphere. Across the room, CNN provided a broader narrative, blending international events with the crisis at hand. The laughter of children echoed softly from the corner with Disney cartoons, while a few adults, perhaps the most fatigued by the constant flood of updates, lost themselves in the nostalgic comfort of the old movies.

Caleb glanced around, seeing the fractured reality reflected in each screen. The makeshift setup was a microcosm of the world outside—some looking for answers, some desperate for distraction, and some clinging to memories of a time when things made sense.

Still restless, perhaps driven by a nervous energy, the radio astronomers added yet another TV beside the first, where the muted drone feed of NBC was playing. On the new TV, they tuned into the ABC network, but this time the sound was on. The host, a well-groomed commentator with a somber expression, was interviewing yet another expert about the strange and unsettling markings on Alohanui.

"I'm here with Dr. Morrison, an archaeologist from the

University of Georgia," said the host, his voice calm but charged with anticipation.

"Thanks for having me," said Dr. Morrison, adjusting his glasses and leaning in toward the camera, clearly eager to delve into the topic.

"You're going to help explain these markings that have everyone talking," the host prompted.

"Yes, well, I'm going to try," Dr. Morrison said, clearly ready to launch into his analysis. "The markings on Alohanui are writings in ancient Greek and Hebrew, which is… unexpected, to say the least."

The screen split, with Dr. Morrison and the host on the left side, while the right side displayed a high-resolution close-up of Alohanui. The image focused on the enigmatic steps that had been generating so much speculation.

Dr. Morrison continued, "Let's start with the Greek inscriptions. As you can see, there's no writing on the 'bottom,' the massive quartz square face. But along the sides, where there are these twelve enormous steps—each about 216 feet high and 216 feet deep—we can see names. And these names, written in characters about 150 feet tall, are, well, proper names. Easily recognizable to anyone who reads modern Greek, they are the names of Jesus' apostles."

The screen zoomed in on one of the steps, highlighting a name that even some non-Greek speakers could now recognize: Σίμων Πέτρος—Simon Peter.

Dr. Morrison pressed on, his tone cautious but precise. "Now, I want to be clear: people are going to jump to all kinds of conclusions about the significance of these names. But let's stick to what we know."

The host, silent, seemed transfixed, as did the viewers at home.

"One," Dr. Morrison began, counting off his points with a professor's clarity, "Alohanui has been traveling through space for at least 60,000 years. It left its last port of call—wherever that was—a long time ago.

"Two, Jesus appointed his apostles about 2,000 years ago. So, these names must have been added much more recently than when Alohanui first set out.

"Three, we've been broadcasting television signals for almost a hundred years. That means, conceivably, whoever —or whatever—added these names could have received information from Earth during that time. That's another possible explanation for how these inscriptions got here."

"Fascinating," the host said, but before he could steer the conversation, Dr. Morrison continued, not missing a beat.

"I just want to emphasize that, while the presence of these names might seem like a cosmic message or a sign from God, we don't yet know what they mean or why they're there."

The host, regaining control, finally interjected. "Thank you, Professor Morrison. We're short on time, but we appreciate your insights. Now, for a different perspective, we turn to the Reverend Dr. Nough, a familiar face to many of our viewers from his weekly program here on ABC."

Reverend Nough, sitting in a different studio, smiled graciously as his introduction wrapped up. His demeanor was calm, but his eyes sparkled with intensity.

"Reverend Nough, what do you make of all this?" the host asked, clearly eager to hear a religious interpretation of what had just been revealed.

"Well," the Reverend began, his deep voice filled with measured wisdom, "I can't disagree with what Professor Morrison has said. I also know a little Greek," he added, with a slight grin, "and I don't mean George Stephanopoulos." His quip earned a chuckle from the host, acknowledging the small-statured TV personality.

"The apostles' names are there, clear as day, written for anyone to see. I can't debate that," Reverend Nough said. "But I do want to address this growing rumor that Alohanui is the New Jerusalem prophesied in the Bible, specifically in the Book of Revelation, chapter 21, verses 2 and 10."

The screen shifted again, showing an illustration of the New Jerusalem, a radiant cube descending from the heavens.

"There's no denying that Revelation describes the New Jerusalem as a cube," Reverend Nough continued. "But—and this is an important distinction—the New Jerusalem is described as 1,500 miles high, long, and wide. That's much, much larger than Alohanui, which is only 18 miles wide."

He paused, letting the gravity of his words sink in before delivering his closing thought. "So, while I understand why people are making this connection, I would encourage everyone to read the scriptures carefully. Alohanui is not the New Jerusalem, not by biblical standards. Whatever Alohanui is, we'll have to wait for more information before we can understand its true significance."

"Thank you for that, Reverend Nough," the host concluded. "Alohanui continues to baffle both scientists and religious scholars alike, and we'll bring you more updates as they come."

The broadcast returned to the drone footage, but Caleb and Emma were already lost in thought, the weight of what they had just heard sinking in.

As they continued watching, the white spacecraft descended slowly, hovering just above the ground in the war-torn Middle East. The combatants on both sides, momentarily distracted from their violent conflict with one another, turned their attention to the enigmatic white craft. RPGs were fired relentlessly, rocket after rocket aimed at the strange vessel. But something unexpected happened.

The rockets, which would have typically exploded on impact, instead crumpled in midair. It was as if they had struck an invisible wall—a force field surrounding the craft. Each grenade collapsed inward, crushed under some unseen pressure before it could detonate. The white spacecraft remained unscathed, its protective field deflecting the barrage with effortless precision.

Soon, both sides of the conflict seemed to reach an unspoken agreement: the white craft and its mysterious pilot were now their common enemy. The RPGs, the bullets, even the mortar shells—all were redirected toward the craft. And yet, none of them came close to their mark. The force field was impenetrable, and the projectiles were neutralized before they could do any damage.

Caleb and Emma watched in stunned silence, their eyes glued to the TV screen as the chaos unfolded. The combatants had abandoned their war with each other, focusing all their firepower on this new, otherworldly arrival. The pilot, humanoid in shape but obscured by the craft's brilliant glow and the shimmering force field, seemed utterly unfazed.

"They've stopped fighting each other," Emma whispered, as the sheer strangeness of the situation sank in.

Caleb nodded, his mind racing. "What's the pilot trying to do? Why come here, to the middle of a war zone?"

The TV commentator seemed to echo Caleb's thoughts. "It's baffling. The craft isn't attacking, it's not firing back—it's just… hovering. And the pilot? Completely unphased by the assault. This isn't an offensive maneuver. So, what *is* it?"

Though all sides continued to fire relentlessly at the pilot, some projectiles veered off course, and while the commentator avoided addressing it directly, the TV audience could clearly see the carnage unfolding. Friendly fire and stray bullets were wreaking havoc on the combatants, who were inadvertently decimating their own forces.

The battlefield had morphed into something unrecognizable. Gunfire and explosions rang out in a chaotic symphony, yet the white craft remained untouched, hovering above the destruction like a ghost. The fight had shifted—no longer between warring human factions, but now between mankind and something entirely beyond their comprehension.

Caleb, transfixed by the scene, muttered under his breath, "What are we witnessing?" The weight of the moment pressed down on him and Emma. Whatever was unfolding, it was clear—this was just the beginning.

CHAPTER 8 FIERY RED AND FLAT BLACK

As if things couldn't get any worse, another portal on Alohanui, one of its massive, mysterious openings, rotated open and spat out a second craft. This one was a deep, menacing red, and it looked as though flames danced along its surface. Unlike the white craft, which had hovered calmly, this one sped with unimaginable speed toward the upper edge of the atmosphere before slowing and beginning a calculated descent over Richmond, Virginia.

Almost immediately, chaos erupted. Riots spontaneously broke out across the city. Gangs brandishing Confederate flags swarmed the federal building, setting it ablaze as if the arrival of the red craft had ignited more than just flames—it had ignited a storm of hatred and fury. U.S. flags, once proudly waving, were torn down and set alight by the rioters, the stars and stripes burning in the streets as the crowd chanted slogans of defiance and division.

The TV coverage flickered between shots of the red craft descending and the escalating violence on the ground. "It's madness," Caleb whispered, watching in disbelief. The eerie calm of the white craft in the Middle East stood in stark contrast to the destructive energy now swirling around

Richmond.

"What does this mean?" Emma asked, her voice shaky. Caleb didn't have an answer. Whatever the purpose of these strange arrivals, one thing was clear: their world was unraveling at a pace no one had anticipated.

The local ABC news team abruptly cut into the national Alohanui coverage, switching to chaotic scenes of riots and looting in Honolulu. The streets, once peaceful, were now a battlefield of shattered storefronts, rising smoke, and overwhelmed police officers struggling to contain the unrest. Among the rioters, to Caleb and Emma's shock, several carried Confederate flags—an eerie and baffling sight, given that the Kingdom of Hawaii had remained neutral during the Civil War. It made no sense, but sense seemed like a thing of the past in this world turned upside down.

Emma's eyes filled with tears as the destruction unfolded on the screen. Her shoulders began to shake, overwhelmed by the weight of everything. "I can't believe this is happening," she whispered, her voice barely audible as the first tear slipped down her cheek.

Caleb pulled her into his arms, holding her close as her tears began to flow more freely. "Hey, it's okay," he said softly, though he knew the words sounded hollow even to his own ears. "We're safe here. Oahu made it through Pearl Harbor—it'll get through this too."

Emma buried her face in his chest, sobbing quietly. "It's just all too much… everything, all at once," she said, her voice thick with emotion.

Caleb stroked her hair gently, trying to soothe her as the TV continued to broadcast images of rioters waving those strange Confederate flags. "I know, I know… but we'll get through this," he whispered. Yet even as he said it, the chaos on the screen and the growing uncertainty in their lives pressed down harder.

Caleb watched in stunned silence as the fiery red spacecraft left Richmond, Virginia, leaving a trail of chaos and violence in its wake. The news cut to maps and live updates, and within minutes, reports came flooding in that the craft had reappeared—this time over Sarajevo. No immediate drone footage accompanied the news, but the grim reality was pieced together through shaky cellphone videos and frantic reports from journalists on the ground.

Clashes between the Muslim Bosniaks, Orthodox Serbs, and Catholic Croats had escalated into an all-out war. Riots and fires spread like a contagion, with scenes of shootings, men wielding axes, and even fabricated swords and spears tearing through the fragile fabric of an already war-torn region. The city, already a historical symbol of ethnic tension and bloodshed, was once again plunged into darkness.

Caleb could barely comprehend what he was seeing. As the footage streamed in, showing burning buildings and bodies littering the streets, a cold chill ran down his spine. Emma, still emotionally drained, clung to him as she watched the violence unfold, her tears returning with a fresh wave of grief.

Then, in a sudden change of tone, the screen cut to a live broadcast from the Vatican. The Pope, his face pale and solemn, addressed the world from his balcony. His voice, usually calm and measured, was thick with sorrow.

"I call for peace across the world," he implored, his voice echoing over the images of burning cities. "My heart aches to see Christians killing one another. This violence between the Serbs and Croats—our brothers and sisters—must cease. I beg you, in the name of God, lay down your arms, and remember that we are all children of the same Creator."

His plea was genuine, but it felt distant—like a faint cry in a world that had spiraled too far into chaos to hear reason.

Caleb gently led Emma toward the center of the auditorium, his mind racing with a sense of helplessness. The world was unraveling before them, and it felt like everything was spiraling out of control. They needed to regroup, to focus on what mattered most.

"We need to think," Caleb said quietly, his voice tense but calm. "I don't see how watching more of this news is going to help us. I mean, sure, we need to know about the riots nearby, but the rest? It's just endless noise—riots, wars, fires—none of it is helping."

Emma nodded, her brow furrowed with concern. "I still can't reach Mom or Dad," she said, her voice trembling. "The phones are down."

"That's our priority right now," Caleb agreed, squeezing her hand. "Let's talk to the National Guard, see if they can help."

The two of them left the auditorium, weaving their way through the chaos until they found the tent serving as a command post for the National Guard. As they approached, Caleb spotted a National Guard Sergeant deep in conversation with what appeared to be a Military Police Captain in the Air Force. The Sergeant, noticing Caleb, motioned toward him.

"Captain, is this who you're looking for?" the Sergeant asked.

Captain Thomas MacDonald, USAF, glanced at Caleb, then back at the Sergeant. "Yes, I'm pretty sure it is."

Caleb's stomach dropped. His immediate thought was that they were here to arrest him for his failed attempts to hack into NASA's classified archives. Panic swelled in his chest.

When my parents died, I thought that was the worst day of my life,

Caleb thought bitterly. *Then Emma's cancer diagnosis came, and that was the worst day. Now I'm going to jail, and Ted and Star might be in danger, and Emma is hanging on by a thread.*

But running wasn't an option. They were still within the secure grounds of the Institute. Plus, Emma wouldn't be able to flee with him, and they couldn't leave her parents behind. No, he had to face this head-on.

"Are you Dr. Caleb Jacobson?" the Captain asked.

"There's no point in denying it," Caleb said, trying to keep his voice steady.

The Captain then turned to Emma. "And you must be Dr. Emma Kanoa?"

Emma nodded, her grip tightening on Caleb's hand.

The Captain returned his attention to Caleb. "Well, I have an offer from your government," he said.

Caleb blinked, thrown off by the unexpected shift. "You mean like a plea bargain?" he asked, his confusion evident.

The Captain looked puzzled for a moment before he chuckled. "Oh, you're joking," he said, shaking his head. "No, nothing like that. I'm a lawyer, so I can see how you might jump to that conclusion. How did you know I was a lawyer?"

Caleb let out a small, relieved laugh. *So I'm not going to jail.* "Sorry about that," he said, feeling a bit more at ease. "I know how awkward it can be meeting someone new, and I didn't want to come off as defensive."

Captain MacDonald smiled and nodded. "No harm done."

"Right now, we're more worried about finding Emma's parents," Caleb continued. "The phones are down, and we think they're still at home. We're getting pretty desperate."

"Do you have any other family here on the Islands?" the Captain asked.

"No," Emma answered, her voice quiet. "I'm an only child, and Caleb's sister is in Oklahoma City. His parents passed."

The Captain sighed, then looked at them both seriously. "All right, here's the situation. Have you ever heard of Raven Rock?"

"No," Caleb said, looking to Emma for any recognition.

Emma, surprisingly, nodded. "It's the president's post-apocalyptic bunker in West Virginia, right?"

Caleb hesitated, momentarily stunned that Emma knew about it, but he quickly pushed his surprise aside, filing it away for later. He glanced at her, his eyes searching hers for permission to share more. She met his gaze and gave a small, reassuring nod.

"OK," said Caleb. "What is the job offer?"

"The offer is for *both* of you to work in SPEOC, the Satellite Presidential Emergency Operations Center. You would be working on teams which advise the President. You would be doing similar work to what you do now. Especially you Dr. Jacobson, when you were spokesman for the IfA about Alohanui. You'd probably be answering the same kind of questions that the press asked then except no podium and no cameras. Same with Dr. Kanoa, she would also advise. There's much more to it, of course. The offer is for you and your families, are you interested?" asked Captain MacDonald.

"Before we answer, what about medical care?" Caleb asked, his voice steady but tinged with urgency. "Emma's been fighting liver cancer. She needs a transplant, and while we wait for a donor, she might need additional chemotherapy. The care she's been receiving is top-notch, and I can't just uproot her unless I'm absolutely certain she'll get the treatment she needs—

treatment that could save her life."

The Captain's expression softened. "I understand your concern," he said. "Let me assure you that the best doctors, nurses, and medical professionals will be working at Raven Rock. You'll have access to the most advanced equipment and treatments available—far beyond what's accessible in most civilian hospitals. Transplants, chemotherapy, surgery, any medical procedure—it's all there. We've already brought in top specialists in oncology, cardiology, and practically every field of medicine."

He paused, allowing the gravity of the situation to sink in. "The facilities at Raven Rock are state-of-the-art, equipped to handle anything. Your well-being will be in the best hands possible, so you and Emma can focus on the work at hand without worrying about anything else."

Caleb exchanged a look with Emma, who seemed to visibly relax at the Captain's assurances.

The Captain nodded. "Your parents, Caleb's sister—everyone will be well taken care of. They'll have the same access to the best care. Physiotherapists, social workers, counselors—whatever support they need. Your family will be in good hands so that you both can fully concentrate on the task at hand. The government is sparing no expense to ensure the well-being of key personnel and their families."

Caleb let out a breath he didn't realize he had been holding. The weight of the offer, the chance to be a part of something this monumental, and the knowledge that Emma would get the care she needed—it was overwhelming, but for the first time, it felt manageable.

"Okay," Caleb said, after a moment of thought. "We're in."

Caleb felt the weight of the decision bearing down on him. He glanced at Emma, seeing her concern for her parents and their safety mirrored in her eyes.

"We'll go," Caleb finally said, his voice steady. "But only if you bring Ted and Star with us."

The Captain nodded, already signaling his team. "We'll collect them. Pack your things. Time's running out."

As the Captain left, Caleb turned to Emma, his mind still spinning. They were about to leave everything behind—their work, their home, their lives as they knew them. But together, they would face whatever came next.

Caleb stood there, dumbfounded by the offer. Raven Rock? Presidential Emergency Operations Center? This wasn't a conversation he'd ever imagined having. He glanced at Emma, whose expression mirrored his disbelief. But beneath the shock, he could sense her worry for her parents—Ted and Star—who were still unreachable.

"We need to think," Caleb said, his voice sounding distant to his own ears. "This is... a lot to take in."

Captain MacDonald, sensing their hesitation, stepped forward. "I understand this is overwhelming. But let me be clear: this is a one-time offer. The world is falling apart, and we're giving you a way to not just survive, but to contribute. You'll be safe, and your expertise will be invaluable to the government. But time is not on our side."

Caleb's thoughts raced. He glanced around the tent, feeling the oppressive weight of the chaos outside—the rioting, the wars, the unknown threats looming in every corner of the world. And yet, here they were, offered a lifeline to safety. But how could he abandon everyone else? How could they just leave?

"I don't know what to say," Caleb muttered.

Emma, despite her mounting worry, turned sharply to Captain MacDonald. "We need to find my parents first," she insisted.

"They must fly with us."

The captain nodded without hesitation. "Understood. That's part of the deal."

He then turned to the lieutenant standing at attention behind him. "Take a squad, locate Ted and Star Kanoa at their home. I'll be at the landing strip coordinating our other guests. Call me on the Sat phone once you've reached them, and put Dr. Kanoa's parents on the line. She'll be able to persuade them to join us. Afterward, meet us at the airstrip."

With that, Captain MacDonald shifted his focus back to Caleb and Emma. "You two are in a unique position. You've studied Alohanui more deeply than anyone else, and while the government and NASA may have kept certain things from you, your knowledge is still vital. We need your insights, your instincts. No one else is better equipped to help us figure out what's really happening."

He paused, letting the gravity of his words settle. "But understand this: it's no longer just about Alohanui. It's about survival now. It's about managing the chaos that's coming."

His words felt like a gut punch. Caleb had known the situation was deteriorating, but hearing it spelled out so starkly left him shaken. Everything felt like it was on the brink of collapse, and the thought of walking away—from his work, his colleagues, the pursuit of the truth—was suffocating. This wasn't just a crisis anymore. It was a defining moment, one that carried a weight too heavy to ignore.

Emma's gaze met Caleb's, and in that moment, they both realized the enormity of what lay ahead. There was no going back.

Emma squeezed his hand, her eyes searching his. "What do we do, Caleb?"

For a moment, Caleb didn't know. The world seemed to be asking too much of them. But then he looked at Emma, thought of her parents, and thought of his sister back in Oklahoma. He realized that despite everything, despite the confusion and the fear, there was a chance to keep those he loved safe. And maybe, just maybe, they could still find the truth about Alohanui.

"Okay," Caleb said, his voice steady. "We'll go with you. But you need to get Ted and Star first. Then we'll talk about what comes next."

Captain MacDonald nodded, a slight smile of relief on his face. "I'll send a team right away. Prepare yourselves. This is just the beginning."

As the captain left to make arrangements, Caleb and Emma stood there, holding onto each other as the weight of their decision sank in.

Caleb, Emma, Ted, and Star left Hawaii with nothing but the clothes on their backs, as per government orders. They were evacuated swiftly, their personal belongings to be handled later by a government contractor. When and if the fires and riots subsided, the contractor would remove all of Caleb's apartment contents and place them in secure government storage. Ted and Star's home would receive the same treatment. Caleb's rental agreement was canceled, and the government promised to cover any penalties and forward his damage deposit. As for Ted and Star's house, it would be maintained in its current condition until they were able to return, though when—or if—that would be was anyone's guess.

The evacuation itself was a whirlwind. The family was picked up in a convoy of black SUVs, driving them under tight security to the National Guard Air Base outside Honolulu. There, a

C-17 Globemaster III, a massive military transport aircraft, was waiting to whisk them away. As they boarded, the sight of the plane's cavernous interior left an impression—rows of strapped-down cargo crates lining the walls, with rows of seats fitted in the center for other evacuees like themselves. The flight was tense and silent. Emma, always calm in the face of chaos, gripped Caleb's hand as the plane roared down the runway, lifting them away from their lives in Hawaii.

The plane flew through the night and landed at a National Guard Air Base just outside Charleston, West Virginia, under the cover of dawn. It was colder than they had expected as they stepped off the ramp, the brisk mountain air a stark contrast to the tropical warmth of Hawaii. Soldiers were waiting, escorting them into a line of armored vehicles that transported them through the winding, forested roads toward Raven Rock.

Raven Rock was a behemoth of underground architecture—sprawling enough to house 100,000 people, with miles of tunnels and cavernous rooms. Caleb, Emma, Ted, and Star were assigned identical two-bedroom apartments. Caleb and Emma's apartment was on one floor, while Ted and Star's was a few floors above them. Caleb's sister, Bethany, had already been evacuated from Oklahoma City and was set up in a one-bedroom unit on another floor. The apartments were compact but fully furnished, all designed with a sterile efficiency that reminded Caleb of military barracks. Everything was brand new, and they needed nothing. Every resident received a government-issued supply of clothing and essentials, so there was no need for a day off to unpack. If anything, they needed time to mentally adjust.

There were even department stores inside Raven Rock—scaled-down versions of what they were used to on the surface. As strange as it felt, there was a sense of forced normalcy about the place. Here, beneath the mountains, life was continuing, though the weight of the world's chaos still pressed heavily on their shoulders.

As soon as Caleb and Emma were settled into their new apartment, they wasted no time in checking on Ted and Star. Their apartment, located a few floors above, was a mirror image of their own—functional, clean, and secure. Ted and Star were already starting to settle, adjusting to the strange new reality of living underground.

Once Caleb and Emma were assured that their families were safe and settled, a message arrived summoning them to their first briefing at SPEOC—the Satellite Presidential Emergency Operations Center.

The phrase "no plan survives contact with the enemy" came to mind. Coined by 19th-century Field Marshal Helmuth von Moltke, a brilliant war strategist, it seemed to perfectly capture their situation. Their initial expectations—working in and beneath the West Wing—had already shifted. But aside from missing out on a chance to meet the president in person, there were undeniable advantages to their new reality. With no need to commute, they'd have more time to focus on the task ahead, something far more valuable than proximity to power.

PMOSS was one of the key facilities inside Raven Rock, serving as a mirror to the operations happening above and below ground at the White House. The president and his cabinet were still physically located in Washington, but the work done in Raven Rock was a seamless extension of the decision-making happening in the West Wing. High-ranking military officials, intelligence officers, and key scientists were relocated to Raven Rock to ensure continuity, and now Caleb and Emma were joining their ranks.

They were escorted by two military officers through a maze of tunnels and hallways until they arrived at a set of heavy, reinforced doors. The moment they stepped through, they were met with the low hum of high-tech equipment, the glow of monitors, and the constant flow of information being processed and analyzed. The room was vast, with rows of desks, large digital displays showing real-time maps, satellite images, and classified data streams, all overseen by key personnel who monitored the situation both on Earth and in space.

Caleb couldn't help but feel a strange sense of awe as he took it all in. This was the nerve center of the nation's emergency operations, and he and Emma were now part of the team. A nearby officer gestured them to a briefing room where a small group was already gathered.

"Welcome to the Satellite Presidential Emergency Operations Center," the officer said. "You'll be working here, in coordination with the White House. This is where the real decisions are made, and it's where you can provide the expertise we need. The president may be working out of the White House, but in many ways, this place is the heart of operations now."

Caleb and Emma exchanged uneasy glances, the weight of their situation settling over them like a thick fog. This wasn't just about understanding Alohanui or surviving the chaos—this was something far bigger, more complex. They were now key players in a global crisis, and the stakes had never been higher.

They stood in the clean, fluorescent-lit corridor of the Satellite Presidential Emergency Operations Center (SPEOC) facility. (Jokingly pronounced *Spock* as in the first officer of the *Enterprise* from *Star Trek*.) The air was cool, sterile, with a faint chemical scent, likely from industrial-strength cleaners. They had been ushered here by military escorts, their boots echoing on the polished floors as they led Caleb and Emma through the labyrinth of the underground complex. The complex buzzed with the quiet hum of machinery and distant voices, all underscored by the urgency that permeated the place.

Waiting for them was a man in a plain gray T-shirt and faded blue jeans—a sharp contrast to the military precision of their surroundings. His short-cropped brown hair and five-o'clock shadow gave him a rugged, unpolished look, but there was an intensity in his eyes that spoke of someone who'd seen too much. His posture was relaxed, but his sharp gaze betrayed his deep focus.

"My name's Greg Neuman," he said, his voice carrying a low, calm authority. He shook their hands, his grip firm but not aggressive. "I'm heading your team—the one tasked with studying Alohanui and the three spacecraft that have come out of its portals. Unless you're clairvoyant," he added with a wry smile, "you're going to need a serious briefing."

Caleb and Emma exchanged another glance, both eager for the answers they knew were coming.

Greg wasted no time. "Before you ask any questions, let me catch you up. I doubt you've heard about the black spacecraft Alohanui released about three hours ago." He motioned for them to follow as he led the way into a sterile briefing room. The faint aroma of freshly brewed coffee lingered in the air, mingling with the slightly stale coolness of the air-conditioning. The room was starkly functional—dominated by a long metal table, a handful of chairs, and a large screen projecting high-resolution satellite images.

Greg didn't sit. Instead, he leaned against the edge of the table, arms crossed, his expression a mix of urgency and disbelief. "Right now, that black craft is lifting off from Weyburn, Saskatchewan," he began. "It's enormous—at least two orders of magnitude larger than anything we've seen so far."

Emma's brow furrowed as she processed the scale. "Two orders of magnitude?" she repeated, her voice tinged with incredulity.

Greg nodded gravely, his gaze locked on the screen. "Imagine something the size of forty supertankers combined."

Caleb sat forward, shaking his head. "Forty supertankers?" His voice carried a note of skepticism. "The gates on Alohanui are what—200 feet in diameter? A single supertanker is over 200 feet wide. How on Earth did something that massive fit through the gate?"

Greg's lips curled into a faint, grim smile. "It didn't 'fit.' It changed size. That craft can manipulate its dimensions at will."

Emma exchanged a stunned look with Caleb as Greg pressed on. "And that's not even half of it. Remember how we thought Alohanui was using sunlight and solar wind to adjust its orbit around the Sun? Well, turns out, that's just part of the story. Alohanui doesn't need detectable propulsion. It rotates and alters its trajectory effortlessly—completely beyond anything we understand."

A heavy silence filled the room, punctuated only by the steady hum of the air conditioning. The implications of Greg's words hung in the air like a storm cloud, charged with tension and awe.

Greg straightened, his voice steady but loaded with meaning. "The only plausible explanation is that they've mastered gravity—and, by extension, space-time itself. They're curving space. Think about that. This isn't just antigravity we're talking about; this is control over mass and its manifestations—momentum, weight, inertia. Instantaneous acceleration. Deceleration. No inertia effects. They've achieved something that completely defies what we thought were the limits of physics."

Caleb leaned back in his chair, running a hand through his hair, his mind racing. *Control over gravity? Manipulating mass and momentum? Instantaneous changes in velocity without inertia?* The sheer scale of what Greg was describing left him reeling.

"What kind of civilization are we dealing with?" Caleb muttered, more to himself than to anyone else.

The weight of the question settled heavily over the room. Whatever humanity thought it knew about technology, power, or dominance, it was clear: Alohanui and its creators existed on an entirely different level.

And, get this—it negotiated a deal. It bought 20 *million* tonnes of wheat in exchange for 84 tonnes of gold."

Caleb's jaw nearly dropped. "They're... trading? Like, actually buying stuff?"

Greg smirked, clearly enjoying their reactions. "Exactly. This isn't an invasion. It's trade. The black spacecraft negotiated the deal just like any foreign country would. "Now," Greg went on, "back to the Black spacecraft. We watched it load wheat, and it looked like something straight out of *Star Trek*. No visible beams, no flashy lights—just wheat floating up into the ship's hold like it was caught in an invisible inverted tornado."

"That's... incredible," Emma said softly, her eyes wide with amazement.

Greg nodded, but his tone turned more serious. "Here's the kicker: the ripple effect this will have on our economy. Alohanui is draining our wheat reserves and simultaneously devaluing gold. Our economists are in a panic and, as soon as they see it on the 6 o'clock news, every economist will panic. It's like they're deliberately destabilizing everything."

Caleb, still trying to grasp the gravity of the situation, narrowed his eyes. "What about the gold? Is it real?"

Greg chuckled. "Yeah, the FBI's on it. They sent a team from Crosby, North Dakota. Plain clothes, unarmed—they missed the transfer, but we've got tons of cell phone footage. The Canada Wheat Board thought they were dealing with another foreign buyer. While payment in gold is rare, it's not unheard of. The entire deal was handled through encrypted financial channels, facilitated by the Chicago Mercantile Exchange."

Emma raised an eyebrow. "They've figured out and hacked the global financial system?"

Greg shrugged. "Seems like it. The deal was smooth—like they'd been doing it for years. And once it was done, they dropped off 2,100 blocks of pure gold—40 kilograms each—right next to a wheat elevator. Then they sucked up every grain of wheat from Weyburn and continued across Alberta, Saskatchewan, and Manitoba, emptying railcars and silos. But here's the thing—they were completely honest. All tests so far confirm the gold is 100% pure and they took only what they paid for."

Caleb frowned, the confusion evident in his voice. "Why would they drop the gold at the wheat elevator? That's crazy—it can't be right."

Greg leaned back, nodding slightly. "Yeah, I thought it was strange too. But Eric, the finance lawyer, had some thoughts about it."

Scanning the bustling situation room, Greg spotted Eric near the coffee machine. "Hey, Eric! Over here!" he called out, his voice cutting through the chatter and drawing a few curious glances.

Eric approached, his tie slightly loosened but his demeanor professional. "What's up?" he asked, sipping his coffee.

Greg gestured toward Caleb. "Caleb's trying to make sense of why the Alohanuis dropped the gold next to the elevator. Can you explain it again?"

Eric chuckled softly, setting his coffee down. "Ah, yes, the infamous gold drop. It baffled us too—at first. Then I dug into the standard grain futures sale contract used by the Chicago Mercantile Exchange (CME)." He adjusted his glasses and continued. "The contract specifies that unless alternative payment arrangements are explicitly agreed upon, payment is required to occur at the FOB location of the grain being sold. This clause aligns with UCC Article 2 provisions for contracts involving the sale of goods."

Caleb's eyebrows shot up. "So, you're saying they followed the contract to the letter?"

"Exactly," Eric replied, nodding. "The Canadian Wheat Board, on the other hand, had its own clearing specifications, which included wire transfer procedures. However, CME contract terms take precedence unless expressly overridden. In this case, no additional agreements were made specifying a different payment method. That means, legally, payment in full was required at the elevator."

"So *that's* why the Alohanuis just dropped the gold there." Emma interjected, her voice laced with wonder.

Eric grimaced, his expression tinged with sympathy for the workers at the elevator. "They didn't just drop it—they delivered 84 metric tonnes of pure gold bars, perfectly stacked in the parking area, right next to the elevator. The only 'security' on site? A half-dozen Wheat Board employees, armed with nothing more intimidating than a couple of brooms and a few square mouth shovels."

He leaned forward, his voice lowering for emphasis. "Imagine it: an alien spacecraft so massive it blocked out the sun across a five-square-mile area. Add to that the inverted tornadoes swirling and vacuuming up the grain. Those poor employees must have been scared out of their minds. And yet, somehow, they stayed there, doing their best to guard the gold until the RCMP arrived."

Eric shook his head, his tone growing more somber. "Honestly, I wouldn't be surprised if they're all suffering from PTSD after what they witnessed. But you know what? Those six are absolute heroes. They faced the unimaginable and held their ground."

The room felt colder as Eric's words hung in the air. This wasn't just an alien visitation—they were engaging in high-level trade, manipulating economies, and showing off technological capabilities that defied human comprehension.

The white, fiery red, and black spacecraft continued their mysterious missions, each with a distinct and unnerving purpose. The white craft, gliding from one war-torn region to another, brought with it a message of peace—but not the kind the world expected. The pilot offered terms of total, unconditional surrender to the armies of the world. Yet, in every case, no army had accepted. Instead, the presence of the craft seemed to escalate the violence. Rather than laying down arms, the intensity of the conflicts only increased. Tensions between China and Russia, which had been relatively peaceful, began to boil over. Both nations built up massive armies along their borders, and sporadic gunfire turned into near-constant skirmishes.

Meanwhile, the fiery red craft was no less menacing. It, too, moved from place to place—but where the white craft stirred up conflict between nations, the red craft incited civil unrest. In its wake, cities erupted into chaos. Terrorism, violent protests, riots, and race wars flared up wherever it appeared. Countries that had once been stable teetered on the brink of collapse, as civil wars broke out, fueled by the malevolent presence of the fiery red craft.

With little to distract them, Ted and Star were struggling

with the move. They felt disoriented, out of place, and deeply homesick. The news that their home on Oahu had been burned to the ground, just hours after they'd left, weighed heavily on them. Marauding bands of arsonists had thrown a Molotov cocktail through the window, setting the house ablaze the very night they departed. The thought of their home, the place they'd built their lives around, reduced to ashes only intensified their sense of loss, making it even harder to adjust to life at Raven Rock.

Ted, especially, was haunted by guilt. He kept replaying the "what-ifs" in his mind—if he had been home, maybe he could have put out the fire, or at least saved some cherished belongings before everything was lost. The idea that their house had burned down in his absence gnawed at him. He never said it out loud, but the regret and helplessness showed in his every expression and weighed on his heart like a stone.

Emma, worried for her parents, recalled that Captain MacDonald had mentioned the availability of social workers on-site. She made a few inquiries, and by that afternoon, a social worker arrived at the Kanoa's apartment. The social worker wasted no time, gently encouraging Ted and Star to get involved in community activities and introducing them to some of the other relocated families. She also suggested daily walks along the network of trails that wound through the forested areas surrounding the bunker—a way to reconnect with nature and escape the claustrophobic feeling of being underground.

Slowly, the couple began to find their footing. The fresh air, the towering trees, and the company of others who were also adjusting to their new reality helped ease their homesickness, one small step at a time. But Ted's guilt lingered, a silent shadow that would take much longer to fade.

Ted and Star unofficially adopted Bethany, Caleb's younger

sister, filling a void that had grown in their lives as Emma became more consumed with her work and relationship with Caleb. This newfound connection did wonders for Ted and Star, giving them a sense of purpose and helping them heal from the trauma of losing their home. At the same time, Bethany found comfort in their presence. Still reeling from the loss of her parents in the tragic plane crash over the Atlantic, she had been struggling—unsettled and deeply shaken by the news that her parents, en route to the Holy Land, were gone forever.

Though Ted and Star's spiritual views were vastly different from the devout Christianity that had shaped Caleb and Bethany's upbringing, their warmth and steady presence provided Bethany with a familiar solace. The differences in belief were overshadowed by their shared values of kindness, love, and support. In many ways, Ted and Star reminded Bethany of her parents—steadfast, nurturing, and willing to offer her the care she so desperately needed. Together, they began to form a new kind of family, one built on mutual understanding and the comfort of shared grief.

The news from Oahu was devastating. Ted, Star, Caleb, and Emma learned that a race and class war of sorts had erupted on the island. The older neighborhoods—small houses packed tightly together, built during World War I and shortly after—had become tinderboxes. Fires, once started in any home, would quickly leap from house to house, consuming entire blocks. In contrast, the wealthier areas, with sprawling estates and wide spaces between properties, seemed relatively untouched by the spreading infernos.

But the marginalized communities of Oahu were not content to let that disparity continue. They took matters into their own hands, marching through affluent neighborhoods and making sure no mansion was left unscathed. Armed with Molotov cocktails, they rationed out one per house, turning even the most fortified estates into blazing ruins. Meanwhile, firefighters—overwhelmed and stretched thin—focused their efforts on saving high-rise apartments and densely packed areas. The rich and famous were left to fend for themselves.

The chaos brought back haunting memories of the recent fires in Maui. Just as before, desperate residents of Oahu had no choice but to flee toward the ocean. People waded into the waters off Waikiki Beach, waiting, hoping for rescue, as the flames devoured their homes and the island's skyline was choked with smoke. Help seemed a distant hope as the fires raged unchecked, and the situation on Oahu spiraled further into destruction.

Fortunately, the Manoa Campus of the University of Hawaii, home to the Institute for Astronomy (IfA), was spared from the widespread fires and violence, thanks in no small part to the swift intervention of the National Guard and military forces. The government had made the protection of key scientific assets a top priority, ensuring that the world-class telescopes atop Mauna Kea and Haleakalā, as well as the IfA itself, remained secure. With the island in turmoil, these military units formed a protective shield around the campus, recognizing the critical role the Institute played in monitoring Alohanui and safeguarding humanity's future.

4,600 miles away from Raven Rock, Pan-STARRS continued its relentless sweep of the night sky, uncovering new moving objects in space. Its Moving Object Processing System (MOPS) quickly processed 30- to 60-second time-lapse images, flagging any objects not yet recorded in its vast database. While this automated discovery process thrilled astronomers, it had its limitations. MOPS could detect motion but lacked the ability to determine key information such as distance, speed, or trajectory. For that, human expertise was critical—and every second mattered.

Astronomers had to act fast because, with every passing second, the detected object would have moved, and unlike objects on Earth, those in space rarely traveled in a straight line. They followed complex, parabolic, or elliptical paths, which meant that the longer it took to start analyzing a moving object, the more difficult it became to track. Additional images and longer observation times were required to relocate the object and accurately plot its course.

To determine these key details, IfA astronomers frequently relied on follow-up observations from the Canada-France-Hawaii Telescope, which allowed them to calculate the object's distance, velocity, and direction, and ultimately predict its trajectory through the vastness of space.

But Caleb and Emma were no longer at the Institute for Astronomy (IfA). The IfA itself was running with a skeleton crew, leaving many of the discoveries from Pan-STARRS in need of urgent classification. With their expertise, it made perfect sense for Caleb and Emma to assist in processing these moving objects remotely from their new base of operations at Raven Rock. However, the workstations they were assigned in the Satellite Presidential Emergency Operations Center (SPEOC) were far from ideal for their work.

The glaring brightness of the situation room was jarring compared to the dim, tradition-steeped environment of the IfA's "warm room," where they were accustomed to working in near-darkness. While the low light at IfA wasn't strictly necessary, it had been a comforting part of their routine, a quiet atmosphere conducive to deep focus. At SPEOC, the situation was entirely different—bright, bustling, and loud, with continuous news coverage and constant chatter that made it very hard to concentrate.

After some complaints about the harsh lighting, Caleb and Emma were able to get anti-glare privacy screens installed on their monitors, reducing some of the distractions. But the chaotic energy of the situation room was still a far cry from the quiet intensity of tracking distant objects in space. Their work was more vital than ever, but adapting to the environment proved to be a challenge.

CHAPTER 9
SPRING GREEN

A portal on Alohanui rotated precisely 90 degrees, and from it emerged yet another craft—this one a vibrant yellow-green, the fresh, luminous color of new shoots pushing through the soil in spring. Unlike the previous crafts, its arrival seemed almost peaceful, as if its very hue signaled something different. With barely a moment's hesitation, it shot toward Earth, descending rapidly from the sky.

Meanwhile, the three earlier spacecraft from Alohanui continued their missions with terrifying efficiency.

The white craft, its pilot calm and unwavering, hovered along the tense boundary between China and Russia, as well as over Mongolia. Here, the largest armies ever assembled in human history were massing, prepared for a conflict that could change the geopolitical landscape forever. The white craft's presence loomed over them like a harbinger, offering terms for peace—unconditional surrender—but no army had yet accepted. Instead, the conflict only intensified in the face of its silent, unmoving witness.

The red craft was a different story altogether, continuing its chaotic journey across the globe. Wherever it went, it left devastation in its wake. Riots, looting and arson erupted in city after city. Race wars, class wars, and civil wars erupted in country after country. Streets were aflame, buildings collapsed, and societies tore themselves apart under its baleful influence. The pilot of the red craft, like a grim reaper of strife, reveled in the chaos, stirring up discord and violence as it moved from continent to continent, leaving no corner of the world untouched by its hand.

The black craft, ever pragmatic, made continuous trips between Alohanui and Earth, its hold filled with gold bricks as it landed, and returning to space with cargoes of food such as wheat, barley, olive oil, and wine. These exchanges occurred with clockwork precision, seemingly devoid of emotion, as if part of some larger cosmic transaction. All the while, the black craft and its pilot were deeply engaged in Earth's economic systems, conducting seamless trades on every mercantile exchange, effortlessly controlling the ebb and flow of Earth's resources from a place far beyond human understanding. What was clear: gold was being devalued while food was becoming scarce.

The President entrusted SPEOC with the urgent task of predicting Alohanui's reflective sunlight events—rare but catastrophic occurrences where its reflected beams could incinerate the Earth's surface. Despite their relentless efforts, accurate forecasting proved nearly impossible due to the object's erratic movement and intricate sunlight interactions. To mitigate the threat, air raid sirens were repurposed to warn the public of imminent sunlight surges. While these warnings couldn't protect those already exposed, they effectively kept others indoors, minimizing further casualties.

The reality was far graver than Caleb could fathom. Alohanui was fine-tuning its solar sail-like thrust using gravity waves focused on the Sun's core, compressing it and exponentially increasing its solar output. The horrifying consequence was the vaporization of people caught in its intensified rays. With precise control over sunlight-powered thrust, Alohanui was set to achieve geosynchronous orbit in mere days instead of years—at the devastating cost of a million lives.

What troubled Caleb even more was the realization that Alohanui's mindless actions might push the Sun toward a supernova. He understood that the Sun would eventually die, transitioning into a white dwarf that would engulf the Earth. Yet, in his gut, Caleb was certain that tampering with the Sun in such a way could only accelerate its natural aging process, hastening both its demise and the end of the Earth.

Now, with the green craft hurtling toward Earth, it was unclear what new purpose this latest arrival would bring—whether it, too, was an agent of chaos, commerce, or perhaps something more ominous still.

Sitting at his desk in SPEOC, still mulling over Alohanui's use of gravity waves, Caleb waited for a replacement keyboard. The cable on his old one had frayed and finally stopped working, forcing him to call IT. Fortunately, IT support at SPEOC was about 100 times faster than at the Institute for Astronomy, his previous workplace. Within five minutes, Glen from IT arrived with a new keyboard in hand.

Glen unplugged the damaged keyboard and plugged in the replacement. Just as he was about to take the old one away, Caleb noticed something odd—the exposed wires where the cable met the keyboard. White, red, black, and green. The same colors as the ships from Alohanui. *How strange,* Caleb thought. *Am I dreaming?*

Is this all a horrible nightmare? My parents' death, Emma's cancer, wars, riots fires, scorching. Wake up Caleb, wake up! But Caleb didn't wake up. It wasn't a dream.

-

The next morning, Emma met her new oncologist at Raven

Rock. Though anxious, she couldn't help but feel a sense of relief knowing that this phase of her treatment was beginning. Her oncologist, Dr. Margaret Baron, came highly recommended—one of the top specialists in her field. Dr. Baron was a soft-spoken but incredibly sharp woman, with a warmth that immediately put Emma at ease. She had trained at Johns Hopkins and spent years in clinical oncology before focusing on advanced liver cancer treatments. Her expertise was complemented by a caring bedside manner, something Emma had come to appreciate over the past months.

The office where Emma met Dr. Baron was pristine, minimalist in design with soft, neutral tones that gave it a calming, almost spa-like atmosphere. Although they were hundreds of feet below ground, state of the art floor-to-ceiling artificial windows provided simulated natural light that flooded the waiting area, casting a peaceful glow on the light gray walls. Small potted plants sat in the corners, their green leaves a reminder of life thriving even in a place so closely associated with illness. The air smelled faintly of lavender, calming Emma's nerves as she sat beside Caleb, who squeezed her hand reassuringly. Across from them, another patient sat quietly, reading, waiting for their appointment.

Dr. Baron greeted them with a warm smile and ushered them into her private office for a more personal discussion. The office had the same light, neutral palette, but was decorated with framed diplomas and certificates, evidence of her prestigious career. A small bookshelf behind her desk held medical textbooks and a few personal mementos—a photo of her family and a framed quote: "Hope is stronger than fear." The desk itself was sleek and modern, but uncluttered, with only a few neatly arranged files.

"Emma, I've reviewed your medical records thoroughly," Dr. Baron began, her tone calm but firm, radiating both empathy and authority. "The good news is that your doctors caught this early, which gives us a significant advantage. However, liver cancer can be unpredictable, so we need to act decisively. I recommend starting you on a six-cycle chemotherapy regimen as your team in Hawaii suggested, but you didn't get a chance to start."

"We'll use GEMOX—a combination of gemcitabine and oxaliplatin—which is often the best choice for patients in good overall health who can tolerate a dual-drug protocol. I believe this regimen is the most effective option for you."

Dr. Baron paused, letting her words sink in before continuing. "To remain on the transplant list, it's critical that you achieve complete remission. Chemotherapy is our best—and sometimes only—tool to get there. The transplant committee won't even consider you for candidacy until you've completed at least one full course of treatment. Each course includes six cycles, so we'll take it step by step, keeping a close eye on your progress."

Caleb sat quietly, absorbing the information, but Emma had a million questions running through her head. She'd read about chemotherapy and had heard horror stories from friends of friends who'd gone through it, but now that it was her reality, the weight of it felt more crushing.

"What should I expect in terms of side effects?" Emma asked, her voice steady but tinged with worry.

Dr. Baron leaned forward slightly, her expression gentle. "Everyone reacts differently, but with gemcitabine plus oxaliplatin, you can expect some fatigue, nausea, and hair loss. We'll also monitor you closely for any other side effects. We have medications to help manage the nausea, and our team will be with you every step of the way."

After answering a few more of Emma's questions, Dr. Baron stood up. "If you're ready, we can start your first session this afternoon. We've prepared everything so that you can settle in and begin your treatment right here in Raven Rock."

Emma nodded. It was happening so fast, but she knew there was no time to waste. Dr. Baron led them down a bright, clean hallway toward the chemotherapy treatment area. Along the way, she explained more about what to expect during each session, outlining the schedule of treatments—three weeks between each cycle, with regular blood tests and checkups to monitor how her body was handling the drugs.

The chemotherapy room was a large, open space divided into smaller, semi-private sections by pale blue curtains. Each station had a comfortable, reclining chair upholstered in soft gray fabric, with a small table next to it for personal belongings. Emma spotted a basket of magazines and a TV mounted on the wall in each section, along with headphones for patients who wanted to distract themselves during treatment.

Emma was directed to one of the recliners. She sank into the chair, grateful that it was more comfortable than she had imagined. The chair was adjustable, and with a press of a button, she found herself reclining, able to rest more comfortably. A nurse, who introduced herself as Lisa, appeared and smiled warmly, hooking up Emma's IV while chatting lightly to ease the tension.

The smell of antiseptic and the faint hum of air purifiers filled the room. Nurses moved quietly between Emma and the one other patient there, adjusting IVs, checking vitals, and offering words of encouragement. Lisa, with practiced ease, began the infusion of gemcitabine. As the drug entered Emma's system, she felt a cold sensation creep up her arm from the IV. She closed her eyes, focusing on Caleb's presence beside her, his hand resting gently on her arm.

"You're doing great," Lisa said, her voice calm and reassuring. "This will take a few hours. Just try to relax, and let us know if you need anything."

Next came the oxaliplatin. By now, Emma was starting to feel a little groggy, a slight wave of fatigue settling over her. Lisa explained that the treatment room also offered light snacks and drinks for patients. Emma, not feeling up to eating, politely declined, but Caleb grabbed some tea from a nearby station and offered her sips.

The hours passed in a blur. The rhythmic beep of monitors and the quiet conversations between nurses and patients were the only sounds that punctuated the soft atmosphere of the chemotherapy room. Emma felt a heaviness settle in her bones, not painful, but exhausting. The fatigue was different from anything she had experienced before, but she knew this was just the beginning.

When the infusion was complete, Lisa gently removed the IV and handed Emma some paperwork with instructions on what to expect over the next few days. Emma leaned on Caleb as they left the clinic, the exhaustion hitting her harder than expected. But despite the fatigue, there was a quiet strength in her gaze. This was the first of many battles, but she was ready to fight. Dr. Baron had assured her that the treatment plan was aggressive, but effective. They would be monitoring her progress every step of the way, adjusting as necessary to ensure the best outcome.

Emma and Caleb made their way back to their apartment in Raven Rock. The world felt quieter, heavier, but there was a sense of purpose that hadn't been there before. They were in the fight now, and there was no turning back.

Despite Caleb's protests, Emma firmly insisted that he continue his work while she underwent chemotherapy. "You need to stay focused on Alohanui," she said gently, her voice resolute even as fatigue from the treatment weighed on her. "There's nothing you can do for me by sitting in the chemo room all day. I need you to stay sharp, keep working. The world still needs you."

Caleb wanted to be there for her during every session, but he couldn't argue with her reasoning. As much as he hated the idea of leaving her side, the work they were doing to understand Alohanui and its implications for Earth was critically important. It was what had brought them to Raven Rock in the first place, and the discoveries being made were pivotal to the fate of the planet.

Emma also had the comfort of family. Star, Ted, and Bethany quickly organized a rotation system, ensuring that Emma was never alone during her chemotherapy sessions. Each of them would take a day, sitting by her side in the sterile, cool chemotherapy room, providing her with company, comfort, and the moral support she needed. Star, with her quiet strength, would often bring homemade soups and herbal teas, nurturing Emma with warmth and care. Ted, although awkward at first, learned to offer reassuring words, reading aloud to her from her favorite books or simply holding her hand when the treatments took a toll on her energy. And Bethany, with her vibrant, youthful spirit, would chat animatedly, filling the space with stories and light-hearted humor to distract Emma from the fatigue and nausea.

On days when Emma felt too drained to talk, they simply sat together in silence, offering companionship without the need for words. The sounds of the chemotherapy room—a gentle hum of medical equipment, the occasional beep of a monitor, and the soft shuffling of nurses moving between patients—became familiar, and though Emma would leave each session feeling worn and exhausted, she never left feeling alone.

Meanwhile, Caleb tried to juggle his responsibilities, torn between the weight of his work and his desire to be with Emma. But knowing that she was surrounded by people who loved her—people who would keep her safe and cared for—gave him the strength to push forward. Each time he arrived at the Satellite Presidential Emergency Operations Center, his thoughts would drift to her, but he stayed focused on the task at hand. The weight of both worlds pressed down on him: the monumental task of decoding Alohanui's presence and the immense personal struggle of watching Emma endure the ravages of chemotherapy.

It wasn't easy for him to compartmentalize, but Emma's unwavering strength inspired him. She had fought so hard to survive, and now she was urging him to fight on a different front—the one that held the future of the world in balance.

Caleb, sitting at the foot of Emma's bed one evening after a particularly grueling round of chemotherapy, watched as she fought off the fatigue that seemed to weigh down her every movement. She was trying to smile, to reassure him that she was okay, but he could see through it. The dark circles under her eyes, the pallor of her skin, and the thinness of her once-luxuriant hair all told a different story. Caleb knew she was tough—tougher than anyone he had ever known—but he also knew when to step in, when to protect her from herself.

Emma had always been the one to push through. Even in the middle of her treatment, she had continued to monitor Pan-STARRS updates, read reports, and analyze data when she could. She even managed to submit a few newly discovered asteroids to the Minor Planet Center at the International Astronomical Union. Caleb admired her for that, for her resilience and her refusal to let cancer dictate her life. But at some point, it was enough. If Emma could decide for him that he needed to keep working during her chemo, then Caleb figured he had the right to make some decisions for her, too.

That's it, he thought, his resolve hardening. *No work for her until at least three weeks after her last dose of chemo.*

The next morning, as they sat together sipping tea, Caleb brought it up. "Emma, I've been thinking... no more work for you for a while. Not until three weeks after your last chemo session."

She looked up, frowning slightly. "Caleb, I can't just—"

"No," he interrupted, his tone firmer than usual. "You've been deciding things for me—telling me to keep working while you're in chemo, telling me not to worry. Well, I'm deciding this for you. No more work. You need time to recover properly."

Emma, taken aback by the rare assertiveness in Caleb's voice, blinked. "But... Pan-STARRS still needs—"

"Pan-STARRS will survive without you for a few months," Caleb countered, setting his tea down and leaning forward. "You need to survive. You need to rest, Emma. You've been through hell, and I'm not going to stand by and watch you push yourself any further than you already have."

She opened her mouth to argue, but then paused. The determination in his eyes was unmistakable, and as much as she hated to admit it, Caleb was right. She had been pushing herself far too hard. Between the chemo sessions, the exhaustion, and the emotional toll of it all, the last thing she needed was the pressure of work on top of everything else.

Caleb reached for her hand, his grip warm and comforting. "You've been so strong, Em. You've carried so much. But it's okay to let go for a while. It's okay to take time for yourself."

She sighed, a mix of frustration and acceptance in the sound. "Three weeks, huh?"

"Three weeks after your last chemo session," Caleb said, nodding. "You need that time to heal, to rest. No more looking at reports, no more logging into work and maybe most important of all no watching the news! Just focus on getting better."

Emma leaned back into the couch cushions, her tired eyes searching his face. She could see how much he cared—how much he wanted her to be okay. And in that moment, she realized that maybe, just maybe, it was okay to let someone else take the reins for a while. She had been strong for so long, but now it was time to let Caleb be strong for her.

"Okay," she finally said, her voice soft. "Until three weeks after my last dose. No work. No news."

Caleb smiled, relieved, and leaned in to kiss her forehead. "Thank you."

As the days wore on, Emma found herself resisting the urge to check her phone for news, emails and to follow up on the latest astronomical findings. But each time she felt the pull, she remembered Caleb's words. She needed this time to recover. She deserved this time. And with Caleb by her side, reminding her to rest and recharge, she knew that, for once, it was okay to let go and just focus on herself.

Unknown to Emma and only partially understood by Bethany, Star, and Ted, the world outside the safe walls of Raven Rock was descending into chaos. What had started as political and civil unrest had grown into something far more uncontrollable, and soon, the ripple effects of societal collapse began to stretch into every corner of daily life.

The Centers for Disease Control and Prevention (CDC) found itself crippled by the widespread upheaval. What was once a meticulously organized and efficient system to contain and combat diseases was now suffocating under the weight of fractured communication networks, broken supply chains, and a world on the brink of collapse. The once seamless movement of medical personnel and resources became almost impossible, choked by blockades, rioting, and the chaos of closed borders. Planes grounded, trains halted, and highways became dangerous corridors, patrolled by desperate mobs more interested in survival than civility.

Yet, ironically, there was a brief, razor thin, silver lining to this dark cloud: fewer people were traveling, which meant fewer opportunities to spread diseases from place to place. Airports emptied out, tourist hotspots became desolate, and for a time, diseases that relied on human carriers to jump borders slowed their spread. But this brief reprieve came with a terrifying new reality—wherever the spring green spacecraft visited, new diseases began to emerge. These weren't just mutations of old ailments; they were far more sinister, deadlier, and unlike anything humanity had seen before.

The first of these new plagues was a virulent, vaccine-resistant strain of rabies. The infected didn't just show symptoms of fear or confusion; they were driven to aggression unlike anything seen in recorded outbreaks. Animals and humans alike, once bitten or scratched, rapidly became frenzied attackers, spreading the virus with terrifying speed. Bites, scratches, or even saliva transferred the disease, and within days, entire towns were quarantined—often too late to prevent total loss of life. Governments and scientists scrambled to find treatments, but the strain had morphed, rendering standard vaccines useless. Victims died painfully, their brains ravaged by fevered violence.

Just as the world was struggling to comprehend this outbreak, another horror followed. The Yersinia pestis bacterium, known in history as the cause of the Bubonic Plague, reappeared with a vengeance. This time, it spread faster than in any prior epidemic, fueled by unsanitary conditions, overcrowded camps, and the absence of functioning healthcare systems. The haunting images of swollen lymph nodes and blackened flesh once thought consigned to medieval times reemerged in gruesome detail. Hospitals that could still function were overwhelmed with the sick, while field clinics barely scratched the surface of the number of those infected.

In the U.S., the diseases were only one piece of the grim puzzle. As civil unrest escalated and food supplies became scarce, hunger turned from a lingering threat to a dominant killer. Starvation stalked the streets, not only in impoverished regions but in once-thriving cities. Food shipments never arrived, grocery stores were looted, and farms were abandoned or destroyed in the wake of riots. People were dying from malnutrition, their bodies wasting away in a world that could no longer feed them.

But while these horrifying events unfolded across the country, Raven Rock remained insulated. Emma, focused on her recovery, was oblivious to the full scale of what was happening beyond the bunker. She knew things were bad—she had caught bits of conversation here and there, and Caleb had hinted at the unrest—but her days were spent in chemotherapy and recovery, her energy focused inward.

Bethany, Star, and Ted were aware of some of the dangers. They had seen the news before coming to Raven Rock and had heard the reports of diseases and unrest. But they didn't know the full extent. Caleb, struggling with his own responsibilities and concern for Emma, tried to shield them from the worst of it. But even he couldn't fully comprehend the scale of the catastrophe unfolding outside.

For now, Raven Rock stood strong. Its residents were shielded from the deadly diseases and the violence that gripped the world above. But even within its fortified walls, the weight of the outside world pressed in, and everyone knew it was only a matter of time before the full impact of the chaos would be felt.

The black spacecraft had seemingly completed its first, devastating mission: to cripple the global economy and obliterate commerce through the relentless acquisition of vast amounts of Earth's commodities. Grain, metals, oil, rare earth minerals—nothing was spared. What had once been considered untouchable resources, carefully managed and traded among nations, were now stripped from the planet and transported to Alohanui. The world's markets buckled under the weight of these purchases, which, at first, were thought to be a temporary boon. But soon, it became clear that this was no mere economic exchange. The systematic removal of Earth's essential resources was not only choking off trade but leaving nations powerless to recover.

As the black spacecraft siphoned off Earth's reserves, the real-world effects rippled across the globe. What began as a strange new player in the market quickly morphed into economic devastation. Supply chains collapsed, factories shut down, and global trade ground to a halt. Countries that relied on imports for survival were left scrambling, their stockpiles dwindling, while panic set in. Even the wealthiest and most powerful were not spared.

Billionaires, dictators, kings, and princes—the supposed titans of industry and control—realized they could no longer outmaneuver the extraterrestrial force that had commandeered the world's economy. In desperation, they retreated to their fortified mountain bunkers, deep within elaborate tunnel networks carved into remote wildernesses. These hideouts, once mere whispers in conspiracy circles, were now fully operational and outfitted with every imaginable luxury. Family, friends, loyal servants, and private security forces filled these bunkers, each brimming with last-minute shipments of medical equipment, pharmaceuticals, and food supplies.

However, even as these elites secured themselves underground, it became clear that their plans were faltering. The last-minute procurement of essential goods had drained global reserves, stripping the world of any hope for medical treatment or basic necessities. Trained medical professionals—surgeons, doctors, and nurses—were snatched away by these billionaires, leaving the rest of the world bereft of critical care. Hospitals stood abandoned, their halls eerily quiet, while those with money had private clinics within their mountain fortresses.

For years, these rulers of the earth had hoarded gold, believing it to be their ultimate insurance against the collapse of paper currency. They were right—fiat money was rapidly losing value as nations teetered on the edge of insolvency. But the gold they had stockpiled was quickly becoming worthless, too. With the extraterrestrials flooding the market by trading in vast quantities of pure gold, the precious metal's value dropped by the hour. What had once been the ultimate symbol of wealth and security now became a glaring testament to their failure.

The elites' hopes of replenishing their bunker supplies dwindled with each passing day. Finally when the world's commodity traders realized the true extent of the black spacecraft's objectives, they ceased selling to the extraterrestrials altogether. But it was far too late. The damage had already been done. The black craft had drained Earth of its most essential resources. Grain stores that had been hoarded for years, waiting for market prices to rise, were completely emptied. Oil reserves ran dry, leaving pipelines and refineries idle. The once-bustling ports, hubs of international trade and economic activity, now stood desolate—graveyards of rusting containers and motionless cranes, symbols of a global economy that had come to a standstill.

As the global economy collapsed under the weight of these trades, humanity was left in a state of paralysis. What remained was a planet picked clean by the alien presence, its once-vibrant systems of trade and cooperation dismantled in the blink of an eye. There were no more deals to be made, no more goods to be bought. The world had been drained, and in the silence that followed, the consequences of the black spacecraft's mission reverberated like a death knell.

Those in the bunkers had hoarded what they could, but even their preparations could not insulate them from the larger truth: the world they knew was gone. Above ground, nations buckled under the strain of mass shortages and rising violence, as people fought for what little remained. In a twisted irony, the elites who had once controlled the global economy now found themselves as helpless as the masses they had left behind, their gold worthless, their fortresses little more than gilded cages in a collapsing world.

Alohanui's journey through the asteroid belt was anything but smooth. Its head-on collision with Ka'epaoka'āwela, the retrograde asteroid, was nothing short of catastrophic. The impact between the two—a two-mile-wide rock slamming into a 18-mile-wide behemoth, both traveling at a combined speed of roughly 60,000 miles per hour—triggered an explosion estimated at over 2 million megatons, equivalent to 150 million Hiroshima bombs detonating at once.

This explosion dwarfed anything Earth had ever witnessed, even in its most violent moments. During the Cold War, the Soviet Union's Tsar Bomba, detonated in 1961 over Novaya Zemlya island in the Arctic Ocean, had been the most powerful man-made explosion ever recorded. Designed to demonstrate Soviet might, the bomb was originally capable of yielding a 100-megaton blast. However, even the Soviets deemed such force too dangerous to test, reducing the yield to 50 megatons —still the largest nuclear explosion in human history.

But the Ka'epaoka'āwela-Alohanui collision was incomprehensibly larger, the equivalent of forty thousand Tsar Bombas at their full 100-megaton capacity. No force in Earth's history, natural or otherwise, had ever unleashed such unimaginable power.

The full force of the collision was absorbed by the smaller asteroid, Kaʻepaokaʻāwela, which was vaporized and pulverized on impact. The resulting debris, turned into high-speed mini asteroids, was flung in every direction. Some fragments shot out of the asteroid belt entirely, even escaping the solar system. But many others slammed into nearby asteroids, altering their paths—some subtly, others drastically.

Even without this massive collision, Alohanui's mere passage through the asteroid belt had already been wreaking havoc. Its immense gravitational pull disturbed the orbits of nearby asteroids, perturbing their trajectories to align more closely with its own. The terrifying implication of this was simple: a significant number of asteroids, once relatively harmless, were now on altered paths—many of which were now heading straight toward Earth.

The first significant hazardous object from Alohanui's debris field—a 30-meter diameter asteroid—struck Earth with devastating consequences. It entered the atmosphere at a blistering speed, breaking apart and exploding in an airburst high above Beijing. The impact was catastrophic, akin to a 50-megaton hydrogen bomb detonating over the city. In an instant, the explosion killed 3 million people, vaporizing buildings, infrastructure, and everything in its wake. The shockwave flattened vast stretches of Beijing, leaving the once-bustling metropolis in ruins. Fires raged across the city as debris and dust filled the sky, casting an eerie gloom over the surrounding regions.

The Chinese government, already on edge from escalating global tensions, was convinced that the blast was not a natural event but a deliberate attack. With little time for analysis and fearing a nuclear assault from Russia, China retaliated swiftly and with deadly force. In a matter of hours, Chinese military command authorized the launch of a 50-megaton hydrogen bomb targeted at Moscow. The bomb's detonation over the Russian capital unleashed devastation on a similarly unimaginable scale, reducing the city to rubble, and killing millions in its wake.

The retaliatory strike sent shockwaves through the international community, plunging the world into a new phase of global conflict. Without immediate proof that the Beijing explosion had been an asteroid and not a Russian weapon, panic gripped the major powers. Nations scrambled to assess their defenses, while governments issued emergency broadcasts urging their citizens to seek shelter. A chain reaction of retaliations seemed inevitable as the two largest nuclear-armed states stood on the brink of all-out war, not realizing the true source of the disaster was far beyond human control.

Alohanui's debris, once thought to be harmless space dust, was now recognized as a ticking time bomb, with more fragments potentially heading toward Earth.

As tensions between China and Russia escalated, both nations saw the use of tactical nuclear weapons as not only justified but necessary in their ongoing skirmishes along their shared borders. Small, yet deadly, nuclear bombs—similar in destructive power to the one dropped on Hiroshima—became the weapons of choice, each designed to obliterate military camps, strategic bases, and vital infrastructure with terrifying precision.

The first strikes came swiftly, targeting remote military outposts and forward bases nestled in the Gobi desert. The mushroom clouds rose, signaling the grim beginning of a new era of warfare, one in which the use of nuclear arms became a tactical decision rather than a last resort. Entire military camps were vaporized, their occupants lost in the blink of an eye. Nearby forests were scorched black, and rivers boiled as the shockwaves shattered train depots and brought down critical bridges.

China's military, caught between the chaos of Alohanui's asteroid debris and the retaliatory blows from Russia, launched its own nuclear strikes in response. In the borderlands of Mongolia, small nuclear devices were deployed to destroy Russian rail lines and disrupt supply chains, reducing entire sections of the Trans-Siberian Railway to twisted metal and craters. Russian forces, determined to strike back with equal ferocity, targeted Chinese military installations near the Heilongjiang River, their tactical nuclear bombs reducing entire bases to radioactive wastelands.

The once-tense borderlands now became desolate battlefields, dotted with glowing craters, shattered landscapes, and the toxic aftermath of nuclear fallout. Civilian populations in border towns and villages fled in terror, their homes abandoned as radiation spread with the wind. The local flora and fauna perished in the toxic aftermath, turning the once lush and fertile areas into barren exclusion zones.

This new form of limited nuclear warfare, using bombs smaller in yield but still unimaginably destructive, began to feel routine. Each side believed it had the moral and strategic upper hand, convinced that the destruction they wrought was proportional to the damage they had suffered. International observers watched in horror as the conflict escalated, fearing that it was only a matter of time before these tactical strikes would give way to full-scale nuclear war. The entire world stood on edge, waiting to see if the unthinkable would happen next.

Amidst this global tension, a new disaster struck. An iron-and-carbon-rich meteorite exploded high above the Midwest of the United States, creating devastation eerily similar to that of a small nuclear warhead. The force of the explosion flattened the trees in forests directly below, leaving a swath of destruction across a vast area. Pieces of the meteorite rained down over several states, including Illinois, Indiana, Iowa, Kansas, Michigan, Minnesota, and Missouri. At first, the debris seemed like harmless space rock, a strange but natural phenomenon.

But unknown until it was too late, the meteorite had contained lethal amounts of cyanide compounds. These toxic substances, scattered by the explosion, seeped into rivers, lakes, and eventually groundwater. As the cyanide-tainted water infiltrated well systems and water supplies, people across the affected region began to fall ill. Hospitals were quickly overwhelmed with cases of nausea, dizziness, and cyanide poisoning symptoms.

Local authorities scrambled to assess the extent of the contamination, but the damage was already done. In small towns and rural areas where well water was a primary source, the effects were particularly devastating. Dozens fell seriously ill, and tragically, a few died before the extent of the poisoning was fully understood. Entire communities were forced to abandon their homes, their water sources now toxic, as emergency teams worked frantically to decontaminate the affected areas.

This catastrophe, coming at a time when the world was already on edge, only deepened the sense of dread and vulnerability. The meteorite, an unpredictable and unavoidable force of nature, added yet another layer of chaos to a world that seemed increasingly out of control.

Although Caleb, Ted, Star, and Bethany did their best to shield Emma from the relentless flood of bad news, it was impossible to completely insulate her. Despite their efforts to keep the conversations quiet, Emma still overheard whispers in the hallways—strangers murmuring about the outside world, or even her hearing-challenged parents discussing things in hushed tones when they assumed she was asleep. But Emma had always been perceptive, able to read their worried faces and sense the growing tension around her. She knew the world outside Raven Rock was unraveling.

As the days passed, and the chaos outside the bunker worsened, it became harder for them to maintain their careful schedules. Eventually, there came a day when Emma had to face a chemotherapy session alone, the rotating support system they had established for her stretched too thin. The thought of sitting in the cold, sterile room by herself weighed on her mind, amplifying her already fragile emotional state.

Bethany, noticing Emma's unease, approached her gently one afternoon. "Emma, I know how hard this must be for you. I've been thinking—since we can't always be here... would it help if I asked the pastor from my church to come sit with you during chemo? He's a good man, and he's helped a lot of people through tough times. I know it's not the same as having us there, but maybe it could help?"

Emma looked up at Bethany, surprised by the offer. She had never been to a Christian church, but she appreciated the thoughtfulness behind it. The weight of being alone during chemo was a terrifying prospect, and while she didn't know how she felt about having a pastor there, it was better than facing the silence by herself.

Bethany continued, "I've talked to him a few times since we've been here. He's not pushy or anything—just kind. He could be a quiet presence or talk if you need it."

Emma nodded slowly, grateful for her sister-in-law's thoughtfulness. "Maybe... Maybe that would be good, just so I'm not alone."

Bethany smiled softly, relieved that Emma had accepted the suggestion. "I'll reach out to him then. He'd be happy to stop by."

Emma knew it wouldn't solve the overwhelming weight of everything happening outside or the battle raging inside her own body, but it was a small comfort. And sometimes, in the midst of everything falling apart, small comforts were all that kept her going.

On the day of her chemo session, Emma arrived to find Bethany's pastor already waiting. She recognized him from the times she had seen him sitting with other patients during their treatments. He was familiar, but they had never spoken.

"Hi, I'm Emma," she said, unsure how to start the conversation. "Hope you didn't wait too long, Father."

The man smiled warmly, shaking his head. "Oh, don't call me Father. Just call me Ben. I'm not Catholic—actually, I'm kind of from the other end of the Christian spectrum. No clerical collar, no robe."

Emma hesitated, not quite knowing how to respond. There was something disarming about his casual demeanor, and he seemed to pick up on her uncertainty.

"Listen," Ben continued gently, "I know the robe and collar can sometimes be reassuring, like it reinforces the role of a priest. But I'm a bit different. I am a priest, yes, but I don't wear the uniform. In my faith, we believe every member of the congregation is a priest too, in their own way. So, technically, Bethany's a priest as well, though I doubt she goes around telling people that."

Emma couldn't help but smile at the thought. *Bethany, a priest?* She found it oddly comforting that he wasn't what she had expected. His relaxed approach made the idea of having him there for support seem much less intimidating.

Ben smiled back, clearly pleased that he'd broken the ice. "Exactly. It's a bit different from what you might be used to, but it works for us. Now, let's let the nurse get you all set up, and we'll get through this chemo together."

As the nurse busied herself hooking up the IV drip, Emma found herself growing more at ease with Ben's presence. She had been expecting the kind of solemnity that often came with a formal priest, but Ben's laid-back nature felt more like a reassuring friend than someone passing judgment.

Over the course of the next few hours, while the chemo slowly dripped into her veins, the two had a long conversation. Ben listened intently as Emma opened up about the weight on her heart—the uncertainty of her illness, the deep sense of loss after Caleb and Bethany's parents died, and the ever-present fear that lingered in the back of her mind about her own future.

Ben offered comfort, sharing stories of others who had faced the same darkness and found a way through it. His faith was solid but not overbearing, and for the first time, Emma felt a kind of peace she hadn't expected.

Eventually, the conversation turned to Jake and Jean Jacobson, Caleb's parents. Emma had always wondered about some of the plaques in their home, particularly one with a verse from Romans 10:9: *"If you declare with your mouth, 'Jesus is Lord,' and believe in your heart that God raised him from the dead, you will be saved."*

She asked Ben, "Saved from what, exactly?"

Ben paused thoughtfully, his tone gentle but sincere. "Saved from death," he replied. "It doesn't mean that we won't die physically—everyone dies. But those who believe in Jesus Christ as the Son of God, who believe that God raised him from the dead, will be saved in a different sense. It means that death isn't the end for them. They'll be raised again, brought out of the grave, to live forever."

Emma considered his words carefully. It wasn't something she had thought much about, at least not in that way. She had always associated faith with the rituals she'd seen but never felt a personal connection to it.

As the session continued, Emma found herself asking more questions—not just about the faith that Caleb's parents had, but about how people coped with illness, fear, and uncertainty. Ben's answers weren't preachy; they were simple, practical, and kind, and by the time the chemo was over, she realized that the hours had passed more easily than she had expected.

When it was time to leave, Emma felt lighter, not because her struggles were over, but because she had found a small measure of peace in the midst of them. Ben hadn't offered her any miraculous answers, but he had given her something to hold on to—a sense that even in her darkest moments, she wasn't entirely alone.

The first *planet killer*, perturbed by Alohanui, was a 60-mile-wide asteroid barreling toward Earth. Its calculated impact zone was deep in the South Pacific, precisely halfway between the tip of South America and New Zealand. For weeks, Pan-STARRS had tracked its approach, and Caleb had known the dreadful truth for days. The asteroid hadn't even been named yet, not yet accepted by the Minor Planet Center.

SPEOC, the Satellite Presidential Emergency Operations Center, had pinpointed the exact moment and location of the impact, leaving no doubt about the devastation it would unleash.

"It's a blessing," Rachel Timmins remarked, her voice calm yet filled with an underlying tension. "It's planet-killer size but it's going to hit the middle of the ocean. So it's not going to completely destroy civilization. For simplicity, let's call it the Annihilator." A brilliant paleontologist who had transitioned into asteroid impact assessment, Rachel had become a key figure in their operations. She was more than just a scientist—she led her team with precision, using complex simulations to predict the consequences of cosmic collisions. She stood at the front of the room, laser pointer in hand, directing everyone's gaze to the pulsating red circle on the map.

"What about DART—the Double Asteroid Redirection Test? Can't we use that?" Caleb asked, his voice barely masking his desperation.

"Unfortunately, we'd have needed at least a ten-year warning to put something like that in place," Rachel replied with a sigh, shaking her head. "And we have seventy-two hours."

She took a breath before continuing, her words tinged with grim resignation. "If this asteroid were going to hit anywhere else, it would end civilization as we know it. We're lucky—if you can even call it that—that it's set to strike the South Pacific. It's not the best-case scenario, but it's the least catastrophic we could have hoped for. If it hit land—anywhere on a continent—there wouldn't be anything left. This gives us a slim chance. But it's still going to be devastating."

She pointed her laser at the screen, tapping it to emphasize the impact zone. "The Pacific Rim is going to feel the brunt of this. Enormous tidal waves—mega-tsunamis—will radiate outwards in all directions. Coastal cities are... gone. There's no way around it. We're talking waves that will reach heights of a thousand feet or more, traveling at unimaginable speeds."

Caleb felt a chill run down his spine as he listened. The weight of Rachel's words settled over the room like a suffocating fog.

"San Diego, Los Angeles, Tokyo, Sydney, even Hawaii... they'll all be obliterated. There won't be anything left standing," Rachel continued. "The entire coastlines will be swept away. The evacuation of those cities needs to start now, but..." She paused, swallowing hard. "There's no way to get everyone out in time."

A heavy silence followed her words. Caleb leaned forward, burying his face in his hands, trying to comprehend the magnitude of the disaster that loomed over them. This wasn't just another close call. This was the one—the asteroid they had feared for years.

Rachel cleared her throat, breaking the tension. "We have seventy-two hours to clear millions of people from the coasts. The logistics are beyond overwhelming. But we have to try. The alternative is unthinkable."

"How big are we talking? How high will these waves get?" Caleb asked, finally lifting his head, his voice thick with disbelief.

Rachel turned toward him, her face drawn but resolute. "Some estimates put them at over 1,000 feet, depending on the location. The size of the waves will vary, but coastal areas like California, Japan, and parts of South America are looking at 1,000 feet or more. And it won't just be one wave. Aftershocks, secondary impacts, and the ocean disturbances will send waves crashing in for hours—possibly days."

"And what about inland? How far will the destruction go?" another voice asked from the back of the room.

Rachel's gaze darkened. "The tsunamis will penetrate inland by up to fifty miles, maybe more depending on the topography. Even cities not directly on the coast could be at risk. Rivers will back up, lakes could overflow. The damage will be far-reaching, way beyond what we've ever seen. But... it could have been worse. If this hit land, it would be the end of everything."

"Fortunate," Caleb muttered under his breath. He knew Rachel was right—this could have been far worse. But the thought of hundreds of millions of lives being lost, even with the ocean impact, felt like a hollow blessing.

He straightened in his chair, his resolve hardening. "We need to start evacuating now. California, Australia, Japan—every coastal city needs to be evacuated. We have to tell them."

"Evacuations are already underway," called out one of the logistics officers. "But let's be honest—there's no way we're getting everyone out. The roads are going to be jammed, airports overwhelmed. It's impossible."

"Then we get as many out as we can," Rachel interjected, her voice steely with determination. "We tell the people the truth. And the rest... the rest comes down to chance."

For a few agonizing moments, no one spoke. The enormity of what was coming sat heavily on their shoulders. They were scientists, strategists, and decision-makers, but even they were helpless in the face of nature's wrath.

"One more thing," Rachel added, her voice quieter now. "The impact is going to trigger earthquakes. Massive ones. The shockwaves will travel through the Earth's crust, causing tectonic shifts. We can't predict exactly where, but every fault line is going to feel it. The world is going to shake."

The team exchanged glances, struggling to digest the full scope of the catastrophe.

"We need to get the message out globally," Caleb said, breaking the silence. "This isn't just about the coasts. Everyone's going to feel this."

Rachel nodded. "We will. But no matter how much we warn people, no matter how loud we shout... some won't listen. Some won't believe it. They'll stay. And they won't survive."

As the reality of the impending asteroid impact sank in, global governments and emergency agencies launched the largest evacuation efforts in human history. The race against time had begun, and every second counted.

In the United States, the Federal Emergency Management Agency (FEMA) declared a nationwide state of emergency. Coastal cities along the Pacific—San Diego, Los Angeles, San Francisco, and Seattle—became ground zero for evacuation efforts. The highways, already notorious for traffic congestion, were turned into one-way roads out of the cities, directing millions of vehicles inland. Military convoys and National Guard units were deployed to maintain order and assist with logistics, but the sheer volume of people overwhelmed the system.

Television screens across the country flashed evacuation maps and routes, urging citizens to head east, away from the coast. Public transportation was commandeered, with buses, trains, and planes repurposed to ferry people inland. Emergency shelters were set up in the deserts of Nevada, Arizona, and New Mexico, far enough away from the expected reach of the tsunamis.

Hospitals in coastal cities were evacuated, with critically ill patients airlifted to facilities farther inland. But not everyone could be moved. The sight of hospitals working frantically to save those who couldn't leave the city, combined with the endless streams of cars inching along the freeways, painted a stark picture of desperation.

In Japan, the situation was even more dire. The country, with its densely packed population, had little room to move inland. Evacuations from cities like Tokyo, Yokohama, and Osaka were underway, with people heading north into the mountains and south toward less densely populated areas. The government mobilized every available resource, urging citizens to leave the coast. Bullet trains were packed, buses were overloaded, and even fishing boats became makeshift ferries for those trying to escape.

The Japanese Self-Defense Forces (JSDF) worked tirelessly to keep roads clear and assist in moving people away from the coastlines, but the sheer number of evacuees meant that many families had to make difficult choices about what to leave behind. Shinkansen (bullet trains) ran at maximum capacity, shuttling millions toward safety, while the government issued instructions for those stuck on foot to make their way to higher ground and hope for the best.

In Australia, cities like Sydney and Brisbane faced the same struggle. The Australian government called in the military to assist with evacuations, with helicopters and cargo planes lifting people to safety inland. People were evacuated to the Blue Mountains and other high-altitude regions, where makeshift camps were being set up in the open countryside.

Chile and Peru, countries that had seen their share of natural disasters, began preparing to move entire populations inland. Evacuation efforts along the west coast of South America faced severe challenges as cities like Lima, Santiago, and Valparaíso struggled to move people out of harm's way. Chilean naval ships were used to transport coastal communities up rivers into the Andean foothills.

New Zealand, positioned directly in the path of the incoming tsunamis, mounted its own evacuation efforts. The government urged people to head inland and to higher ground. In cities like Wellington and Auckland, residents packed up their homes and businesses, abandoning everything they couldn't carry in a mad rush to get away from the coast. Ferry services between the North and South Islands were suspended as ships were reassigned to evacuate coastal communities. The mountainous regions of New Zealand were flooded with evacuees seeking refuge.

Despite the coordinated efforts, chaos reigned in many

places. Roads clogged with cars, families packed together, and arguments broke out over fuel and supplies. Grocery stores were emptied in a matter of hours as people stockpiled whatever food and water they could find. Tempers flared as fuel became scarce, and some people were left with no choice but to abandon their vehicles and continue on foot.

Airports were flooded with people desperate for flights to anywhere that seemed safe, but the overwhelming demand for flights left most people stranded. The skies above California and Japan were crisscrossed with the contrails of military and civilian aircraft as airlifts became the last hope for many.

In the coastal cities, not everyone was willing—or able—to leave. Elderly citizens, people in poverty, and those without access to transportation were left behind. In some cases, police and National Guard units went door-to-door, urging people to evacuate, but the scope of the disaster meant that not everyone could be reached.

The media played a critical role in keeping the public informed, broadcasting live coverage of the evacuation efforts and giving constant updates on the asteroid's trajectory. Emergency broadcasts on radio stations urged people to remain calm, though panic was becoming a common sight in many places. For those without access to the news or the internet, military trucks with loudspeakers roamed the streets, blaring evacuation orders.

In rural areas, local radio stations were critical in getting the message out. Government agencies set up emergency call centers to coordinate rescue efforts, though the lines were frequently overwhelmed with people asking for help.

Despite the despair and chaos, moments of human resilience and cooperation shone through. Strangers shared their vehicles with those without transportation, and communities came together to help each other pack up and leave.

Doctors and nurses volunteered to stay behind to help those who couldn't be moved from hospitals. In many cities, ordinary citizens became impromptu leaders, organizing groups to make sure no one was left behind.

Shelters inland quickly filled up, but churches, schools, and community centers opened their doors to take in evacuees. Volunteers handed out blankets, water, and food, offering what little comfort they could to those who had left everything behind.

The evacuation efforts, despite their Herculean scope, were insufficient. Too many people, too little time. As the countdown to impact ticked closer, the true extent of the destruction to come weighed heavily on the shoulders of every government leader, military officer, and civilian watching the unfolding disaster.

Looters and arsonists, undeterred by the evacuation orders and widespread panic, stayed behind in the cities, convinced that the looming catastrophe was either exaggerated or wouldn't reach them. In their minds, the government warnings were just another tactic to control the masses. As residents fled inland, abandoning homes, businesses, and entire neighborhoods, the opportunists moved in.

They struck first in the wealthier districts. With law enforcement stretched thin and focused on managing the evacuations, luxury stores, high-end boutiques, and vacant mansions were easy targets. Looters broke into homes, prying open safes, emptying drawers, and smashing through storefront windows with an eerie sense of calm. Expensive electronics, jewelry, and art were carried off in broad daylight. Some looters arrived in trucks and vans, loading them up with stolen goods.

As dusk fell and the cities became eerily silent, the

arsonists followed. Without fear of retaliation, they lit fires indiscriminately—starting in abandoned stores, and then homes, setting entire blocks ablaze. Some set fire to buildings just for the thrill, using Molotov cocktails and gasoline. Flames spread quickly, especially in the densely packed neighborhoods. The already thin line of firefighters left behind to protect critical infrastructure was overwhelmed, forced to abandon the burning districts as the fires grew uncontrollable.

The looters saw opportunity in the chaos. They broke into supermarkets and pharmacies, stripping shelves bare of food, alcohol, medicine, and even baby formula. In their desperation to capitalize on the temporary lawlessness, they took anything they could carry, ignoring the warnings of the impending disaster. Some even laughed at the idea of fleeing, believing that they could ride out whatever was coming. They sat in high-rise apartments, their loot piled around them, watching the horizon as smoke filled the sky.

But the fires quickly spiraled beyond their control. Once the arsonists had torched half a neighborhood, they realized too late that the flames were spreading faster than they anticipated. Buildings collapsed, entire streets became firestorms, and in some cases, the looters who had chosen to stay behind found themselves trapped in the very cities they thought they would plunder.

In the heart of the cities, once grand and bustling areas became ghostly and apocalyptic. Thick smoke choked the air, blocking out the sun. The distant rumble of the approaching asteroid only added to the sense of impending doom, yet still, many refused to leave. For some, it was greed; for others, sheer disbelief that the end could really be near. And for a few, it was defiance—a refusal to be driven out by what they saw as the government's scare tactics.

As the countdown to impact drew closer, chaos and

fear gripped the cities and countryside alike. Fires blazed uncontrollably, fueled by the dry heat and the sheer terror of the impending destruction. Looters, who had initially believed they could take advantage of the lawlessness, soon realized—far too late—that there was no escape from the devastation that was about to come. Their stolen goods, clutched tightly in their arms, seemed meaningless in the face of the apocalypse bearing down on them. There was no hiding, no running fast enough, no place safe from the obliterating force descending upon the Earth.

While the Pacific had its own catastrophe brewing, Europe and the Atlantic Ocean faced a different kind of nightmare. Rather than a singular, cataclysmic asteroid, they were bombarded by a relentless meteor shower. Thousands of meteorites—ranging from 100 feet in diameter to the size of a football—rained down from the heavens, each one a fiery messenger of doom.

Most of these meteorites exploded before they hit the ground or a body of water, creating a sky alight with explosions, each blast more violent than the last. People across Europe, from London to Paris to Berlin, witnessed the terrifying spectacle of bright streaks of light hurtling toward the Earth, only to detonate with thunderous force. The larger meteorites, those that managed to reach the ground, unleashed devastating shockwaves upon impact, leveling buildings, tearing through infrastructure, and killing thousands instantly. Craters dotted the landscape where homes and businesses once stood, now reduced to smoldering ruins.

The smaller meteorites, though less immediately destructive, brought a slow, creeping doom. These fiery rocks, numbering in the tens of thousands, fell over an area of 4 million square miles, raining down like a fiery storm. They impacted rivers, lakes, and the Atlantic Ocean, their iron-rich cores sinking into the waters.

At first, the damage seemed purely physical—the burning of forests, cities, and farmlands—but soon, the true horror began to unfold. The influx of iron into the waters triggered an environmental disaster unlike anything seen before. Red toxic algae blooms spread across Europe's rivers, lakes, and coastal waters, their crimson hue turning the waters the color of blood. The algae, thriving on the iron deposits, released deadly toxins that poisoned the aquatic life, killing fish, plants, and anything that depended on oxygen in the water.

The once-clear waters teemed with death, suffocating entire ecosystems. Fishermen who had managed to survive the initial strikes now found themselves surrounded by lifeless seas, the air heavy with the stench of decay. Boats bobbed aimlessly, their nets empty and useless. What had once been a source of life and sustenance for Europe had become a poisoned wasteland, spreading its toxicity into the coastal regions and threatening the food supply for millions.

Communities that relied on freshwater sources now faced a grim reality—there was no safe water to drink. Entire towns were evacuated, their populations fleeing not only the fire raining from the sky but also the poisoned waters creeping inland. The death toll mounted, not just from the direct impacts of the meteorites but from the silent killer that spread through the waterways. In the aftermath, Europe was left to grapple with not only the immediate destruction but the long-term ecological collapse unfolding before their eyes.

The telescope optics component of Pan-STARRS was still in good condition but the human component was in pretty bad shape. With the asteroid induced tidal wave destroying the Institute for Astronomy at the University of Hawaii, there was nowhere for astronomers to work. The irony of the destruction of the Institute by an asteroid was not lost on the astronomers. Most survived the tidal wave - they were smart enough to get to high ground but many had had their homes destroyed. Just finding food moved to the top of their to-do list every day and tracking asteroids moved to the bottom. Clearly, if tracking asteroids became important at some time in the future, the hardware at the tops of Hawaiian volcanoes would be there waiting for the astronomers.

In a desperate attempt to continue their work, a handful of dedicated astronomers managed to make the arduous drive up Mauna Kea, determined to access the warm rooms at the summit to analyze images of asteroids. However, the journey to the top of the dormant volcano was far from simple. Mauna Kea, with its 40% lower oxygen levels and air pressure than at sea level, posed a dangerous challenge. Altitude sickness was a real threat—brought on by the rapid ascent and the body's inability to adjust to the thinner air. Headaches, nausea, vomiting, insomnia, and impaired coordination were common symptoms, and they could severely reduce performance.

In addition to the physical strain, practical issues compounded the astronomers' efforts. The struggle to find fuel for their vehicles, the scarcity of safe water, and the sheer difficulty of securing enough food made the idea of commuting to the summit more than just impractical—it bordered on impossible.

Given the mounting challenges, it wasn't a shock when the world failed to notice a looming disaster. A ten-mile-wide asteroid, slingshotting around Venus, went undetected by astronomers. This enormous space rock, hurtling towards Earth, positioned itself directly between the sun and the planet, casting a massive shadow across one-third of the globe. The world plunged into pitch-black darkness—a sudden, unanticipated eclipse that spanned continents.

The response was swift and devastating. As darkness

enveloped the land, fear and panic took hold, plunging cities and towns into chaos. Uncertainty spread like wildfire, fueling waves of hysteria. Riots erupted as people, gripped by desperation, looted stores and homes, scouring for supplies in what felt like an unfolding apocalypse. Windows shattered, alarms blared, and once-thriving neighborhoods devolved into lawless battlegrounds.

Flames erupted from burning buildings, filling the air with dense, acrid smoke that seared the lungs of anyone who dared remain in the streets. The poisonous haze choked the city, extinguishing any hope of peace. Gunshots echoed—a grim reminder of the desperation and violence that surged through the darkness as frantic mobs fought to secure dwindling resources.

Looters smashed barricades and raided stores for food, water, and anything that promised a measure of safety. The crackling roar of fires and the wail of sirens formed a relentless, chaotic soundtrack. In the suffocating darkness, every shadow seemed a threat, leaving people trapped between the burning streets and an unknown terror lurking beyond. What had once been orderly society had unraveled into a nightmarish scramble for survival, exposing humanity at its most desperate.

In major cities, entire districts fell to the frenzied mobs, looting whatever they could find. Police and emergency services were powerless, overwhelmed by the tide of violence. The streets, once filled with cars and bustling crowds, were now overrun by rioters smashing their way into storefronts, grabbing electronics, food, and water—anything of value. Fires spread unchecked, filling the air with thick smoke that made breathing even more difficult.

Amid the chaos, the darkness pushed people to the edge, their fear twisting into violence as a means of survival. Society teetered on the brink, oblivious to the even greater disaster hurtling toward it from the depths of space.

No one knew what the next few days would bring or how much of the world would survive.

CHAPTER 10
ABDUCTION

The Hanga Roa impact—that's what they called it after the closest inhabited land, the largest town on Easter Island. Hanga Roa lay about 2,300 miles from Chile and nearly 3,000 miles from ground zero in the vast South Pacific. The impact site itself was equidistant from the southern tips of South America and New Zealand, both around 3,000 miles away.

As predicted, colossal tidal waves—some towering up to 1,000 feet—obliterated coastal communities all around the Pacific Rim. Casualty estimates ranged anywhere from 100 million to 1 billion lives lost, a grim toll that left the world gasping in disbelief. Entire cities vanished beneath the unstoppable surge, and the devastation reached every corner of the Pacific.

Though Emma was aware that bad things were happening beyond the walls of Raven Rock, the full scope of the disaster was kept from her. She knew her family was hiding the worst of it, but she had no idea just how severe the catastrophe had been.

For example, she had no idea that Caleb's apartment, her parents' home, and entire swathes of Oahu had been flattened and washed away by the monstrous waves. She couldn't know that the University of Hawaii at Manoa, along with the Institute for Astronomy buildings, had been completely destroyed—ripped from the earth and swallowed by the ocean. The lucky ones who heeded the warnings and moved to high ground survived, but those who stayed behind—whether out of disbelief, defiance, or greed—perished in the chaos. Looters and arsonists, once so brazen in their refusal to leave, were among the countless lives lost, their final acts rendered futile in the face of such overwhelming destruction.

The world outside Raven Rock was unrecognizable, and while Emma's body fought cancer, the world outside was fighting to survive. But inside, the truth was kept at bay for just a little longer, and Emma remained sheltered from the unimaginable horrors unfolding in the wake of the Hanga Roa impact.

SPEOC, pronounced "Spock," the Satellite Presidential Emergency Operations Center, had its experts working around the clock to assess the damage and strategize. They figured it would take several months to get Pan-STARRS, along with the massive telescopes on Mauna Kea and Haleakala, operational again. This was a devastating blow, especially considering that ATLAS (Asteroid Terrestrial-impact Last Alert System), which was designed to provide last-minute warnings of incoming asteroids, also relied on the same infrastructure. With both systems offline, the world had lost over 70% of its capability to detect hazardous asteroids.

The chilling reality was that Earth was now far more vulnerable to asteroid impacts, with no early detection systems in place. Pan-STARRS had been humanity's decades-ahead warning system, while ATLAS was designed to give immediate alerts just before impact. Without them, it felt like the world was flying blind.

Zero hour arrived at 6:15 p.m. local time in the SPEOC bunker. The first tremor, traveling straight through the Earth's core, was felt at 6:26 p.m. It was a deep, unsettling rumble that seemed to come from beneath their feet, a reminder of the sheer magnitude of the forces at play. Just six minutes later, at 6:32 p.m., the shockwave that had traveled along the surface reached them. It crashed through like a violent ripple, jarring the walls and sending a collective shudder through the room. For the rest of the evening, the shockwave continued to circle the Earth, returning every 34 minutes, each pass slightly weaker as it dissipated over time. Similarly, the deep tremor echoed back every 22 minutes, fainter with each recurrence, as if the Earth itself was trying to shake off the blow.

When the first tremor hit, Dr. Rachel Timmins, leader of the Impact Team, stood up and addressed the group. "Quiet, please. Quiet." Her voice was firm, but her expression betrayed the weight of the moment. "It's happened, just as predicted. But right now—this very minute—there is nothing more we can do. So I'd like us to take a moment. A minute of silence, to remember the dead and those who are destined to die in this catastrophe, no matter how well or how poorly we do our jobs."

The room, already tense with dread, fell into a heavy silence. Heads bowed, the faint hum of machinery the only sound, each person lost in their own thoughts, aware of the enormity of the disaster unfolding across the globe.

-

Meanwhile, Caleb's role at SPEOC was diminishing. As the situation became more dire, his expertise in asteroid detection was becoming less relevant, and he found himself spending more time staring at the screens in the operations center than actively contributing. There was a growing sense of futility—his years of study and work seemed almost irrelevant now, with the observatories offline and chaos taking over.

When Emma suggested a family outing—a hike around the grounds of Raven Rock—Caleb had no real reason to refuse.

They had successfully shielded Emma from learning about the devastating Hanga Roa impact. Knowing the destruction it brought to Oahu—a place so deeply intertwined with her identity—would have shattered her spirit. Such grief could have hindered her recovery from chemotherapy, burdening her already fragile state. Protecting her from the knowledge served as an act of love; there was nothing she could do to change the past, and sparing her the weight of that sorrow felt like the only kindness they could offer.

With his workload shrinking, and the increasing sense of helplessness settling in, the idea of getting out into the open air, even for a short while, felt like a welcome reprieve.

Caleb, Emma, Star, Ted, and Bethany decided to celebrate the day before Emma's final week of chemotherapy. It had been three weeks since her last session, and Emma was feeling better than she had in months. The heaviness of the treatments had lifted just enough for her to remember what it felt like to be normal. Her energy was returning, even if it was temporary. For that brief moment, the cancer seemed like something she could overcome—or at least something she could live with. This was a day worth celebrating, despite the looming uncertainty of her future.

Liver cancer, she knew, had a way of coming back. That dark thought lingered at the edges of her mind, but she pushed it away. If this was her life now—fighting cancer, always on guard for its return—then she might as well seize the good moments when they came. And today was one of those moments. Even when the world outside was unraveling, and no one else could understand why she'd choose now, of all times, to celebrate, she insisted. She wanted to be surrounded by the people she loved, on this fine fall day, and feel alive.

They made their way up to the surface, behind the heavily guarded fences of Raven Rock. The fresh air hit them as soon as they stepped outside, crisp and cool, carrying the unmistakable scent of fallen leaves and pine needles. The sky was a brilliant blue, dotted with a few wispy clouds that looked like they had been painted there on purpose. It was the kind of fall day that made you forget, just for a moment, that anything could be wrong with the world.

The trail they chose was wide and well-maintained, winding gently through the forested grounds. The trees were in full autumn splendor—rich reds, vibrant oranges, and bright yellows cascading down from the branches, some leaves fluttering gently in the breeze to the ground below. Every step crunched beneath their boots, the sound of dried leaves breaking the peaceful silence that surrounded them.

Emma, though weaker than the rest, was determined. She pushed herself harder than she probably should have, but no one said anything. They all knew why she wanted to keep going. She needed to feel strong, if only for today.

"Let's go to the lowest lookout," Emma suggested with a faint smile, glancing up at Caleb. She could sense the concern in their eyes, but no one voiced their doubts. This was her day, and they were here for her. The lookout wasn't far, but it was a steep incline. She was going to feel it later—she knew that much—but right now, it didn't matter. She wanted to see the world from above, to take in the full beauty of the fall landscape.

The climb was slow and deliberate, with Emma pausing here and there to catch her breath, but she didn't complain. Caleb stayed close, always ready to lend a hand if she needed it, but he respected her desire to do it on her own. Star, Ted, and Bethany followed behind, chatting quietly, though their eyes often flickered to Emma, watching her with a mixture of pride and worry.

When they reached the lookout, the view was breathtaking.

The trees stretched out for miles, a rolling sea of autumn colors that seemed to glow in the soft afternoon light. The horizon was a blur of fading green and distant mountains, and far below, a winding river sparkled in the sun like a silver thread. The breeze was cool but gentle, carrying with it the faint scent of pine and earth.

Emma stood at the edge of the lookout, gripping the wooden railing, her chest rising and falling heavily as she caught her breath. But her eyes were bright, and for the first time in a long time, she felt truly at peace. She looked out over the vast landscape, letting the view sink into her soul.

"This," she said softly, her voice barely above a whisper, "is what I wanted. To see the world like this. To remember how beautiful it can be." She glanced over her shoulder at Caleb and the others. "I know what's coming. I know the fight isn't over. But right now... I just want to feel this. I want to celebrate this moment."

Caleb moved to her side, resting a hand on her shoulder. "You need this, Em. Every second of it."

-

Pan-STARRS was offline that day, its usual steady gaze at the cosmos interrupted when the Institute for Astronomy completed its mothballing of their mountain top facilities days ago. Every telescope and piece of equipment on Mauna Kea and Haleakala had been meticulously powered down, following strict protocols in the hopes that, after the tsunami passed, they could restart operations. Even the backup generators, typically left on for emergencies, were silenced. It was a grim precaution, one that symbolized how serious the threat was.

The Big Island of Hawaii, usually buzzing with activity, was eerily quiet. The entire population had been moved to higher ground, up beyond the 1,000-foot elevation mark on the slopes of the dormant volcano. What had once been home to a vibrant community and some of the most important astronomical equipment in the world now sat deserted, waiting for the oncoming waves.

So for Caleb, there was no astronomy today and probably not for weeks to come. There was no scanning the heavens for new discoveries, no data to pore over. The hum of technology that usually filled his life had been replaced by silence. A gnawing sense of helplessness settled in as he realized how fragile their work truly was. Alohanui was still out there, and he should have been tracking it, monitoring it—doing something. But all he could do now was wait.

It seemed like the hike couldn't have come at a more convenient time. With Pan-STARRS offline and the world around them in disarray, the simple act of walking through the forested trails around Raven Rock offered a temporary reprieve from the chaos. Caleb, Emma, Star, Ted, and Bethany had spent weeks inside the bunker, immersed in news updates, scientific reports, and the constant hum of fear. Today, however, felt different—a break from it all, even if it was just for a little while.

The five of them stood there in silence, taking in the view together, the quiet broken only by the sound of the wind rustling through the trees and the occasional distant birdcall. For just a little while, the world beyond their trail—beyond the chaos and destruction—ceased to exist. It was just them, the trees, the sky, and the colors of fall.

Emma stood quietly at the edge, taking it all in, her hand wrapped tightly around Caleb's. This hike, this view, this moment—it was hers. A small victory against the cancer that had stolen so much from her. For a brief moment, it didn't matter that the world was unraveling. It didn't matter that

Alohanui loomed in the background of every thought. Today, they were here, together, in the midst of this beautiful, fleeting fall day.

As they stood there, Emma allowed herself a rare moment of hope, even if it was fleeting. Today was for living. And she had no regrets for choosing this day to celebrate, even with everything else crumbling around them.

And that was enough. For now.

As they stood at the lookout, watching the strange cloud draw closer, an eerie stillness settled over the group. The cloud was no ordinary formation, brilliant in the sunlight but unnatural in its movement. Ted's casual comment about the storm coming now seemed chilling in light of what they were witnessing.

"Is that an air raid siren?" Ted asked, his voice filled with concern. Then, after a pause, he added, "Actually, it sounds more like a trumpet."

"Yeah, sometimes they play the trumpet through the outside PA system," Caleb replied. "It's all military out here, no civilians. But I don't have a clue what that trumpet call means. What about you, Ted?"

Ted shook his head, squinting into the distance. "I was too young for World War II and too old for Korea and Vietnam. So no, I don't know."

"Call to quarters," said Emma. "The trumpet is playing *Call to Quarters*. No time to explain how I know that. It's a long story, I'll tell you later. I think we need to return to Raven Rock right now."

The distant sound of the trumpet echoed through the forest, eerie and unfamiliar. As they turned to head back down something caught their attention and sent a cold chill down

Caleb's spine. High above them, objects—too many to count—were rising into the cloud, figures that looked disturbingly human were being pulled up, as if by some invisible force. Caleb had never seen anything like it.

His phone buzzed in his pocket, the vibration urgent against his leg. He answered immediately, his expression darkening as he listened to the voice on the other end.

"Like Emma said, we've got to get underground, now!" he exclaimed sharply, turning to the group.

They scrambled down the trail as quickly as they could. Emma, still weak from her chemotherapy, did her best to keep up, with Caleb holding her arm to support her. Each step was slower than the last, but they couldn't afford to stop. As they pushed forward, Caleb kept glancing back at the sky, unable to shake the terrifying sight. The figures—thousands of them—were rising into the clouds like grain sucked into a thresher.

"They might have the Rock locked down before we get there," Caleb muttered, panting from the effort. "If they do, we'll wait at the entrance. There'll still be soldiers there to keep us safe."

But his eyes kept drifting back to the sky. Among the floating bodies, he glimpsed a figure, glowing with a radiant white light. And nearby, unmistakable even at this distance, was the black spacecraft from Alohanui. The way it hovered, effortlessly drawing people into the sky, was disturbingly similar to the footage he'd seen of the black craft siphoning wheat from the grain elevators in Weyburn. Only now, it wasn't wheat being lifted—it was people.

"Where are these people coming from?" Caleb whispered to himself, confused. "This area is just forest... There shouldn't be anyone here."

His phone buzzed again. He answered quickly, listening with growing intensity. When he hung up, his face was pale.

"Raven Rock is secured. The vault's sealed tight," he told the others. "There's no point in rushing now. Reports are coming in from all over the world, and the strangest part? No one's missing. This... whatever it is, it's not taking the living."

They stopped, exchanging bewildered glances, the tension between them palpable. Ted frowned and glanced back at the swirling cloud above.

"Not the living?" Ted asked, his voice low and uncertain. "Then what...?"

Caleb's phone buzzed once more. The pre-recorded message was brief but chilling. When he put the phone down, his expression had grown even grimmer.

"They're robbing graves," he said, his voice flat with disbelief. "Funeral parlors, mausoleums, morgues... all the places where the dead are kept. It's not the living they're taking. It's dead bodies in various degrees of decomposition and not all of them, only a few from each place, many dead bodies left. All over the world."

The air seemed to grow heavier with each passing second, thick with the weight of the revelation. The extraterrestrials weren't here to abduct the living—they were hand picking the dead. And that truth, more than anything else, left them feeling helpless and horrified.

Though camouflaged from a distance, up close the tunnel entrance into the mountain housing Raven Rock was an awe-inspiring sight. It looked like an enormous bank vault, a fortress of thick steel reinforced with beams that could withstand almost anything. The door itself, wide enough for semi-trucks to pass each other effortlessly, towered over anyone standing near it. It wasn't just a door—it was a barrier, designed to protect those inside from whatever disaster raged outside.

At the moment, the vault was sealed tight, locked in place with no chance of opening for the next 48 hours. No exceptions.

Guarding the entrance were two National Guard soldiers, standing at attention with the kind of stern focus that spoke of long hours of training and an unspoken readiness for anything. They were clad in full combat gear, helmets gleaming under the overcast sky, their rifles resting across their chests. Though they stood still, there was a tension about them—like coiled springs waiting for the moment to act. Every now and then, one of them would speak into a radio, his voice low and controlled as he received updates or passed along status reports.

Nearby, hidden among the thick trees of the forest, stood antennas disguised as foliage. These deceptively simple structures were vital, ensuring communication between those inside Raven Rock and those outside. Although the vault door was closed, Caleb could still speak to personnel within the mountain, but nothing could change the fact that the door wouldn't budge for two days. It was protocol—a security measure whose reasoning was beyond Caleb's knowledge, but he knew well enough that it wasn't negotiable. The delay meant Emma's final round of chemotherapy would be postponed—two long days of waiting and worry.

Emma, however, had more immediate concerns on her mind. "Where will we sleep? What will we eat?" she wondered aloud, her voice carrying the exhaustion of a woman who had already been through too much.

Fortunately, the National Guard had anticipated these needs. The guards escorted Caleb, Emma, Ted, Star, and Bethany to a temporary shelter nearby. It was a reinforced tent, sturdy and functional, set up at the base of the mountain. Inside, the setup was simple but practical—cots lined up against the canvas walls, each one with a folded blanket waiting at its end.

The lighting was soft, casting a warm glow across the space, lending an unexpected coziness to the otherwise spartan accommodations. A small table in the corner held essentials—bottled water, MREs, and basic toiletries—enough to keep them comfortable while they waited for the vault to reopen.

Outside, the soldiers continued their silent vigil, the murmur of their radios blending with the rustling leaves of the forest. The air was thick with an odd mix of tension and calm. They were safe, for now, but the real safety—the fully protected underground city—was still locked behind that impenetrable door, just out of reach.

For now, all they could do was wait, hoping that the 48 hours would pass without further incident.

"I knew we were going for a hike, but I didn't realize we were going camping," Ted quipped when he laid eyes on the tent. His voice carried a surprising lightness, a brief reprieve from the heavy reality they had all been living in. "Hope there will be a campfire where we can roast marshmallows and weenies. Oh, and where's the beer? What's camping without beer?"

The sergeant who had escorted them chuckled softly, a smile pulling at the corners of his weathered face. For a moment, even he seemed to drift into nostalgia, wishing for the simpler times Ted alluded to—back when camping trips were just about fresh air and good company, not sheltering from the end of the world.

Caleb smiled, though it didn't quite reach his eyes. The memories Ted's words triggered in him were bittersweet. He could almost see it—those weekends when his parents had loaded up the family car with tents, sleeping bags, and coolers full of food. Bethany, always the first to run ahead, eager to find the perfect spot by the lake where they'd set up camp. His father would be lighting the fire, teaching them how to toast marshmallows just right, while his mother handed out snacks and drinks, her laughter filling the air.

Now, standing at the edge of a temporary shelter set up to stave off the chaos of the outside world, those carefree camping trips felt like memories from another life. He glanced over at Bethany and saw a faraway look in her eyes. He knew she was thinking about the same thing—the warmth of those fires, the sound of crickets at night, and the feeling of safety they had all taken for granted.

Emma, leaning on Caleb for support, let out a soft sigh, pulling them all back to the present. The tent was no cabin in the woods, no weekend retreat. It was a refuge from the uncertain world they now lived in, where a walk through the woods could turn into a sprint for survival. The humor in Ted's voice was a fleeting glimpse of hope—a reminder that they could still find something to laugh about, even if it was just a small, shared moment of levity in the face of so much uncertainty.

The sergeant, still smiling, gave a brief nod as if to acknowledge that they all could use a little of that lightness. "Well, sir, if I could conjure up a campfire and some cold ones, I would. But for now, all we've got are MREs and bottled water." He gestured to the makeshift supplies table. "Afraid that's as close to a campout as we're gonna get today."

Caleb's gaze lingered on the table—a far cry from the spread they used to enjoy on those family trips. Yet here they were, making do. "Looks like we're roughing it," he said quietly, his smile just a little stronger this time, as he squeezed Emma's hand.

Bethany stepped forward, her face softening as she added, "Maybe we can save the marshmallows and beer for when this is all over. When things are... normal again."

The words hung in the air, tinged with a fragile hope. Ted gave a small chuckle, patting Bethany on the shoulder. "I'll hold you to that," he said warmly.

The sergeant nodded, wishing them well before returning to his post. As he left, a silence settled over the group, but it wasn't heavy with fear or dread this time. Instead, it was the kind of silence that often followed after a good laugh—a pause that gave space for everyone to breathe, to remember that no matter how strange the world had become, they were still together.

Caleb glanced at Emma, her tired smile giving him all the motivation he needed to keep going. They would make it through this, somehow. Maybe, one day, they really would have that campfire again. But for now, they would take this moment for what it was—a small, fleeting piece of normalcy in the middle of all the chaos.

Emma, of course, was exhausted, as were her parents, so everyone quietly retired to their cots, dousing the lights. Despite their fatigue, sleep came slowly, slipping through fitful dreams as the weight of the world pressed down on them.

Emma rose before dawn, sensing that she wasn't the only one awake. In the dim light, she could see Bethany stirring on her cot as well. With a soft motion, Emma signaled for her sister-in-law to follow. They grabbed their coats, slipping out of the tent into the cool, early morning air.

"Maybe we can catch the sunrise," Emma whispered, the crispness of the air clearing her thoughts.

They approached one of the guards standing watch outside the shelter. "Any chance you know a good spot to see the sunrise?" Emma asked.

The guard, an older man with tired eyes, nodded and pointed to a nearby rocky outcropping. "Climb up there, you'll get a good view. I'll keep an eye on you from here."

"Thanks," they murmured, as they started their short trek. The world was quiet, the earth still dark, but the sky was slowly brightening with the promise of dawn. As they reached the outcropping, the horizon began to glow faintly, with the sun still hidden just below. The undersides of the clouds ahead were tinged with the first light, turning from a deep blue-gray to a brilliant white, streaked with pink and gold.

Emma pointed toward the horizon. "Look there," she said, eyes widening in surprise. "That cloud... it looks like a man standing."

Bethany followed Emma's gaze, her voice catching slightly. "It reminds me of...," she trailed off, words lost to a mix of awe and memory.

Suddenly, with a soft smile and a mischievous glint in her eyes, Emma stretched her arms toward the sky. "I can fly!" she said, laughing softly.

Bethany smiled, the lightness of the moment breaking through the heaviness of the night before. For a brief, fleeting moment, as the sky continued to brighten, it felt like there was still a world of possibilities ahead of them—something to hope for, even with all that was happening around them.

-

Only the guard witnessed the abduction, and what he saw would haunt him for the rest of his life. It was a quiet, crisp morning, and everything had seemed so peaceful as Bethany and Emma climbed the rocky outcropping to watch the sunrise. The soft glow of dawn was just beginning to paint the landscape in warm hues, the world around them still asleep. He had kept a casual eye on them, watching as they chatted quietly, their figures silhouetted against the brightening sky.

Suddenly, without warning, a strange hum filled the air. The guard straightened up, squinting toward the horizon.

His hand instinctively reached for his rifle, but there was nothing immediately visible to explain the sudden shift in the atmosphere. The hum grew louder, and the air itself seemed to vibrate.

It all happened so fast.

The guard's breath caught in his throat as he saw the wind pick up around Emma and Bethany, swirling violently like an invisible vortex. He blinked, thinking it was just a trick of the light, but before he could react, both women were lifted off the ground as if they weighed nothing. Their arms flailed briefly, instinctively reaching out for something solid, but there was nothing to hold onto. In a matter of seconds, they were no longer standing on the rocky ledge, but rising into the sky, pulled upward by an unseen force.

The clouds overhead darkened, swirling in unnatural patterns. The guard shouted, his voice hoarse and frantic, but no one else was around to hear him. He watched in stunned horror as Emma and Bethany were sucked higher and higher, their bodies drawn into the rolling mass of clouds. The brilliant sunrise now seemed ominous, as the two women vanished into the swirling vapor, swallowed by the sky itself.

He stood frozen, rifle still in hand but utterly useless. His heart pounded in his chest as he radioed frantically for help, barely able to speak through the shock. The only thing he could manage was a disjointed report—"They're gone... Emma Kanoa and Bethany Jacobson... they were taken... into the clouds."

When reinforcements arrived minutes later, there was nothing left but the morning light and the lingering echo of the hum. Emma and Bethany were gone, vanished without a trace. The guard was left staring into the sky, trying to make sense of what he had just witnessed.

All he could say, over and over, was, "They were taken... right up into the sky." His voice trembled, but no one could quite believe it until they saw the security footage from the hidden cameras near the outcropping.

The footage was grainy, distorted by the strange energy surrounding the abduction, but it showed enough—a sudden gust of wind, Emma and Bethany rising off the ground, and then nothing. They were gone.

In the following hours, the entire Raven Rock facility was on high alert. Every available guard, scientist, and military officer was called in to analyze the incident, but no one had any answers. What force had taken them? Why? And most terrifying of all—would it come back?

CHAPTER 11
INVASION

For Caleb, Ted, and Star, the moment Emma and Bethany were taken, it was as if their lives were snuffed out along with them. They had survived so much already—the uncertainty of the world unraveling, the chaos of the looming asteroid, the relentless trials of Emma's illness—but nothing had prepared them for this. The sudden, violent abduction of their loved ones into the sky was something beyond comprehension, something that felt more like a nightmare than reality.

Caleb, who had spent his life searching for answers in the cosmos, now found himself helpless in the face of something inexplicable, something that defied every law of science he had ever known. He replayed the moment over and over in his mind, the guard's frantic report, the chilling image of Emma and Bethany being pulled into the sky. No matter how hard he tried to grasp it, there was no logic, no reason that could explain what had happened. His mind, once a sanctuary of rational thought and problem-solving, was now consumed by grief and disbelief. The vastness of space, which had always been his ally, now felt like a cruel enemy, stealing away the people he loved most.

Ted and Star were shattered. They had already lost their home, seen the world around them descend into madness, and now they had lost their daughter and *adopted* daughter. Ted, once so steady and grounded, now wandered aimlessly through the days, his mind trapped in a haze of guilt and regret. He blamed himself for not acting sooner, for not protecting his family, for not somehow foreseeing this unimaginable event. He had watched helplessly as his family was torn apart, and now he was left with the empty, hollow feeling that he had failed in his most sacred duty as a father.

Star, always the emotional anchor, was adrift. The weight of the loss was unbearable, and she felt it physically, like a crushing force on her chest. She would sit for hours, staring blankly into space, her thoughts lost in memories of Emma as a child, of Bethany's laughter, of family dinners that now felt like they had happened in another lifetime. Star had always been strong for her family, but this—this was too much. The pain was relentless, seeping into every part of her being, leaving her fragile and broken.

The days following the abduction passed in a blur, a never-ending cycle of grief, anger, and numbness. Caleb stopped eating, stopped sleeping. Every time he closed his eyes, he saw Emma and Bethany, floating helplessly into the clouds, just out of reach. He spent hours in front of the screens in the SPEOC bunker, watching the sky, waiting for something, anything, that might explain what had happened. But there was nothing—just the cold, indifferent silence of the universe.

Ted and Star withdrew into themselves, their once-vibrant personalities dulled by the overwhelming sorrow that had enveloped them. They barely spoke, their conversations reduced to whispers of shared pain, a language only they could understand. They had lost their daughters, and in losing them, they had lost themselves.

For Caleb, Ted, and Star, the future felt like a hollow, meaningless stretch of time. Their purpose, their reason for fighting, was gone. Emma and Bethany had been their light, their hope, and without them, the world felt dark and empty. There was no moving forward, no healing from this kind of loss. The grief was too deep, too all-consuming.

They were still alive, still breathing, but in every other way, their lives had ended the moment Emma and Bethany were taken into the sky. And no amount of time or explanation would ever bring them back.

-

Alohanui was back in the headlines, and this time the news was impossible to ignore.

After months of continuous monitoring by the nations of earth, the massive cube, Alohanui, had finally settled into geosynchronous orbit. Unlike Earth's traditional geosynchronous satellites, which maintain a stable position 22,236 miles above mean sea level directly over the equator, Alohanui defied convention. It took up a position 2,200 miles north of the equator in what scientists termed an "offset geosynchronous orbit." This location should have been impossible for any Earth-made object, as such an orbit would typically require a continuous lateral force to maintain—something no known human technology could achieve.

However, Alohanui once again displayed its mastery of physics far beyond anything humanity was capable of. To generate the necessary lateral force, it rotated its enormous bright white square base—essentially functioning as a solar sail. By carefully angling this base towards the sun, Alohanui harnessed the gentle yet constant pressure of sunlight to maintain its unnatural orbital position. It was a subtle but profound reminder of the technological and scientific prowess of whatever civilization had constructed this impossibly advanced structure.

The fact that Alohanui could not only sustain such an impossible orbit but also manipulate natural forces with pinpoint precision left Earth's scientists in a state of awe and growing unease. Each new discovery about the cube's capabilities deepened the unsettling realization that humanity was facing a power whose grasp of the universe far exceeded anything known to human science. The sheer sophistication of Alohanui's technology was a stark reminder that Earth's most advanced theories were primitive in comparison to the knowledge wielded by those who had sent the cube.

Its chosen location? The volatile region of the Middle East, hovering directly above the West Bank—a contested area that included the Arab state, Israeli West Jerusalem, and Palestinian East Jerusalem.

The arrival of Alohanui over one of the most religiously and politically sensitive places on Earth sparked immediate chaos. Riots broke out in the streets, escalating into full-scale war between Israel and its surrounding neighbors. The sight of the alien object looming overhead acted as both a symbol of divine prophecy to some and a harbinger of doom to others.

Then came the real terror. Alohanui, which had remained a distant and ominous presence for so long, suddenly began a rapid descent, as if waiting for the perfect moment to make its move. The cube, once floating serenely in space, now appeared to have a deliberate agenda. Its descent was direct, intentional, aimed squarely at the contested land below.

More than one million people lived beneath the area where Alohanui seemed to be heading. Panic spread like wildfire. The descent was swift at first, taking only an hour for the cube to reach the edge of Earth's atmosphere. Then, in a terrifying display of its mastery over mass and gravity, Alohanui slowed almost to a stop. To the naked eye, it appeared to have halted completely, but closer observation revealed it was still moving—just at an excruciatingly slow pace of about one mile per hour. At that rate, it would take approximately 60 hours to reach the ground.

As Alohanui decelerated at the edge of the atmosphere, over two hundred satellites traveling at 17,000 miles per hour smashed against its forcefield. Most of these were Starlink satellites, a devastating blow to SpaceX's network. The sudden loss of the Starlink system left millions of people, particularly in remote areas, without access to the internet for weeks. This included the U.S. military, one of Starlink's largest clients. As a result, the military's secure communication network was crippled, and only the most critical surveillance data and operations regarding Alohanui were prioritized. The disruption severely limited the real-time surveillance feeds, leaving the US military partially blind in monitoring the object's every move.

Meanwhile, on the ground, the situation was spiraling into chaos. Evacuating a million people from an area 18 miles square in 60 hours was an impossible task under normal circumstances. Now, with streets clogged by war refugees and ongoing conflict, it became a nightmare beyond comprehension. There simply wasn't enough time. People caught in the shadow of Alohanui could do nothing but watch in helpless terror as the massive cube loomed larger and larger in the sky, edging ever closer to the earth.

During the day, the bright white base of Alohanui was barely visible in the sky, blending in with the sunlight. But as the sun set and the sky darkened, the cube became impossible to miss. Alohanui, still illuminated by the rays of the sun from space, stood out like a massive, glowing monolith in the twilight. To those on the ground, it appeared to be descending ever closer, its size increasing dramatically hour by hour.

It was a terrifying sight. The massive cube, already an object of fascination and fear, now became something far more menacing. As it descended, casting an enormous shadow over the land below, the entire region braced for what seemed like an inevitable disaster. Yet no one knew what Alohanui's true intention was. Was this the end, or just the beginning of something even worse?

In Jerusalem, mosques, synagogues, and churches filled with people praying for deliverance, each hoping that their god would intervene. But the slow, deliberate descent of Alohanui continued, indifferent to their prayers. The atmosphere became thick with tension, the air heavy with the uncertainty of what was to come.

And as the massive, glowing object inched closer and closer, it seemed as though the very earth was holding its breath, waiting for the inevitable.

Caleb entered Ted and Star's dimly lit apartment, and the weight of their grief hit him immediately. Star lay curled up on the bed, her face hidden beneath a blanket, while Ted sat slouched in a chair, staring blankly at the TV. The flickering screen reflected off his glasses, but it was clear he wasn't paying much attention to whatever program was on.

Caleb stood in the doorway for a moment, uncertain. He hadn't expected to find them like this. The sadness in the room was almost tangible, like a fog that clung to everything. He wanted to turn back, to leave them in peace, but he couldn't. Not with what he had to say.

"Hey, Ted. Star," Caleb said gently as he stepped inside.

Ted turned his head slowly, blinking as though surfacing from a deep reverie. "Caleb? You here for something?"

Star stirred but didn't look up. The sight of her like this—a woman who had always been so full of life—hurt Caleb in ways he hadn't expected.

"I need to talk to both of you," Caleb said, his voice steady but soft. He pulled up a chair and sat down across from Ted. "There's... something I've been asked to do. And it's dangerous."

That got their attention. Ted leaned forward slightly, his brows furrowing. Star, still not looking at him, shifted under the covers.

"I've been asked to volunteer for a mission," Caleb continued. "They need someone to go to where Alohanui is set to land. They want someone there when it touches down, someone who isn't military. It's in a war zone, no guarantees of safety, and I'd be on my own."

Ted's face went pale. Star finally uncovered her face and looked at Caleb with wide, tear-streaked eyes.

"But why you?" Star asked, her voice shaky but insistent. "You don't have to do this, Caleb. You're not a soldier."

"No, I'm not," Caleb agreed. "But they need someone who can get close without being detected, someone who understands what Alohanui might be, what it represents. And, to be honest, I'm probably one of the few people willing to go."

There was a long, heavy silence. Ted rubbed his temples, his jaw clenched tightly. "It sounds like a suicide mission," he said finally, his voice rough. "And you've already lost so much. Don't throw your life away, Caleb. Not like this."

Caleb looked at him, struggling with the same thoughts. But deep down, he knew this was something he had to do. "I don't want to throw my life away," he said quietly. "But I can't just sit here and do nothing either. I feel like... maybe I could find them. Maybe Emma and Bethany are on Alohanui. I know it sounds crazy, but every instinct I have is telling me that I have to go."

Star sat up slowly, looking between Ted and Caleb. Her eyes were filled with grief but also understanding. "You think... they might be up there?" she asked softly.

"I don't know," Caleb admitted, his voice cracking slightly. "But I have to try. I can't just... give up on them. Not yet."

Ted and Star exchanged glances, their sadness deep but their love for Caleb even deeper. They knew that nothing they said could truly dissuade him, and perhaps, in their own way, they understood. Star reached out, her hand trembling, and took Caleb's hand in hers.

"If this is what you need to do," she whispered, "then you go. Find Emma. Find Bethany. We'll be here, waiting for you, no matter what."

Ted cleared his throat, his voice thick with emotion. "We've already lost so much, Caleb. But we know you wouldn't take this lightly. If this is what your heart tells you to do, you have our blessing. Just... come back to us. Please."

Caleb nodded, his eyes stinging with unshed tears. "Thank you," he whispered. "I don't know if I'll come back. But I'll do everything I can to find them. I promise."

He stood to leave, but Ted grabbed his arm. "Caleb, remember—whatever happens out there, you're family. And family doesn't disappear. We'll always hold a place for you, no matter what."

Caleb squeezed Ted's arm in return. "I'll come back," he said, though he wasn't sure if he believed it. But as he walked out of the apartment and back toward Rachel's office, he felt a renewed sense of purpose.

Star and Ted had given him their blessing. He didn't know exactly how or why, but the idea of finding Emma and Bethany up there, on Alohanui, didn't seem as far-fetched anymore.

When Caleb returned to Rachel's office, she was already standing, her arms crossed, her expression a mix of patience and determination.

"Well?" she asked, her tone calm but her eyes searching his face for an answer.

Caleb drew in a deep breath, steadying himself. "I'm in," he said firmly. "But I have a favor to ask. Can you reach out to Pastor Ben? I don't know his last name, but he often visited Emma in the chemo ward. Could you ask him to check in on Star and Ted while I'm gone?"

Rachel's expression softened, a hint of a smile tugging at the corner of her lips. "Of course," she replied. "I'll contact him and make the request. He'll look after them."

"Thank you," Caleb said, his voice hiding his fear of the mission but tinted with quiet gratitude.

"Good luck, Caleb," Rachel added, her voice steady and sincere as she extended her hand. Caleb shook it firmly, their shared understanding unspoken but palpable.

-

Caleb stood on the tarmac, staring up at the massive C-130 Hercules that would take him on the first leg of his journey to Alohanui's projected landing zone. The plane's engines rumbled, a deep, throaty sound that seemed to vibrate the very ground beneath him. Soldiers moved around him, loading supplies, coordinating equipment, and preparing for departure. This was a military operation, but for Caleb, it felt deeply personal.

The mission was simple on paper: travel to the war-torn area where Alohanui was set to descend, land, and wait. The reality, however, was far more complex. He would be alone, deep in hostile territory, with no military support once he arrived. The C-130 would get him close, but he'd have to make his way on foot through an area currently embroiled in all-out war.

He adjusted the straps on his backpack, feeling the weight of the supplies he carried—just enough to keep him going for a few days, along with equipment for documenting what he saw and communicating back to SPEOC. His mind raced with questions, fears, and a faint glimmer of hope.

"Caleb," Rachel's voice brought him back to the present. She was standing beside him, her expression a mix of concern and resolve. "This is your last chance to back out. You know that, right?"

Caleb nodded, but his mind was made up. "I know. I have to do this."

Rachel sighed, handing him a small tablet. "This is a direct link to SPEOC. Satellite uplink. Use it only when absolutely necessary. We can't risk the signal being intercepted."

He took it, sliding it into a pouch on his belt. "Got it."

The pilot called for boarding, and Caleb turned to face the plane. The massive, olive-drab aircraft looked intimidating, but it was his only way to get where he needed to go. He shook Rachel's hand, gave her a nod, and made his way up the ramp into the belly of the Hercules.

Inside, the cargo bay was dimly lit, lined with rows of seats along the walls. Soldiers, strapped in with harnesses, barely glanced at him as he found his seat. The plane was filled with supplies—rations, medical gear, and other essentials bound for military outposts closer to the landing zone. Caleb settled into the webbed seat, securing the harness over his chest.

The engines roared to life as the plane taxied down the runway, and within minutes, they were airborne. The flight was long, grueling, and tense. The Hercules was not built for comfort—its metal floors cold, the constant rumble of the engines loud enough to make conversation nearly impossible. Caleb pulled his jacket tighter around himself and tried to focus on the task ahead.

As the plane climbed higher, he stared out through the small window, watching the landscape below grow smaller and more distant. Somewhere down there, in the chaos of war, was the place where Alohanui would touch down. The thought filled him with a strange mixture of dread and anticipation.

The hours passed slowly, punctuated only by the occasional murmur from the flight crew or the shifting of the soldiers nearby. Caleb dozed off at some point, only to be awakened by the descent of the plane as they neared their destination.

The interior of the plane was stark and utilitarian, its unadorned walls and sparse seating arrangement reflecting its purpose as a military transport rather than a commercial jet. The hum of the engines filled the cabin, a steady background noise that seemed to heighten Caleb's sense of unease. He was caught off guard when a man in plain overalls slid into the seat beside him. The overalls bore no insignia, rank, or badge—no indication of any military branch or government agency.

Without introducing himself, the man leaned in and spoke in a low, firm voice, his tone leaving no room for argument. "What I am about to tell you is classified at the highest level. You are not to share this information with anyone."

Caleb tensed, his pulse quickening as the man continued.

"The President, Vice President, and the surviving Cabinet members have relocated to Raven Rock. The mountain has been sealed per presidential order. Charges, installed years ago for this contingency, were detonated to collapse the rock above and around the entrance, blocking it completely. Thousands of tons of debris now seal the complex. Everyone inside is there for the long haul. For now, the communication cables and camouflage antennas are operational, but no one can say for how long."

The man's voice grew heavier, his expression unchanging. "Lastly, and with great sympathy, I must inform you that your fiancée's parents, Ted and Star Kanoa, have been reported missing. Raven Rock is in utter chaos. It's possible they are lost somewhere in the labyrinth of tunnels, but it's equally likely they figured out what was happening and slipped out just before the doors were sealed and the charges detonated."

Caleb stared at the man, his mind reeling. The weight of the revelation left him speechless, his stomach churning with dread and disbelief. The thought of Ted and Star trapped—or worse—was almost too much to bear.

The man's tone softened but remained resolute. "Finally, I must remind you of the gravity of your mission. It is of supreme importance to the United States of America. Please do not abandon it to try and locate Ted and Star. You will serve as our only eyes and perhaps the sole representative of America at what may be the most significant event in human history. Rest assured, we are doing everything possible to locate the Kanoa family, and you will be informed as soon as we have any news."

Without waiting for a reply, the man stood and walked briskly toward the back of the cabin, disappearing into the shadows. Caleb remained frozen in his seat, the hum of the engines now a hollow echo in his ears as he grappled with the enormity of what he had just learned.

"We're about an hour out," the pilot's voice crackled over the intercom. "We'll be landing at a military forward operating base just outside the war zone. After that, you're on your own."

Caleb nodded to himself, bracing for what was to come. The

base would be the last bit of relative safety before he entered the chaos on foot. He wasn't sure what to expect once he arrived, but he knew he couldn't afford to hesitate.

The plane touched down with a jarring thud, bouncing slightly on the rough airstrip. As the engines powered down, the ramp at the back of the plane lowered, revealing the dusty, barren landscape of the military base. Soldiers were already moving to unload supplies, but Caleb wasted no time. He grabbed his backpack, adjusted his gear, and made his way off the plane.

The air outside was dry, hot, and filled with the acrid scent of smoke. The base was a sprawling complex of tents and makeshift buildings, with soldiers moving in and out in a constant state of motion. Humvees rumbled past, their tires kicking up clouds of dust. In the distance, Caleb could hear the low rumble of artillery—evidence of the ongoing conflict not far from where he stood.

A sergeant approached him, clipboard in hand. "You're the civilian, right?"
"Yeah," Caleb said, tightening his grip on his pack.

"Good luck out there. You're heading straight into a hot zone." The sergeant handed him a map, marked with the route he'd need to follow. "Keep your head down and stay off any main roads. We'll get you as close as we can by vehicle, but after that, you're on foot. Got it?"

Caleb nodded, slipping the map into his jacket pocket. He followed the sergeant to a waiting Humvee, where two soldiers stood ready to take him as far as they could. The vehicle roared to life, and within moments, they were speeding away from the base. The scenery outside the window painted a grim picture—vast stretches of scorched earth, skeletal remains of bombed-out buildings, and the flickering glow of fires stretching across the horizon like distant, unrelenting beacons of destruction.

The lieutenant in the passenger seat turned toward Caleb, his face grim, illuminated by the faint light from the dashboard. "This will be your final briefing," he began, his tone measured but heavy with urgency.

"Reports indicate that the Euphrates River has either dried up or been intentionally rerouted. This has paved the way for the unthinkable: a mobilization of 200 million troops from China, Russia, and North Korea, all converging toward a mustering point at Megiddo, in Northern Israel."

Caleb's pulse quickened, the enormity of the situation pressing down on him. The lieutenant continued, his voice unyielding.

"The city of Hillah, historically known as Babylon, has been completely annihilated—flattened without a trace. While its strategic significance remains unclear, the symbolic weight of its destruction cannot be ignored."

The lieutenant's expression darkened further, and he leaned slightly closer as though the next piece of information required added gravity. "Finally, and perhaps most critically, there is an outbreak of what the doctors are calling 'fistulous skin ulcers.' It's a highly infectious disease—these ulcers form channels, or fistulas, that drain pus directly to the skin's surface. The design is grotesquely efficient, turning the afflicted into unintentional agents of contagion."

The air inside the Humvee felt heavier, oppressive with the grim litany of catastrophes unfolding in real time. Caleb stared out at the darkened landscape, the lieutenant's words replaying in his mind. Each piece of information seemed like another step toward an unimaginable reckoning, yet he knew there was no turning back.

When the Humvee finally stopped, the soldiers exchanged grim looks with him. "This is it," one of them said. "Good luck."

Caleb stepped out of the vehicle, slinging his backpack over his shoulder. The heat was oppressive, and the air was thick with tension. He glanced up at the sky, knowing that somewhere above him, Alohanui was descending ever so slowly. He could feel it—like a weight pressing down on the world, growing heavier with every passing hour.

With a final nod to the soldiers, Caleb turned and began walking toward the landing zone. The landing zone, once the most sacred city of Jerusalem, now resembled a scene from an apocalyptic nightmare. It was not bombs or missiles that had reduced the city to ruins just hours ago, but an unprecedented earthquake—one so powerful it split the city into three sections along fault lines, turning its ancient masonry buildings into piles of rubble. The devastation was total. Many who had defied evacuation orders perished, while those who survived were left with no reason to remain. Food, water, and shelter were gone, forcing them to flee in search of basic necessities. Yet escape was fraught with danger. Caleb had been warned that soldiers from the surrounding armies, driven by fear and chaos, were indiscriminately shooting any refugees they encountered.

By the time Alohanui began its slow descent, the city was utterly abandoned.

The earthquake, the most powerful ever recorded, exceeded a magnitude of 10 on the Richter scale—a measurement so colossal it defied the capacity of conventional instruments, which capped at 9.5. It was an event of such violence that it literally reshaped the region. Mountains shifted, some rising, others collapsing, while entire island nations, including Cyprus and Crete, were displaced hundreds of feet eastward. The seismic activity also triggered volcanic eruptions, spewing vast amounts of ash and particulate matter into the atmosphere. For weeks afterward, the moon hung blood-red in the sky, an eerie reminder of the catastrophe.

The destruction extended far beyond Jerusalem. The earthquake's impact reverberated across the region, leaving behind a fractured and desolate landscape. The scars of war, both human and natural, marked the earth. Yet, amidst the devastation, Alohanui descended with an air of deliberate precision, indifferent to the chaos it had amplified.

Caleb could feel the weight of the moment as he made his way through the ruined terrain. Every step felt like walking on the bones of history, the sacred ground of Jerusalem now unrecognizable. He thought about the people who had once lived here—pilgrims, worshippers, families—and the lives that had been lost in the quake or at the hands of the soldiers patrolling the perimeter. The eerie silence, broken only by the distant hum of Alohanui's approach, underscored the profound emptiness of the city.

Scientists at SPEOC described the quake as a once-in-an-era event, likely triggered or exacerbated by Alohanui's gravitational manipulation. Caleb knew the numbers: millions displaced, hundreds of thousands dead, and entire ecosystems disrupted by the tectonic upheaval. The sight of the devastated city, combined with the reports of Alohanui's gravitational influence, painted a grim picture of a world pushed to its limits.

As Caleb scanned the horizon, the ruins of Jerusalem stretched out before him, a shattered testament to human history and resilience. He couldn't shake the feeling that Alohanui's arrival was more than an invasion or occupation—it was a rewriting of the Earth's story.

Every step felt like a march toward the unknown, but Caleb didn't hesitate. He had to be there when Alohanui arrived.

He had to find Emma.

Some expert, tucked away deep in the labyrinthine tunnels of Raven Rock, had proposed that the East Portal would be the ideal entry point. Alohanui, with its faces perfectly aligned to the cardinal directions, had an east-facing portal right in the center of the east wall. The expert's theory was that if any side opened to allow an ambassador—or anyone else—inside, it would be this one. Caleb hoped they were right. One miscalculation and he'd be crushed if Alohanui rotated even slightly before it touched down.

Caleb glanced down at his satellite-linked tablet, which updated him in real-time. Alohanui had slowed to a crawl, moving at just over half a mile every two hours. It was eerie to think that something so massive—18 miles per side—could hover so quietly, so deliberately. With the perimeter of the cube stretching 72 miles, Caleb knew that if the expert was wrong, he could be facing a 3 to 7 mile trek to the next potential entry point.

The landing area, scarred by war, was mountainous. A jagged range of peaks ran roughly north to south, cutting through the middle of what would soon be Alohanui's vast base. Caleb's tablet showed him the terrain's elevation, with a 3,000-foot difference between the highest and lowest points. If the cube stopped when its first point touched the ground, enormous gaps would exist between the base of the structure and the earth below. It was impossible to predict exactly what would happen once the extraterrestrial object made contact with Earth.

Caleb's only plan of action was the expert's suggestion so he had made his way to the spot where he hoped Alohanui would welcome its first human emissary. The air was thick with tension, not just from the impending landing, but from the uncertainty that gripped the world. Every second that ticked by felt like an eternity, and the weight of the moment pressed down on Caleb as heavily as Alohanui itself.

He took a deep breath and scanned the horizon. To the east, the Jordan River Valley stretched out in the morning haze, a peaceful contrast to the tension filling the air. To the west, the silhouette of Jerusalem stood solemn against the horizon, its ancient stones bracing for whatever would come next.

Suddenly, the ground beneath Caleb's feet trembled—Alohanui had made its first contact with Earth, touching down on the sacred ground of the Temple Mount. The tremor rippled through the landscape, more like the deep rumble of an earthquake than a simple landing. Caleb staggered slightly as the earth groaned beneath the immense weight of the extraterrestrial cube.

What followed was unlike anything he had ever experienced. The friction of rock against rock generated static electricity that exploded into the sky. Thunder and lightning, violent and unnatural, lit up the heavens. Streaks of blinding light lashed across the sky, splitting the horizon with deafening cracks of thunder. It felt as though the heavens themselves were reacting to the intrusion, a cosmic protest at the sudden arrival of something beyond comprehension.

Caleb stood frozen, staring at the apocalyptic display. This was no ordinary storm; it was as if the very fabric of the Earth was fighting back against the invasion. The air crackled with electricity, making the hairs on his arms stand on end. Every flash of lightning illuminated the towering cube of Alohanui, casting jagged shadows across the mountainous landscape, transforming it into an alien world that felt both awe-inspiring and deeply hostile.

"What am I doing?" Caleb's mind snapped back to survival mode. "I've got to get flat to the ground."

With a swift, instinctual dive, Caleb threw himself into a shallow hollow nearby, the rocky ground unforgiving against his ribs. From his position, he rolled over just in time to witness lightning firing back and forth between the earth and Alohanui's immense, gleaming base. The blinding flashes tore through the sky, creating an almost strobe-like effect, making it impossible to gauge the true distance of the strikes.

His ears were ringing from the deafening cracks of thunder, so Caleb quickly jammed foam rubber earplugs into his ears, hoping to preserve whatever hearing he had left. Alohanui's base hovered ominously about 1,500 feet above him, casting a menacing shadow, while its edge loomed roughly 2,000 feet to the west. The sheer scale of it made Caleb feel infinitesimal, like an insect crouched beneath a skyscraper.

The lightning was relentless, each bolt leaving searing afterimages that burned jagged patterns into his retinas. Squinting against the storm's fury, Caleb fumbled for the dark glasses in his pack, slipping them on to dull the glare. Even with them, the intensity of the electrical storm was overwhelming. He grabbed the tablet he'd been using to record everything, angling it toward Alohanui. Whether or not he could focus through the chaos didn't matter—there would be experts back at SPEOC who could extract something useful from the footage, no matter how shaky or disjointed it was.

The earthquake, lightning, and thunder might have actually been a blessing in disguise, pushing the estimated one million people who had ignored the U.S. government's urging to flee the danger zone. The terrifying display of nature's fury—earth trembling beneath them, the sky erupting in flashes of blinding light—served as a final, desperate warning. It was as if the universe itself was urging them to escape before it was too late.

Hezbollah, Hamas, and a swarm of splinter factions launched

an unrelenting barrage of missiles at Alohanui, driven by the fierce belief that the alien structure was an elaborate Israeli-American plot to seize more land for Israel. Ironically, they remained unaware that Israel was also firing missiles at Alohanui—perhaps even more than the Arab factions. Missiles of varying sophistication, from crude makeshift rockets to advanced warheads, streaked across the sky like fiery arrows, each leaving behind a thick trail of smoke. The barrage, relentless and chaotic, filled the sky with arcs of destruction aimed at the monolithic structure.

As the missiles neared Alohanui, their fiery trails illuminated the night, painting the sky in shades of red and orange. But something extraordinary happened as they made contact. Instead of detonating in the brilliant explosions their senders expected, the missiles simply vanished upon impact with Alohanui's surface. There was no dramatic fireball, no deafening roar of destruction—just a quiet, unsettling absorption. Each missile was swallowed by the cube as if it had hit an invisible barrier, its mass and energy dispersed into nothingness.

Despite the escalating intensity of the missile strikes from both sides, the colossal structure remained untouched, its very invincibility provoking frustration and desperation among those launching the attacks. Each faction, convinced of their righteousness, watched as their efforts evaporated into the sky, realizing too late that no human force could challenge this alien entity.

The bedrock beneath Alohanui as it made its slow, deliberate descent was limestone, a relatively soft rock compared to the unyielding force of the colossal structure. Under the sheer pressure of Alohanui's massive weight, the limestone crumbled into powder, crushed into a fine, pale dust that began to rise into the air. The winds, as usual, were blowing from the west, but Alohanui was an immovable dam, forcing the wind to split and flow around it but also creating powerful updrafts around the massive base.The structure generated its own force fields, protecting itself from the relentless barrage of missiles, mortars, RPGs, and gunfire.

These swirling air currents interacted with the moisture in the atmosphere, triggering the formation of thick, roiling clouds that clung to the edges of Alohanui like a stormy veil. The already chaotic weather was further exacerbated by these newly formed clouds, which churned with intense lightning and deafening thunder. The violent electrical activity, amplified by the presence of the alien structure, lit up the sky in an apocalyptic display of nature and technology colliding.

And then came the rain—torrential downpours, as if the heavens had opened up in response to the chaos below. Sheets of rain battered the ground, turning the powdered limestone into a wet slurry that mixed with the growing rivers of mud. The constant thunder and lightning crackled overhead, accompanied by the steady rumble of earthquakes caused by the crushing weight of Alohanui as it ground its way down into the Earth.

Caleb, stationed on the east side of the landing site, remained unaware of the deadly hailstorm ravaging the west. There, a massive updraft fueled the formation of gargantuan hailstones—some as large as small cars. These ice behemoths plummeted to the ground with explosive force, shattering anything in their path and claiming the lives of thousands of stragglers caught in the storm's merciless grip.

It was a scene of unrelenting devastation: earthquakes shaking the ground, lightning tearing through the sky, and rain pouring down in torrents, all while Alohanui descended with an eerie calm, indifferent to the chaos it left in its wake. The forces of nature, it seemed, were powerless in the face of the alien cube's incomprehensible strength.

Caleb was soaked to the bone, every inch of his body chilled by the relentless rain. The cold cut through his wet clothes, making him shiver as he trudged through the muddy terrain. His thoughts were clouded with worry about the people who had once lived in the area that Alohanui was now slowly consuming. He hoped desperately that most had managed to escape before the alien structure fully embedded its base into the ground, covering the entire 18-mile by 18-mile square area.

The experts at SPEOC had grimly estimated that somewhere between 100,000 and 300,000 of the roughly one million residents in the region would likely perish during Alohanui's descent. But those numbers hadn't factored in the additional deaths from hail, lightning strikes or the torrents of debris and mud that had begun to surge through the area.

Caleb's tablet buzzed with an urgent message, its screen flickering through the rain. "Move back five miles from the perimeter of Alohanui immediately!" the message read. He glanced at it, squinting through the wet blur as he began running, trying to put more distance between himself and the landing zone.

As he ran, the rest of the message flashed across the screen: "The Laser Interferometer Gravitational-Wave Observatory (LIGO), The Virgo Interferometer, and Kamioka Gravitational Wave Detector (KAGRA) are all reporting gravitational waves originating from Alohanui."

The mention of gravitational waves made his heart pound faster, and not just from the exertion. He knew what that meant—Alohanui was manipulating gravity on a massive scale. That was enough to make Caleb focus entirely on running, putting every ounce of energy into escaping the disaster zone.

He had already been a mile back from the projected edge of Alohanui's base when he started sprinting, and now, he managed to push himself another three miles before his legs gave out. He collapsed onto the muddy ground, gasping for breath, his chest heaving. The rain still pounded down on him, but he ignored it. After a minute, he rolled over onto his back, staring up at the dark, swirling clouds above, trying to collect his thoughts.

When he looked back toward Alohanui, his eyes widened. Massive, upside-down tornadoes—dark, swirling columns of debris—were forming along the edges of the alien structure, spinning with impossible precision. The funnels seemed to be depositing what looked like pulverized limestone, creating a perfectly flat surface beneath the base of Alohanui. From Caleb's perspective, it appeared that the structure was hovering about 1,500 feet above the original ground level. Around the perimeter, he could see the beginnings of what looked like gentle slopes forming. He guessed the grade to be around 10%, a smooth downslope stretching outward.

The top of the upside-down twisters was too far north for Caleb to see, but he reckoned that the base of these newly formed slopes would end about five miles from the original edge of the square.

"Oh," he muttered to himself, realization dawning. "That's why they told me to move five miles back."

Panting, Caleb knew he couldn't stop for long. He pulled himself up, his legs aching from the exertion, and started walking toward a group of limestone outcroppings he had spotted about a mile away. They would provide some shelter from the elements and, hopefully, a better vantage point from which to observe Alohanui's bizarre construction process. The massive structure was reshaping the very earth beneath it, and Caleb felt like a witness to something both extraordinary and terrifying.

He moved as quickly as his tired legs would allow, driven by the urgent need to stay ahead of whatever came next.

When Caleb reached the limestone outcropping, he paused to catch his breath and immediately checked his tablet. It confirmed that he was now exactly five miles away from Alohanui's massive base—just outside the danger zone, or so he hoped. He was here to observe, and despite the surreal danger around him, that was exactly what he intended to do.

The tablet displayed a detailed contour map, something Caleb found particularly useful since the terrain around him, dominated by slopes and debris, made it difficult to fully grasp what was happening in the landscape beyond. According to the map, there was a dry moat that stretched out below Alohanui's base, one that he hadn't been able to see from his previous vantage point. The moat was about a thousand feet wide and a hundred feet deep, and as it continued south, it widened and deepened, and turned east.

The weather, which had been nothing short of apocalyptic earlier, was now starting to settle down. The rain had reduced to a light sprinkle, and the once deafening thunder had faded to occasional rumbles. The lightning, which had been fierce and concentrated around the tornado-like funnels that descended from Alohanui, was now mostly confined to the southern half of the landing zone. The north side appeared to be mostly finished—no more tornadoes or violent electrical storms in that direction.

The westward winds, which had caused clouds to pile up on one side of Alohanui, were still blowing strong, but now Caleb, stationed on the eastern side, watched as the clouds above him began to dissipate, allowing patches of sunlight to filter through. The sunlight illuminated the landscape, casting an eerie glow on the strange and unsettling scene before him.

As he continued to watch, something remarkable happened. The tornadoes, having finished the task of grading the area beneath Alohanui, shifted gears and began constructing roadways in front of each of the giant portals. These roads were unlike anything Caleb had ever seen before—wide and perfectly smooth, about 200 feet across, supported on base layers and sub base layers roughly 200 feet above the graded slopes below them. They stretched out from the portals, creating a network of pathways that seemed to link various sections of the landing zone together.

Where the roads crossed over the dry moat, beautiful, intricate bridges began to form. These weren't ordinary bridges—Caleb marveled at the construction, watching as the materials swirled together in mid-air before solidifying. The bridges appeared to be made of a substance that resembled quartz, though it was blended with other compounds that gave it a rainbow-like translucency. The colors shimmered in the sunlight, casting vibrant reflections across the landscape, creating a mesmerizing contrast to the devastation that had occurred just hours before.

The material looked both delicate and incredibly strong, its smooth surface gleaming under the now-calmer skies. Caleb couldn't help but admire the alien craftsmanship—it was a testament to Alohanui's mastery of not only mass and gravity but also material science far beyond human comprehension. The structures were simultaneously otherworldly and breathtakingly beautiful, a strange juxtaposition to the destruction they had wrought.

After losing one General Atomics MQ-9 Reaper drone to one of Alohanui's inverted tornado-like gravity marvels, the U.S. military waited cautiously for the strange atmospheric phenomena to subside before deploying another. Once the tornadoes had dissipated, they deployed a fresh drone, this time hoping to capture clearer images of the mysterious transformations happening below.

When the high-resolution aerial photographs finally arrived, Caleb was stunned by what he saw. In addition to the roads and bridges that had been constructed, the previously barren dry-bed watercourses were now meticulously lined with smooth river rocks. The precision of the work was startling. The stones appeared perfectly arranged, as if placed by unseen hands, each fitting seamlessly together to form natural yet deliberate channels.

"When did that happen?" Caleb muttered to himself. The last time he'd focused on those areas, they were nothing but dusty, empty riverbeds. Had he really been so distracted by the construction of the elaborate bridges and roadways that he missed this? The whole area now looked like it had been landscaped by some master designer, with attention to even the smallest details. It was almost as if Alohanui had a plan not just for its landing, but for the entire terrain surrounding it.

The photographs showed more than just river rocks. Alongside the newly smoothed paths, there were large, neatly spaced boulders, almost like markers or waypoints leading from one section of the area to another. Caleb zoomed in, fascinated by the careful arrangement. These weren't just natural formations—the placement seemed intentional, as if guiding something or someone toward a destination yet unknown.

It was clear now that every change, every alteration to the landscape, was part of something far bigger. Alohanui was not just descending—it was reshaping the land beneath it, preparing the area for... what exactly? Caleb had no idea, but the precision and scale of it were unlike anything he'd ever imagined.

Caleb had spent years studying countless images of Alohanui, captured from distances ranging from thousands to even millions of miles away. Those images, fuzzy and distant, had painted only a rough picture. But now, standing just five miles away with the rain and fog finally cleared, Caleb could observe Alohanui directly with his own eyes. It was awe-inspiring in a way that no satellite or radar image could have prepared him for.

From afar, radar images had led people to describe Alohanui as a cube. The shape had prompted comparisons to the infamous *Borg Cube* from *Star Trek*. But standing this close, Caleb could see how far from the truth that analogy was. Alohanui didn't resemble the cold, mechanical cube of sci-fi lore. If anything, it looked more like an ancient, walled city, a metropolis with towering skyscrapers. Some of these skyscrapers soared 18 miles high, with the tallest clustered near the center of the structure. Their gleaming surfaces shimmered in the sunlight, giving the entire structure an otherworldly appearance.

Everything within the walls of Alohanui had a distinct golden tint, as though bathed in a translucent layer of gold. Caleb recalled that spectroscopic analysis had confirmed a strong signature for gold, though this didn't look like solid metal. Instead, the gold seemed almost ethereal, like a mist or a delicate coating that shimmered and glowed depending on the angle of the light. The walls themselves, towering over 200 feet, added to the sense that this was not a simple cube but a fortified city, protected by advanced technology far beyond human comprehension.

Caleb had already seen the force field in action. Missiles, planes, and even satellites disintegrated before they could touch Alohanui, as if they were being torn apart by an invisible barrier. The consensus from the Raven Rock Brain Trust was that this was an intense gravitational field, similar to the forces around a black hole. Anything that came too close would be ripped apart by gravitational waves, much like an object approaching the event horizon of a singularity.

The foundation of Alohanui was equally as impressive as its towering heights. It consisted of twelve massive, roughly 200-foot-thick layers, which looked like enormous steps. Each layer was set back about 200 feet from the one below, forming a colossal stairway leading up to the city's base. Beneath the portals, the foundation was filled with brown-black pulverized limestone, a stark contrast to the pristine golden layers visible elsewhere. Caleb could see these steps clearly, their massive proportions dwarfing everything around them, a testament to the unimaginable forces that had constructed them.

Beyond the 200-foot wall, Caleb couldn't see the inner workings of the city from his vantage point, but the General Atomics MQ-9 Reaper drone flying several miles above him provided detailed images. Inside the walls, there was a carefully planned urban layout, with wide roads, parks, and sprawling city squares. The drone's camera captured a network of beautifully designed spaces—far from the cold, alien architecture one might expect from an extraterrestrial megastructure.

One of the most striking features was a vast highway that ran the full length of Alohanui from north to south, connecting the center west portal to the center east portal where Caleb hoped to enter the city. This was no ordinary road. It was a separated highway, with two wide lanes of travel in each direction, divided by a broad, landscaped median. And in the center of that median flowed a river, its waters shimmering under the golden light. Groves of trees lined the riverbank, creating a stunning park that ran through the heart of the city. The trees looked almost Earth-like, their green canopies offering shade and beauty to the alien metropolis.

It was clear that Alohanui was not just a fortress or a vessel; it was a fully realized city, teeming with infrastructure, designed with both function and beauty in mind. Yet, its purpose remained shrouded in mystery. Caleb, standing in its looming shadow, knew that whatever was happening inside Alohanui was far beyond anything humanity had ever encountered.

Caleb stood at the edge of the outcropping, staring up at the towering, otherworldly structure of Alohanui. It was magnificent in every sense of the word—a monolith of gleaming golden hues and intricate, geometric patterns that shimmered under the pale light of the sky. Its sheer size and flawless symmetry were awe-inspiring. The translucent golden towers, piercing the heavens, and the seamless integration of form and function made Alohanui seem more like a work of art than a mere alien artifact. It was a masterpiece, something no human could ever have imagined, let alone created.

But as Caleb's tablet vibrated in his hand, alerting him to the latest SITREP from SPEOC, the gravity of its existence weighed heavily on his heart. According to the latest reports, Alohanui's arrival, and the events it had set in motion, had already caused the deaths of one-third of the world's population. Billions of lives snuffed out—entire families, cities, and nations plunged into chaos, famine, disease, and war.

He looked down at the numbers on the screen, unable to comprehend the sheer scale of the devastation. One third. It was an incomprehensible loss, a statistic too large for the mind to grasp, yet it was the harsh reality of the situation. For a moment, Caleb closed his eyes, trying to process the conflicting emotions that churned within him. How could something so breathtakingly beautiful, so flawlessly designed, be responsible for such unprecedented destruction?

Alohanui was, without question, a marvel. Its towering spires were like needles piercing the sky, their walls so high and seamless that they seemed to defy the laws of physics. From a distance, it resembled a utopian city suspended in the air—an architectural dream that could captivate even the most jaded observer. Its translucent golden skin reflected the colors of the sky, making it look alive, almost sentient, as if it were aware of its surroundings and adapting to the light around it. There was a serenity in its stillness, a kind of quiet majesty that made Caleb want to appreciate it, to marvel at it.

But the beauty was deceptive. Beneath that stunning facade lay a cold indifference to the lives it had disrupted, to the millions it had annihilated without hesitation. How could such a thing of wonder coexist with the horror it had unleashed on the world? How could something so perfectly constructed be so utterly devoid of compassion?

Caleb's thoughts were a tangled mess. He had spent his entire life studying the cosmos, searching for answers in the stars, hoping that humanity might not be alone in the universe. Now, staring up at this alien creation, he wasn't sure he wanted the answers anymore. Alohanui had come not as a beacon of hope, but as a harbinger of death and destruction. It had disrupted the natural order of things, triggered conflicts, and ushered in disasters that mankind had never imagined possible.

He had seen the footage—cities wiped out by tidal waves, people scrambling for safety as the skies darkened, governments crumbling under the weight of impossible decisions. All of it, in one way or another, traced back to Alohanui.

"How could something so beautiful be so devastating?" he whispered to himself, unable to shake the question that had been haunting him since the cube's arrival. "How can such callousness exist alongside such beauty?"

Caleb's mind struggled to reconcile the two opposing realities. Alohanui represented the pinnacle of technological and aesthetic achievement—something no human had ever thought possible. Yet, it was also the greatest source of suffering the world had ever known. Could something so magnificently constructed truly be void of empathy, of any consideration for the fragile lives beneath it?

He knew he had to find answers. The surface-level awe he felt for Alohanui's beauty was no longer enough. It wasn't just an alien artifact to be studied and admired—it was something far more dangerous, something that demanded understanding. Caleb felt the weight of responsibility settle on his shoulders. He couldn't just be a passive observer anymore. He had to seek the truth behind this beautiful, terrifying thing before it was too late.

And yet, standing there, in the shadow of the behemoth, all he could think about was the sheer wonder of its existence. Alohanui was a paradox—a symbol of both creation and destruction, a thing of awe and terror. It was a reminder that beauty could, indeed, be deadly.

CHAPTER 12
OCCUPATION

As Caleb stood gazing up at the wonder that was Alohanui, his tablet buzzed, interrupting the surreal calm that had fallen over him. He glanced down at the screen.

Battalion headed your way. Missiles inbound. Take cover.

His stomach dropped as he read the message. The tension in the air thickened, a stark contrast to the still beauty of Alohanui looming ahead. The screen on his tablet began scrolling with an overwhelming display of data—troop numbers, tanks, missile counts, aircraft positions—all converging on his location. He felt as though he were standing at the epicenter of an impending storm.

The armies were coming, likely they had bided their time until Alohanui made contact with the ground. It was impossible to escape the magnitude of what was happening. Caleb was trapped between the impenetrable alien city and the largest army ever assembled. If he stayed where he was, he'd eventually be caught in the crossfire. *Maybe not immediately,* he thought, *but soon enough.*

SPEOC had promised that the General Atomics MQ-9 Reaper

drone was monitoring the area and would provide him cover. The drone's surveillance and protection were the only reasons Caleb had survived this long, but he knew its fuel and ammunition wouldn't last forever. He glanced back at the hills behind him, now dotted with the shadows of marching troops and the faint glint of armored vehicles. They were coming fast.

He was out of options. Running towards the oncoming battalions meant certain death. Running toward Alohanui seemed the only viable option, even though it felt like running toward the unknown. He could only hope that hiding under the bridge beneath the road near the portal in the center of Alohanui's east city wall would provide some shelter. The closer he got to the wall, though, the greater the risk of being struck by debris from the missile attacks being fired at the alien structure. The remnants of shattered projectiles might rain down at any moment.

Caleb's heart pounded, not just from fear but from physical exhaustion. He had already pushed his body to the limit, sprinting away from the landing zone earlier. His muscles burned, his legs heavy like lead. But the tablet's warning left him no choice. He turned and ran as fast as he could toward Alohanui, toward the alien city's east gate. The freshly constructed road leading to the east portal was wide and smooth, offering an easy path, but the incline was punishing—a grueling 10 percent uphill grade that slowed his pace.

Breathing hard, his legs screaming for relief, he was forced to slow to a walk. Every step was an effort, each breath a labored gulp of air. He could feel the weight of his exhaustion. Glancing over his shoulder, Caleb knew the MQ-9 Reaper was still overhead, its sharp eyes surveying the vast landscape, protecting his back from the approaching soldiers. The sound of distant engines, the rumble of artillery, and the marching of thousands of boots echoed across the hills, a constant reminder of the death that was chasing him.

Alohanui's gleaming walls loomed larger and larger as he moved closer, but his mind raced with doubts. What if the drone was shot down before he reached the bridge over the moat? What if Alohanui's defenses didn't recognize him as anything but a threat? He wasn't sure what was more dangerous—the alien city or the battalions closing in from behind.

Still, he pressed on, knowing that retreat wasn't an option. The sky above was filled with clouds darkened by the aftermath of explosions. Missile trails streaked across the horizon, their targets set on Alohanui. Caleb quickened his pace, adrenaline fueling his weary legs as he aimed for the only place that might offer a shred of hope—the mysterious, beautiful gates of Alohanui.

He had no idea what would await him there. Would the alien city welcome him, or would it cast him aside like all the other threats it had so effortlessly shrugged off?

The MQ-9 Reaper drone continued its silent surveillance, relaying high-resolution images to Caleb's tablet. As he scanned the latest feed, something unexpected drew his attention—water flowing through what he had initially assumed to be a dry moat.

"It's not a moat at all," Caleb murmured, leaning closer to the screen. "It's a river. But not part of the city's defenses. It doesn't look like it's meant to slow or impede attackers, though it might still do that. So... what's its purpose?"

His gaze lingered on the flowing water. Outside the walls, the river was a massive, natural torrent, wide and deep, its currents swirling with barely restrained energy. Yet, inside the city walls, it was entirely different. There, the river became a controlled stream, channeled with perfect symmetry down the median of a grand boulevard, as if it were part of a carefully designed park or urban feature. The contrast was stark, almost unsettling.

The outside river's sheer size dwarfed the city's controlled stream, creating an odd imbalance that Caleb couldn't quite reconcile. Shouldn't the flow remain consistent, he wondered? Why was the river outside the walls so expansive, while inside it appeared almost ornamental?

He paused, staring at the shimmering waters on his screen. "This doesn't make sense," he whispered, his mind racing. The shimmering translucence of the bridge above, the way the river seamlessly integrated into the city's layout—it all hinted at an intentional design, something far beyond human capability.

The drone's feed flickered momentarily, showing the river's path weaving through the city like an artery. Caleb felt a growing unease. "What's it for?" he asked himself again, his voice barely audible. "And why does it feel like the river knows something we don't?"

His fingers quickly tapped out a message to SPEOC: *"Can you determine the width of the river inside the city and compare it to the width of the river outside the wall?"*

It didn't take long to answer his request.

"Approximately 1%. The river inside the walls is roughly 10 feet wide, while the river outside the walls is approximately 1,000 feet wide. Similarly, the humanoids inside the city average around a half an inch tall—about 1% the size of an average human. But there are also humanoids walking on the top of the walls, averaging 5 feet 6 inches tall, roughly equivalent to the height of an average human."

Caleb stared at the words in disbelief. *One half inch tall?* The beings inside the city were miniature, but the ones patrolling the walls were normal human size. The disparity left him momentarily baffled, but his mind quickly latched onto something else—the possibility that the figures walking the walls might be human.

His heart raced. Could Emma be there? Could Bethany? The thought electrified him. The river, the strange size differences—it all melted away in the face of this possibility. *If there are human-sized figures on the walls, they could be prisoners, hostages, or worse...* But the faintest glimmer of hope bloomed within him. What if they were survivors? What if Emma and Beth were among them?

Without wasting another second, Caleb's mind was made up. He had to reach them. *Whatever the risk, whatever the cost, I need to find them.* His thoughts raced ahead, forming a plan. He had already come this far—there was no turning back now.

The drone's live feed continued to map the terrain ahead, showing the towering walls of Alohanui and the slowly expanding river beneath them. Caleb realized the walls weren't just architectural marvels—they were boundaries between worlds. A world where giants roamed the walls and miniature beings moved within the city.

He took a deep breath, feeling the cold air fill his lungs. His legs, though aching from the earlier sprint, were ready for another push. With the vast river between him and the city's interior, and no clear idea how to cross it, he knew getting inside wouldn't be easy. But none of that mattered now.

Caleb began moving toward the eastern side of the wall, where he hoped to find a way in. His thoughts lingered on the figures patrolling the city's massive perimeter. *What if they aren't human at all? What if...* He shook the thought away.

No. Emma is here. She must be here.

Steeling himself for what lay ahead, he pressed onward, determined to get closer to Alohanui and discover the truth behind its impenetrable walls.

At that moment, Caleb's attention snapped to the screen of his tablet just in time to witness the last moments of the MQ-9 Reaper, or what remained of it, nose-diving into the ground. A quick flash followed, and then the tablet's display showed the ominous words: *Signal Lost*.

On my own, Caleb thought, feeling a cold wave of dread wash over him. The reassuring hum of the Reaper's protection, however fragile, was now gone.

He pushed forward, moving as quickly as his weary body would allow, heading toward the nearest portal in the towering wall of Alohanui. As his boots pounded against the unfamiliar terrain, he strained to recall the exact orders he'd been given for this kind of situation.

They had been blunt, leaving little room for misinterpretation.

"You shouldn't count on the U.S. military undertaking any rescue attempt," they'd said in that no-nonsense tone that echoed in his mind now, louder than ever. *"The largest army in history is mustering in the area. Do not assume that any English-speaking troops are friendly. We've had reports of numerous desertions from the U.S. armed forces in recent days. There's a real possibility that American soldiers you encounter may be deserters, or worse—turncoats."*

Caleb swallowed hard, the implications heavy on his mind. It wasn't just the loss of the Reaper that stung—it was the chilling realization that he was truly alone out here, surrounded by hostile forces, and with no clear allies.

The tablet, now his sole lifeline, buzzed in his hands as he maneuvered it while running. *"The tablet will relay communications between SPEOC and you through U.S. assets in the theater of war,"* he remembered them telling him. *"If any of these assets become non-functional, attempts will be made to reroute communications through other assets. This may take days or even weeks."*

Weeks? He hadn't considered that possibility deeply before, but now the weight of those words pressed down on him like a boulder.

Glancing at the tablet, he mentally ran through its features. *"The back of the tablet is a solar cell. If you're cut off for an extended period, place the tablet face-down to charge during sunny days. It can receive local commercial radio signals like AM and FM, as well as TV, CB, ham radio, and shortwave broadcasts."*

As he looked up, the towering silhouette of Alohanui grew closer, casting a long, imposing shadow. His mind raced through contingency plans—what he would do if he lost contact for days, how he would ration his water, and whether the rumored "force fields" around Alohanui would even allow him to get close.

The road ahead stretched endlessly, but the massive alien city loomed larger with each step. He was on his own now, and he had to figure out how to survive—not just against the extraterrestrial forces of Alohanui, but in a war zone where friend and foe were impossible to distinguish.

With nothing but the tablet, his backpack and his wits, Caleb pressed on, trying to shake off the weight of uncertainty that clung to him.

But the sudden loss of communication with SPEOC hit Caleb hard. It made him temporarily forget the very reason he had volunteered for this mission—Emma and Beth. How could he have let himself get so rattled by the destruction of the drone and the severing of his link to the command center?

I was almost suicidal when they abducted Emma, he thought, chastising himself. *I felt that without Emma, life wasn't worth living. There is one, and only one, reason why I'm here—to find her.*

He took a deep breath, regaining focus. *I can't afford to fall apart over a drone or lost communications.* Again, he reminded himself of what mattered. Emma was out there—somewhere—and he was the only one who had any chance of finding her. *Emma and Beth.* That thought brought him back to his purpose. He had to keep going, no matter what.

He had been so consumed with the tools that were supposed to support him—the tablet, the drone—that he hadn't even realized how dependent he'd become on them. *Two machines,* he thought bitterly. *And I let them nearly strip me of my purpose.*

He shook his head, trying to push those thoughts aside. The wall of Alohanui was now only 500 yards away, its looming presence reminding him of the enormity of his mission. Caleb realized just how useful the drone had been. From the ground, about 200 feet below the top of the wall, he couldn't see the walkway that the drone had revealed in previous scans. The wall was like a castle parapet, with gaps in the top—narrow slits where archers fire arrows to defend the city. He wondered if someone, or something, might be peeking through one of those gaps, watching his approach.

His reverie was shattered by the scream of a missile overhead. The sound was deafening, the engine's roar filling the air with a crushing intensity. Caleb's instincts took over as the missile struck the wall above the portal. He braced for the impact, expecting debris, an explosion, something—but nothing happened. No crash, not even a thud. The missile simply disappeared as it made contact with Alohanui's unyielding surface.

Caleb's heart pounded in his chest, and he glanced toward the river ahead. *Move, now.* He sprinted, his boots splashing through the shallow water as he aimed for the safety of the bridge—a massive 1,500-foot arch of translucent material spanning the river like something out of a dream. The bridge's deck glowed faintly, the light passing through it dispersing into shimmering rainbows. But Caleb didn't have time to marvel at its beauty. He needed cover.

The portal was just beyond the bridge, barely visible through the prismatic colors filtering down. Caleb pressed himself up against the smooth bulkhead under the bridge, which felt like polished quartz under his hands. The surface was cool and slick, almost unnatural in its perfection. The cobble-sized egg shaped river rocks sloped up to the bulkhead at a point about six feet below the bridge deck, and they were loose, moveable.

With shaking hands, he began shifting the rocks, moving them around to create an indentation where he could hide. He needed to disappear from view, to make sure no one—or no thing—could see him. The bridge's arch provided some cover, but he knew that anyone curious enough to peer under it could easily spot him.

Just let me stay hidden, he thought, feeling his pulse race as he pressed himself into the small hollow he'd made. His breath came in shallow bursts, and he forced himself to slow down, to focus. *Emma and Beth.* They were all that mattered now. Not the drone, not the tablet, not even the armies marching toward him.

When Caleb felt he had done everything he could to conceal himself under the deck of the bridge, his attention shifted to the river flowing quietly beside him. His canteen was bone dry. He needed water desperately, but as he stared at the glowing current, he hesitated. The water looked strange—almost radioactive. It glowed faintly, like the eerie blue light emitted by heavy water in a nuclear power plant spewing Cherenkov radiation.

Yet, despite the unnatural glow, life thrived in the river. Caleb noticed fish darting through the water, not the trout or bass he might expect in a freshwater stream, but creatures more reminiscent of the tropical fish he had seen around the reefs of Waikiki—though these were far less colorful. One, however, stood out, a familiar shape that brought back memories of home: tilapia. *An invasive species in Hawaii, but delicious,* he thought. *How strange to see it here, of all places.*

The memory of Hawaii tugged at his heart. He could almost feel the warm sun and the salt spray on his skin as he recalled surfing with Emma on the North Shore. But those days felt like another lifetime, especially after the asteroid-induced tidal waves that had wiped out much of the Hawaiian coastline, leaving destruction in their wake.

Even if I find Emma, Caleb wondered, *how will we ever make it back to Hawaii? Is there even anything left?*

He quickly shook off the thoughts of the past and the future. He knew better than to dwell on what had been or what might be. *Focus on surviving right now. To survive, I need safe drinking water and food.* The glowing river made him wary. *I wish I had brought a Geiger counter.*

The thought sparked an idea. *Had someone told me the tablet had a radiation sensor built into it?* Caleb grabbed the tablet from where it lay just outside the bridge's shadow, where he had placed it to soak up the weak sunlight for charging.

When he turned the tablet on, the familiar *NO SIGNAL* message appeared, along with icons similar to those on a smartphone. Among them was a magnifying glass icon. Caleb tapped it, and a keyboard popped up on the screen. He quickly typed, "Geiger counter."

Instantly, the tablet responded, displaying a screen titled Nuclear Radiation Detector along with the date, time, and battery charge. Below, a small chart showed radiation levels:

Min: 0.14 uSv/hr
Max: 0.23 uSv/hr

Current Dose Rate: 0.31 uSv/hr.

A bar chart filled the rest of the screen, with a green-to-red gradient, signifying safe to dangerous levels. All the readings were firmly in the green.

That's good, Caleb thought, relief washing over him as he read the tablet's display. *No harmful radiation. Maybe the glow in the water wasn't radioactive after all. Maybe it was just light refracting through the translucent bridge deck above, creating an illusion.*

Feeling a small measure of reassurance, Caleb crouched by the river's edge and filled his canteen, dropping in a water purification tablet. He shook it vigorously, then waited, keeping his eyes fixed on the distant horizon, where he could see armies gathering like dark clouds before a storm. Artillery fire rumbled in the distance, a deep, unsettling sound that seemed to vibrate through the very ground beneath him. Every few moments, the whistling shriek of missiles overhead pierced the air, forcing him to flinch. He could sense the tension in the air—he knew the armies were closing in, advancing steadily from both the west and the east. Yet here, beneath the shelter of the bridge, he found a temporary refuge, an uneasy calm amidst the brewing chaos.

The massed armies were an ominous sight to behold—millions of soldiers converging, their weapons lighting up the horizon in a relentless barrage. Yet something about their movements puzzled Caleb. They were firing continuously—rifles, mortars, RPGs, missiles—each weapon aimed at the great alien city of Alohanui. But there were no visible defenders, no soldiers fighting for Alohanui, no indication that their attacks had any effect at all. Despite the intensity of their assault, they didn't seem to advance. They just kept shooting, their fury directed at a target that remained completely indifferent to their efforts.

After what felt like an eternity, the thirty minute water sterilization period passed. Caleb picked up the canteen and cautiously took a sip. The cool liquid slid down his parched throat, instantly soothing it. Despite his fears, the water tasted fresh and pure, a welcome respite in an otherwise hostile world.

I must have been more dehydrated than I realized, Caleb thought, as he gulped down more. *This is the best-tasting water I've ever had.*

He leaned back for a moment, savoring the feeling. The world around him was chaos, filled with thunderous artillery, the clash of armies, and the looming, enigmatic presence of Alohanui. But for now, he had water, he had shelter, and he still had a mission—to find Emma and Beth. Whatever came next, he was ready. He just needed to survive long enough to see his chance.

He leaned back against the cool quartz bulkhead, listening to the distant rumble of tanks and the occasional crack of artillery fire, growing ever closer. *I may need to move*, he thought. But for now, in this brief moment of stillness, the water, and the chance to catch his breath, were enough.

His tablet vibrated, signaling a new message. It was an email from Rachel, sent two weeks ago. *Lucky it even made it here at all*, he thought as he opened it.

Caleb,
I'm so sorry to bring you bad news. I asked Pastor Ben to check on Ted and Star, and he did, but now they've been missing for several days. From what I can gather, Ben, Star, and Ted went for a walk outside and never returned. As much as was feasible, a search of the grounds was conducted, but it turned up nothing. They're not at Raven Rock.

I know this news comes at the lowest point in your life, but please know my thoughts are with you. Wishing you all the best.

Rachel

Ever since the anonymous man on the plane informed him that they were missing,.Caleb had hoped for good news. But this news was devastating. The words hit him like a blow, leaving him so stunned he couldn't move. For a long moment, he just sat there, paralyzed. Then the tears came—unstoppable, overwhelming. He cried and cried, the pain of it all finally breaking through. At least, he thought numbly, he was safe and hidden for now.

-

His sorrow gradually began to ease.

For the first time, Caleb had a chance to unpack his knapsack—a moment that felt oddly cathartic. When it was handed to him after stepping off the plane, they'd mentioned it contained a tent, a sleeping bag, clean socks and underwear, a stove, MREs, and a first aid kit. He couldn't quite remember if there was anything else, but the thought of Meals Ready to Eat was somehow somewhat comforting in his sorrow. Turning the pack upside down, he dumped its contents onto the river rock pad he had carefully laid out.

To his incredulity, nestled among the gear was a compact fishing kit that fit neatly in the palm of his hand. It had folding scissors, fluorocarbon line, floats, hooks, weights, flies, and a leader. No fishing pole, but the fiberglass tent pole could easily double as one in a pinch.

Fishing would have to wait, though. The MREs would last him for at least a week, and water wasn't a problem. His most pressing concern was finding Emma and Beth. He needed more information, more perspective, and the first place to look was on top of the wall. Avoiding the extraterrestrials inside Alohanui's walls—the ones who were barely half an inch tall—was critical.

Caleb was running on pure adrenaline, his body exhausted but his mind unwilling to rest. Night had fallen, and after forcing himself to eat and drink, he assessed the situation. The armies were no closer than before, giving him a fleeting sense of reprieve. Deciding it was safe enough, he prepared his makeshift bed, tucking himself into his sleeping bag at the base of a depression in the riverrock. Pressed tightly against the bulkhead under the bridge, he felt well-concealed—hidden from sight unless someone ventured directly beneath the structure.

As he lay there, the coolness of the rock against his back, Caleb closed his eyes and let his thoughts drift. Inevitably, they found their way to Emma. Her laugh, her strength, the way her presence could make even the bleakest moments bearable. He smiled faintly, his weariness softening at the memory of the night he proposed—a proper date for once, one filled with joy and hope. He tried to recall every detail: the way she looked at him, the words they exchanged, the promise they made to each other. It was a memory he clung to, a light in the darkness that surrounded him.

Caleb smiled at the memory, a rare, radiant moment in a world that often felt on the brink of collapse. It had been a night unlike any other, planned meticulously to give Emma something magical, something to hold onto when the weight of their lives grew too heavy.

The evening began with a drive along Oahu's coastline, the setting sun painting the sky in vivid hues of orange and pink. Caleb had insisted on driving, claiming he had "something special" planned. Emma had laughed at his uncharacteristic enthusiasm, her curiosity piqued as the familiar roads led them to an elegant, secluded restaurant perched on a cliff overlooking the ocean.

The entrance to the restaurant was framed by lush tropical gardens, with torches flickering gently in the breeze. Inside, the atmosphere was intimate and warm, with soft lighting casting a golden glow over tables draped in white linen. The sound of a live ukulele player filled the air, his music weaving seamlessly with the rhythmic crash of waves below. The scent of plumeria flowers mingled with the aroma of exquisite cuisine, heightening the romantic ambiance.

Their table was set on the open terrace, offering an unobstructed view of the moonlit ocean. A gentle breeze carried the scent of salt and blossoms as they were seated. Emma's eyes sparkled as she took it all in, her hand finding Caleb's across the table. "This is incredible," she said softly, her smile lighting up the evening more than the twinkling string lights above them.

The meal was a culinary journey—a parade of delicate appetizers, freshly caught fish, and rich desserts, each plate as beautiful as it was delicious. Caleb found himself captivated not by the food, but by Emma. She laughed easily, her long black hair catching the candlelight as she leaned forward to talk about the stars overhead and the future she sometimes dared to imagine.

When the dessert arrived—a decadent chocolate soufflé adorned with edible gold—Emma was about to take her first bite when she noticed something sparkling on her plate. Her breath caught as she looked closer and saw a ring, nestled in a delicate flower petal. She glanced up at Caleb, who had moved from his seat to kneel beside her.

"Emma," he began, his voice steady despite the emotion

shimmering in his eyes. "You've made every challenge we've faced worth fighting through, every moment brighter just by being you. I can't imagine a future without you in it. Will you marry me?"

The world seemed to stand still as Emma's eyes filled with tears, her hand flying to her mouth in disbelief. She nodded before she could find the words, her voice breaking as she whispered, "Yes, Caleb. A thousand times yes."

Applause erupted around them as the other diners cheered and clapped, though Caleb and Emma hardly noticed. He slid the ring onto her finger, its delicate design catching the light as she pulled him into an embrace. For a moment, it was just the two of them, the ocean, and the stars, their love transcending everything else.

That night, as they walked hand in hand along the moonlit beach after leaving the restaurant, Caleb had felt an unshakable certainty. No matter what challenges lay ahead, he and Emma would face them together. It was a memory he cherished, a beacon of hope that shone even in the darkest times.

With those cherished memories vivid in his mind, Caleb finally drifted off to sleep. His exhaustion carried him into a dream—a dream so vivid it felt more like a memory.

He was back in the car with Emma, driving home after the night she had said yes to his proposal. The atmosphere between them was electric yet calm, a perfect balance of excitement and contentment. The cool evening air streamed through the cracked windows, carrying the scent of the ocean. They didn't talk much, but their glances spoke volumes, their eyes meeting every chance they could steal without him taking his focus off the road.

Emma sat beside him, radiant and serene. She wore a flowing

white dress that shimmered faintly under the soft light of the dashboard. The fabric, delicate and airy, seemed to catch the moonlight whenever they passed under an open sky, making her appear ethereal. Her dark hair, loosely cascading over her shoulders, framed her face, and the simple gold necklace she wore reflected her understated elegance. The ring Caleb had just given her glinted on her hand as she rested it lightly on his arm, her touch warm and reassuring.

Caleb couldn't help *but* steal glances at her, his heart swelling every time their eyes met. She was his fiancée now—his future—and the thought filled him with a joy he hadn't known was possible. She turned to him, her expression soft but serious, and broke the silence.

"I'll wait for you," she said, her voice steady and filled with a quiet resolve. "As long as it takes, I'll wait for you."

Her words confused him, a flicker of doubt piercing the perfect moment. "What do you mean?" he asked, his grip tightening on the wheel as he tried to read her expression.

Emma's gaze grew distant, her smile fading slightly, though her tone remained gentle. "We're all here, nearby. Your entire family and mine. Waiting for you."

Caleb's chest tightened as her words lingered in the air, an unspoken truth hanging between them. He turned to look at her, but her figure seemed to blur, the dream shifting as if reality were trying to intrude. Before he could ask anything more, the dream began to dissolve, pulling him back into the darkness of his makeshift camp.

He woke with a start, Emma's words echoing in his mind, leaving him both comforted and deeply unsettled.

The next morning after an MRE breakfast, Caleb took out his binoculars and focused on the massive portal embedded in the wall. It was clearly closed, probably even hermetically sealed.

He wondered if it would be possible to scale the smooth surface of the wall. There had to be a small gap between the quartz wall and the spherical portal, right? Maybe he could wedge something into that gap, using it to gain enough grip to climb. He imagined a slow, deliberate process—alternating between placing wedges and pulling himself up, using the tent pegs as wedges and the small ax as a hammer. His goal would be the narrow slits in the parapet, through which he could hopefully pull himself up onto the wall.

As an afterthought, he attached the tablet to his vest so its camera could record everything. *If communication with SPEOC is ever restored, I am sure they would appreciate a close up of the gate.*

As Caleb crossed the translucent bridge toward the portal, he wondered if he had the courage to see this through. The idea of scaling the enormous, alien structure filled him with a mix of dread and determination. He had come this far—now he had to trust that the path forward would reveal itself.

One hundred yards from the gate, the unimaginable happened. The portal rotated without a sound, revealing a tunnel that opened directly toward Caleb. Emerging from the tunnel was a humanoid figure, striding confidently toward him.
Caleb froze.

The being wasn't the half-inch-tall entity he might have expected from the previous drone observations. No, this extraterrestrial stood at least six feet tall, towering and imposing. It had two arms, two legs, and, bizarrely, four bat-like wings that flared out from its shoulders and its back. Its face, eerily human, gazed directly at Caleb. But there were two other faces—one on each side of its head. One looked like a bull, with dark, menacing eyes, while the other resembled a lion, its mane flowing as if caught in an unseen wind. If those extra faces were meant to terrify, they succeeded.

But even more frightening was the lightsaber—or rather, what looked like a flaming sword—gripped in its hand, flickering with fire and otherworldly light.

The extraterrestrial stepped into the center of the gate and stood still. A sentry. A guard.

Caleb didn't move, his body locked in place, eyes wide. The guard remained motionless as well, a statue with wings and faces.

After what felt like an eternity, Caleb dared to take a step forward. The guard's flaming sword shifted, rising slightly, as if preparing for action. Caleb immediately stepped back. After a minute, the sword lowered.

He tested the creature's response, stepping sideways this time. No reaction. Another step back—again, no movement from the guard. With a shaky breath, Caleb took a step forward again, inching toward the portal. This time, the sword lifted higher, the flames roaring slightly louder. Caleb halted.

Another step back. The sword lowered once more.

They continued this strange dance for what seemed to Caleb like an hour—him inching forward, the guard reacting with subtle movements of its sword, and then Caleb retreating. The being seemed to be giving a clear message: come no closer.

Frustration and fear welled up inside Caleb, but there was nothing more he could do. Finally, with no way to bypass the guard and no clear path forward, he retreated fully, returning to his makeshift campsite beneath the bridge near the bulkhead.

His mind raced with confusion. *What is that thing? What is its purpose? And how am I ever going to get inside?*

Exhausted, he leaned back against the smooth quartz surface and closed his eyes, the image of the three-faced guardian and its blazing sword still burning in his thoughts.

He retrieved the tablet from his vest and realized it had been recording the entire time. *Might as well shut it off*, he thought. But something made him pause. *I should review the footage. I was so focused on the guard—who knows what else might have been happening while we were playing that game of 'go, go, stop.'*

Caleb opened the recorded video and fast-forwarded to the moment the portal had opened. As he scrubbed through the footage, something caught his eye. The view through the tunnel beyond the gate... it was mind-blowing. There, on the other side, people were walking. They looked exactly like human beings.

His mind raced, jumping to the only thing that made sense. *Parallax and pixels*, he thought. If there was anything he was certain of as an astronomer, it was the science of measurements. He paused the video and zoomed in on the figures walking near the end of the tunnel, just inside the city. He knew from countless hours studying the external images of Alohanui that the gate opening was almost exactly 200 feet high.

He carefully coaxed the tablet into analyzing the video. *How many pixels from the floor to the ceiling of the tunnel?* He calculated quickly—1,260 pixels. Then, he measured the height of the humanoid figure at the entrance to the tunnel —36 pixels. The math was elementary for an astronomer: 36 pixels out of 1,260 pixels meant the figure was about 5'9", not the half-inch tall beings that the MQ-9 Reaper drone had indicated.

Something's off, Caleb thought, his heart racing. *Was there an error with the MQ-9 Reaper? Or had SPEOC made some massive miscalculation?*

As Caleb pondered the implications, he realized with a jolt that he had been so engrossed in the drone footage—and so rattled by his close encounter with the extraterrestrial guard—that he had failed to notice something critical. The relentless barrage of missiles, mortars, and artillery had stopped. In their place was a heavy, eerie silence that blanketed the landscape like a suffocating shroud.

Cautiously, Caleb crawled out from his hiding spot under the bridge, his movements deliberate and slow. He peered to the east. At first glance, nothing seemed out of place. The terrain looked as barren and war-torn as before. But when he raised his binoculars, a cold wave of dread washed over him. Scattered across the battlefield were bodies—scores of them—motionless, abandoned where they had fallen.

"Dead," Caleb muttered to himself, his voice barely audible. The sight unnerved him. He wasn't naive; he knew these soldiers would have shot him on sight without hesitation. Yet seeing them like this—lifeless, discarded—it struck him with a deep unease. What could have done this? How had an army of this magnitude, the largest ever assembled, been wiped out so completely and so suddenly?

Then, the scene shifted from unnerving to utterly apocalyptic. The sky began to darken unnaturally, clouds swirling in chaotic patterns overhead. Lightning cracked across the heavens, illuminating the desolate battlefield in sharp, blinding flashes. Yet, bizarrely, there was no accompanying thunder. The absence of sound made the lightning all the more surreal, as if the universe itself were holding its breath.

The battlefield was eerily silent, save for the soft rustle of the wind as it carried the acrid scent of death across the expanse. The armies, once teeming with life and purpose, now lay motionless, a sea of bodies sprawled across the blood-soaked earth.

After a half an hour, the silence was broken by a faint sound he couldn't place. An ominous shadow darkened the horizon. At first, it seemed like a storm cloud, but as it drew closer, the shapes became distinct—hundreds, then thousands, of them.

Birds of prey filled the sky, their numbers blotting out the fading light of the sun. Every kind of scavenger imaginable had gathered: vultures with their bald, sinister heads; hawks with their keen, piercing eyes; and majestic eagles gliding with a deadly grace. Their cries pierced the air, a cacophony that echoed over the desolate plain, a grim announcement of nature's inevitable claim over the remnants of humanity's folly.

One by one, they began to descend, their powerful wings slicing through the air as they landed atop the lifeless forms. Vultures tore at the flesh with their hooked beaks, their movements efficient and unrelenting. Hawks darted in, ripping smaller morsels from exposed limbs, while eagles —larger and more imposing—staked out their territories, defending choice sections of the carnage with shrill cries and threatening postures.

The ground became a chaotic mosaic of feathers and blood, the scavengers working in relentless harmony to strip the remains of the fallen. They worked methodically, their instincts overriding any sense of hesitation, as if summoned by some primal force to cleanse the earth of its dead. The smell of decay mingled with the sharp scent of iron from the blood-soaked soil, a nauseating reminder of the price paid in the final battle.

Above it all, the sky remained thick with circling birds, their shadows dancing across the battlefield. From the tallest corpses to the broken remnants of war machines, nothing escaped their scrutiny. Nature, indifferent to the tragedy of human ambition, had reclaimed the field in its own brutal way. The feeding frenzy continued as dusk gave way to night, the haunting sounds of flapping wings and tearing flesh persisting long into the darkness.

To Caleb's horror, the ground began to tremble. Twenty miles away, a massive hole yawned open in the earth, its edges crumbling away like a festering wound tearing beneath the battlefield. The sky seemed to react in kind, the swirling clouds above forming a vortex that mirrored the chaos below. Silent bolts of lightning danced across the heavens, casting eerie, flickering shadows over the fractured land. This time rolling thunder followed.

From the pit emerged a colossal funnel, a swirling, otherworldly tornado of darkness and force. It spun with a malevolent energy, its currents twisting violently as it reached upward toward the chaotic sky. The pit became a voracious maw, consuming everything in its path. Dead soldiers, tanks, artillery, entire battalions of war machines—all were pulled into the vortex as though drawn by an irresistible, unseen hand.

The scene was like a nightmare brought to life. Each flash of lightning illuminated the grotesque spectacle, painting the battlefield in harsh, unnatural light. The massive funnel worked tirelessly, its eerie silence amplifying the horror. It consumed the remnants of the largest army in history with clinical precision, never harming any of the birds still trying to feed on the flesh of the fallen, leaving no trace behind. Tanks vanished into the void like toys, bodies disappeared without a sound, and the land itself seemed to flatten under the relentless force of the phenomenon.

Caleb watched, frozen in place, as the funnel continued its grim task. The sky grew darker, the oppressive clouds swirling ever closer to the ground. The silent lightning persisted, a mocking illumination that revealed the utter desolation of the field as it was scoured clean.

By the time the funnel finally dissipated, there was nothing left. The birds of prey, completely satiated, flew away and left the land eerily pristine, as though the battle, the soldiers, and even the war itself had been nothing more than a fevered dream. Alohanui had erased every trace of conflict.

Caleb's mind struggled to process the sheer enormity of what he had just witnessed. The scene played over and over in his head—a massive void opening up, an entire army vanishing, the sky darkening as if the Earth itself had decided to erase history. It was as though everything he knew about the rules of the universe had been torn apart and rewritten before his eyes. He stood there, stunned, his thoughts a tangled mess, struggling to decide what to do next.

Had Alohanui just eliminated war? The prospect loomed large in his mind, but he couldn't allow himself to be overwhelmed by the magnitude of it all. He couldn't forget why he was here—Emma and Beth. That was the mission. He had promised himself that nothing else would matter until he found them. He couldn't let go of that purpose.

The question of his own survival began creeping in. Should he even stay here now that the armies were gone? Was it now safe to return to Raven Rock, to Ted and Star? If he wanted to leave, where would he even begin? The Middle East had become a war zone of unthinkable proportions—were there even any functioning airports left? And if he stayed, how could he ever hope to enter Alohanui? The extraterrestrial cube seemed both majestic and impenetrable, towering above him like a fortress beyond reach.

His heart twisted with indecision. The possibility of failing to reunite with Emma and Beth tore at him. But then, how could he help them if he didn't find a way to understand Alohanui? If he didn't find a way in?

Suddenly, a voice within his mind spoke, clear and calm amidst his turmoil.

Wait. Just wait for a while.

He took a deep breath, allowing the words to resonate. Perhaps he needed to let the dust settle—both in the world outside and within his own mind. Maybe there was no clear path yet, but patience might be his best ally. His gut told him there was more to come; Alohanui wasn't finished with them yet. He just needed to wait, to watch, and when the opportunity presented itself, be ready to seize it.

"Emma, Beth, I will find you," he whispered, the words carrying his determination into the swirling winds around him. Whatever it took, wherever he had to go, he wouldn't give up. He'd come this far, and he wasn't about to stop now.

Under the sheltering arch of the bridge, Caleb sat hunched, staring intently at the river's faint, otherworldly glow as it wound its way eastward. His thoughts churned with uncertainty and exhaustion, but the rhythmic murmur of the water offered a small, unexpected comfort. Against the chaos of the outside world, this quiet refuge felt like a fragile sanctuary, a rare moment of stillness amidst the storm.

Gripping his tablet, Caleb activated its shortwave radio function and tuned into the faint, crackling signal of the BBC's emergency broadcast. Even with its skeleton crew, the steady cadence of the English language provided a tenuous lifeline to normalcy, however grim the updates might be. He adjusted the volume, leaning closer as the broadcaster's voice came through the static.

"The river flowing from Alohanui has been identified as toxic waste effluent from what experts believe to be the extraterrestrial city's radioactive power source," the announcer declared, their voice carefully measured but tinged with alarm. "Reports indicate that the river poses a radiation hazard. As it continues to flow into the Dead Sea, it has created what experts are calling an ecological catastrophe, diluting the unique salt content of this ancient body of water."

Caleb frowned, his gaze shifting back to the water. Toxic? Radioactive? He knew that couldn't be true. He'd tested the water himself with the tablet's radiation detector, and the readings had been clear—no radiation. The river wasn't hazardous, at least not in the way the report described. And the changes in the Dead Sea? They weren't destructive; they were transformative.

The water glowed faintly, yes, but Caleb suspected that was an optical illusion caused by light filtering through the translucent bridge deck above. It wasn't the dangerous blue glow of Cherenkov radiation in nuclear reactors, and he had even drunk the water—carefully purified first, of course—with no ill effects. Far from being toxic, the river seemed to breathe new life into the desolate environment. The salt in the Dead Sea was diluting, its waters becoming less harsh and more akin to those of the Sea of Galilee. Fish—actual fish—swam in the current now, darting through what had once been an inhospitable brine.

"The extraterrestrials are guilty of destroying a unique ecosystem," the broadcaster continued. "Their actions have erased millennia of geography, geology, and topography. While some salt marshes remain, sustaining a small salt-harvesting industry, the transformation of the Dead Sea is irreversible. The so-called 'living sea' is now teeming with fish similar to those found in the Sea of Galilee, but at the cost of an irreplaceable natural wonder."

Caleb snorted softly at the dramatization. A crime against Earth's natural heritage? Perhaps, but was this really a catastrophe? The Dead Sea, a lifeless expanse of hypersaline water for thousands of years, was now capable of sustaining life. To Caleb, it wasn't an erasure—it was a rebirth.

He stared at the glowing river, its flow relentless and purposeful, and wondered what other changes Alohanui might bring. It had caused so much devastation, so much death. Could this be its way of giving something back? Was this a deliberate act of restitution—or simply another step in its incomprehensible agenda?

Above him, the wind rustled through the surrounding terrain, carrying faint whispers of distant artillery and the acrid scent of burned earth. The sky remained heavy with bruised clouds, pressing low over the landscape as though mourning the shattered world below. The river, gleaming faintly in its unnatural glow, coursed steadily onward, a silent witness to the transformations unfolding in its wake. Caleb watched its flow, the questions piling in his mind as the BBC's crackling broadcast faded into the static once again.

Caleb didn't realize it, but Raven Rock had shifted its focus, transitioning from the Satellite Presidential Emergency Operations Center (SPEOC) to a Brain Trust. This was no abrupt change; it was a gradual evolution, an adaptation to the realities of a world that was crumbling faster than anyone could have anticipated. From the very beginning, Raven Rock had been designed with a dual purpose: to act as a command center during crises and, if necessary, to preserve the collective history and knowledge of humanity in the event of a civilization-ending cataclysm. That secondary mandate had now become its primary mission.

It had always been understood that operations might become impossible. There were contingency plans for a time when there would be no more National Guardsmen to deploy, no government employees to manage resources, no soldiers to carry out orders. What no one anticipated was that SPEOC would end not with a climactic event but with a slow, creeping collapse. Communications with the outside world had grown more sporadic, then increasingly fragmented, until finally, they stopped altogether. Resources outside Raven Rock dwindled, and the number of people available to direct or assist dwindled with them. One by one, the lines of connection between Raven Rock and the outside world fell silent, leaving the facility isolated.

Outside, chaos reigned. The global infrastructure that had once kept nations functioning dissolved into lawlessness and desperation. The world beyond Raven Rock had become a grim reality of "every man for himself." As SPEOC's directives became meaningless in a world with no one to follow them, Raven Rock's leadership made a difficult but necessary decision: it was time to shift gears.

Raven Rock transitioned fully into its Brain Trust mandate. Its mission now was not to lead but to preserve. The facility's vast archives were meticulously maintained, containing records of human history, science, art, and technology. Libraries of digital and physical resources were cataloged, alongside survival knowledge that could one day help rebuild civilization. The Brain Trust was no longer concerned with the immediate crisis—it had become a repository for humanity's collective wisdom, a seed bank for a future world.

As part of this transition, Raven Rock sealed itself off completely. Specially placed explosives were detonated to collapse the mountain's entrance, burying the massive vault door under tons of rock. It wasn't an act of cowardice but a calculated measure to ensure survival. The goal was simple: wait out the chaos. When the world outside became habitable again—when the storms passed, and the remnants of humanity were ready to rebuild—the people of Raven Rock would dig themselves out and emerge, carrying with them the keys to rekindle civilization.

Inside, life took on a new rhythm. The atmosphere,

once buzzing with urgent activity, settled into a quiet determination. Scientists, historians, and thinkers focused on their tasks, safeguarding knowledge and preparing for an uncertain future. They worked under the belief that, someday, the Earth would heal, and their efforts would matter.

Caleb, still unaware of Raven Rock's shift in purpose, continued his mission in the outside world, not realizing that the facility he had once depended on was no longer directing operations but preparing to become a beacon for a distant future. Raven Rock was no longer fighting the battle of the present; it was ensuring the survival of the past and the possibility of tomorrow.

The sun dipped low on the horizon, painting the sky with streaks of amber and crimson as Caleb sat by the riverbank, taking stock of his dwindling situation. His MREs had long since run out, leaving him with the stark realization that he was utterly on his own. The air was cooling rapidly, carrying with it the fresh, earthy scent of the river and the faint, lingering metallic tang of the distant battles still raging somewhere in the east. The occasional pop of artillery fire reminded him of the chaos he had temporarily escaped.

Caleb's decision to follow the river to the Dead Sea was both strategic and practical. Roads created by Alohanui, with their eerie precision, felt too exposed and unnatural—perfect ambush zones. The river, while more treacherous to navigate, offered clean water, food, and a semblance of natural cover. The water was remarkably clear, shimmering under the fading daylight, its surface broken occasionally by the flick of a fish's tail. Yet the journey along the riverbank was not without its challenges. Smooth river stones were slippery underfoot, and the constant danger of turning an ankle kept Caleb vigilant.

He was grateful for the quiet, though it carried its own sense of unease. Not a single person had crossed his path all day. He wasn't sure what he would do if someone did.

His hand brushed the pouch tied to his belt, feeling the reassuring weight of the forty silver dimes inside. Minted in 1955, each coin was 90% silver and worth far more than its face value—about $40 to $50 each. They were a relic of old-world preparedness, issued to him by those at Raven Rock who foresaw a time when paper currency would become worthless. Caleb knew they might save his life, though the engraving, "United States of America," could just as easily get him killed in the wrong hands.

When the sky deepened into twilight, Caleb decided it was time to set up camp. The chirping of crickets began to rise, blending with the soothing murmur of the river. A gentle breeze carried the smell of water and wet earth, mingling with the faint, acrid scent of distant fires.

His stomach growled as he pulled out his makeshift fishing kit from his knapsack—a compact collection of hooks, line, and weights, simple but effective. Using a flexible tent pole as an impromptu fishing rod, Caleb cast his line into the glowing river. The luminous water reflected the starlight, creating an almost magical atmosphere.

It didn't take long. A tilapia, sizable enough for one meal, tugged at the line almost as soon as the hook hit the water. Caleb pulled it out with a mix of relief and amazement. He hadn't expected such quick success.

With no wood or twigs nearby for a campfire, Caleb resorted to the white gas stove from his pack. The tilapia sizzled in the pan, filling the air with the rich, savory aroma of cooking fish. He ate slowly, savoring every bite. It was the best meal he'd had in days, even without sides.

The next morning, as the pale light of dawn began to break through the treetops, Caleb heard a voice calling from the riverbank above.

"Hey, American! How are you feeling?"

Startled, Caleb looked up to see a man silhouetted against the sky, his posture casual but his tone wary.

"How was your fish last night?" the man asked.

Caleb's pulse quickened. He realized that this stranger—clearly a deserter—had been watching him for hours, perhaps even since the night before. He felt exposed but knew he couldn't run or hide now. Gathering his courage, he replied.

"I'm Caleb," he called out. "Who are you?"

"George," the man replied. "Where are you from?"

"Oklahoma City, originally. Hawaii, most recently. You?"

"Gaza, originally. Austin, Texas, most recently."

"What do you want?" Caleb asked, his voice steady but cautious.

"I saw you eat radioactive fish," George said. "I want to know if you're okay. I'm starving, and, if the river's not radioactive, I'd like to try some of those fish."

Caleb hesitated. He didn't fully trust this man, but something in George's tone—earnest and desperate—made him feel a sliver of trust. "The stories about the river being radioactive are wrong," Caleb said. "Why don't you come down here? We can try catching breakfast together."

George made his way down the steep bank carefully, his movements deliberate. Up close, Caleb saw a man who looked exhausted but determined. His clothes were worn, his eyes sharp.

"Do you know how to fish?" Caleb asked.

"Not really," George admitted. "Do you?"

"Not really."

Despite their lack of expertise, they managed. Caleb cast his line into the glowing water, pulling out another tilapia within minutes. George, clearly impressed, took over the cooking, expertly handling the white gas stove.

As the fish sizzled, filling the air with its delicious aroma, George said, "You know, the river's not just clean—it's full of life. It's almost like it's been purified, not poisoned."

Caleb nodded. "There's a lot we don't understand about Alohanui or this river."

They ate in relative silence, the tension between them easing with each bite. By the time the second fish hit the pan, they had begun to talk, cautiously sharing bits of their stories, their fears, and their plans. Caleb still didn't know if George could be trusted, but for now, having company felt like a luxury he hadn't realized he needed.

However, the conversation crackled with tension, a subtle undercurrent of suspicion running beneath the exchange. Caleb kept his eyes on George, scanning him for any sign of deceit or ulterior motive. George, for his part, seemed relaxed, though Caleb couldn't help but feel that his calm demeanor was calculated—a front designed to disarm.

"Turns out the army was looking for a few good men who could write and speak Arabic," George said, his tone casual as he poked at the fire. His eyes flicked briefly to Caleb, gauging his reaction.

Caleb hesitated before replying, unsure if he should press for more details. "Is there still a U.S. Army?" he asked, trying to keep his tone neutral. The idea of finding some semblance of organization or assistance sent a flicker of hope through him, though he tried not to let it show.

George let out a dry chuckle, shaking his head. "Not for me," he said, his voice carrying a trace of bitterness. He met Caleb's gaze then, and for a moment, Caleb thought he saw a flicker of something—anger, regret, maybe both.

"After most of my friends were abducted—taken by the Alohanuians—everything changed," George continued, his voice lower now, almost a murmur. "It was defeat after defeat. Our troops were decimated. The ones left behind felt abandoned, betrayed. So most of us—including me—left the Army. The abductions, the casualties, and then the desertions... It all unraveled. So, no," he said, his voice tinged with finality. "There's no U.S. Army anymore. Not like you're hoping."

Caleb nodded slowly, his mind racing. If there was no military, no organized force to rely on, what hope did he have? He needed allies, resources—anything to help him survive and carry out his mission. But George's answers offered none of that.

"How have you managed to find food to eat?" Caleb asked cautiously. He kept his tone even, but the question was loaded. He needed to know if George could be trusted—or if his survival had come at someone else's expense.

George leaned back slightly, his posture casual but his eyes sharp. "Believe it or not, there are still a few farms left," he said. "But you need something to trade for food. Barter's the only currency now. You might be able to trade fish for vegetables, but that'll only last until the farmers realize the river and even the Dead Sea are full of delicious, non-radioactive fish."

Caleb caught the faintest glimmer of a smirk on George's face, but he couldn't tell if it was genuine humor or something darker. He felt a knot tightening in his stomach. Was George testing him? Did he know about the silver dimes in Caleb's pack?

"And what happens when people find out?" Caleb asked, carefully watching George's reaction.

George shrugged, his expression unreadable. "Then the game changes, doesn't it?" he said, his voice light but his words heavy. "When everyone knows the river isn't toxic, it won't be long before they come looking for their share. And when they do…" He let the sentence trail off, leaving Caleb to fill in the blanks.

Caleb didn't respond immediately. He kept his face neutral, though his thoughts churned. Was George warning him? Threatening him? Or was this just the cynical musings of a man who had seen too much? Caleb couldn't tell, and that uncertainty gnawed at him.

The two men sat in uneasy silence for a moment, the crackling of the fire the only sound between them. The smell of cooking fish hung in the air, mingling with the damp, earthy scent of the river. Overhead, the night sky was clear, the stars glinting like distant beacons in the darkness.

Caleb finally spoke, his voice steady but guarded. "If you've managed to survive this long, you must know your way around," he said, testing the waters. "Any advice for someone who's just trying to keep moving?"

George looked at him for a long moment, his expression unreadable. Then he leaned forward, spearing a piece of fish with his knife. "Yeah," he said, his tone matter-of-fact. "Trust no one. Not me. Not anyone. If you're lucky, you'll stay alive long enough to figure out who's worth trusting."

Caleb nodded, unsure whether to feel reassured or more wary. One thing was certain—he'd have to watch his back around George. For now, though, he had no choice but to eat, plan, and keep moving forward.

"I suppose I could live for a while on just fish," said Caleb. "But it would be nice to have some fruit and vegetables occasionally."

The fire crackled softly between them, providing warmth against the early morning chill as the scent of cooked fish mingled with the faint plumeria-like aroma of the river. Caleb stared into the flames for a moment, gathering his thoughts. He felt the weight of his next words, knowing they could shape his survival in this harsh, war-torn landscape.

"You know, George," Caleb began, his voice steady but tinged with emotion. "You've helped me immensely. I'm not sure I have what it takes to live like this—like a vagabond, a stranger in a strange land." He glanced up at George, who was calmly chewing a piece of fish, his expression unreadable.

George raised an eyebrow but said nothing, letting Caleb continue.

"How about this as a proposal?" Caleb asked, leaning forward slightly. "I go back to living under the bridge at the gate. I'll fish, and I'll live off that. You come and check on me once in a while, bring some food, and I'll trade you fish for vegetables. Of course, you could fish for yourself, but here's what I'm going to do."

Caleb reached into his pack, pulling out a small pouch. His hands trembled slightly as he opened it, revealing the glint of the forty silver dimes inside. He held them out to George, the coins catching the firelight like tiny mirrors.

"I'm going to give you these," Caleb said, his voice firm now.

George's eyes narrowed as he looked at the coins, then back at Caleb, suspicion flickering across his face. "What's the catch?" he asked, his tone cautious.

"No catch," Caleb replied. "I've decided to trust you. This is all I have to trade with—these coins and my life. I'm putting my life in your hands, George."

George's face softened slightly, though his guarded demeanor remained. He took the pouch carefully, weighing it in his palm before peeking inside at the coins. "Silver," he murmured, almost to himself. "Real silver. This could be worth something... maybe."

"I think you could do something with them," Caleb said. "Trade for food, or maybe other supplies. I don't have a clue what's valuable anymore, but you do. You speak Arabic and English, and you've been surviving here for months. Meeting you might be the best thing that's happened to me since I came to this place."

For a long moment, George didn't respond. He stared at Caleb, as if trying to read his soul, before finally nodding. "You're either incredibly naive or incredibly brave," George said, his voice tinged with reluctant admiration. "But I'll take you up on this. I'll check on you. I'll make sure you don't starve to death under that bridge."

"Deal," Caleb said, relief washing over him. He stood, shouldering his backpack. The weight felt lighter now, as if he'd shed more than just the coins. "I guess I'll see you around, then."

George nodded, tucking the pouch into his jacket. "Stay safe, Caleb. This place isn't kind to dreamers."

As Caleb turned and began the trek back toward Alohanui, the first stars began to emerge in the darkening sky. For the first time in days, Caleb felt a spark of hope. Maybe, just maybe, he could find a way to survive—and perhaps, a way back to Emma and Bethany.

As Caleb retraced his steps toward Alohanui, the once barren landscape around the river began to reveal subtle, but undeniable, signs of transformation. The dry, dusty banks he had passed on his initial journey were now dotted with fresh green shoots. Grasses swayed gently in the breeze, bulrushes clustered near the water's edge, and even small tree seedlings were sprouting, their delicate leaves reaching skyward as if in silent gratitude to the life-giving river.

"I suppose I could try eating grass if things get desperate," Caleb muttered to himself, a faint smile tugging at the corners of his mouth.

Just as he spoke, movement caught his eye. A gazelle stood by the river, its graceful neck bent low as it nibbled at the tender new growth. Caleb froze, watching it. The animal raised its head briefly, its large, dark eyes meeting his gaze, but it showed no fear, no instinct to flee. That struck Caleb as odd. The gazelle behaved as though it had never encountered a human before.

"Strange," he whispered. "You're not afraid of me, are you?"

He continued walking, his eyes now attuned to the growing greenery around him. The closer he drew to the bridge, the more vibrant the landscape became. Patches of green spread outward like ripples in a pond, overtaking the previously lifeless plain. The riverbanks were no longer just streaks of wet earth; they were transforming into lush, fertile ground.

Caleb paused, crouching down to touch the soil. It was damp, rich, and teeming with the promise of life. He realized that it must have taken time for the river's waters to saturate the parched earth beneath and around the riverbed. Days, perhaps, since the river had first begun flowing from Alohanui, carrying with it not just water, but something transformative, something that seemed to bring the land itself back to life.

As he approached the city, he noticed how the river meandered in graceful curves across the plain outside the walls, its path carving a natural, life-giving artery through the land. Near the city, the river ran almost parallel to the wall, its waters calm and wide, gently lapping at the edges of the burgeoning greenery. The banks here sloped gradually, the flow serene and steady, as if inviting the new life to settle and thrive.

Farther away, however, the character of the river changed. The bed grew steeper, and the water's flow became more turbulent, churning with restless energy as it tumbled over stones and down inclines. Caleb stopped to watch it for a moment, marveling at the contrast. It was as though the river carried the dichotomy of its source—Alohanui's imposing, unyielding structure—and the promise of renewal in its waters.

By the time Caleb reached the bridge near the eastern gate, he couldn't help but feel a flicker of awe. The land was changing, reshaping itself under the influence of Alohanui's river. Soon, he thought, the entire plain might become a verdant expanse, watered and nourished by this strange, alien gift. But as the gazelle's unafraid gaze lingered in his mind, Caleb couldn't shake a growing suspicion: Was this transformation entirely natural, or was there something more deliberate—more controlled—at play?

As Caleb neared the bridge—his sometime home and the place he'd come to regard as a tenuous safe haven—something caught his eye. Floating near the edge of the river, half-submerged in the gentle current, was a leaf. Its vivid green hue stood out against the silvery sheen of the water, drawing his attention.

"A leaf?" Caleb muttered, halting in his tracks. His heart quickened. A leaf meant a tree, and a tree meant potential fuel for a campfire. The thought was a relief—his white gas supply was nearly depleted. While the gas stove had served him well for cooking fish, it was a luxury quickly running out. Eating the tilapia raw wasn't appealing, even though he'd enjoyed the same fish as sushi in a Japanese restaurant with Emma back in Hawaii. That memory, bittersweet, nudged at his resolve to carry on.

Determined, Caleb waded into the river, careful to keep his footing on the smooth stones below. The water, cool and invigorating, lapped around his knees as he reached for the leaf. As his fingers brushed its surface, he realized something surprising—it wasn't just a lone leaf. It was attached to a twig, and the twig, in turn, was connected to something else: fruit.

Caleb froze for a moment, staring at the treasure in his hands. A piece of fruit! He examined it closely, his mind racing. The fruit was small and golden, smooth-skinned, and firm. It resembled a miniature apple but carried a faint citrus scent. His stomach growled as he considered its potential as a meal—or at least a tantalizing snack.

He scanned the surrounding landscape, his eyes darting along the riverbank. A fruit-bearing tree, outside Alohanui? That seemed impossible. He had seen the carefully manicured trees inside the city, lining the river's edge in organized groves, but outside? He hadn't noticed anything even remotely resembling a tree in this barren expanse. The river had brought life to the land, yes, but this—this was something new.

Caleb waded back to shore, the fruit still in his hand, his mind swirling with questions. How far upstream had this come from? Was there a tree nearby, or had the river carried it from inside the city itself? He studied the twig more closely. It was green and supple, not brittle or dried out. Whatever tree had produced it couldn't be far.

His curiosity sparked, Caleb decided to investigate. If there was a tree nearby, it could mean more than just fuel for a campfire. It could mean shade, sustenance, and the promise of something alive—something thriving—in this harsh and desolate place. Clutching the twig and its precious fruit, he set off along the riverbank, scanning the horizon with renewed determination.

After carefully studying the landscape outside Alohanui's towering walls, Caleb confirmed his suspicions—no tree had miraculously sprung up in his absence. The barren plain outside the city remained treeless as when he had left on his brief journey. Any hopes that the river's rejuvenating waters had fostered new growth were dashed. If the fruit and leaf had come from a tree, it was not one growing anywhere outside the city walls.

Resigned to this realization, Caleb turned his attention to the peculiar path of the river. Just before reaching the massive eastern gate—the gate near which Caleb had been camping—the river split, flowing in two separate channels that flanked the gate. It was a deliberate and unnatural design, the water bypassing the portal like a moat guarding an ancient fortress, though it was anything but medieval.

As he studied the leaf and fruit again, a memory stirred. Caleb suddenly recalled the high-resolution video footage he had captured during his earlier reconnaissance. The video had provided a rare glimpse through the open gate into the city beyond. Eager to confirm his hunch, he pulled out his tablet and accessed the footage.

Fast-forwarding to the key moments, Caleb scrutinized the images of the city's interior. There, flanking the riverbanks just inside the gate, he found what he was looking for—rows of trees, their branches heavy with leaves and fruit identical to the one he now held in his hand. The comparison left no doubt in his mind. The leaf and fruit he had fished from the river must have come from one of those trees within the city walls.

He paused, considering the implications. The river had carried the twig, leaf, and fruit from inside Alohanui, bypassing its fortified walls to deliver this small token to the outside world.

This realization reignited Caleb's curiosity—and his hope. The river was an unguarded way out of the city, could it be a way in? The possibilities swirled in his mind as he tucked the twig carefully into his pack. Whatever secrets Alohanui held, this fruit and leaf were proof of one thing: life flourished inside. And perhaps Emma and Beth did too.

Before stowing the tablet, Caleb double-checked the radiation levels again, still grappling with the disbelief that "experts" quoted on the BBC shortwave could lie so blatantly about such a critical issue. The tablet displayed the same reassuring result: *No radiation.*

Relieved but still wary, he set aside his unease and focused on setting up camp. The air was cool, carrying the faint scent of the river mingled with the aroma of wet stones and distant greenery. Overhead, the fading light of dusk painted the sky in soft purples and deep oranges, a brief moment of serenity before the encroaching night.

Caleb unpacked the rest of his backpack, his movements methodical. He baited his hook, cast his line into the water, and once again, almost immediately, caught a fish. This one was different from the tilapia he had caught before. It looked familiar, but he couldn't quite place the name. Regardless, it was large enough to provide a good meal for one man.

As he began cleaning the fish with his small knife, his focus wavered for just a moment, and the blade slipped. A sharp pain shot through his hand as he sliced his finger deeply—so deeply, in fact, that he could see the white gleam of bone beneath the crimson. Blood flowed freely, dripping onto the stones by the riverbank.

"Damn it!" Caleb hissed, clenching his jaw against the pain. He grabbed the first aid kit from his pack and fumbled with its contents, his hands trembling. He pulled out a bandage, but his vision blurred as tears of pain and frustration welled up in his eyes. He knew this wound needed stitches. But where could he possibly find a doctor in this desolate land? The realization that he might have incapacitated himself in such a critical moment filled him with a surge of anger. His hands shook so badly he couldn't properly bind the wound.

As he searched blindly for a gauze pad, his hand brushed against the leaf he had fished from the river earlier. Without thinking, he pressed the pliable leaf against his bleeding finger, just to temporarily stop the flow. The possibility of toxicity didn't even cross his mind in his frustration and desperation.

What happened next stunned him. The bleeding stopped instantly. It wasn't just slowed—it *stopped*, as if some miraculous styptic agent had been applied. The leaf felt cool and soothing against his skin, far more effective than any first-aid product he'd ever used. He held it there for several moments, half-expecting the bleeding to resume, but it didn't.

"Could this really be happening?" he muttered to himself, bewildered. The pain in his finger began to subside, replaced by a strange tingling sensation. After five minutes, Caleb gingerly unwrapped the leaf from his finger.

What he saw made him freeze. There was no blood, no wound, no scar—nothing to indicate that his finger had ever been cut. The skin was completely unblemished, as if the injury had never occurred.

Caleb stared at his hand in disbelief, his mind racing. Was this some property of the leaf? Some advanced healing mechanism tied to the extraterrestrial nature of Alohanui? He examined the leaf more closely, now treating it with a reverence usually reserved for ancient relics.

"What *are* you?" he whispered, holding the leaf up to the

fading light. The implications of its healing power sent a shiver down his spine. This wasn't just an ordinary plant. This could change everything.

As Caleb finished tending to his wound, the sun dipped below the horizon, leaving the sky painted in deep indigos and faint streaks of orange. A crescent moon hung low, its silvery light just enough to reveal the rippling surface of the river and the faint outlines of the alien landscape around him. Stars began to pierce the darkening sky, glittering like distant beacons in the vast expanse above. The air was cool now, carrying a slight dampness from the river, mingled with the faint metallic tang he associated with Alohanui's peculiar aura.

His stomach growled, reminding him of the fish he had caught earlier. The smell of the river still clung to his hands—a mix of clean water and the faint scent of aquatic life. The fish, fresh and ready to cook, would be his dinner, but there was a problem: his stove's flame might give him away. Caleb hesitated, weighing the risks. He wasn't overly concerned about the extraterrestrial guard, who seemed content to stay near the gate, but the unpredictability of Alohanui loomed large in his mind. If the alien city decided to act, everything could change in an instant.

Deciding to press on, he dismissed his fears about radiation or poison. He hadn't experienced any ill effects from the river fish or the strange fruit he had found. Holding the fruit in his hand, he brought it closer and inhaled. Its aroma was sharp and citrusy, with a hint of something floral—exotic and unfamiliar, yet somehow enticing. It reminded him of lemons, and the idea of squeezing its juice over his fish was too tempting to resist.

Caleb ignited the small white gas stove, its hiss and blue-orange flame breaking the stillness of the night. He placed his pan over the flame and fried the fish, its flesh sizzling and releasing a mouthwatering aroma that mingled with the clean, crisp scent of the river. As the fish cooked, he carefully sliced the fruit, its bright flesh releasing a burst of tangy perfume into the air. He squeezed the juice over the fish, the acidic scent mingling with the savory aroma of the frying fish.

The first bite was heavenly. The flesh of the fish was tender and flaky, its natural sweetness perfectly balanced by the tangy brightness of the fruit's juice. Caleb ate slowly, savoring each bite, the flavors heightened by his hunger and the surreal setting.

Once he finished the fish, he eyed the remaining pulp of the fruit. It was soft and sticky, glistening faintly in the moonlight. Scooping a piece into his mouth, he found it surprisingly sweet, with a flavor that reminded him of a blend between orange and pineapple, but with an unfamiliar twist. It left a pleasant aftertaste that lingered as he sat back, looking up at the now fully starlit sky.

The night was quiet save for the gentle murmur of the river and the occasional distant rustle of wind through sparse grasses. The cool air carried the faintest hint of the fried fish he had cooked, mingled with the residual citrusy aroma from the fruit. Caleb stretched out, letting the moment sink in. For now, he was full, the wound on his finger miraculously healed, and the sky above offered a fleeting sense of peace in a world that had otherwise descended into chaos.Caleb's dreams that night were unsettling, though he slept soundly. In his dream, he was lying on his pillow, spitting out teeth one by one as they loosened and fell from his gums. Each tooth landed softly beside his head in a growing pile, the strange sensation vivid enough to wake him. He jolted upright, the dream still lingering in his mind.

Rubbing his eyes, Caleb felt oddly refreshed despite the bizarre images that had haunted his sleep. Then he noticed it: a small pile of objects on his pillow. His heart skipped a beat as he leaned closer. At first glance, the objects were small, hard, and white—similar to teeth but much smaller. Among them was something that made his stomach drop: his dental crown.

The sight took him back in an instant. He had gotten that crown years ago after a trampoline accident left one of his molars shattered. He had been attempting a somersault and landed on the steel ring of the trampoline, smashing his knee into his jaw. The damage had been severe, and the dentist had given him two options: extract the tooth, which could lead to lifelong bite issues, or get a crown—a much more expensive solution. His parents, who didn't have dental insurance, had been forced to borrow money from Caleb's grandparents to pay for the crown, an ordeal that took his father, Jake, a year to repay.

Caleb vividly remembered the dentist showing him the crown before it was installed. It was small, almost weightless, and yet incredibly expensive. How could something so tiny cost so much? Now, staring at the object on his pillow, he recognized it immediately.

He felt a wave of panic. *Where am I going to find a dentist here?* Rubbing his tongue along his teeth, he braced for the worst—an empty gap where the crown had been. But to his astonishment, all his teeth were intact. No gaps, no missing molars. Every tooth was present and in perfect condition. Confused, he ran his tongue over them again. They felt smooth, natural. He wasn't sure whether to feel relieved or alarmed.

Turning back to the pile on his pillow, Caleb picked up the crown. It wasn't just similar to his crown—it *was* his crown. The porcelain was fused to a metal base, the distinctive wear pattern unmistakable. The other objects, which he now realized were tiny fragments, looked familiar too.

Fillings, he realized with growing unease. They were his old fillings.

He rummaged through his pack, pulling out a small magnifying glass and a mirror. Holding it up to the sunlight filtering into his tent, he examined the crown and fillings closely. They were undeniably his. Yet, when he probed his mouth with his tongue again, every tooth felt flawless—smooth, unblemished, as if the fillings had never been needed.

Positioning the mirror and angling his mouth just right proved to be a challenge. He struggled to align everything so that the sunlight illuminated his teeth while still allowing him to see clearly in the mirror. After several awkward adjustments and a few minutes of trial and error, he finally managed to get a proper view. The realization hit as he inspected his reflection —his crown was gone.

His mind raced. *My crown fell out. My fillings fell out. But my teeth... healed themselves?*

The realization hit him like a bolt of lightning. Somehow, the leaf or perhaps the fruit had caused his teeth to regenerate. Not only had his fillings and crown fallen out, but the teeth beneath them had completely restored themselves to perfect health. The thought was equal parts thrilling and terrifying.

Caleb leaned back, his eyes fixed on the small pile of discarded dental work resting in his palm, the weight of his discovery pressing heavily on his chest. His mind churned with questions and possibilities. *What else could this leaf heal?* The thought gripped him, refusing to let go. His thoughts turned sharply to Emma, to her battle with cancer, to the pain and fear she had endured.

If this leaf could repair my teeth so perfectly, could it do more? Could it heal her?

And then, like a sudden flash of light in the dark, a new

thought struck him. *If Emma is inside Alohanui, perhaps she's already been healed.*

The possibility ignited a flicker of hope within him, fragile yet profound, pulling him from the edge of despair. Whatever awaited him next, he knew one thing—he had to find her. And he had to find out if the miracles of this place extended to the one he loved most.

CHAPTER 13 THE BEGGAR AT THE GATE

Caleb spent his days fishing and scavenging along the steadily greening riverbanks, finding solace in the routine. Nobody approached him, and as long as he stayed away from the imposing guard at the gate, the guard paid him no attention. That uneasy truce was enough for Caleb to focus on survival. He couldn't help but wonder how George was faring with the silver dimes he'd given him. Was George managing to trade and barter successfully? And if they ever crossed paths again, would George bring something useful in return?

Caleb began to think about trade. If anyone comes by, fish might be valuable. But preserving fish for trade was a challenge. He needed a way to keep them from spoiling. Every day, the banks of the river and the surrounding plain grew lusher. Bamboo, not the tropical variety but the hardy kind suited to this latitude, had begun to flourish. It was an unexpected blessing, and Caleb quickly discovered its many uses.

His first project was crafting drying racks. Using the versatile bamboo, he built sturdy frames where he could butterfly and spread fish to dry in the sun. The process worked, but something was missing. *Salt,* Caleb thought. *I need salt to make this work—something tasty enough to trade if I ever meet George again, or anyone else, for that matter.*

As Caleb busied himself collecting kindling for his campfire and casting his line into the river, he kept one eye trained on the water, always alert for leaves or fruit floating downstream. He was certain they would be valuable for trade, far more than the fish he caught. But he couldn't risk parting with the single leaf he already had. It was his lifeline, a miraculous treasure that had healed his wound and left him awestruck by its power.

The fruit he had found previously seemed almost mythical now. Dense and heavy, it had barely floated, kept above the water only by the attached twig. Caleb had been lucky to spot it before it sank. Since then, the river had carried no such gifts. He knew the odds were slim that another piece of fruit would drift by—it was far more likely that any future fruit from Alohanui's trees would sink to the riverbed, lost to him forever.

Leaves, on the other hand, could float for a time before becoming waterlogged. That small fact gave him a glimmer of hope. He felt fortunate to have set up his camp under the bridge closest to where the river emerged from Alohanui's walls. If anything valuable were to float out of the city, he was perfectly positioned to find it. Yet, two months had passed since his last discovery, and the river had offered him nothing more than fish and smooth stones.

It had also been two months since George had gone east when Caleb went west. Caleb had all but given up on ever seeing him again, resigning himself to solitude. Then, on a day like any other, as Caleb tended his campfire, he spotted a figure in the distance. Emerging from a dense patch of foliage along the riverbank, a man strode onto the road. Caleb squinted, his heart leaping when he recognized the silhouette. George.

Without hesitation, Caleb ran to greet him, relief and joy washing over him in equal measure. "I was beginning to think I'd never see you again," Caleb said, a grin spreading across his face. "Good to see you, my friend."George smiled back, his face thinner than Caleb remembered but his eyes just as sharp. He raised a hand in greeting and replied with the traditional Arabic salutation, "As-salaam 'alaikum."

"Wa 'alaikum as-salaam," Caleb answered, stumbling over the words but meaning them sincerely.

The two men stood there for a moment, taking in each other's presence. For Caleb, it felt like the first warm connection he'd had in months, a reminder that he wasn't entirely alone in this strange and hostile world. For George, it was a chance to reconnect with someone who had shown him unexpected kindness in a time of desperation.

"Come on," Caleb said, motioning toward his camp under the bridge. "I've got fish. Let's catch up."

The sight of George walking toward him had brought an unexpected swell of relief. For two months, Caleb had survived on fish, bamboo, and the occasional edible plant he scavenged along the riverbank. The solitude had begun to weigh on him more heavily than he'd realized.

George looked thinner, his face more weathered, but his eyes still held a spark of determination. He carried a small bundle slung over his shoulder, and Caleb noticed the glint of something metallic in George's hand.

"I didn't think I'd make it here either," George admitted, smiling faintly. "The world out there is... well, you know."

Caleb nodded, his thoughts flashing to the ominous stillness of Alohanui towering behind him. "Did you have any luck with the dimes?" Caleb asked, motioning toward his small campfire.

George crouched by the fire, untying the bundle slung over his shoulder. The firelight cast flickering shadows across his face, worn thin by months of survival. "Luck? Not exactly," he said, his voice low and tinged with fatigue. "But I did manage to trade some of the coins for this."

From the bundle, he pulled out a small leather pouch. He opened it carefully, revealing its contents: a handful of seeds of various shapes and sizes. "They say these are vegetable seeds—carrots, lettuce, beans. Hard to trust anyone these days, but the guy I traded with seemed genuine enough."

Caleb's eyes lit up as he leaned closer to inspect the seeds. The sight of them filled him with a surprising sense of hope. "This is incredible!" he exclaimed. "I've been trying to figure out how to preserve fish for trade, but growing vegetables... that could be even better. A real game changer."

George grinned, but there was a hint of caution in his expression. "Don't give up fishing just yet," he said, reaching into his bundle again. With a grunt, he hefted a forty-pound sack onto the ground beside Caleb. The sack bore faint markings that had once read "Dead Sea Salt."

Caleb blinked in surprise. "Salt? Where did you—"

"There's a thriving salt harvesting operation in the marshes of the Dead Sea," George explained, brushing dust off his hands. "The topography has shifted a lot. The whole area's well above sea level now. During the earthquake that destroyed Jerusalem, the whole area around the Dead Sea and the Sea of Galilee rose a couple thousand feet. It's no longer cut off—it flows out to the Red Sea. And thanks to your Alohanui River, it's not dead anymore. The water's getting fresher by the day."

Caleb's mind raced at the implications. A sustainable source of salt and seeds meant he could begin to trade in earnest, building something that might help him survive longer—and maybe even thrive—in this desolate, unpredictable landscape.

"Salt and seeds," Caleb murmured, shaking his head in amazement. "George, you've done more than I could have ever hoped for."

"Just trying to stay useful," George replied with a smirk. "We've got to adapt, right? This world isn't what it used to be. We're not what we used to be."

Caleb nodded, his grip tightening around the sack of salt. As the fire crackled between them, it wasn't just warmth they shared—it was something long missing in both their lives: possibility.

Caleb paused, his voice tinged with curiosity. "What else have you seen out there?"

George's face darkened, shadows from the flickering fire accentuating the weight of his words. "The world's unraveling, Caleb. Someone told me over five billion people have died since Alohanui entered our solar system. And while the 200 million soldiers who died in the battle for Alohanui are a staggering number, the fighting hasn't ended. The so-called Allies have turned on each other. It's chaos—every man for himself. People are scavenging, bartering, doing whatever they can to survive."

He hesitated, his gaze flicking to the glowing river and then toward Alohanui, its walls catching the faint glimmers of twilight. "But there's more. Rumors. Strange stories about the city."

Caleb leaned forward, his pulse quickening. "What kind of stories?"

George's eyes narrowed as he stared at the alien structure looming in the distance. "They say those alien guards with flaming swords are letting some people enter the City of

Alohanui. Not many, but some. And not everyone comes back out. Those who do… they're different. Healed, completely whole in ways you wouldn't believe. But there's more to it than that. Some folks swear they've seen loved ones, long dead, walking along those walls."

A chill ran down Caleb's spine as George's words sank in. "The dead?" he whispered, his voice barely audible.

George nodded slowly. "Yeah. Alive, moving around like nothing ever happened to them. And I'm not talking about ghost stories, Caleb. These are people who were dead and buried—brought back."

Images flashed through Caleb's mind: the videos he had seen of the upside-down tornadoes ripping open graveyards, the corpses being drawn into the clouds like leaves on the wind. It all made sense now. They weren't robbing graves or dissecting bodies for some macabre experiment.

"They're bringing the dead back to life," Caleb murmured, his throat dry. The thought was equal parts horrifying and hopeful, his mind turning immediately to Emma and Bethany. Were they inside Alohanui? Could they have been healed, restored—even if they were dead?

The two men sat in silence, the fire crackling between them. Above, the stars emerged one by one in a sky darker than Caleb had ever remembered. Alohanui stood unmoving, its enigmatic walls guarding secrets too vast and alien for the human mind to grasp.

George leaned forward, his voice dropping to a conspiratorial tone. "There's another rumor going around. They say the fruit from the trees inside Alohanui can cure anything. Disease, injuries, you name it. People are desperate to get their hands on it, but so far, I haven't met anyone who's actually succeeded."

Caleb's hand moved instinctively to the small pouch hanging

around his neck. Inside were his treasures: the single leaf, the twig, and the peel from that miraculous piece of fruit he had found floating in the river. His fingers brushed the pouch's surface, his mind racing with possibilities.

If what George said was true, then this fruit wasn't just rare—it was life itself, a beacon of hope for a broken world. But it also meant that if anyone found out what he carried, his life could be in even greater danger. Caleb tightened his grip on the pouch and glanced toward Alohanui, its walls casting an ominous silhouette against the deepening night.

"Desperate, you say?" Caleb murmured, his voice low. "They don't even know what they're chasing."

Caleb and George sat by the fire that night, hashing out a plan to improve their chances of survival and maybe even carve out a small foothold of stability in the chaos. George agreed to stay for a few days to help Caleb plant and water the seeds, construct more drying racks for fish, and assist in salting the fish Caleb had already dried.

The stretch of land they had at their disposal was vast, a fertile plain along the riverbank. But their resources were limited; they had only a few seeds to work with. They decided to space the seeds out strategically near the top of the riverbank, where the soil was moist but not waterlogged, and where sunlight was abundant. The men worked side by side, loosening the soil with improvised tools made from split bamboo and stones. George's hands were calloused but steady as he pressed each seed into the earth, while Caleb fetched water from the river to moisten the newly planted rows.

While George focused on the planting, Caleb turned his attention to fishing. The river's bounty seemed endless, and Caleb had become adept at catching, cleaning, and butterflying the fish for preservation. As George watched Caleb work, he marveled at the ingenuity Caleb had shown in crafting tools and supplies from the bamboo growing along the riverbank. Caleb demonstrated how he peeled long strips of 'bark' from young bamboo shoots, twisting and knotting the pliable strips into a surprisingly strong and durable twine. Once hardened, the twine created firm, permanent connections between the pieces of bamboo that made up the drying racks.

The two men worked with focused efficiency, seamlessly dividing their tasks. Caleb added freshly caught fish to the bamboo racks George had skillfully assembled. The process was straightforward but effective: butterflied fish were laid flat on the racks, positioned to catch the sun's drying heat and the river's steady breeze. Meanwhile, George salted some of the already dried fish, hoping the added preservation would increase their shelf life and trade value. As they worked, Caleb reflected on the salting process. He knew that applying salt only after the fish had dried wasn't ideal. With a steady supply of salt now available, salting the fish immediately after cleaning and butterflying them would yield a far superior product. This method would allow the salt to penetrate the flesh more deeply during the drying process, enhancing both flavor and preservation.

Still, there was no point in dwelling on what couldn't be changed. This batch, even if less than perfect, had to suffice for now. Caleb figured that improving the process was a task for the future. For now, their priority was to produce enough fish to make the trade worthwhile. *That's George's challenge to handle when he's out there bartering,* Caleb thought. *My job is to make sure he has a product to trade when he gets back.*

"This is pretty good work for a couple of guys who've never fished or farmed before," George said with a chuckle, stepping back to admire the neatly arranged racks and the carefully planted rows of seeds along the riverbank.

Caleb nodded, wiping sweat from his brow. "We're learning.

Let's just hope it's enough to keep us going."

After a few days, with the seeds planted and a new and improved batch of fish salted and in the process of drying, George prepared to set out again. His goal was to trade some of the first batch of salted fish for more supplies—tools, seeds, or even news about the world beyond the river. Caleb watched him pack up the dried fish into a sturdy woven bag, his movements purposeful but unhurried.

"Stay sharp out there," Caleb said, handing George the bag. "Make some good trades."

George smirked as he slung the bag over his shoulder. "I'll give it a shot. By the time I'm back, maybe you'll have managed to grow something worth eating."

Caleb laughed, though he wasn't sure how long it would take for the seeds to sprout. "Here's hoping, my friend."

As George disappeared down the road, Caleb returned to his camp, now feeling a bit less isolated. Together, they had laid the groundwork for something that felt almost hopeful, a fragile sense of purpose amidst the surrounding desolation. Caleb knew the days ahead would be tough, but he was determined to make this patch of land thrive.

"It must be the water," Caleb muttered to himself, his voice breaking the silence of the deserted landscape. The seeds were sprouting faster than he had ever expected. The river, teeming with fish before its channel had fully filled and long before it reached the Dead Sea, clearly carried more than just water—it carried life.

"This is good," he said, half-smiling, though his thoughts were already turning practical.

He powered on his tablet for the first time in weeks, a soft glow illuminating his face as he navigated the menus. He needed information—anything to teach him how to grow vegetables from seed in this unfamiliar environment. To his relief, the tablet's memory held an offline copy of Wikipedia, compressed for efficiency. It also contained the Quran in classic Arabic, the King James Bible, the complete works of Shakespeare, and, amusingly, *The Hitchhiker's Guide to the Galaxy*. He chuckled at the odd assortment of knowledge at his fingertips.

As he sifted through Wikipedia, Caleb came across a critical detail about growing vegetables: pollination. Many plants, particularly pumpkins, cucumbers, gourds, and melons, required pollinators to "bear fruit." Caleb froze, realizing a problem—he hadn't seen a single insect anywhere near the city or the plain. No bees, no butterflies, no beetles. Nothing.

He leaned back against the smooth quartz bulkhead, pondering the implications. Without pollinators, these plants would grow but never produce anything edible. But further reading offered a solution that startled him in its simplicity: *He could be the pollinator.*

Armed with this knowledge, Caleb waited. When the first flower on what he hoped was a watermelon plant appeared only a week after planting, he examined it closely. It turned out to be a pumpkin plant, but Caleb didn't mind. He recognized the flower as male—a brightly colored bloom with a pollen-dusted stamen at its center. Days later, more flowers appeared, including female ones with their distinctive bulb-like base.

Carefully, Caleb cut the male flower, its vibrant petals soft and fragrant in his hand. He gently shook its stamen over the pistils of the female flowers, watching as the pollen dusted the delicate surfaces.

"Here's hoping this works," he murmured, stepping back to admire his handiwork. The plain around Alohanui was eerily silent except for the sound of the river flowing nearby. The absence of insects, birds, or any other creatures except the fish seemed unnatural, but Caleb focused on his small victories.

If this method succeeded, the pumpkin plants would bear fruit in record time. He didn't have the luxury of nature's help here, but he would do what he could with what he had.

Every single seed that George had brought to Caleb germinated, as if the Alohanui River's water carried some kind of life-giving magic. Although George and Caleb had spaced the seeds generously far apart when planting, just two weeks later, the young plants were crowding each other, their lush green leaves already sprawling across the pale soil. The transformation of the plain was startling, a burst of life where barren ground had stretched for as long as Caleb could remember.

Caleb spent countless hours tending to the plants, his fingers coated in the peculiar, chalky soil that seemed to contradict everything he thought he knew about agriculture. At first glance, the soil appeared lifeless—nothing more than pulverized limestone, dry and barren. He had doubted it could support any kind of growth, let alone sustain the thriving greenery that now surrounded him. Yet, to his astonishment, the soil was more fertile than the richest organic compost he had ever worked with, even surpassing the dark, nutrient-rich earth of Emma's little garden in Ted and Star's backyard back in Hawaii.

Once the plants were established with just a few careful waterings from the Alohanui River, they became nearly self-sufficient. Caleb realized that the water table was astonishingly shallow, likely no more than a couple of feet below the surface, allowing the plants' roots to reach moisture on their own. They thrived with minimal intervention, their roots delving deeply into the ground and anchoring themselves firmly.

The transformation was breathtaking. Where once there had

been barren ground stretching to the horizon, there were now vibrant green shoots growing taller and fuller each day. Caleb marveled at how effortlessly life had taken hold here, defying the grim, desolate nature of the world outside this patch of the plain.

When the crowding became an issue, Caleb experimented with transplanting some of the seedlings. He had low expectations, bracing for withered leaves and drooping stems. But to his amazement, the Alohanui River water seemed to nullify any transplant shock. The transplanted seedlings didn't just survive—they flourished, growing stronger than ever in their new locations.

Then Caleb made another discovery: cuttings. On a whim, he snipped a branch from one of the thriving plants and plunged it into the soil, watering it with the river's water. Within days, the cutting sprouted roots and began growing new branches and leaves, quickly establishing itself as a fully independent plant. Caleb stared at the thriving cutting, incredulous. Was there anything this water couldn't do?

With these discoveries, Caleb's modest planting efforts exploded into something far greater. From the one hundred seeds George had brought, Caleb now had over 2000 plants flourishing across ten acres of the plain. The once-sterile expanse now had a square patch of vibrant green in addition to the overgrown riverbanks, the plants standing tall against the stark backdrop of the pale soil and the quartz and gold structures of Alohanui looming in the distance.

The air was heavy with the scent of the burgeoning plants, mingling with the faint, mineral tang of the river. A gentle breeze carried the sounds of rustling leaves and the soft murmur of the river's flow, creating a serene atmosphere that belied the chaotic world beyond the plain. Overhead, the sky stretched wide and blue, with only a few wisps of clouds drifting lazily above the scene of near-miraculous growth.

Caleb stood at the edge of his expanding garden, wiping the sweat from his brow and gazing over the rows of thriving plants. Despite the eerie quiet of the plain—no insects buzzed—he felt a cautious sense of hope. Here, amidst the chaos of a collapsing world, life was flourishing. If he could sustain this, it might not only feed him but offer something to trade, a tangible resource in a world starved of hope.

Caleb had started to expand his diet beyond the endless supply of fish, introducing fresh vegetables from the thriving garden he and George had brought into being. It began with a single baby carrot—crunchy, sweet, and full of flavor. He snapped the top off and removed the four stalks from it and carefully replanted the top and the four stalks, confident that he would gain five carrots in his garden and one in his stomach as a result, marveling at how quickly they regrew in the fertile, limestone soil. Next came snap peas, their pods crisp and refreshing, perfect for a quick snack or a hearty addition to his meals. Even the immature peas inside the pod could be used as seeds, ensuring the cycle of growth continued uninterrupted.

Before long, cherry tomatoes began to ripen, their bright red skins glowing like jewels in the sunlight. They were an indulgent treat, bursting with sweetness and acidity with every bite. And then, it seemed, everything started yielding. Cucumber vines twisted up from the soil, their fruits hanging heavy and cool to the touch. Squash plants sprawled across the ground, their blossoms transforming into rich, golden gourds. Even herbs like basil and cilantro began to thrive, adding flavor and fragrance to his meals.

The garden flourished beyond Caleb's wildest expectations, producing an abundance of fresh produce that never seemed to stop. Each day brought new surprises, new additions to the growing bounty of their farm. Caleb found himself overwhelmed by the generosity of the land, grateful for every morsel it provided.

Still, the thought of winter lingered at the back of his mind. Would this miraculous garden survive when the temperatures dropped? Would the river, with its life-giving properties, slow or freeze? He didn't have answers, but for now, he decided to focus on the present. "Make hay while the sun shines," he muttered to himself, embracing the old adage as his personal mantra.

Caleb kept himself busy tending to his plants and collecting material for his campfire. But as he worked, he couldn't shake the feeling that someone might eventually discover his garden and take advantage of his efforts.

Early one morning, Caleb stirred from his sleep to find a man standing at the edge of the bridge, watching him. His heart raced as he sat up, staring at the stranger who looked back at him with a calm yet unsettling demeanor.

"Hi," the man said in English, smiling. "You've got a fine-looking garden here. I was wondering if I could sample some of it. It's been a while since I've had fresh produce."

Caleb blinked, caught off guard. "Well, I suppose so," he said cautiously, his voice masking his rising anxiety. "Come with me."

The man didn't appear armed, but there was something bulky in his pocket. Caleb couldn't tell if it was a weapon or just some random object, but the man didn't seem overly threatening. He looked older than Caleb, though it was hard to tell exactly how old.

"Anything in particular you're interested in?" Caleb asked as he led the man toward the garden.

"Carrots and peas," the man replied, glancing around as if

appraising the crops.

"Do you live around here?" Caleb asked, trying to assess the situation further.

"Oh yes, very close," the man said. "But we don't have a source of produce right now. Maybe you could be it."

Without waiting for permission, the man bent down, pulled up a carrot, wiped it on his sleeve, and bit into it with a crunch. "Oh, sweet. You've quite a garden here."

Caleb's unease grew. Summoning his courage, he finally asked, "How do you expect to pay for this?"

"Well, aren't samples free?" the man said, smirking.

"Are you some kind of wise guy?" Caleb shot back, growing more assertive.

"I guess I am," the man admitted with a chuckle. "But you're right—I shouldn't joke about a man's livelihood." He straightened up, brushing dirt off his hands. "How much for all your peas and all your carrots?"

"I don't know. You're my first customer," Caleb admitted, trying to figure out how to navigate this barter. "What's being used for money these days?"

The man considered this for a moment. "Well, I don't have any cash. What I can offer are leaves and fruit."

Caleb's eyes narrowed. Could this man be talking about the same kind of fruit and leaves he had retrieved from the river? "What kind of fruit?" he asked, keeping his tone neutral.

"Fruit and leaves from the tree of life," the man said matter-of-factly.

Caleb's pulse quickened. "Samples are free, right?" he said, throwing the words back at him. "Let me see one."

The man grinned and pulled a small piece of fruit from his pocket. Caleb examined it closely. It didn't look like the fruit he had fished out of the river.

"That's not from the Alohanui tree," Caleb said firmly.

"Alohanui?" The man raised an eyebrow. "Is that what you call it?" He gestured toward the city.

"Yes," Caleb said. "That's Alohanui."

"Well," the man said, smirking again. "This fruit comes from the tree that grows on either side of the river inside the city."

Caleb shook his head. "It's not the same. I've seen the fruit myself."

The man leaned in conspiratorially. "The tree produces twelve kinds of fruit, one for every month. This piece here is July's. June's fruit is golden and firm, kind of like a crab apple but with the scent of lemon."

"How am I supposed to know you're telling the truth?" Caleb challenged.

"Have you ever seen a leaf?" the man asked, pulling a few stacked leaves from his other pocket. Caleb's breath caught. They were identical to the leaf he had retrieved from the river, their unique almost-square shape unmistakable.

"They stack nicely, don't they?" the man joked. "Fit right in your wallet."

Caleb nodded slowly. "Those are the leaves."

"Well, I can barter in leaves or fruit," the man said, his tone turning businesslike. "Currently, the exchange rate is 75 leaves for one piece of fruit. Your peas and carrots are not worth a piece of fruit. So the best I can do for your entire crop of peas and carrots is 20 leaves."

Caleb hesitated, weighing his options. "By the way, what's your name?" he asked, hoping to distract the man and gain more information.

"Jacob," the man said. "And you?"

"Caleb."

"Where are you from originally, Caleb?" Jacob asked.

"Oklahoma City," Caleb replied. "And you?"

"Horse Creek," Jacob said. "It's not on any map, it didn't even have a post office."

Caleb froze. "My dad was born in Horse Creek."

Jacob raised an eyebrow. "What's his name?"

"Jake Jacobson," Caleb said.

Jacob laughed softly. "Jacob Jacobson? That's funny. I think he's my grandson."

Caleb frowned, his disbelief apparent. "That's impossible. My great-grandfather died before I was born."

Jacob's expression softened. "I was born in 1925."

Caleb stared, stunned. "Are you telling me you're my great-grandfather? Or is this just a ploy to get me to trade all my peas and carrots for 20 leaves?"

"Maybe both," Jacob said with a sly grin, his tone teasing but not unkind.

Caleb narrowed his eyes, determined to test him. "What's my mother's name?"

"Jean," Jacob replied without hesitation.

Caleb felt a chill run through him. "I want to see her."

Jacob shrugged, his expression unreadable. "Well, go see her then. I'm pretty sure she's still in there—in the city you call Alohanui. But think about it, Caleb. If she wanted to see you, don't you think she would've come out by now? The gate guards know you're here. If she had asked them about you, they'd have given her a full report."

Caleb's jaw tightened, but Jacob held up a hand, his tone softening. "But I'm kidding with you a bit. I could think of many reasons why she hasn't come to see you yet. Timing, circumstances, maybe even rules we don't fully understand. Don't lose hope. I'm sure she'll get around to it."

The words didn't ease Caleb's frustration. "Please," he said, his voice dropping. "Give me, your great grandson, a piece of fruit from the tree of life."

Jacob studied him for a long moment before nodding. "Of course, Caleb. Since you asked so earnestly..." He reached into his pocket and handed Caleb a small, smooth fruit. "Here you go. This one ripened in July."

Caleb stared at the fruit in his hand, its faint aroma like a mix of peach and citrus. For a moment, he forgot where he was, overwhelmed by the significance of what he held.

"Now," Jacob said, breaking the spell. "I hope that little gift establishes some rapport between us. How about you give me all your peas and carrots for 20 leaves?"

Caleb blinked, grounding himself in the present. "Fine," he said, his mind already calculating his next move. "But I need the stalks from the carrots. I'll need to propagate them, since you're taking all of them."

"Fair enough," Jacob agreed with a nod.

Caleb set to work, harvesting every pea pod and carrot from his garden and bundling them into a burlap sack. The weight of the bag felt significant, not just in pounds but in the value of his labor. He handed it over to Jacob, who slung it over his shoulder with ease.

"Good doing business with you, Caleb," Jacob said, tipping an imaginary hat. Then, without another word, he turned and walked down the road away from the city, his silhouette fading into the horizon.

Caleb's pulse quickened. *He must have come from the city. Maybe the city is finally open for business,* he thought. The idea of getting inside, of finding Emma and Beth, propelled him forward. He immediately moved to follow Jacob, but the guard's reaction was swift and unmistakable.

With a deliberate motion, the guard raised its flaming sword, the blade crackling with a fiery intensity that lit up the night. The heat was palpable, forcing Caleb to halt in his tracks. The figure stepped into his path, its multi-faced visage as unreadable as ever, but the message was clear: *You shall not pass.*

Caleb took a step back, frustration bubbling within him as he watched Jacob's silhouette disappear into the depths of the city.

That's a lot to process, Caleb thought, but it'll have to wait. Do what needs to be done first, thinking and reflection can come later.

Pushing his musings aside, he turned his attention to the carrot stalks. One by one, he pressed them into the fertile soil along the riverbank, ensuring each one was firmly planted and upright. The rich, clear water from the Alohanui River soaked into the ground as he carefully poured it around the stalks. The damp earth gave off a faint, mineral scent that mingled with the cool night air. He glanced up at the sky, now streaked with purples and deep blues as twilight gave way to night. *By morning, I'll know if this works,* he thought.

Beneath the bridge, Caleb settled onto his makeshift seat, unwrapping a piece of salted fish from his second batch. He bit into it, savoring the difference. Salting the fish before drying had been a game changer, giving it a rich, savory flavor that was deeply satisfying after the day's work. The faint crunch of the salt crystals and the tasty fish made the meal feel like a small victory.

With his hunger satisfied, Caleb turned his attention to his precious stash of leaves. He reached into the hollowed-out space beneath a cluster of rocks, pulling out the small, carefully wrapped bundle. Twenty-one leaves in total—each one a potential lifeline. He traced the edge of one leaf with his finger, marveling again at its unique texture and perfect symmetry. After inspecting them, he returned them to their hiding spot, packing the rocks securely around the cache.

The moon was high now, casting its silvery glow over the river. Caleb leaned back, letting his mind wander as the gentle sound of flowing water filled the air. The night was cool and calm, a peaceful contrast to the tension of the day. He exhaled slowly, watching the faint mist rise off the river's surface, and for the first time in hours, he allowed himself to relax. *Tomorrow's another day,* he thought, his eyes fixed on the shimmering water under the moonlight.

Caleb drew in a deep breath, the crisp night air sharp and cool against his skin. He closed his eyes, replaying Jacob's words in his mind. *A different fruit every month to remind people to eat them regularly. Was he joking? Or was that some sort of rule?* Caleb frowned, his thoughts tangling. *What happens if you miss a month? Would it matter? Why would anyone even risk it?*

The fruit was still in his hand, its smooth surface catching the faint silver light of the moon. Caleb turned it over in his palm, examining it again. *No point in hesitating,* he thought.

With a decisive motion, he bit into the fruit, the skin, and flesh yielding easily.

It was delicious—unexpectedly so. Sweet and tangy, with just a hint of citrus and something he couldn't quite place. He ate it all, every last bite, savoring the taste as the juices ran over his tongue. When he finished, he wiped his mouth with the back of his hand, staring at the empty rind in his palm.

His thoughts turned back to Jacob. *Was that really my great-grandfather? Or was it an Alohanuian pretending to be him?* The idea sent a shiver down his spine. *If it wasn't him, how could he know my mother's name? How could he know about Horse Creek?*

Caleb shook his head, trying to process it all. *And if it was Jacob, how could he still be alive? My Great-Grandfather died five years before I was even born.* His mind flicked back to George's words about the rumors. *Had the aliens actually brought the dead back to life? Or was it something darker, like in 'Invasion of the Body Snatchers?' Copies of people, but not the people themselves?*

The thoughts swirled in his mind, refusing to settle. He leaned back, staring up at the night sky. The stars twinkled like scattered diamonds, their distant light cold and indifferent to the turmoil in his heart. Somewhere in that city—Alohanui—was the truth he desperately needed to uncover.

The next day, Caleb heard the low rumble of an engine long before he saw George. His pulse quickened, and a wave of relief washed over him as an old, battered Nissan pickup truck crested the hill and rattled toward his camp. The sight of George behind the wheel was reassuring in a way Caleb hadn't expected.

As the truck rolled to a stop, George leaned out the window, grinning. "Miss me?"

Caleb walked over, shaking his head with a smile. "Where'd you get this thing?" he asked, giving the truck's faded blue paint and dented hood a once-over.

George hopped out, slamming the creaky door shut. "Dead Sea Market," he said, stretching his back. "Near the saltworks. There's a mechanic down there fixing up abandoned cars and trucks, selling them cheap. People are getting back organized."

Caleb arched an eyebrow. "Organizing? You mean like trade unions or something?"

George let out a dry chuckle, leaning casually against the truck. "Not quite. No one's forming unions or drafting constitutions if that's what you're thinking. But people are trading, making things, figuring out how to get by without a government breathing down their necks." He gestured back toward the truck. "The market's crazy, though. Salt traders, mechanics fixing up old cars, even a couple of blacksmiths hammering out tools. It's like stepping into a time machine. Bartering, trading—it's straight out of the Middle Ages."

"Sounds... surprising," Caleb said, crossing his arms. He gave George a scrutinizing look.

"And you're telling me people are just—what's a better word than organizing? Oh, I've got it—cooperating now? Since when?"

George shrugged, a faint grin tugging at the corner of his mouth. "I wouldn't say it's all sunshine and rainbows. But honestly? People seem different. Kinder. Not so quick to pull a knife or a gun just because you looked at them wrong. Maybe they've realized there's no cavalry coming. If we're going to make it, we've got to figure it out ourselves."

Caleb tilted his head, still skeptical. "That's a big turnaround from your 'don't trust anyone' speech last time you were here. What gives?"

George sighed, scratching the back of his neck. "Look, I still think it's smart to keep your guard up. But after everything that went down during the war for Alohanui—the abductions, the battles, the chaos—the worst of the worst didn't make it. They burned themselves out. What's left... well, it's people just trying to survive. Maybe even rebuild something."

Caleb nodded slowly, digesting the words. "Sounds like a start, at least."

Caleb folded his arms, skeptical. "That's a pretty big change from what you were saying before. Weren't you the one telling me not to trust anyone?"

George nodded, a flicker of seriousness crossing his face. "And I stand by that. But honestly, Caleb, it feels like the worst of humanity burned out during the war for Alohanui. The truly violent ones? The arsonists, looters, violent criminals, terrorists, fanatics and maybe even drug dealers and thieves? As far as I can tell, most of them are gone. What's left are people just trying to survive. Maybe rebuild."

Caleb mulled over George's words, glancing at the river flowing steadily past their camp. The world might actually be healing, even in small, halting steps.

"That's good news," Caleb said. Then, with a smirk, he added, "Guess what? I met my dead great-grandfather yesterday and sold him some peas and carrots."

George blinked, his face a mix of confusion and disbelief. "Wait. What?"

"You heard me," Caleb said, leaning casually against the truck. "Jacob Jacobson. Born 1925, Horse Creek, Oklahoma. My great-grandfather. He's alive—or at least something that looks and acts like him is—and he bought my entire crop of peas and carrots."

George whistled low, shaking his head. "And I thought I'd seen it all. What did he pay you with? Ghost money?"

Caleb chuckled softly, trying to mask his unease. "No, and not gold or jewels—leaves. From the tree of life inside Alohanui. He says they're valuable, and half of them belong to you."

George raised an eyebrow, leaning against the pickup, the quiet rustle of the river filling the silence between them. "Leaves from the tree of life? You're sure it was him? Your great-grandfather? If the leaves turn out to be the real deal, that would go a long way to proving his claim."

Caleb's smile faltered as the weight of the encounter settled over him again. "That's the thing—I don't know. I never met him. He looked like my grandad and talked like him. He knew things about my family, stuff no one else could have known. But he's been dead for decades..."

George rubbed his chin, his expression unreadable. "So you're thinking the Alohanuians brought him back?"

"Maybe," Caleb murmured, his voice subdued as his eyes fixed on Alohanui's towering silhouette in the distance. The city's gleaming walls caught the fading sunlight, casting elongated, surreal shadows across the plain. Its immense, otherworldly presence seemed to pulse with silent power, as if it were alive. "Or maybe it's something else entirely. Either way, it's hard not to wonder."

He paused, the weight of his thoughts bearing down on him. "Jacob said he knew my mother. He talked about her like she's in the city, like she's alive. If they brought her back..." His voice trailed off, a flicker of hope and fear mixing in his expression. "Could they have brought back Emma and Beth too?"

The air around him felt charged, as if Alohanui itself was listening. The faint rustle of the river and the whisper of the breeze through the growing greenery seemed almost conspiratorial, a quiet reminder of the mysteries the city held. Caleb's heart ached with the possibilities, both wondrous and terrifying, as he stood staring at the distant, enigmatic walls of the alien city.

George finally broke the silence, his voice cutting through the weight of Caleb's thoughts. "If these leaves are what he claims—and the same ones I've been hearing whispers about in the market—then you might be sitting on something bigger than either of us can imagine." He paused, his gaze steady. "So, what's our next move? What are we going to do with this?"

Caleb tightened his grip on one of the drying racks, his knuckles whitening. "I don't know yet. But I'm not giving up, I'm going to keep farming and I'm going to keep fishing and I'm going to talk to everyone who comes by. I'm not going to stop until I know the truth about Emma and Beth."

George placed a hand on Caleb's shoulder. "That's a lot to process. But hey, you've got me curious now. Let's keep this trade going: produce for leaves, if they are the real thing and if the rumors are true you made an incredible trade, he paid you way way more than the peas and carrots were worth."

Caleb nodded thoughtfully. "Thanks for the vote of confidence, George. And thanks for getting the truck. We're gonna need it if we're serious about hauling all this produce to the market."

George leaned casually against the truck, a grin spreading across his face. "Not just produce to the market," he said, gesturing toward the truck bed. "Today, it brought supplies back here to you. Salt, tools, and a few things to make life out here a bit less… primitive." He paused, his expression turning mischievous. "But, uh, you've got the wrong idea about the truck. It's not exactly mine. Think of it more as a… lease."

Caleb raised an eyebrow, curiosity sparking. "A lease?"

George chuckled, the sound carrying over the quiet plains. "No. Not a lease, maybe a better description of our arrangement is a no down payment, layaway plan. Yeah. Turns out, a backpack full of salted fish and wilted produce doesn't quite cut it when you're trying to buy a truck. Even one as beat up as this. But…" His voice dropped conspiratorially, "the promise of a leaf—one of those leaves from the tree of life? That sealed the deal."

Caleb's stomach tightened, his eyes narrowing. "You traded a leaf? Where did you even get one?"

"Not a leaf," George clarified, holding up a hand. "But the promise of one. Look, I didn't know you were planning to hand me ten leaves, and that completely takes care of trying to sell enough produce to earn a leaf. Anyway I made a deal with the mechanic: one leaf on my next trip to the market. That was his price. If you hadn't given me the leaves, I would have had to avoid him for a few trips or give him back the truck until I had managed to obtain a leaf for him. So here's how the truck deal went: He had me sign for the truck—just the number '1.' No dollars, no gold. The dollar's dead, and gold's useless if you're starving or dying. Leaves are the new currency."

Caleb let out a slow breath. "One leaf is worth one well used truck. I had no idea. And nothing down and he took you at your word. That's amazing too. Like you said, a kinder and gentler world."

George nodded, his grin fading into something more serious. "Think about it, Caleb. Word's getting out about those leaves. Everyone's desperate for a cure. Cancer, heart disease, allergies—hell, even a bad back. Everyone has something. If these leaves are as miraculous as they say, they're more than just valuable—they're life-changing. And if you've got access to a steady supply…"

Caleb's thoughts lingered on Jacob, the cryptic conversations they'd had, and the precious leaves now hidden securely away. "If I can get more," he murmured, almost as though speaking to himself.

George clapped him firmly on the shoulder, pulling him back to the present. "And if your great-grandfather—or anyone else inside that city—gets a taste for fresh produce, we're in business. This could be massive. Bigger than fish, bigger than veggies. We've got the rarest commodity in the world sitting in our hands. Now we just have to figure out how to play our cards right."

Caleb nodded but hesitated, a thought bubbling to the surface. "Well, there's something you might be able to help me with," he said, his tone more serious. "From everything you've told me, it sounds like people are talking about others going in and out of Alohanui. But here's the thing—my great-grandfather is the only person I've ever seen actually enter the city. Can you ask around, see if anyone else has seen people coming and going? Because if I'm going to sell produce to Alohanuians, I'm going to need more... foot traffic."

George raised an eyebrow, considering. "That's a good point. If this place is open for business, it's not exactly advertising itself. And if people aren't getting in and out, it's not much of a market, is it? I'll dig around, see what I can find. Someone's bound to know more than the scraps I've been hearing."

"Thanks," Caleb said, his voice steady but his thoughts racing. If Alohanui was the key to everything—Emma, Beth, the leaves, maybe even the future of humanity—then understanding who could enter and why was critical.

George tossed him a grin. "No promises, but I'll do my best. And hey, if you do start getting customers from Alohanui, let me know if they need a ride." He patted the side of the battered truck, then added with a laugh, "Maybe we can start a taxi service."

The amount of produce produced from their garden warranted a daily trip from Caleb and George's garden to the Dead

Sea Market. So Caleb was only mildly surprised when George arrived the very next day. What did surprise him, though, was the vehicle George was driving—a larger, newer, and noticeably faster truck.

"This," George said, climbing out with a grin, "is what two leaves will get you. Much smoother ride on the way to the market. The Alohanui section of the road is smooth as glass, like fresh asphalt. But the Dead Sea half was still pretty rough."

Caleb took a moment to inspect the truck, noting its spacious cargo box. "Bigger box, that's for sure," he said, patting the side of the truck. "It'll definitely come in handy."

George nodded. "We'll need it if the market keeps growing the way it is. Plenty of demand for fish and produce. People are starting to realize how rare fresh food is."

Caleb cut straight to the question on his mind. "Did you come up with an explanation for why I can't go into Alohanui?"

George leaned against the truck, his expression turning serious. "Yeah, it's pretty simple. Only the abductees and the revived dead—those brought into Alohanui by the Alohanuians—are free to come and go. You and I? We're not welcome. Every gate is guarded by one of those gargoyles. They keep people like us out."

"That makes sense in some bizarre way, I suppose." Caleb frowned, his gaze drifting toward the distant city. "Did you learn anything else?"

"I did," George said, his tone dropping as if he were revealing a secret. "I asked around about the east gate—your gate, the one in the middle of the east wall. Apparently, it's reserved for the Prince. That's what they told me."

"The Prince?" Caleb repeated, his brow furrowing. "What prince? Alohanui has royalty now?"

George shrugged. "That's all I got. No one seemed to know who this Prince is, but they said the Gate is sacred or something. No one uses it."

Caleb stared at the city, the faint shimmer of its walls catching the morning sun. "Sacred? Reserved for royalty? What does that even mean?"

George sighed, rubbing the back of his neck. "Beats me. But it's a good thing you didn't try pushing past that gargoyle at the gate. Sounds like they don't mess around when it comes to keeping the wrong people out."

"I guess," Caleb muttered, his thoughts spinning. The mystery of the east gate and the so-called Prince only deepened his curiosity about Alohanui—and his determination to find a way in.

George clapped him on the shoulder, breaking his train of thought. "Look, we've got plenty to keep us busy. The garden's producing more than ever, and I've got leads on some bigger trades. Let's keep building what we've got here, and maybe—just maybe—we'll figure out how to crack the Alohanui code."

The air was heavy with the scent of freshly tilled soil and the faint metallic tang of the river as Caleb leaned against the truck, his eyes narrowing in thought. The late afternoon sun cast long shadows over the bridge and the rows of thriving plants stretching along the riverbank.

"Alright, I've got another question," Caleb said, his tone taking on an edge of urgency. "Is there a way to drive to the next gate? Maybe we could expand the business—sell more produce, learn more about what's happening inside. More leaves, more knowledge."

George leaned back against the truck, crossing his arms, his face thoughtful. "It's about six miles to the next gate," he said, rubbing his chin. "You told me that before. Anyway, if you're talking about the gate to the south, there's a problem. You'd have to cross the Alohanui River. And let me tell you, that's no small feat."

Caleb frowned, the river's broad expanse flashing in his mind. "Too deep?"

George gave a short laugh. "Way too deep even with a snorkel and way too wide to even think about driving across it. And I wouldn't try swimming it unless you're part fish yourself. That current is no joke, and who knows what's under the surface. So that leaves the northernmost east gate."

Caleb's expression lightened slightly. "Could we drive there?"

"Yeah," George said, nodding. "The plain is pretty flat and, I think, drivable—at least in my four-wheel drive. If the soil changes as you move north or if it starts to rain—which seems unlikely—you could always drive back south to this road. From there, you could take it to the Dead Sea, then follow the Dead Sea's west coast road north for about 10 miles and take the North East Gate road to the North East Gate. Or, you could walk across the plain, or even try walking along the city wall's foundation. Each step in the foundation is more than 200 feet wide. We could even drive on it, except that in some places, parts of the wall's foundation are buried."

Caleb glanced toward the horizon, where the towering walls of Alohanui loomed, casting long shadows across the plain. "Driving seems like the better option—quicker, and the produce stays fresher. If we can set up a vegetable stand at another gate, it might double our opportunities. More customers, more information. And if the city dwellers show up, we might end up trading with people who are flush with leaves." A flicker of excitement lit his face.

George leaned against the truck, adjusting his weathered cap with a skeptical grin. "Alright, we'll scout it out tomorrow, see if it's worth it. But don't get your hopes too high. Just because it's another gate doesn't mean they'll roll out the red carpet. Your friend at this gate"—he nodded toward the motionless gargoyle guard with its faintly glowing flaming sword—"doesn't seem like the welcoming type."

Caleb smirked, a mix of determination and humor in his expression. "I'm not expecting a welcome parade, George. But even if the reception's icy, we'll at least know what we're dealing with. And knowing more than we do now? That's always worth the trip."

George chuckled and gave Caleb a pat on the shoulder. "Alright then, looks like we've got ourselves a plan."

They set out from the bridge at the east gate in George's pickup just as the morning sun began to gild the horizon. The air was cool, the sky a soft gradient of colors, promising a clear day. Caleb leaned back in the passenger seat, watching the towering walls of Alohanui fade into the rearview as George navigated the truck north across the plain.

"Six miles," George said, adjusting his cap. "Shouldn't take long."

He started out cautiously, keeping the truck at a steady ten miles per hour. The plain was unexpectedly cooperative—no soft spots, no hidden wet patches, and the soil felt solid under the tires. The ride was smooth, the hum of the engine blending with the faint rustling of the wind across the open land. After a few minutes, George glanced at Caleb, who gave a small shrug, signaling he was comfortable with a bit more speed. George nudged the truck up to twenty miles per hour.

Still, the drive remained surprisingly easy. The tires kicked up little dust, and the plain seemed almost eerily pristine. George was just beginning to think they could push the truck faster when something appeared on the horizon—a narrow ribbon of dirt cutting through the plain.

"There's the Northern East Gate Road," George said, gesturing toward the straight path leading toward the city. He veered slightly, pointing the truck toward Alohanui, and slowed as they approached.

Finally, George brought the truck to a stop about 1,000 feet from the gate, pulling off the road and onto the shoulder. The shimmering walls of Alohanui loomed ahead, their smooth surface gleaming faintly in the morning light. Unlike the east gate they had left behind, there was no bridge or river here—just the road and the towering gate, its massive frame dominating the landscape.

"Well, here we are," George said, stepping out of the truck and surveying the scene.

Caleb followed, his eyes widening. "Lots of people."

And indeed there were. A steady flow of travelers moved through the gate—men, women, and children, some carrying bundles of goods, others walking with empty arms. The scene was bustling but orderly, the road alive with chatter in multiple languages. The gate guard, a figure similar to the one at the east gate, stood watchful but didn't intervene as people came and went.

George wasted no time. Standing by the truck, he cupped his hands around his mouth and called out, "Free samples! Fresh produce just picked this morning! All you can carry for just one leaf!" He repeated the offer in Arabic, his voice carrying across the open plain.

The reaction was immediate. Heads turned, and within moments, people began making their way toward the truck. Some were cautious, eyeing the unfamiliar sight, while others moved quickly, their curiosity piqued.

A small crowd gathered, inspecting the array of carrots, peas, and other produce laid out in the truck bed. One man, dressed in a worn but clean tunic, stepped forward and picked up a handful of snap peas, examining them closely before popping one into his mouth. He smiled broadly, the crisp crunch echoing faintly in the quiet.

"Good," he said in heavily accented English. "Very good."

More people began reaching for the produce, and soon the truck was surrounded by eager hands. George grinned, exchanging a look with Caleb. "Told you this might work," he said.

Caleb nodded, already scanning the crowd for potential leads —anyone who might have knowledge of the city, its gates, or, more importantly, Emma and Beth.

Caleb kept repeating,"Anybody know Emma Kanoa, Beth Jacobson, Jacob Jacobson or Jean Jacobson?" Meanwhile George was doing a goodly number of transactions and collecting a lot of leaves.

A man heading for the Dead Sea heard Caleb and came over, "Brother, if you are looking for someone just ask the guard," he said.

It occurred to Caleb that the guard at the East Gate may have just been preventing anyone from using the gate except the Prince. And Caleb admitted to himself that he was asleep when his great grandfather had approached him and so Caleb had just assumed that he wasn't welcome in the City, not that no one but the Prince could use the East Gate.

"Thanks, friend, I'll go ask him," Caleb said, trying to keep his voice steady as he moved toward the imposing guard.

The guard stood motionless at first, but as soon as Caleb got within a few feet, he unsheathed his sword. The blade burst into flames with an audible hiss, the heat radiating outward like an invisible wall. The guard raised the fiery weapon and pointed it directly at Caleb.

The people passing through the gate reacted with alarm, a few gasping and pulling back, but the guard was precise. He moved with meticulous care, keeping the blade high above the heads of the travelers and ensuring their paths remained unblocked. His movements were deliberate, never touching Caleb or anyone else, but the message was unmistakable—Caleb was not to approach the gate, let alone enter the city.

Caleb stopped in his tracks, his pulse racing as the guard's fiery gaze locked onto him. He took a hesitant step back, realizing he had underestimated just how unwelcome he was.

The man who had encouraged Caleb earlier appeared at his side, looking sheepish. "I'm sorry. I thought you were a citizen," he said quickly. "I've never seen survivors of the plague this close to the city. Tell me those names again, and I'll go ask the guard."

Caleb hesitated, still feeling the heat from the sword lingering in the air. "Emma, Bethany, Jean, and Jake, Jacobson," he said cautiously. "They're my family."

The man nodded and moved toward the guard, his steps hesitant at first but gaining confidence as he approached. He spoke to the guard in a low voice, gesturing occasionally back toward Caleb. The guard remained silent, standing as still as a statue, but his fiery sword dimmed slightly as he listened.

The conversation stretched on for what felt like an eternity. Caleb shifted on his feet, his nerves fraying with every passing moment. The distant hum of activity at the gate seemed muted compared to the tension buzzing in his ears.

Finally, after about ten minutes, the man returned. His expression was thoughtful, but Caleb couldn't read whether it was good news or bad.

"Well," the man began, "it's pretty clear your name isn't in the book. That means you're not allowed in the city."

Caleb's stomach sank, but he didn't interrupt.

"But," the man continued, "your mother, father, sister, and fiancée are in the city. The guard confirmed it. Jacob—your great-grandfather, I take it—has let them all know you're here and looking for them. They said they'd come and see you, but it might take some time."

Caleb blinked, absorbing the information. Relief and frustration clashed within him like opposing tides. *They're alive—or something like alive—and they know I'm looking for them,* he thought. But his relief was tempered by a nagging question: *Why couldn't they come to me now? What's stopping them?*

He glanced back at the towering walls of Alohanui, their smooth, gleaming surfaces offering no answers. "Did they say how long it might take?" Caleb asked, his voice quiet, almost hesitant.

The man shook his head, sympathy flickering in his expression. "No, but… they'll come when they're ready. No. No. That's wrong, they actually said they will come when *you* are ready. That's all I know."

Caleb exhaled, his shoulders sagging slightly as he processed the cryptic reassurance. *When I am ready.* It wasn't much to go on, but it was all he had. He looked back at the man, a new thought surfacing.

"Hey, do you have any fruit on you?" Caleb asked, his tone almost casual, though his curiosity was anything but.

The man raised an eyebrow, then chuckled. "Of course I do. It's like an American Express card—I never leave home without it."

He paused, a playful grin spreading across his face. "Although, truth be told, I don't even know what an American Express card looks like. I'm just quoting something my father used to say."

Caleb managed a faint smile, despite the weight of the conversation.

The man reached into a small satchel at his side and pulled out a piece of fruit. Its smooth, golden skin caught the light, gleaming faintly in the late afternoon sun. "This is from the August vintage. I can spare one."

He extended the fruit toward Caleb, his expression turning serious. "Here you go. Promise me you won't sell it. In fact, eat it right now. I have no idea how long you might have to wait, but trust me, you'll want to be at your best."

Caleb hesitated for a moment before accepting the fruit, its cool, firm surface smooth against his fingers. He turned it over, inspecting it closely. There was an almost otherworldly quality to its appearance—a perfection that seemed too precise to be natural.

"Thanks," Caleb said, his voice subdued. He took a deep breath, then bit into the fruit. It was like nothing he'd ever tasted—sweet and tangy, with a burst of flavor that seemed to invigorate him with every bite.

The man watched him with a faint smile. "Good, right? Now you're ready for whatever comes next. And if I were you, I'd try to stay close to that gate." He nodded toward the imposing structure before disappearing back into the crowd.

CHAPTER 14
REUNION

The small produce market that George and Caleb started just outside the Northern East Gate flourished beyond their wildest expectations. What began as a simple stand with baskets of vegetables quickly expanded into a vibrant hub of commerce. A bamboo stand with a woven roof was the first improvement, shielding their produce from the relentless sun. Then came another stand, and another, until the area outside the gate transformed into a bustling marketplace.

Though the Northern East Gate lacked a reliable water source, George and Caleb decided not to relocate their cultivation operation. The rich fields near the river at the East Gate were too fertile to abandon, and the journey between the gates was short enough to keep their produce fresh.

Their success enabled them to hire workers—locals desperate for stability—whom they paid in precious leaves or traded goods. The produce they sold was in high demand among the citizens of Alohanui, and they rarely dealt with anyone from outside the city. Over time, the fishing arm of their business faded, though it didn't disappear entirely. The fish they now offered were both salted and smoked, a high-quality product sought after by those outside the walls.

Their cultivated area expanded rapidly, growing to 100 acres of lush, thriving farmland, with no signs of slowing down. Caleb marveled at the transformation: what had once been barren plains was now a patchwork of greenery that defied the surrounding landscape.

George proved to be a natural businessman, skilled at selling, recruiting workers, and procuring supplies. He scouted new opportunities with the same enthusiasm he had when they first started, returning from each trip to the Dead Sea Market with stories, tools, and the occasional nugget of valuable information. Caleb, on the other hand, found his role at the market. He supervised their growing number of employees and, more importantly, talked to anyone willing to share a conversation. Every interaction felt like a chance to learn something new, to piece together the puzzle of Alohanui and the enigmatic citizens who inhabited it.

Caleb couldn't shake the words of the citizen who had spoken to him: *"They will come when you are ready."* Those words haunted him, echoing in the back of his mind as he worked. He still held onto the hope that one day his mother, his father, his sister, and Emma would walk through the gate to find him. But when? And why did he have to wait?

George had become Caleb's closest friend, a steadfast ally in an uncertain world. Caleb made it his mission to ensure that George ate a ripe piece of fruit from the tree of life every month. The fruit wasn't for sale—not unless circumstances drastically changed and it became widely available outside the city walls.

Yet, strangely, Caleb found it easy to acquire the fruit. All he had to do was ask a citizen, and almost without exception, they would hand him a piece without hesitation or question. It was a curious dynamic. The citizens seemed devoid of judgment or self-interest when it came to Caleb. They treated the fruit not as a commodity but as a gift, one that carried a profound significance Caleb was only beginning to understand.

As the market thrived, Caleb often gazed at the towering walls of Alohanui in the distance, wondering what lay beyond them. The citizens seemed to live by an entirely different set of rules, ones Caleb yearned to grasp fully. *Maybe, just maybe,* he thought, *I'm getting closer to being ready—whatever that means.*

One crisp morning, Caleb broke the quiet rhythm of their work at the market. The sky was a sharp, unbroken blue, and the air carried the faint scent of the river and fresh produce. Caleb hefted a basket of carrots onto a stand, then glanced at George, who was stacking a crate of tomatoes. "George," he asked, his tone contemplative, "how long has it been since we met?"

George paused, setting the tomatoes down and leaning against the truck. "It's been fifty years since Alohanui touched down," he said, his voice calm but laced with a touch of wonder. "The citizens are calling it the Jubilee. We met just a few days after the landing." He tilted his head, giving Caleb a measured look. "And by the way, you look younger than the day we met."

Caleb barked out a laugh that echoed through the quiet marketplace. "So do you. Thanks to the tree of life, huh? The leaves keep us alive, and the fruit keeps us young. No aches, no pains, no wrinkles, no gray hair—and yet, no pimples." He smirked at his own humor.

George chuckled, shaking his head. "Not a bad deal at all."

The two fell into a comfortable silence, the hum of activity around the market filling the air—the soft murmur of distant voices, the occasional creak of carts, and the rustle of fresh vegetables being moved. After a few moments, George broke the quiet. "So," he said, a curious edge to his voice, "what values did you share with your family? And what set you apart from them?"

Caleb straightened, his brow furrowed in thought. He rested his hands on the edge of the stall. "We all shared a strong work ethic," he said finally. "And we loved each other deeply. Emma and I shared a lot—a love of astronomy, surfing, and a real appreciation for the beauty of the natural world. But there were differences. Mom, Dad, and Beth—they never went to college. Emma and I both got doctorates. They never held it against us, though. The biggest difference..." He hesitated, then continued, "was religion."

George raised an eyebrow. "Let me guess—your family were devout Christians?"

Caleb nodded, his gaze distant. "Yeah. Mom, Dad, and Beth were unwavering in their faith. I grew up in the church, but as I got older, I couldn't reconcile what I heard from the pulpit with what I learned in the lab and lecture halls. It just didn't add up for me."

"And Emma?" George prompted, his voice softer now.

Caleb's expression shifted, a hint of nostalgia in his eyes. "Emma wasn't raised Christian. Her beliefs were eclectic—a mix of new age and a bit of Buddhism. Her dad was Hawaiian, and he followed traditional Hawaiian religion, which was polytheistic and animistic. They revered dolphins, ocean waves, and the natural world. But Emma..." He trailed off, a faint smile tugging at the corner of his lips. "She was fascinated by the scripture plaques my mom had all over the house. There was one she spent minutes reading, over and over. It said, 'For God so loved the world, that He gave His only begotten Son, that whosoever believeth in Him should not perish but have everlasting life. John 3:16.'"

George frowned, his curiosity deepening. "Do you think she

converted?"

Caleb shook his head, his hands gripping the edge of the stall. "Not that I ever knew. Why do you ask? Do you think the abductees—and the ones they brought back from the dead—were all Christians?"

George scratched his chin, his gaze drifting toward the towering silhouette of Alohanui in the distance. "It's crossed my mind. What about your great-grandfather? Was he a Christian?"

"As far as I know," Caleb replied. "A long line of Christians… until me."

George turned to him, his voice low, almost conspiratorial. "So, do you think that's why they won't let you in? Because you're not a Christian?"

Caleb exhaled sharply, his jaw tightening. "I really don't like that idea. But I can't think of any other reason. I wish I could talk to my great-grandfather again."

George clapped Caleb on the shoulder, his touch grounding. "Be careful what you wish for," he said with a crooked grin. "Just kidding. Honestly, I can't see any downside to talking to Jacob again. It's been years, hasn't it?"

Caleb nodded, his gaze distant, the towering walls of Alohanui casting long shadows over his thoughts.

The following day, as Caleb stacked crates of freshly harvested vegetables under the bamboo roof of their produce stand, he spotted a familiar figure browsing the market near the gate. He froze, the sunlight catching on his great-grandfather's distinctive features. Coincidence? Caleb wondered. Or had Jacob been coming to the market regularly, unnoticed? Perhaps Caleb simply hadn't been looking.

Dropping the handful of snap peas he was holding, Caleb

hurried toward him. Jacob looked younger than the last time Caleb had seen him. His hair was darker, his skin smoother, his posture more relaxed. The simple, well-tailored clothes Jacob wore—a crisp white shirt tucked into khaki trousers with polished leather shoes—stood out among the more rugged and practical attire of the market visitors. Caleb couldn't help but marvel. Of course, he thought. He has direct access to the tree of life.

The sky above the market was overcast, a thick layer of gray clouds muting the sun's warmth and casting a pale, diffused light over the bustling stalls. A cool breeze swept across the plain, carrying with it the faint scent of rain and rustling the bamboo roofs of the produce stands. Caleb and Jacob stood near a stack of crates filled with freshly harvested vegetables, their conversation wrapped in the quiet hum of the market around them.

"Great-grandfather," Caleb said, a mix of awe and curiosity in his voice, "I've been wanting to ask you some questions."

Jacob turned to face him with a warm smile. "Just call me Jacob," he said, waving off the title with a flick of his hand. "We look about the same age, don't we? Inside the city, I've met relatives going back ten generations. The 'greats' get tedious after a while. So, Jacob it is. What's on your mind?"

Caleb hesitated for a moment, suddenly feeling the weight of the questions he wanted to ask. The spiritual implications gnawed at him, and he wasn't sure he was ready for those answers. Best to start with something technical—something grounded.

"How big is Alohanui?" Caleb finally asked.

Jacob's smile widened slightly. "Ah, I thought you'd already know that by now." He gestured toward the towering city walls, their smooth surfaces gleaming in the morning sun.

"Alohanui is 1,500 miles by 1,500 miles by 1,500 miles inside. Outside, it's only 18 miles by 18 miles by 18 miles. Bigger inside than outside. But you already suspected that, didn't you? Your reconnaissance drone gave you a good peek over the walls."

Caleb's mind raced. He remembered the drone footage, the impossibly expansive interior glimpsed through the gate, the buildings stretching beyond the horizon. "I remember back at Raven Rock," he said, his voice laced with nostalgia and intrigue, "one of the astrophysicists theorized that Alohanui could manipulate mass, momentum, gravity, and space-time itself."

Jacob nodded thoughtfully. "They were right. The City isn't just a city—it's a marvel of engineering, science, and something you might call artistry. Its control over the fabric of space and time is beyond anything humanity could achieve on its own. But," he added with a twinkle in his eye, "that's just scratching the surface."

The air between them seemed to hum with unspoken questions. Caleb wanted to dive deeper but felt the need to choose his words carefully. Around them, the bustle of the market carried on—people bartering produce, the faint rustle of vegetable leaves in baskets, and the occasional clang of tools being repaired in nearby sheds. Caleb could smell the earthy aroma of freshly dug carrots mingling with the faint metallic tang of the city's proximity.

"Well, you were right," Caleb said, his voice steady despite the whirlwind of thoughts in his mind. "I suspected that the builders of Alohanui were—and are—in complete control of space-time."

Jacob's expression was calm, but his eyes twinkled with an unspoken depth of understanding. Caleb hesitated, the cool breeze brushing against his face as he grappled with the weight of his next question. Might as well ask him, he thought.

"Jacob," Caleb began, his voice quieter now, "are you a Christian?"

Jacob straightened slightly, his tone unwavering and filled with conviction. "Absolutely. Jesus Christ is my Lord and Savior, and I believe He died to make me whole and that God raised Him from the grave on the third day."

Caleb felt a knot tighten in his chest. That's confirmed, he thought. He looked toward the city walls, looming in the distance like a fortress shrouded in mist. The clouds above shifted slightly, letting through a faint streak of light that illuminated the top of the towering structure.

"Almost fifty years ago," Caleb said, turning back to Jacob, "you told me, 'They will come when you are ready.' What I really want to know is—what do I need to do to become ready?"

Jacob smiled gently, the lines on his face softening. His voice was steady, almost reverent as he replied, "I think you already know. 'If you confess with your mouth, "Jesus is Lord," and believe in your heart that God raised Him from the dead, you will be saved.' That's the truth. And when you do, you can enter the City—the New Jerusalem."

Caleb's breath caught as Jacob continued, his tone taking on an almost prophetic weight. "You call it Alohanui, which means 'eternal love' in English. Emma was right when she named it. She wasn't just naming an asteroid; she was prophesying. Everything she saw, everything she felt—it all led to this."

A faint rumble of thunder rolled in the distance, the promise of rain hanging heavy in the air. Caleb felt the enormity of Jacob's words sink into him, the implications as vast as the towering city before him. Alohanui—eternal love. The name took on a deeper meaning, resonating with a truth he hadn't yet dared to fully embrace.

Although the East Gate remained guarded but unused, Caleb had long since abandoned his spot beneath the nearby bridge. The bridge, like the gate itself, was a place of reverence, reserved for the Prince. Out of respect for this custom—and with a growing sense of purpose—Caleb chose to build a proper home. What started as a modest shelter gradually evolved into a sprawling, well-appointed compound that reflected his evolving life and aspirations.

The compound was a self-sustaining haven. Hot and cold running water flowed from a shallow well next to the river of life, its crystal-clear water a constant reminder of Alohanui's miraculous presence. A solar panel array on the roof provided abundant energy, charging a massive battery pack that powered the pumps and everything else in the house. The entire system was remarkably efficient, ensuring the compound remained off-grid and independent.

A state-of-the-art but compact sewage treatment plant served both Caleb's home and the restrooms at the bustling market he ran with George near the East North Gate. It was a thoughtful addition, designed to maintain a pristine environment around the river and the plain.

Surrounding the main house were smaller structures. A guesthouse offered accommodations for traders or visitors. A workshop for repairs, while a storage shed housed tools, equipment, and supplies. Outside, a covered veranda wrapped around the house, providing a shaded spot to sit and watch the plains or the distant, gleaming walls of Alohanui.

It was a sanctuary not only for himself but also for Emma, should she ever choose to leave the city and join him.

The compound stood just off the paved East Gate road, a two-lane stretch of smooth asphalt that cut through the compacted pulverized limestone plain, connecting the East Gate with the East North Gate road. George had contracted its construction, ensuring it was a seamless, well-engineered route for the shuttles they ran daily. The road saw constant use, ferrying both Alohanuins and non-Alohanuins alike to and from the bustling market at the East North Gate—all free of charge.

George, ever practical, had chosen not to build near the market. He rarely lingered after sundown, heading back to what Caleb suspected was a quiet life in the town near the bustling salt market on the shore of the now-living Dead Sea. Caleb often wondered about George's family. He suspected George had a loving home—perhaps a wife or even children—but George never spoke of them. Caleb assumed it was out of deference to his own situation, knowing how deeply Caleb had yearned for Emma, Bethany, and the rest of his family to visit him. If George had shared the reasons for his happiness, Caleb would have felt joy for his friend but sadness for himself.

That evening, as the sun dipped below the horizon, painting the plain in hues of gold and violet, Caleb walked back to his compound. The night air was cool, carrying with it the faint scent of the river. The lights from the distant city walls of Alohanui twinkled like stars, their glow casting long shadows across the plain. As he entered the gates of his compound, the familiar comfort of his sanctuary wrapped around him. He glanced toward the bridge in the distance—a place of memories and beginnings—before heading inside.Tonight, there was no music, no video, no reading—just silence. Caleb sat on his veranda under the canopy of stars, wrestling with Jacob's words. He needed to process, to ponder, to sift through the weight of what had been said.

Only Christians allowed into the City? *It felt wrong, selfish even. Exclusionary and inhospitable. It didn't seem like the Jesus he remembered from Sunday School. That Jesus had welcomed sinners, outsiders, the broken. This... this felt like the opposite.*

*And the thought of **dropping asteroids on Earth, unleashing plagues, riots, wars, and the deaths of perhaps six billion people?** That, too, seemed alien to the loving God he had learned about as a child. A God of love who proclaimed care for every soul on Earth? How could such a God be behind all this devastation? It didn't add up.*

He leaned back in his chair, staring at the infinite expanse of the sky. **How could a God of love do this?** The question echoed in his mind like a relentless drumbeat.

To enter Alohanui, to see Emma, he would have to **acknowledge Jesus as Lord.** Caleb let out a bitter laugh. *The same Jesus—or his Father—responsible for the death of six billion people? And he was supposed to swear allegiance to Him?* The thought tasted bitter, like ash in his mouth.

"I could do it if my life depended on it," Caleb muttered to himself. "Just like swearing loyalty to Adolf Hitler if the alternative was a firing squad." The comparison unsettled him, but he let it hang in the air.

And then there was the second requirement: **to believe that God raised Jesus from the grave.** Could he do that? Could he believe in something so far removed from logic? Caleb shrugged. "I suppose I could convince myself that extraterrestrials, far more advanced than humans, could've engineered all of this," he thought aloud.

But the more he turned it over in his mind, the less sense it made. Maybe he was looking at it all wrong. Maybe he needed to focus on what he had personally witnessed. Not rumors, not stories from the market, but what his own eyes had seen.

Had he seen anyone crushed by Alohanui's landing? No. *Maybe he arrived too late for that—or maybe it never happened.* **Had he seen the asteroid strike the Pacific?** *No. Just a tremor. That could've been anything—a subwoofer in the Raven Rock situation room, for* all he knew. And the claim of six billion dead? Gossip. Nothing he had seen firsthand.

What he had seen—**really seen**—was the army attacking Alohanui. Missiles slamming into its walls, mortars exploding day after day. For the longest time, Alohanui had simply absorbed the blows, unmoving, silent. Its patience had seemed almost infinite. Only after days of relentless assault had it responded.

But when it did, it was... devastating.

He closed his eyes, the memory vivid. **The funnel, the abyss, the dead swept away.** Many of those soldiers had died from friendly fire or factional infighting. Caleb had seen that with his own eyes. The chaos of war had claimed more lives than Alohanui itself.

Do I believe Alohanui has the right to defend itself? The question surprised him, piercing through the fog of his thoughts.

Or, if it wasn't extraterrestrials—if it was truly God—then: ***Do I believe God has the right to defend Himself?*** *But maybe, the more accurate question would be:* ***Do I believe that God has the right to defend a city full of his children?*** *That's what it was:* ***God defending his children in the City and me, outside the Gate.***

The night deepened around him, the stars burning cold and bright above. Caleb let the question hang, unanswered, as the river murmured in the distance.

Caleb woke to a sharp knock at the door, the sound pulling him from a restless sleep. He had fallen asleep fully dressed on the couch, lost in the haze of soul-searching and unanswered questions from the night before. Rubbing his eyes, he stumbled to the door and opened it to find George standing there.

Before Caleb could say a word, George cut to the chase. "There's someone in the market asking for you."

Caleb blinked, shaking off the remnants of sleep. "What, someone looking for a better deal on leaves?" he joked, stepping out into the crisp morning air. Caleb's reputation as the softer of the two often drew customers hoping to haggle.

George shook his head. "No, not this time. They say they're a friend of yours."

Caleb stopped in his tracks. "A friend? Do *you* think they're a friend of mine?"

"Oh, yeah," George said, his tone uncharacteristically serious. "You'll want to meet them."

Suspicion flickered in Caleb's chest. "I doubt it. Probably just some rando hoping to sweet-talk your soft-touch business partner."

But George didn't respond, merely gesturing toward the market. Caleb's curiosity got the better of him, and the two men headed off together, the morning sun casting long shadows across the plain.

When they arrived at the market, Caleb's eyes scanned the bustling stalls. Amid the familiar movement of buyers and sellers, one figure stood out. A woman in a long, pure white dress, the kind he had occasionally seen female Alohanuians wearing, stood by a stall. She turned at their approach, her gaze locking directly with Caleb's.

His breath caught. His chest tightened. He felt as though the world had tilted on its axis.

It was Emma.

"Emma…" Caleb whispered, his voice trembling, his eyes involuntarily welling with tears. The noise of the market seemed to fade, replaced by the deafening beat of his heart. Her smile was radiant, her eyes shimmering with warmth, love, and something deeper—something he couldn't quite name.

Before he could say another word, she stepped forward, pulling him into an embrace. Her arms around him were solid and real, grounding him as much as they unraveled him. She kissed him, and for a moment, time ceased to exist. The market, the world, even the looming walls of Alohanui—all of it melted away.

When they finally broke apart, Caleb's voice came out as a hopeful whisper. "Does this mean that I'm ready?"

Emma's expression softened, though a shadow of seriousness flickered across her face. "Not yet," she said gently. "But you're getting closer. Jacob said you still have questions."

"I do," Caleb admitted, his voice steady but tinged with urgency.

"Is there somewhere we can talk?" Emma asked, glancing around at the bustling market.

Without hesitation, Caleb took her hand, leading her away from the crowd. Together, they walked across the plain to the verandah of his house. The air was cool and crisp, the gentle rustling of leaves and the distant murmur of the river providing a tranquil backdrop. They sat facing the horizon, where the market buzzed below and Alohanui shimmered in the distance.

Caleb leaned forward, his hands clasped together. "I've got so many questions," he began, his voice low with anticipation.

Emma turned toward him, her expression calm and knowing. "I could ask you to tell me what your questions are," she said, her voice soft but firm, "but I think I already know. Let me start with the answers you need."

She took a deep breath before continuing. "Caleb, you've judged God. Don't be afraid of that; don't shy away. Everyone does, in their own way. But that judgment—it gets in the way of understanding. Deep inside, you know there's a Creator. You're an astronomer, an astrophysicist. You believe in the Big Bang, and you know, as Stephen Hawking once said, that the cause of the universe lies outside the universe itself. And yes, I know you'd argue that Hawking recanted that later in life. But you also know the steady-state theory, the idea that the universe is infinite, was proven wrong. And yet, how often do you hear people talk about the universe as if it's infinite and eternal?"

Emma paused, letting her words settle before pressing on. "We both learned in university that the universe will come to an end. The Big Freeze, the Big Rip, the Big Crunch—pick your poison. But the point is, everything ends. Everyone dies. Everything is destroyed. It's written in the stars."

She leaned closer, her voice softening. "What a strange contradiction, isn't it? To embrace a godless universe where everyone dies, yet judge God for letting someone die too soon. Caleb, you've been willing to hold God accountable for all the wrongs in the world, yet if there were no God, you'd accept those same wrongs as just part of the natural order."

Caleb opened his mouth to speak, but Emma held up a hand, her expression patient but resolute. "Does that make sense? Is it fair? Caleb, you don't have to stand in judgment of God. You don't have to demand that He right every wrong in the world. Because He already has. Jesus made everything right—at the cost of His own life."

The words hung in the air, their weight settling over Caleb like a blanket. The sky above them began to shift into the colors of twilight, deep purples and golds spilling over the horizon. Caleb looked out at the river, at Alohanui in the distance, and then back at Emma.

"I think you're ready," Emma said, her voice soft but steady. "Let's walk over to the river."

Caleb hesitated for only a moment before nodding. "Alright," he said, his voice low. He didn't fully understand what was about to happen, but Emma's words carried a quiet authority he couldn't ignore.

As they approached the river, Caleb's eyes widened. A crowd had gathered along its edge, their figures framed by the golden glow of the morning sun. The river shimmered, its crystal-clear waters catching the light in dazzling patterns. A sandy beach had formed near the bridge over the past fifty years, its soft, inviting slope a testament to the passage of time and the river's gentle transformation.

"Who are all these people?" Caleb asked, his heart pounding.

"Just look," Emma replied, her voice warm and encouraging.

Caleb scanned the crowd, his breath catching in his chest. At first, he saw unfamiliar faces—men, women, and children, some dressed in the simple yet elegant robes he associated with Alohanuians. But as his gaze moved closer, recognition struck him like a wave.

There, standing among the others, were George, his ever-loyal partner and friend; his great-grandfather Jacob, looking even younger than Caleb remembered; and his grandfather, also Jacob, whose broad smile lit up his face. His parents, Jake and Jean, stood nearby, their expressions a mixture of pride and love. His sister, Bethany, was beside them, her hand resting gently on the shoulder of her old pastor, Ben. Emma's parents, Ted and Star, were there too, along with aunts, uncles, cousins—all of them together, waiting.

"George," Caleb said, his voice cracking as he turned to his friend. "Were you in on this?"

George grinned, his eyes twinkling. "Fifty years ago, Emma asked me to watch out for you. I've just been keeping my promise."

Caleb's gaze returned to Emma, his heart swelling with gratitude and a profound sense of purpose, something steady and unshakable. She smiled warmly and took his hand, leading him to the edge of the shimmering river.

Jacob, his great-grandfather, stepped forward, his voice resonant and unwavering. "Caleb, do you believe that Jesus Christ is Lord, the Son of God, who died for your sins and rose again on the third day?"

The question settled heavily in Caleb's chest, a culmination of years of searching and longing. *Do I believe?* The words reverberated through his mind, unearthing an old memory from Sunday School—a father pleading with Jesus to heal his demon-possessed son. The disciples had been powerless, but Jesus had told them that faith could move mountains. Jesus told the man it was necessary he believed that Jesus could heal his son. Faith was required. The father's response had always stuck with Caleb: *"Lord, I believe; help thou my unbelief."* It was a prayer not of certainty, but of raw, honest need.

"Lord," Caleb whispered now, his voice trembling, "I need to believe. Help me believe."

As he spoke, peace washed over him. What had been a burden became a release, a surrender. Caleb inhaled deeply, the cool air filling his lungs and clearing his mind. His voice steadied. "Yes," he said, his words carrying the weight of conviction. "I believe. Jesus Christ is Lord and He is the Son of God."

Jacob's expression softened with quiet joy as he guided Caleb into the river. The water enveloped him, cool and purifying, a tangible reminder of the transformation unfolding within. Jacob's hands rested firmly on his shoulders as he spoke, "I baptize you in the name of the Father, the Son, and the Holy Spirit."

Caleb tilted his head back, letting the river carry him for a brief, timeless moment. The world seemed to pause as the water rushed over him. When he emerged, droplets streaming from his face, the sunlight seemed brighter, the air fresher, and the weight he had carried for so long was lifted. For the first time in years, he felt whole.

Turning toward the shore, Caleb saw Emma already stepping forward. Her white dress rippled in the water like a banner of grace. She smiled at him, radiant and serene, before turning to Jacob. Her voice, clear and unwavering, carried the same heartfelt conviction. "I believe in Jesus Christ as Lord, the Son of God, who died and rose again for me."

Jacob's smile broadened as he led her into the river. Caleb stood nearby, the water lapping at his knees, watching as Jacob spoke the same words that had marked his own baptism. Emma's face shone with quiet strength as she was lowered into the water and then lifted out, her expression a reflection of renewed life and unshakable faith.

The crowd on the shore erupted in joyful applause, their voices rising in a symphony of celebration that echoed across the plain. Caleb met Emma's gaze, his heart full to overflowing.

"Fifty years," he said softly, his voice a mixture of awe and wonder. "And now I finally get it."

Emma smiled, her fingers intertwining with his. "Come with me," she said, her voice playful yet tinged with mystery as she leaned close to whisper. "I want you to meet the man who invented sex. You should see what he's working on now!"

DEDICATION

To my lifetime wife, Allie.

ACKNOWLEDGMENTS

Writing a book is never a solitary endeavor, and I owe thanks to many who made this journey possible.

To my wife, Allie: Your unwavering support and dedication to creating a beautiful and comfortable writing space in every home we've shared have made all the difference. This book exists because of your love and encouragement.

To my children, Becky, Jared, and Tim: Thank you for reading my previous books and writing reviews (or at least saying you did!). Your feedback, encouragement, and belief in my work mean everything to me. A special thank you to my nephew, Jordan, for taking the time to share his thoughts and review as well.

To my lifelong friends, Mike and Rich: Your loyalty as readers and reviewers, not to mention the honest feedback, have been invaluable. Listed in order of the stars you gave me, you'll always have my gratitude—no matter the rating.

To Jeff Bezos and the team behind Kindle Publishing: Your platform has revolutionized the publishing world, allowing writers like me to reach a global audience regardless of connections or status. Thank you for giving everyone a chance to share their stories.

To the Sidney/North Saanich Library Writers Group: Your feedback, camaraderie, and inspiration were invaluable.

Special thanks to Sharon Walker, the Library Manager, for organizing meetings, workshops, and speaker sessions that helped me grow as a writer. To all the fellow writers who pointed out what was obvious to everyone but me—thank you for your honesty and kindness.

To Suzanne Anderson: Your book, *Self Publishing in Canada: A Complete Guide to Designing, Printing and Selling Your Book,* was a treasure trove of knowledge. Your thoughtful response to my question during the Writers Group meeting gave me the clarity and direction I needed.

To Dell Computers: My trusty desktop, built on May 30, 2014, and still running Windows 7 Pro like a champ. It has seen me through countless drafts and revisions.

To Google: For providing the best search engine, free email, and 15GB of cloud storage. Your tools helped keep this project organized and moving forward.

Finally, to every reader, reviewer, and supporter—thank you for taking the time to step into this world I've created. Your encouragement and feedback make all the effort worthwhile.

AUTHOR'S NOTES:

Avoiding the Curse

Revelation 22:18-19
18 I warn everyone who hears the words of the prophecy of this scroll: If anyone adds anything to them, God will add to that person the plagues described in this scroll. 19 And if anyone takes words away from this scroll of prophecy, God will take away from that person any share in the tree of life and in the Holy City, which are described in this scroll.

I sincerely hope no one interprets this book as an attempt to add to or take away from the scroll of prophecy—that is certainly not my intention. My purpose in writing this book is to entertain, perhaps to warn, and to encourage people to read the book of Revelation. After all, a blessing is promised to those who read it, and I want to receive that blessing while avoiding the curse.

Revelation 1:3-20 NIV
3 Blessed is the one who reads aloud the words of this prophecy, and blessed are those who hear it and take to heart what is written in it, because the time is near.

Perspective

This book is a work of pure fiction, precipitated by the disasters, plagues and battles recorded in the book of **Revelation**, chapters 4 through 22. While much of that scripture describes events occurring in heaven, I have chosen to focus solely on the perspective of one man, Caleb, on earth. Consequently, any events in Revelation that could not be observed from an earthly viewpoint are excluded.

Literal Approach to Revelation

I approached Revelation with a literal interpretation, taking its descriptions at face value wherever possible:

- The **river of life** is depicted as a real, physical river. In my story, it transforms the Dead Sea into fresh water, ultimately flowing into and rejuvenating the Red Sea.
- The **New Jerusalem** is a tangible, physical object descending from the sky, designed to house physical human beings.
- The plagues are actual diseases, the earthquakes, real earthquakes and the battles, real battles.

At the same time, I offered natural explanations for certain phenomena:

- The *moon becoming like blood* is attributed to atmospheric dust.
- The *blood* in rivers, lakes, and oceans is caused by toxic red algae blooms.
- The *something like a mountain cast into the sea* is interpreted as a large asteroid.

These creative liberties are intended to ground the story in a blend of biblical prophecy and plausible earthly phenomena.

John's Chronology and Its Influence

John, the author of **Revelation**, is also credited with writing the **Gospel of John**, which differs in chronology from the synoptic gospels. For example:

- In John, Jesus overturns the tables of the moneychangers in the temple at the beginning of His ministry.
- In the other gospels, this event occurs near the end of his ministry.

It's very possible Jesus cleansed the temple more than once, but I suspect John wasn't overly concerned with presenting events in strict chronological order. Similarly, in Revelation, John describes seeing the **New Jerusalem** descend from heaven twice—once in Revelation 21:2 and again in 21:10 from a high mountain. This event is undoubtedly worth witnessing more than once, and the descent could have been a lengthy process, as I portray in my story. However, I again sense that John did not prioritize a rigid chronological narrative.

For this apocalyptic Christian science fiction romance, I created a sequence of events that fits an invented plot. While inspired by the disasters, plagues and battles recorded in Revelation, the story remains entirely fictional.

The Dangers of Overconfidence in One Man's Interpretation

Many Christians believe they fully understand the book of Revelation. Throughout history, some leaders have even gone so far as to predict the exact date of Christ's return, despite Jesus' clear statement in **Matthew 24:36**: *"But about that day or hour no one knows, not even the angels in heaven, nor the Son, but only the Father."*

This presumptuous approach to scripture is fraught with risks. One danger is that Christians may dismiss God's signs simply because they do not align with a rigid timeline or interpretation promoted by egocentric, profit-driven, and misguided individuals. Such attitudes undermine humility and openness to God's plan, replacing them with human arrogance and error.

My Personal Approach to Revelation

My approach to Revelation was to first listen to it repeatedly and then read it many times, allowing the text to speak for itself. I avoided reading commentaries, as they can embed interpretations that color everything you see. I believe it's better to wrestle with the text independently, reflect on it, and give your subconscious time to process and contribute to your understanding.

Avoid taking courses in hermeneutics—God didn't write *that* textbook.

When I have read commentaries, they often seem disconnected from practical realities, as if written by people who have spent their lives in ivory towers or monasteries, far removed from the everyday struggles of life, like managing finances or dealing with real-world challenges. By contrast, Revelation is a text for all people, and I believe its message should resonate with life's realities.

No more sea.

Revelation 21:1 NIV
Then I saw "a new heaven and a new earth," for the first heaven and the first earth had passed away, and there was no longer any sea.

In this fictional interpretation, I took the "sea" mentioned in Revelation 21:1 to refer to the Dead Sea. According to Ezekiel, it will be transformed into fresh water and teeming with fish, no longer a "Dead Sea" but a vibrant, living lake.

Ezekiel 47 NCV
The man led me back to the door of the Temple, and I saw water coming out from under the doorway and flowing east. (The Temple faced east.) The water flowed down from the south side wall of the Temple and then south of the altar. 2 The man brought me out through the outer north gate and led me around outside to the outer east gate. I found the water coming out on the south side of the gate.
3 The man went toward the east with a line in his hand and measured about one-third of a mile. Then he led me through water that came up to my ankles. 4 The man measured about one-third of a mile again and led me through water that came up to my knees. Then he measured about one-third of a mile

again and led me through water up to my waist. 5 The man measured about one-third of a mile again, but it was now a river that I could not cross. The water had risen too high; it was deep enough for swimming; it was a river that no one could cross. 6 The man asked me, "Human, do you see this?"

Then the man led me back to the bank of the river. 7 As I went back, I saw many trees on both sides of the river. 8 The man said to me, "This water will flow toward the eastern areas and go down into the Jordan Valley. When it enters the Dead Sea, it will become fresh. 9 Everywhere the river goes, there will be many fish. Wherever this water goes the Dead Sea will become fresh, and so where the river goes there will be many living things. 10 Fishermen will stand by the Dead Sea. From En Gedi all the way to En Eglaim there will be places to spread fishing nets. There will be many kinds of fish in the Dead Sea, as many as in the Mediterranean Sea. 11 But its swamps and marshes will not become fresh; they will be left for salt. 12 All kinds of fruit trees will grow on both banks of the river, and their leaves will not dry and die. The trees will have fruit every month, because the water for them comes from the Temple. The fruit from the trees will be used for food, and their leaves for medicine."

Judging God *or* Avoiding His Judgement

Caleb, the agnostic astronomer, never fully embraced his parents' beliefs as his sister Beth did. His rejection stemmed more from peer pressure than from grappling with the classic question, "How could a loving God let this happen?" However, the devastating events he witnessed—the destruction of the world, the death of his parents, and his fiancée's battle with cancer—only solidified his leanings toward atheism.

The irony, though, is that God has given clear warnings. The horrors described in Revelation can be avoided by simply heeding them. It's like a parent saying, "Don't touch the stove." The choice to listen makes all the difference.

Isaiah 42:9
See, the former things have taken place and new things I declare;
before they spring into being I announce them to you."

Amos 3:7
Surely the Lord GOD does nothing without revealing His secret plan [of the judgment to come] to His servants the prophets.

Romans 10:9 If you confess with your mouth that Jesus is Lord and believe in your heart that God raised him from the dead, you will be saved.

How many people will die horribly?

Zachariah 13:8 And it shall come to pass, that in all the land, saith the LORD, two parts therein shall be cut off and die; but the third shall be left therein.

Revelation 6:8 I looked, and behold, an ashen horse; and the one who sat on it had the name Death, and Hades was following with him. Authority was given to them over a fourth of the earth, to kill with sword, and famine, and plague, and by the wild animals of the earth.

Revelation 9:15 And the four angels, who had been prepared for the hour and day and month and year, were released, so that they would kill a third of mankind.

Revelation 20:4–6 "And I saw thrones, and they sat upon them, and judgment was given unto them: and I saw the souls of them that were beheaded for the witness of Jesus, and for the word of God, and which had not worshipped the beast, neither his image, neither had received his mark upon their foreheads, or in their hands; and they lived and reigned with Christ a thousand years. But the rest of the dead lived not again until the thousand years were finished. This is the first resurrection. Blessed and holy is he that hath part in the first resurrection:

on such the second death hath no power, but they shall be priests of God and of Christ, and shall reign with him a thousand years.

As Long as You are Alive, It's Never Too Late to Repent

Throughout the apocalypse, every human was given the opportunity to repent.

Revelation 9:20 NASB
20 The rest of mankind, who were not killed by these plagues, did not repent of the works of their hands so as not to worship demons and the idols of gold, silver, brass, stone, and wood, which can neither see nor hear nor walk;

Revelation 16:11 NET
11 They blasphemed the God of heaven because of their sufferings and because of their sores, but nevertheless they still refused to repent of their deeds.

The Rapture

Writing this book has been a learning experience for me, and while I previously discouraged readers from turning to commentaries before trying to interpret Revelation on their own, I must acknowledge the value of the insights offered by many wise commentators. Their works have been helpful to me.

For instance, a commentary on Revelation 14 provided clarity regarding the two distinct harvests described in that chapter: one for the saints (verses 14–16) and another for the rest (verses 17–20). This distinction helped me understand that passages in Corinthians and Thessalonians focus solely on the first harvest.

1 Corinthians 15:51-52 NIV
51 Listen, I tell you a mystery: We will not all sleep, but we will all be changed— 52 in a flash, in the twinkling of an eye, at

the last trumpet. For the trumpet will sound, the dead will be raised imperishable, and we will be changed.

1 Thessalonians 4:15-17 NET
15 For we tell you this by the word of the Lord, that we who are alive, who are left until the coming of the Lord, will surely not go ahead of those who have fallen asleep. 16 For the Lord himself will come down from heaven with a shout of command, with the voice of the archangel, and with the trumpet of God, and the dead in Christ will rise first. 17 Then we who are alive, who are left, will be suddenly caught up together with them in the clouds to meet the Lord in the air. And so we will always be with the Lord.

Revelation 14:14-20 NIV
14 I looked, and there before me was a white cloud, and seated on the cloud was one like a son of man with a crown of gold on his head and a sharp sickle in his hand. 15 Then another angel came out of the temple and called in a loud voice to him who was sitting on the cloud, "Take your sickle and reap, because the time to reap has come, for the harvest of the earth is ripe." 16 So he who was seated on the cloud swung his sickle over the earth, and the earth was harvested.
17 Another angel came out of the temple in heaven, and he too had a sharp sickle. 18 Still another angel, who had charge of the fire, came from the altar and called in a loud voice to him who had the sharp sickle, "Take your sharp sickle and gather the clusters of grapes from the earth's vine, because its grapes are ripe." 19 The angel swung his sickle on the earth, gathered its grapes and threw them into the great winepress of God's wrath. 20 They were trampled in the winepress outside the city, and blood flowed out of the press, rising as high as the horses' bridles for a distance of 1,600 stadia.

Manufactured by Amazon.ca
Bolton, ON